Book One
of the
Mysta Prophecy

The Rise of Xyakah

I hope you enjoy the adventure Cat with love N.L. Osguthorpe 17

By

N.L. Osguthorpe

http://themystaprophecy.weebly.com

DEDICATION

With immeasurable thanks and unconditional love to all my family and friends, for putting up with a dreamer whose head is always partly somewhere else.

Come see where I've been; I hope I've done it justice.

I must also give special thanks to my amazing parents for believing in me and pushing when I needed it. To Maxine, Vanessa and John for telling me it was worth carrying on and to Kate for doing the bits I couldn't do on my own.

CONTENTS

The Kingdom of Maldora

Introduction

A single flicker of pure white light in the perpetual darkness of death...

The entity slept, waiting as ever for the arrival of the souls it tended, this glimmer of a flame the solitary indicator of its presence...

Tentatively the other approached through the vast vaults of the afterlife. Crippled by the exertion she rested, helpless under the enormity of the power surrounding her; overwhelming her.

Unaware of her own importance or purpose she waited - a speck of insignificance in the vastness of eternity...

When the surge came it was unexpected and instant. At first she felt only confusion, but then a mind brushed the edge of her consciousness. She responded by reaching out with her own senses, probing towards the energy on their perimeter. With a fiery surge there came contact, followed by the explosive exhilaration of pure joy, which rushed through her entire being. This is what triggered the change and she began to acquire a form - that of a pale translucent figure. Looking through human eyes she saw the others approaching. Two figures appeared as she did - tall, elegant women surrounded by

1

pale auras of pulsating colour. Just as she emitted silver, so the second radiated bronze and the third icy blue. In an instant the distance between them vanished and the three were reunited.

Not comprehending who or what they were, none thought to ask why this was happening to them but all accepted that they belonged together. Their minds united as the merging powers combined, surging and flooding out into the vacuum, drowning out the flame of the silent entity...

Something was wrong! Why did the Spinner not respond? Something was missing!

Time passed without time. Then came comprehension, and with it pain. Agonizing grief washed over them... They were only three, yet they should be four! Where was the fourth?

Chimes of danger vibrated through the air, mirroring the shivers of warning which rippled down their ethereal spines. Only then did the sleeper stir, feeling the souls of its children cry out to it. Calming their minds, it absorbed their distress and identified its origin...

THIS COULD NOT BE...NO ONE HAD THE POWER TO INTERFERE...NO ONE!

And then with sorrow did the awareness respond, releasing its energy to wrench the three apart. Silently did they fall through the obscurity of time and space, and when the decent ended they were safe. Encased in the warm protective environment of a female womb, where the time of growth would heal their pain, and the trauma of birth erase the dreadful grief still echoing through their minds.

2

Chapter 1
Elayna

Elayna's lustrous, long auburn hair draped across the elegant satin of her pillow. She lay surrounded by comfort, yet still unable to sleep. Her clear blue eyes lingered on the intricately designed wooden panels of the ceiling. The artisan had lovingly sculptured an assortment of woodland animals tumbling around each other in playful glee. This one was Elayna's favourite panel. When she was born her father had commissioned the artist to create a panel for Elayna's room. Each year he was to return and complete another panel, until her eighteenth year when she would be married to a local noble's son and leave her childhood home behind her forever. In a week's time that day would be here, yet four of the panels remained unadorned, a testimonial and constant reminder to the fact that four years ago her mother had died, taking with her everything Elayna had loved about her life here in Galloheart Keep: the cheerful cries of the peddlers calling their wares down in the village; the songs of the barge drivers as they steered their course towards the jetty; the laughter of the servants going merrily about their duties. All the joyfulness of life had seemed to have stopped that day. She often wondered how one small change in her life could bring about so many more.

Gadon, Elayna's father, had been devastated by the loss of his wife, and in his misery had turned to the ale barrel for comfort. Gaylon, her older brother, had taken the situation in hand and ran the family estate as if nothing had happened. *No...* Not quite nothing. The laughter had left all their lives. Even her handsome, carefree brother Gaylon, who had previously spent his days hunting and making merry with his many friends, seemed to visibly age over the following year. Gaylon had been far more than a brother to Elayna. He was her soul mate, mother, father, brother and best friend. He had encouraged the hesitant young girl to take a hand in the running of things about the estate and, in doing so, deal with the dramatic changes in her own life. He had taught her to be strong and composed in public, issuing orders with a confident, commanding tone. Yet at night when she needed to cry he would hold her in his arms, often weeping with her and whisper of how proud their mother would be of them both.

The second family misfortune came the following year when Gaylon had been killed in a freak hunting accident. This time Elayna did not cry. She had no tears left and deep down in her heart she refused to believe he was really gone. Perhaps she had gone mad. Looking back on those days it felt as if she had. Talking to herself in a secret language, sleeping only in the daytime and, at night, searching the stars for a sign of her mother or brother.

Her father, still reeling from the loss of his wife, seemed to fall deeper into his pit of despair. His grief intensified, twisting his pain into rage at all around him, so that he could not bear to be in the same room as his daughter - the one who dared to still live when all else he held dear had left him.

Rumours circled the house that the master had thrown in his lot with the devil, and whispered voices spoke of his sardonic and perverted pastimes. Encouraged by his new friend, Desca, a strange man who he had met in the ale house, and who later revealed himself to be a Xyakahan priest from the secluded temple on the outskirts of the village, Gadon spent more and more of his time away from home. Elayna knew where he was. The servants thought she didn't listen but she did. She heard everything.

"Whoring" the scullery maid had said.

"Animals last night!" the grooms had laughed, making obscene gestures with their hands.

"Little children!" The head cook had announced in a saddened tone, "I believe our master truly is the living dead."

All this Elayna heard and more, but how much was true she had no way of knowing for sure. She knew several stable lads had left suddenly, and three of the chamber maids had been thrown out of the house by Damian the head butler for getting themselves into trouble, but surely her father could not be responsible for every incident! Then there was the gardener's tale of his trip to see his uncle in the next village and how he had seen Gadon entering the Xyakahan temple. Elayna shuddered. She had hoped that tale was a lie, knowing that people believed the priests to be evil magic workers who were suspected to be responsible for the disappearance of several people.

Last night, not more than five hours ago, her father had come to her room. At first Elayna had been pleased to see him, it had been such a long time since he had paid her any attention at all and even that had been to shout at her for "remaining alive in this house of death!" Remembering his words she felt fear; a tingle of panic ran down her spine. She had felt like a trapped rabbit beneath his steel gaze. As he had pushed past her into the room she realised that little remained of the father she had so dearly loved as a child. He seemed smaller; more stooped, and used a stick to help him balance. His hair, what was left of it, was steel grey and his pallid complexion spoke volumes of the drug and alcohol abuse his body had suffered over the last few years. Buried beneath an excess of flesh, his eyes burned with a hate so intense they held her spellbound. His voice, when at last he spoke; had been soft and well controlled, dispelling Elayna's fear that in a drunken stupor he had come to take his sadistic pleasure from her.

"If I am not mistaken daughter," his words slid softly from his thin pale lips, "it will be your eighteenth year within the next few days?"

Heart pounding and mind racing she heard herself answer as if from a great distance. "Yes Father." Her voice had trembled but she forced herself to think of Gaylon and that helped a little.

He had smiled then, though there was no pleasure in it. Neither was it smug; more a sign of resignation, or so Elayna thought.

"Good" the word was a whisper but it seemed to sit heavily in the air. "The arrangements," he continued, his voice strengthening, "are made. You will learn more when you need to know more. For now, understand that you will be married and it will be within the week."

"Who father?" Elayna dared to ask, but it was of no consequence to him. Turning quickly for a man of his size he had strode out of the room slamming the door, leaving only the clicking of the latch as it fell into place behind him.

Elayna had not slept after her father had left. For a long time she had felt numb, but now the tears came and silently she cried. She cried for her mother, her brother, her father but most of all she cried for herself. She didn't know how long she had lain there. The visible tears had long since dried up but inside she still wept. Gradually dawn had come to the world and in the yard below sounds of life came floating up to the open window.

The gentle tapping had been going on for some time when it registered on Elayna's consciousness that someone was knocking at the door. The sound became more urgent and then she heard a voice. "Ela, are you there?" The voice was a whisper but she knew it at once, it was Ly. Lyaren was the one thing good about this nightmare house. He had appeared on the doorstep just days after Gaylon's accident and introduced himself as the tutor Gaylon had summoned to educate Lady Elayna. He had been visibly shocked at the news of Gaylon's death saying that they had been friends at the university in Sidmore, the large city many days' journey to the South, where her brother had studied, and that he had been looking forward to meeting up with his old friend. He had the letter with him that Gaylon had written, and Elayna had to admit that it was unmistakably Gaylon's penmanship. Reluctantly at first Elayna had agreed to his tutorage.

Ly, as it turned out, was just what Elayna needed in a tutor - patient and caring. He seemed to sense her moods and always knew the perfect lesson for each moment, whether it be politics or diplomacy, art or music, hunting or medicine. They had fast become friends and Elayna valued his opinions greatly. Over the last three years he had in his own small way helped her wounds to heal.

7

Despite their friendship it was unheard of for him to come to her room. Wiping her face and composing herself she flung a soft robe around her shoulders and drew open the door.

"I'm sorry Lyaren," she said, avoiding the eye contact which would betray her dismay, "I did not realise the hour was so late, I will be out for our lesson shortly. Shall I meet you in the library?" Her words tumbled over each other in her haste to hide her distress from him, but Lyaren did not seem to notice.

With a finger to his lips he slipped into the room closing the door behind him. Surprised but not afraid by his forward action Elayna took in his appearance. Still dressed in yesterday's hunting clothes, ebony hair dishevelled and face unshaven, she realised that she had not been the only one awake all night. Despite this his emerald eyes shone with life and he wore an easy smile, which served to conceal his unease. Slowly he let the smile fade from his lips and sadness misted over in his eyes.

"Your father has dismissed all the staff," his tone was calm but urgent and he hurried on. "Only Damian and Anna remain and they have been ordered to pack your father's things. I have been ordered to leave also but I dare not go until I know you are safe." Swallowing a lump which, appeared in his throat, he took Elayna by the shoulders and looked deep into her eyes.

"I know your father came to see you last night, Ela, please tell me what is going on."

At first she could not answer. Everything seemed to be happening so fast. Was it really only yesterday they rode down to Fiddlers Field together to collect fresh spring flowers and aromatic herbs to hang in the hallways to freshen the musty air? When she did answer her voice trembled and only with a great effort of self-control did she manage not to cry. "He says I am to

8

be married before the week is out. Perhaps he hopes to be rid of me so he can remarry himself. I know there is one of his women who attends him more often than the others do."

"I see." his tone was angry and curt now. "Did he say who you are to marry?"

"No, just that I would know when the time came."

"Then my fears are justified," he sighed deeply, "Ela, there are many things I need to tell you, things about me and about your father, but for now there is not time. I fear you are in grave danger and I will not leave you to that fate. You mean far too much to me, Ela, you must know that."

"You are a good friend, Ly, and I hate that our friendship must end, but if my father says I am to marry there is nothing I can ..."

"I know who you are to marry." He interrupted; his voice was quiet but held an icy cold edge which sent shivers of panic running down Elayna's spine.

"Who?" Did she really want to know? Her mind was reeling but quickly she gathered her wits and focussed on his words.

"It is not a who, but what you are to marry." Moving her over to the bed he gently sat her down and knelt before her taking both her slight hands in his.

"There has been talk in the village and so I have carried out my own investigations. It is arranged for your father to join the Xyakahan priesthood. One of the conditions is that all your worldly possessions are given over to the church, and any women in your household become handmaidens of Xyakah." He paused a moment to let the implication of his words register. "I believe he intends to marry you to his god. You will become a handmaiden with no life or freedom of your own, living only to serve the priests until the day you are called to

9

join with Xyakah. For the lucky ones that means death. For the others, poor souls, it means a journey to the Eastern desert, to mount Tystar. You would not wish to know their fate."

Elayna looked up into her tutor's face, his eyes welled with tears. "How do you know this?" She asked.

"I have seen the papers. Your father signed them in the library two days ago, I didn't mean to walk in on him, I thought the room to be empty, but it wasn't. As I entered, he quickly moved the documents, but I am from the Far West, you know how sharp my eyesight is. There is no doubt in my mind."

It was true she knew Lyaren's eyesight was a wonder. But perhaps he had made a mistake. She did not need to phrase the question. He had anticipated it and continued with his tale.

"Last night I followed your father. After he left your room, he went to the temple. I slipped in past the guards and watched him make his pledge before the altar. Afterwards there was a ceremony; do you remember Taya, Lord Edrin's youngest?"

"Yes, we were friends as children." She hardly dare listen to what was coming next. The sense of dread in the pit of her stomach grew, twisting into a knot of nausea.

"She's dead! I watched from the shadows for as long as I could stomach it, then I fled, but there is no way she could have survived what I saw them do to her."

"Will they do that to me?" The question came unbidden from her lips.

"No Ela." His voice softened, "They won't do that to you because I won't let them!" Looking deep into her eyes he clasped her hands tighter; lifting them briefly to his lips, he kissed them lightly then said, "If you will allow me, My Lady, I will pledge my life to protect you." The offer hung in the air as the solemnity of it registered in Elayna's mind.

"Lyaren, you are my only friend in the world and so I must trust your word but, even so, I could never ask you to put yourself in danger for me."

"Then don't ask," he smiled "for I offer my help freely and would have it no other way." He stood and took a step back. "For now I think you are safe here but not for long! I will make the preparations and while I am gone I want you to dress in your riding clothes and find your winter cloak, despite the warming of the days the nights are still bitterly cold and we may be on the road for some time. Don't worry, I will take you to my people; they will help us." Turning quickly he strode to the door "I won't be long Ela, I promise." and then he was gone.

His mind swimming Lyaren made his way down the dim corridors. He knew full well the horror of Elayna's fate should the pending marriage occur and the thought of it churned his stomach. How could he have let it get so far? He had been sent to protect her and yet he had not seen this coming. He had allowed himself to enjoy his position as tutor and slipped so easily into the role that he had forgotten to take the most basic of precautions. It would not happen again, he promised himself. They would have to kill him to get at her!

With a grunt Gadon levered himself to his feet leaving the spent, naked body of the stable lad sprawled on the bed behind him. Gadon had checked the boy's pulse, as he always did since the unfortunate incident two seasons ago with the gardener's apprentice. That young man, whose body had appeared in the river several miles downstream, had caused considerable inconvenience!

11

Gadon rubbed the side of his head. The pain was still there burning like a branding iron inside his skull. It was the Tissa; it always did this when he allowed any uncertainty to get the better of him. He had felt no regrets after he had thrown in his lot with Desca and his Xyakahan friends. At first Desca had simply made a good drinking and whoreing partner. Gadon had quickly realised his new acquaintance had a darker side to his nature, but the narcotic Tissa, which he had introduced to Gadon, seemed to deaden the mind to apprehension, fear or concern for oneself or others around you. That first night he had not been troubled at all by the act of brutality the two of them had inflicted on the young bar maid as she made her way home through the fields. He remembered vividly the smell of urine as she emptied her bladder in panic and, as this smell mingled with that of her blood, how his lust grew and he was overcome with a pleasure which far outweighed any sexual encounter he had experienced previously. After that Desca had begun to take him to the temple and Gadon had been introduced to the other priests. They had been only too keen to welcome him to their fold and delighted in his enthusiastic participation of their sacred rights. The rituals all involved sacrifice and pain - it was essential for the magic and Gadon relished every scream and cherished the sight of naked flesh against the dull steel edge of a blade.

As time went by Gadon took more and more of the drug Tissa, which seemed to heighten his darker side. The priests had shown him how to use the drug's effect on the brain to sense the life force of the sacrifice as death drew near, and feed on it as it fled the panic strewn victim. They used this life force for dark magic, but Gadon found it gave him strength and renewed life. He was beginning to feel as if his life was worth living again and he knew with certainty that his future lay with the priesthood.

Not even after his visit to his daughter's apartments last night had his resolve been weakened. He no longer knew or cared for the girl who had become a stranger to him since his involvement with the priests. Now he cherished only the Tissa and the power it offered to him!

After he had left Elayna he had ventured down to the temple to join the priests on their night of praise-giving to Xyakah and to pledge his own existence to the God. Many times had Gadon witnessed the sacred rites with their brutal sacrifices. They talked in the village of the demon priests and their horrific ceremonies, but their stories didn't begin to hint at the true evil of the brotherhood. The ritual began at sunset with chanting and the priests would cut themselves to purify their own blood for the ceremony to come. Then they would eat a meal of raw meats including the hearts of ox, sheep and pig. On special ceremonies such as tonight there would be human flesh too. Gadon did not know the nature of the flesh he ate, but he knew all creatures eaten in this meal must be less than a month in age and more than that he did not need to know!

As the night went on more of the followers had arrived in time for their participation. Only men followed Xyakah, women served other purposes within the temple. This was when Gadon had arrived donning his blood-red robes as the others did, loose fitting for the sexual acts which would follow. Tissa was passed around for all to take, and in large trays around the temple courtyard the Tissa leaves burned giving off an aromatic and addictive odour. Strong mead also laced with Tissa was drunk and slowly the expectation and excitement among the small throng of men began to grow. The first sacrifice had been a lamb and its

13

suffering was relatively short lived. Once dead the creature was drained of blood and this was passed around in the black ceremonial challis for the followers to drink. Gadon had found this hard at first but now he drank deeply, allowing the still-warm blood to trickle down his mouth and chin. Next the priests had brought out the handmaidens of Xyakah and each had fornicated with the girls before they had been sent out to the waiting followers. Gadon passed on the offers made by the dead-eyed girls - he no longer took pleasure from them - but watching his fellow participants heightened his own arousal and he began looking at the girls' auras, searching for any near to death from whom to draw life force and intensify the effects of the Tissa in his blood stream. Most of the women were near to death by the end of the orgy, their bodies torn and bleeding from wounds made by teeth, knife and fist, but only three were actually dead. Still, it had been enough and now he hungered for the next part of the ceremony. The air hummed with the chanting of the priests and the weeping of the women. The smell of blood and other bodily fluids mingled with the Tissa, and a hypnotic trance-like state settled over the gathered worshipers.

The final sacrifice of the night of praise was to be a young human girl of about seventeen. As the priests carried her out it was obvious she had been drugged with Dragath and her eyes held a vacant expression. An unnatural silence gathered over the worshippers as they took in the beautiful, ample curves of the girl's pale flesh; perfect, unblemished in any way. Two young initiates held her naked body upright while the high priest approached chanting the thick nasal chants of the ancient scrolls. The girl did not respond as he approached, Dragath did that to a person, it imprisoned the spirit, the girl may as well be dead. Slowly and with expert precision the priest ran the jagged edge of the blade down the length of the girl's body, applying just enough pressure to reveal a trickle of blood extending from throat to navel. Then one by one the girl's toes and fingers had the skin peeled away from them leaving the tendons and muscles exposed. The girl tensed. Even under the influence of the drug the pain was beginning to register. Turning from the offering to face the gathered throng of worshippers, the priest threw wide his arms and cried out in a commanding voice summoning the power of Xyakah. The oblivious body of the girl was carried to the altar where a second priest approached carrying rope and a large pitcher. When her arms and legs had been securely fastened to the large iron rings at the corners of the altar she was forced to drink from the pitcher, which contained the Dragath antidote. Instantly she was brought to full consciousness! Coherence and understanding sprang to the girl's face and she began to whimper in fear and panic. Despite her struggle the girl was held fast by the ropes and the high priest had then continued his gruesome work peeling away the skin from the girl's body to expose muscle and sinew beneath. Time passed as he expertly exposed the muscle, nerves and bone of her arms, legs and torso. The girl should have been long dead, but black magic held her fragile soul to her body. Three times the girl passed out and each time a little of the Dragath antidote brought her back to consciousness. She had lost control of bladder and bowel so the smell of urine and excrement was mingled with the stench of death which resided in the temple. The followers of Xyakah began to pick up the priests' chant, their voices droning out in a monotonous rhythm. The girl no longer struggled; she had gone into shock. Gadon knew the signs but she would not be allowed to stay in this ignorant state. She had to be fully aware of what was happening to her when she finally allowed to die. The high priest manipulated the blade over the girl's face revealing cheek bone and removing ears. Always the girl was on the rim of life, her aura hovering just above her body giving off more than enough life force to sustain the assembled crowd. Gadon breathed deeply. He could almost taste the life force as it rushed into his body.

The ceremony reached its height. The high priest drew back his blade for the final slashing kill, but as the ritual commanded he stayed his hand. In unison the worshippers began the chant "Xyakah... Xyakah..." Louder and louder the chant grew, faster and faster the words cascaded over each other to form a crescendo of reverence...

Somewhere in the distance thunder boomed, as if announcing his arrival, and from the ceremonial flames which burned beyond the altar a shadowy figure emerged. Xyakah was amongst them. His huge demonic figure hovered above the girl, a carrion preparing to feed. His body was almost completely covered with hair, thick with a black oily sheen, but his chest and head were scaled and in the firelight they reflected the deep crimson of blood. His face was horribly disfigured but the eyes were unmistakably human and only just began to hint at the intellect behind them.

"My children," he began, his voice thick and edged with a deep throated growl. He licked his thin peeled back lips with a reptilian tongue and sticky red spittle ran down his chin. "Thank you for this fine gift, it will feed my body, soul and spirit!" His voice, laced with pleasure, boomed across the assembly, rattling bones with its resonance. Slowly the creature unfurled its body to reveal its already stimulated sexual organ. The priest with the pitcher bowed low before his god and approached the girl's now skeletal glossy face. Only her eyes betrayed her once beautiful features; her mouth gaped like a bloody cavern where her teeth had been removed, and it was into her mouth that the priest poured a large quantity of Dragath antidote - under normal circumstances enough to kill within a few hours, but here that wouldn't matter. Now she looked into the face of Xyakah with total lucidity as the true nature of his evil swamped over her! Rendered mute she struggled to scream, what remained of her face contorting into a mask of tortured terror.

As he entered her she thrashed her body about in an attempt to escape him, but the result only aroused him more and as the struggle continued she began to tear and bleed even more from the ripped flesh. Bearing down on her he licked at her exposed flesh and when he raised his head to his followers his fangs gleamed with the deep crimson of her blood. The chanting increased. The assembled worshippers were on their feet awaiting their lord to reach his climax and end her life.

Gadon knew he should stand too, but he could not. The girls eyes still held him spellbound... he knew her... and with this recognition his whole past life came flooding back. She was Taya, Edrin's youngest. He remembered a happier time in a small fishing boat, sitting back with his friend Edrin as they watched their beautiful daughters play together on the bank of the lake, Taya's black hair complementing Elayna's red. The girls were laughing and so were their mothers, as the small ball was tossed from player to player. Falling deeper and deeper into the girl's gaze the memories flooded back, and then he saw it - recognition of his familiar face watching her torment. Had she any features left he knew she would be pleading with him to help her, and dear god he wanted to.

Xyakah growled as he reached his climax and the spell which bound him to the ceremony ended. He vanished and then she was dead...

The walk home had been a long one, but the pounding in Gadon's head would not clear. Not even an hour with the gardener's apprentice, who enjoyed his masters pleasure as much as he did, had found him any relief from the memory of dead girl's eyes... or were they Elayna's eyes? In his heart he knew he had signed his daughter's death warrant and that no death could ever be more dreadful. There was only one thing he could do.

The fire had burned low in his room but there was still flame enough for his needs. Sitting before the little hearth Lyaren focused on the tiny flames leaping in the grate and summoned the image of Kiam to his mind. The flames leapt higher in response to his power and slowly at first but with increasing speed the soft gentle features of his master's face began to form in his mind's eye. The deep hazel eyes looked directly into Lyaren's soul, betraying his concern, and the dark blue marks beneath told of too many hours spent on study and too few on sleep. His long white hair hung in ringlets framing an angular face with a tight scowl, and so the completed image steadied and the link was formed.

"Kiam, my master, I have little time." Lyaren began.

"I know Lyaren, quickly, tell me of your findings." Kiam's voice always calmed the reeling mind of his student and Lyaren took a deep breath before he replied. "Gadon has agreed to give the girl over to the priests, I cannot protect her here, I must take her away - and quickly."

"Then I pray the Goddess keeps you safe. It will be a hard road but I know you can do it. Be on your guard my student, the Xyakahan priests have much magic; they will know how to use their dark arts to seek you out, and there are many other dangers on the path."

"I know, I have underestimated the dangers here and put the prophecy in jeopardy, but I will not fail again. This I swear!"

"Lyaren, we have every faith in you. You will do as you must." The image began to waver, and then it was gone.

Lyaren rose and walked to the window. Opening the shutters he could see the sun was now high in the sky. With most of the servants gone it had been easy to gather provisions and secure them along with two horses in the winter storehouse to the south of the manor house. It only remained to scout the area for Xyakahan priests and then they would flee.

A figure moving in the courtyard below caught Lyaren's attention. The old stable hand led Gadon's silver mare towards the house where Gadon himself waited by the door. Shunting his bulk awkwardly into the saddle he took the reins and with a flick of the whip raced off through the open gates.

Moving back from the window Lyaren removed his clothes and began the ritual meditation. When he felt the edge of his consciousness tingle with the infusion of power he began softly to chant. He gasped as spasmodic ripples gripped his muscles, twisting and reforming his body. Arms shortened and bent at an unnatural angle sprouting feathers as they transformed into wings. His body also altered, as did his mind. No longer did Lyaren see the world quite like a man.

High above the ground beyond the range of human sight the magnificent white eagle glided on the updrafts of air. Kiam had been delighted when his pupil first took on his animal form and brought about the beginning of the long awaited prophecy. Lyaren had not known of its existence before then but there could be no mistaking that he was to perform one of the key roles as it was played out.

It had taken Lyaren only seconds to locate Gadon as he made his way through the green fields which served the Xyakahan temple. The horse made good speed despite its burden and was not challenged by the guards at the gate as it rushed into the courtyard. Dismounting, Gadon shooed away the man who came to take his horse. "Teysti!" Gadon bellowed as he demanded to see the high priest. Several figures in red robes scurried in and out of the temple with offers of refreshments, bidding him to enter the sanctuary for amusement while he waited, but Gadon stood firm. After some time Teysti, the head priest, appeared dressed in the purple robes of his office, his long solemn face was pulled into a scowl. He was obviously annoyed by the intrusion on his privacy.

"I am here," Gadon's voice was strong and firm like it once had been, "To beg your mercy."

The priest laughed without humour, his voice laced with mirth, "You will find no mercy here, Gadon, and besides," he raised an eyebrow. "You do not sound as if you are begging to me."

"All the same I have made a mistake and I am here to put things right." He spoke plainly; assertively.

"We do not make mistakes Gadon!" Teysti snapped. "What is this about? I am a busy man with no time for foolishness."

"My life and my wealth I have given to the temple; all that I am is yours for I am a true follower of Xyakah."

Bowing his head with raised eyebrow the priest acknowledged the statement.

"But..." Gadon continued. "I must ask that my daughter be allowed to leave before I join with you. I have no right to pledge her life to a God she does not follow."

20

The priest sighed and nodded his head sympathetically. "I understand your distress, Gadon. In fact, I felt the same way about my own daughters. But on the night they became one with Xyakah I knew I had made the right decision. My lord was most impressed with my sacrifice and made a most distinguished place for my girls in his After world."

For a moment Gadon felt confused and disorientated, but the image of the wretched girl's face from the previous night formed strongly in his mind's eye and, changing and shifting, it became the face of Elayna. In frustration his temper rose and with sudden clarity he knew what he must do. "I want her to go free, and if that is not possible then I will withdraw my pledge to the temple!"

Lyaren heard Gadon's anger as he spit out the words to withdraw his pledge. He saw him turn to leave. He did not see the high priest make a simple hand gesture to the archer on the temple roof.

Nor did he see the archer draw his bow, aim and fire. He did see the arrow, true to its mark, slice through Gadon's neck and leave him in a pool of his own blood on the temple floor.

Circling the temple and sick to his stomach the white eagle raced back towards Galloheart Keep; only seconds later a group of armed horsemen, led by a priest in black robes, were dispatched from the temple in the same direction.

Elayna heard the horses enter the courtyard. A cold chill ran down her spine and the hairs on the nape of her neck tingled as though caressed by ghostly fingers. It felt like forever waiting for Ly to return. She had eaten a light breakfast, packed her things then read a little as a distraction. Then several hours ago Anna had brought her food on a tray and they had shared their goodbyes. In dismay the housekeeper, who had been such a good friend over the years, had confessed that the other members of the household staff had already gone, and that her and Damian were also about to depart. After a tearful farewell Anna had fled the room. Elayna listened sorrowfully to the sound of her footsteps diminishing down the corridor for the last time. Within the hour a small wagon piled high with an odd assortment of personal possessions, collected over many happy years of service, twisted its way down the lane until finally only a faint cloud of dust marked its progress on the horizon. Ela had sat on the window seat then to wait for Ly as afternoon passed into evening. He had told her to be ready and wait, but he had been such a long time she couldn't help thinking he had chosen to leave without her. Absently she rummaged through the few small keepsakes she had selected to take with her: an intricately carved bone comb made for her by her brother; the tiny cameo of her mother which sat by her bed, and the slender woodman's hunting knife - a gift from Ly on her last birthday.

The clatter of hooves gave way to husky male voices accompanied by a vigorous hammering on the front door. The violence of the intrusion on the silence of the forsaken house shook Elayna into action and silently she slid back the bolt on her bedroom door. Easing it open she slipped like a ghost out into the corridor beyond, making little sound as she moved towards the stairwell.

"Search the house! The high priest wants her alive!" The voice whipped through the calm of the house like a slaughter man's knife, slashing at a throat to make the kill. By the sound of the echo on the stairway they were inside the house just below the grand staircase. Elayna flattened herself against the wall, thoughts racing. She couldn't fight the panic welling up inside her but, unexpectedly, instincts from childhood games of hide and seek entered her thoughts. Without a sound she dashed along the gloomy corridor towards the servants' stairs. The sound of blood pumping in her ears created a nauseating sensation which she struggled to overcome. Behind her she could hear heavy boot falls on the stone steps and smell the stench of men who spent too much time with horses. Reaching the end of the corridor she came to the green tapestry which concealed an old unused door to the servant stairwell. Heaving it aside, she grasped with trembling fingers for the catch, felt the coarse rusted metal beneath her fingers and tugged down. Groaning with alarming intensity the door swung open.

A shout was let out from somewhere behind and, glancing over her shoulder, Elayna noticed the shadow of several men, cast by the light from the sole window at the top of the otherwise murky stairs. Acknowledging the certainty of her capture, but refusing to accept it all the same, she flung herself through the small doorway, which slid shut behind her, and raced down the stairs. Twisting her way down the spiral stairwell her feet skimmed each step with indifference to danger, reaching her destination before she had registered where she was going.

The servant's stairs continued down below the house and into the large cellar where supplies were stored for the winter. If she could get to the grain store, beyond the wine cellar, there was a tiny door concealed behind the end row of shelves. It led to a narrow tunnel which she and Gaylon had discovered as children, though when their father had found out he had banned them from playing there. The tunnel was old and far from safe, "An accident waiting to happen!" he had said, but if it hadn't caved in it lead beyond the garden walls and opened into a small gully concealed by a dense thicket of gorse bushes on the fringe of the woods to the west of the house.

At the bottom of the stairs she stopped, ears strained for the sound of pursuit but she heard none. In the darkness silence surrounded her like a phantom teasing her very nerves apart. Hastily she felt her way in the murkiness of the cellar, moving easily through the familiar maze below the house. She found the place with ease and wiggled behind the huge shelf stocked high with small sacks of flour. Hidden in the darkness the concealed door opened to her touch, but crawling into the slight passageway was more complex; she had to bend almost double to nudge herself into the total blackness of the dank, disquieting passageway.

Lyaren transformed himself instantly upon reaching his rooms and hurriedly dressed in his riding leathers. Gathering together his few possessions he flung them into a small bag, took one last look at the room which had been his home for the past three and a half years and rushed out of the door. He heard the horses at the front of the house and cursed himself for a fool. He should never have left her, but he had no idea things had gone so far. Ela's room was at the other side of the hall; he would have to run. At the end of the corridor he turned left, making his way as directly as he could without the risk of being seen. He could hear coarse voices coming from all directions both in and outside the house which, by this time, was overrun with Xyakahan hired mercenaries. "Gods," he issued a silent prayer, "let me get to her before they do!"

Just down the corridor stood the door to Ela's apartments; there were men climbing the stairs just beyond. "Ela!" The cry came unbidden as he rushed into the room, only to find it deserted.

Lyaren ran to the window, leaning out as far as he dare for a sight of her in the gardens below. Channelling his powers he scanned the familiar rooms of the house with his mind, reaching out for a sense of her essence. He saw mercenaries, very close to the room now, but he ignored them. The upper levels of the house were empty; his mind's eye plunged down to the floors below. Desperately he searched, as the frantic edge of panic began to rise. Had he failed so soon in his task? And then he found her, safe and unhurt, moving slowly but surely through the shadows of the cellar.

"What do we have here?"

As the voice broke his concentration Lyaren's eyes snapped open and instantly his senses drew back into his body. His hand reached down for his hunting knife as he took in his predicament. Three burly looking men stood in the doorway and a fourth stood just before him, gleaming broadsword drawn and level to his breast. He stayed his hand as the point of the blade pressed deeper into his chest.

"Who are you? What do you want here?" Lyaren feigned ignorance.

It was the priest who answered in a voice laced with honey... "We have come for..." Pushing his way past the guards to enter the room his voice trailed away as he took in Lyaren's appearance. "Ah, and just what do we have here?" Looking Lyaren up and down, the corners of the priest's mouth twitched with malicious pleasure. He noted the slight muscular stature of the man before him, long slender hands and shoulder-length ebony hair. Looking Lyaren straight in the eyes he sneered, "I do believe we have found us some dragon fodder!" He chuckled without humour, placing a gnarled and blackened claw-like fingernail against his own smooth sharp chin.

Lyaren ignored the insult, which was lost on the other men in the room. He could feel the priest's black powers probing his aura; he was strong, not just a showman like most of the fools from the temple. This one was a true Xyakahan high warlock, and Lyaren knew he must act quickly if he was to stand any chance at all.

"I believe I asked my question first." Ly stalled for time.

"And since when have reptile slugs like you had the authority to ask a question of Xyakah's chosen ones!" The priest's voice lay thick with malice. He moved closer, extending his deformed hand to touch Lyaren's sun-browned forearm. "What a pretty coat your hide will make," he crooned. "You are indeed fortunate, slave, for you will be given the ultimate honour; you will lay forth your life force to feed the sacred one."

Then everything seemed to happen at once. The warlock, laughing, reached forward to take the deadly knife from Lyaren's belt. In the same instance Lyaren threw a blinding spell into the eyes of the guards. Turning at the sound of his men's cries the warlock gave Lyaren the chance he needed to catch him off guard. Chanting the words of binding Lyaren released his full power on the warlock, channelling straight into the priest's mind. As Lyaren had anticipated, his adversary was already forming a counter-spell. Grasping the strands of the priest's power Lyaren flipped the spell, redirecting it back to the priest who moaned and fell with a thud to the floor, all his evil powers reversed to work against him, their weight pinning him to the ground more forcefully than any number of warriors could.

Without stopping to think Lyaren leapt across the room kicking the cowering bodies of the guards out of his way with ease. Racing back down the corridor, relying solely on his instincts, he flew in Ela's wake. By the time he reached the underground store his powers were all but spent. His body screamed out against the torture of the exertion he had endured but somehow he found the strength to heighten his sense of smell. In a matter of seconds he had found the small door at the back of the grain store and dragged himself into the tunnel. As the door swung shut behind him Lyaren passed out.

The journey through the tunnel had been like a nightmare. The blackness clung around Elayna like a cloak of doom. Beneath hands and knees the damp earth was covered with a slick film of slime, which moved and wriggled as countless insects scuttled through and over her fingers. The smell of decay hung in the stale, motionless air like a herald of tragedy. Arms and legs protested as she continued her measured progress, dragging herself through the narrow tunnel at a painfully slow pace. Tree roots reached down from the tunnel ceiling, snatching her hair and clawing her shoulders, forcing her to flatten her body against the ground to get by them. All the while the darkness was her oppressive companion, drawing in on her consciousness and forcing fear to rise up and intensify as panic encompassed her whole being.

Afterwards she couldn't tell how long the nightmare had lasted, but as she finally felt the first whisper of fresh air against her skin the malevolent horror of the tunnel began to loosen its hold.

She crawled out of the tunnel mouth as the early evening dusk was falling over the dense, silent woodland surrounding her and, in exhaustion; she curled into a tight ball. Surrendering her will, sleep at last embraced her.

No rest had come with the sleep, only nightmares of demonic abductors, and a fear which coils its victims like a snake, squeezing the mind until sanity fades away. After what seemed a very short time she woke and lay listening to the sounds of the night. Several times she heard men's voices as they searched the woods for her, but terror had overtaken all senses and she lay frozen and rooted to the ground - an ice statue in the gloom. For the past few minutes another sound had held her interest, a rhythmic whisper on the wind. At first she had felt it with her body through the earth she pressed herself against, but now the sound was emerging and growing in volume. A scraping followed by a thud, a rattle and a tapping; Then she understood. Something was moving in the tunnel!

Excruciating cramps crippled Elayna's cold, damp legs as she hurriedly struggled to free her body from the shelter of the tunnel mouth, inhaling large lungfuls of air to smother her pending cry of pain. She had no weapon, but she had survived this far and was not ready to give in now. When they came through the tunnel she would be ready!

By the slight shaft of moonlight emerging through the woodland canopy she could just make out the shape of a large flat rock. Her fingers curled around it and she felt the smooth contours of stone with a pointed bump on its underside. Small insects darted between her fingers, disturbed in their night-time errands, but she didn't even notice them.

She could hear his breathing now, whistling down the tunnel, and then a sigh as he must have realised his journey was close to its end. Long fingers emerged first curling around the tunnel's mouth to pull the body through afterwards. Elayna held the stone high, and as the head appeared she brought the stone down. The man's eyes opened wide, shining emerald in the fading light. Recognition came instantly, but it was too late... She put all her energy into stopping the stone as it thundered down towards its target, but the momentum was too strong. With a stomach churning thud the point of the stone came down firmly on the side of Lyaren's head.

The bleeding lasted only minutes, yet it seemed hours to Elayna as the realisation of what had just happened settled in amongst all the other torments of the past twenty-four hours. An angry contusion began to form, inflaming the side of Lyaren's head, and as the moments dragged by, most of his left eye became buried beneath the swelling. Afraid to make a fire, but aware of the need to keep him warm, Elayna wrapped her own cloak around them both and lay close to share her body heat. Although the voices had now stopped and she prayed that the soldiers had given up their search, she did not sleep.

For most of the night they lay there in the small clearing surrounded by thick gorse bushes, until at last the first early rays of rising sun filtered through the leaves above them and Lyaren stirred.

His head burned like hell, but when he opened his eyes he realised the discomfort was as much from his excessive use of magic as it was from the physical injury.

"Lyaren, are you alright?" Her voice was little more than a breath, yet thick with emotion and on the brink of breaking. He understood that the soft form curled around his back must be her; amongst the odour of leaf mould and damp earth, he could just smell traces of the musty perfume she favoured. "Ly...Ly can you hear me?" Her voice was firmer now. She put her hand on his arm and shook gently, her body trembling slightly as she fought to control her fear.

"It's all right Ela, I'm fine," he answered. He didn't feel fine at all, but it was what she needed to hear. With a slight touch of his power he probed tentatively at his bones and organs, his wizards' sight finding no serious injuries, only bruising. He turned his attention to Elayna; she seemed to be fine, though very frightened.

"What hit me?" he sat up and rubbed his head.

"Oh, I'm sorry Ly" Elayna sat up too, and rubbed at the drying mud which had plastered itself to the side of her face. "When I heard someone in the tunnel I was so afraid, I thought it was those men and..." she turned away at a loss as to what to say.

"It's alright, Ela. I admit my head hurts but I'll be fine in a while, we just have to work out how to get ourselves out of here."

From what Elayna had told him of the voices she had heard throughout the night, Lyaren felt sure the priests would have found the horses and supplies he had concealed by the thicket at the manor house's south gate, which meant they would have to continue on foot. It would be hard on Elayna, but not impossible. The first dilemma was the thicket they were currently in. The gorse bushes were copious and displayed a densely tangled web of vicious-looking thorns. He tried his best to thrash the worst of the branches out of the way, yet for every branch he cut through a second seemed to leap into its place. By the time they emerged from the tangle of branches they both sported ripped clothes and numerous tears and scratches to arms and face. The clearing into which they emerged was a fair distance from the forest proper so, hugging the hedgerows, they slowly made their way to the shelter of the trees. As the sun rose high into the late morning sky, they finally entered the leafy enclosure of the forest and Lyaren visibly relaxed. At least they would have shelter should the priest's men get close. He had been vigilant ever since he woke, using his powers to scout the area ahead and thus lead them away from the numerous detachments of men searching for them. The spell he had worked on that priest back at the house was strong; provided there was not a second with his powers he would be out of it for a few days, but that was all. Once he had horses he would not be far behind. Speed was the imperative!

In silence the two fugitives made their way through the forest, the urgency of the situation quickening their step. Terror gave them the strength to keep up a gruelling pace for the whole of the day. As the first rays of the sun began to set, Lyaren started collecting berries from the bushes they passed. Ela did likewise and so it was on a feast of forest fare the two of them supped that night and then, as the moon rose, Lyaren told Ela of her father and Elayna cried herself to sleep.

When he was sure she slept soundly he transformed himself into the great white eagle, and from the skies he confirmed his suspicions that they were pretty much surrounded by scattered units of mercenaries. About a mile away he located their main camp - a group of about ten men and the priest from Ela's room. Now that Lyaren had revealed his powers to the priest, he doubted he would have the same success against him should they meet again. Making one last circle of the enemy camp he caught a warm updraft and made his way back towards his most precious of charges.

Kizin bowed low before the flickering image of his master, which he had called to the fire. Xyakah, even through the fire, was an imposing image, sitting astride his thrown of human skulls, eyes slit like a snake and wearing armour of blood-red gold.

"What is it Kizin?" boomed the voice of the Demi-god from deep within the fire's heart.

31

"Oh powerful one I have failed you" Kizin prostrated himself before the flames "I offer my life in payment for my incompetence." There was no fear, he knew he had failed and accepted his punishment.

"And tell me, worthless dog, why I should allow your death before you have the chance to suffer for your mistakes?" The image seemed to swell within the blaze and the flames leapt higher into the night sky in response to his anger. "Come, Kizin, tell me how you have failed me."

"Master, the girl was in my grasp yet she escaped me, and with an Elvin sorcerer as an ally."

"Imbecile!" Xyakah spat out his retort, serpentine tongue slithering between his thinly peeled back lips and spittle running down his elongated jaw line. "That one's life belongs to me and I will have her, Kizin. Do you understand me?"

"Yes master... I am your servant."

"That you are, fool! You will find her and kill the elf. Her I need alive. Now rectify your mistake before I tire of your incompetence's..." He turned away, then thought better of it, "And Kizin, you will not fail me again or your punishment will last for all eternity!"

"I hear you master" Kizin bowed low before the image and then Xyakah was gone.

"Ela, wake up!" Lyaren shook her firmly, but the urgency in his voice would have been enough to bring her round to wakefulness.

"I'm awake." She heard her own voice through a sleepy haze.

"Good." Ignoring her obvious lethargy he took hold of her arms and dragged her to her feet.

"Ow!" Ela started to protest but Lyaren's hand was over her mouth before the sound could emerge.

"Shh!" He spoke quietly and close to her ear, his voice barely a whisper. "We must get moving quickly, the guards are very close and I have no intention of getting myself or you killed."

Ela nodded allowing him to remove his hand from her mouth. "How can you be sure, Ly?" she whispered in reply.

"I have no time to explain now, you must trust me! Come on, quickly." And he pulled her in the direction of a small game track which led off through the trees. As she glanced back over her shoulder Ela noticed that all signs of their small camp had been erased. No trace of their presence remained. She couldn't help but be somewhat astounded at Lyaren's apparent knowledge of wood law; it seemed there was more to her schoolmaster than met the eye.

Hurrying to catch up she ran after the quickly disappearing figure before her. Lyaren set a nightmare pace, even greater than the day before, and Ela was rapidly discovering that she was not made for such gruelling jaunts in the woods. Every stone and branch seemed to dig into the soft underside of her riding boots and each step was bringing fresh tears to her eyes. Her clothes torn and dirty from the previous day's flight had become stiff with dried mud and they chafed her skin as she walked, adding to the discomfort of the scratches and blisters she had already accumulated. Ela didn't feel comfortable in the forest, and the periodic howl of wolves which punctuated the silence sent fresh shivers down her spine. In short she was a sorry wretch and as the constant trek showed little sign of relenting she found herself resenting Lyaren and directing the blame for her misery at him. Finally, as the sun climbed high overhead, she threw herself to the ground in total desolation. She had tried so hard to be brave, for her sake and for Ly's, but this was all too much and now she realised she could not hope to escape the forest alive. Rocking silently back and forth she wept without tears; it appeared even her eyes were incapable of cooperating.

Lyaren was instantly aware that Ela had stopped. Every fibre of his being was tuned into the forest, alert for the slightest hint of a presence. In fact their pursuers were all around them and only his heightened senses kept them from stumbling straight into an ambush. The next few days would be vital if they were to escape. But he had made a big mistake and only now did he realise it. Ela didn't truly believe the danger they were in. Yes, she had accepted the reality of yesterday - events had forced her to - yet she didn't know who she truly was and could have no idea of how desperately the Xyakahan priests wanted her. He had to try and make her understand, except there was no time for a full explanation now. He could only hope she would trust him enough to do as he asked and thus keep them both alive!

Turning, he made his way back to the sobbing girl. He took in her sorrowful appearance and sought only to take her in his arms and tell her everything would be all right... But would it?

"Ela," He kept his voice low, "We must keep going, the priest's men are very close and if we stop for long they will be upon us."

Lost in her misery the words meant nothing to her, the sense of danger was nothing more than a dull ache in the back of her head. Lyaren took her hand in his. His voice was full of compassion. "Come, little one, let me help you. I swore a sacred oath to your brother that I would protect you, and that I shall do. Please do not allow your father and brother to have died for naught. You must survive so their memory will live on."

"Why should I live when they are dead?" she sobbed, looking up at him with desolate eyes. Standing swiftly, she turned on her heels and stumbled away from him, back down the slight game track in the direction they had come. Blindly she staggered through the woods; straight into the sight of a startled Xyakahan guard who it appeared had just finished answering the call of nature! Although shocked, the man acted quickly throwing his arms around the girl who was screaming and thrashing like a wild thing.

Then Lyaren was there - eyes alight with fire, energy bristling from every fibre; he hurled himself at the soldier in one fluid motion, hitting him with such momentum that his reaction sent Elayna toppling ungraciously to the forest floor. As the soldier also overbalanced he crashed down hard against the ground, but Lyaren seemed to manipulate the air around him. Twisting his body at an impossible angle, he righted himself before his feet had reached the ground and brought the heel of his boot down on the man's neck, snapping it instantaneously!

The whole encounter had taken less than a minute, yet to Elayna it had all unfolded in slow motion. First she had felt shock as the man grabbed her, then horror as she realised what she had done. Lyaren had saved her; with flawless, perfect movements he had delivered his dance of death. Like a thunderbolt the realisation of her own stupidity crashed down on her. She could have got them both killed!

She didn't argue as Lyaren helped her back to her feet. She expected a reprimand but none came. Protectively he folded her in his arms and then he led her back down the game track and away from the danger. She was never sure if he had heard her whispered apology but she meant it with all her heart. She wasn't really sure what she had just seen, but of one thing she was very certain, Lyaren was far more than a simple tutor... Far more!

Chapter 2
Calin

Calin pulled the heavy cloak tight around his shoulders as the night chill began to settle in, giving a silent prayer to the Earth mother for the good fortune which saw him warm and comfortable. For the past three years he had been apprenticed to a master ironsmith. Now he returned home, a guildsman in his own right, with a letter of recommendation from Master Ellis himself, head craftsman of the Tarrow guild of forge workers. His cart was loaded high with a good supply of tools, a gift from his tutor to help him establish his own business. He smiled as he imagined the look on his mother's face upon his return. A poor widow, she was always so proud of her son and had never doubted his ability to make something of himself. Calin knew she would glow with pride to see him a wealthy man.

He had been on the road for almost a week now and with the cart and his heavy-set carthorse, Greg, he had made good speed. From time to time he'd encountered fellow travellers, but any out to cause trouble took one look at the well-muscled youth with a huge broadsword strapped to his back and gave him a wide berth. In short his journey had been wholly uneventful. Despite this Calin was no fool, and felt very strongly the need to take precautions against the bandits who stalked these parts. Tonight he had chosen to take refuge in the forest, choosing the location for his camp with a care for both isolation and seclusion. With a large tree at his back and his horses and wagon concealed by a thicket of rhododendrons, Calin blended expertly into the forest. And so it was, confident in his own judgment, that Calin nodded off to sleep.

Instantly woken by the sound of movement Calin sprang to his feet, wielding his massive broadsword like a child's toy. Patiently he stood his ground, waiting as the intruders approached. When they did finally emerge through the murky darkness of the forest Calin could have laughed with relief. Only the pitiful state of the two bedraggled figures before him stayed his mirth. Somewhere beneath the mud and grime there appeared to be a man and young girl; however, they were so filthy it was hard to be sure. In the dying firelight their eyes were gaunt with exhaustion, their clothes hanging like rags from their slight frames. The child looked like a startled rabbit, ready to bolt at any moment, yet the man had a firm determination in his eyes betraying the strength remaining in his tortured physique.

It was the man who broke the silence; his voice strong and calm. "We did not mean to intrude on your camp though, if you would allow us, we would share your fire?" he smiled, "If not we will be on our way." Calin lowered the sword and gestured with his free hand for the two to approach. "My fire is almost burned out, and with the bandits I'd rather not rekindle it, but I've a little food left, and by the look of y'r, your needs are greater than mine."

"Thank you," the man whispered gratefully. "We are indeed very hungry," he inclined his head towards the girl. "My charge has not eaten a decent meal in the last few weeks."

"Then come and sit," Calin smiled. "My name is Calin, and my camp is yours."

The tension seemed to dissipate and Calin fetched the remainders of the thick venison stew and a large chunk of bread. The two strangers sat meekly by the embers of the fire, too fatigued to attempt conversation, their bearing expressing total exhaustion.

Elayna had been enthralled by the fearsome giant who challenged them in the clearing. After her initial assumption that he would kill them in their tracks, his kindness had come as some surprise. Since the incident with the Xyakahan guard, Lyaren had led her through a maze of tangled foliage for more days than she cared to remember. The forest had provided food, but as Lyaren would not light a fire they had lived on roots and berries. They stopped only when they could walk no further and ate only when hunger demanded. They had not talked about what Ly had done, although she felt sure he had wanted to on more than one occasion. It was as if the incident had happened to someone else and they had simply been observers from far away.

As she looked at the young man; *'Calin, was that his name? Not a giant but a friend,'* she thought to herself. The meat he had offered had been delicious and filling. Despite his fear of the bandits he had piled more wood on the fire, and for the first time since she'd left home Elayna felt warm, full and able to relax, just a little. She smiled and Calin smiled back, transforming his stern broad features into those of roguish youthfulness. Self-consciously, he swept his thick blond hair from his face and allowed his eyes to wander towards the canopy above.

Calin felt uneasy. The strangers appeared grateful for his help and the girl seemed to be grinning at him, but her hollow eyes spoke an untold tale of terror and wretchedness. The man had fallen silent, encasing himself in his own thoughts. With an inward shrug Calin decided to shoulder his unease for the time being. Maybe they would be more conversational after a good night's rest. Decisively, he stood and wandered over to where he had concealed the wagon and ponies. He returned carrying two thick blankets which he handed to his guests as he bid them a good night.

Lyaren felt nauseated. This young stranger was undoubtedly an honest man and should he become entangled in this mess the guilt would lie firmly on his own shoulders. Ela had needed rest and warmth; he chided himself, but what else could he have done? The last two nights had seen a frost and, without blankets, he was sure she would not survive another night. When his scrying had detected the lone traveller, Lyaren had begun to feed a concern for bandits into the man's subconscious. This had ultimately baited Calin into spending tonight in the forest just where their paths would meet. Lyaren had been able to conceal Ela and himself from the Xyakahan priest, but he could not conceal a fire or the smoke it would create. Yet without warmth they would both be dead within the week. Their only chance was to meet a legitimate traveller who would set up a camp, which they could share. When the priests scried they would see only Calin and, with a bit of luck, choose not to investigate further. He had lured the poor man into this predicament to use him, but now he was finding himself liking him! Had he found himself another charge to protect? There was only one option open to him. He would rise early in the morning, before Calin, and rouse Ela. It would be easy to lose themselves in the forest and that would leave Calin to continue his journey in safety... Despite this good intention, sleep found Lyaren and demanded its due. He awoke to find

Calin mixing a thick sausage and herby-smelling stew for breakfast. The young man sang happily to himself as he tended the fire and made ready to break camp.

"Good morn" Lyaren folded the blanket and handed it to his host.

"Keep it," Calin grinned. "I've plenty and, besides, y'r stench has no doubt lingered." He raised his eyebrows and screwed up his nose, but didn't quite smile. "There's a stream just beyond them trees. If y' want to wash I'll keep me eye on your young'n for ya."

Feeling somewhat humbled by the big man's gentle and generous nature, Lyaren followed the game trail Calin had indicated until he came to a fast-running, waist-deep stream. After undressing he lay in the icy shallows of the waters and for a short time let his qualms be washed away.

It was the smell of food, which finally roused Ela from her slumber. As she placed her own folded blanket upon the one Lyaren had left she realised only Calin was present at the camp.

"Good morn, Lady." His voice had a strong accent similar to that of her father's villagers, but with more of a sing-song quality which seemed to soften the vowels. "I trust y' slept well?"

"Very well, thank you."

Calin laughed. "So she does have a voice, I was starting to wonder,"

He smiled a genuine smile. "And perhaps I could tempt y'r to be sharing a name?" Elayna felt profoundly embarrassed; this stranger had offered them nothing but benevolence and in return they had not even extended to him the courtesy of their names.

"My name is Elayna, sir" Ela dropped her eyes and bobbed an awkward curtsey in her tattered skirts. "I must apologise for my tardiness in not introducing myself sooner."

"No matter" Calin waved the apology away. "But now you've found a voice you've got me a little curious. How comes a lady like y'self finds herself in this pretty pickle?" He coloured slightly and coughed to hide his embarrassment. "Pardon me bluntness and such?"

She knew Lyaren would be cross with her for talking about their plight, yet she could not help but trust Calin. He was the first normal person they had encountered since this nightmare began, and by the Earth mother she had to tell someone! She felt so alone and so wretched. So, without dwelling on the consequences, Ela found herself telling Calin the whole story. As she spoke her tale, reliving the horror of their flight from the priests, her eyes welled with tears and for the first time since the night they fled the house she began to weep.

Feeling refreshed and invigorated, Lyaren dressed and turned back to the stream. Squatting on the bank, he traced a circle of power over the waters; instantly an unnatural calm possessed the water of the streams, creating a mirror-like surface. Fixing an image of the white eagle firmly in his mind he began the meditation exercises which opened his power centre. Slowly the energy flowed over him and his soul soared through the canopy, breaking out into the clear, crisp morning sky above. Opening his eyes, Lyaren saw a flawless bird's-eye view of the forest reflected in the sparkling still water of the stream. Mostly he saw only vegetation but some movement over to the southeast caught his attention. He followed the movement until he found his soul hovering just above the enemy camp. He knew the priest and his men couldn't be more than five hours behind them, but at least they were gaining distance on their pursuers and once again Lyaren felt he was in control of the situation. He dispersed the water image with his hand and made his way back to the camp.

Retracing his steps through the forest, Lyaren strolled back into the small clearing to find Calin awkwardly trying to comfort a distraught Ela. She must have heard his approach because, as he drew closer, she pulled away from the big man and ran into his arms. Instinctively Lyaren pulled her towards him, enveloping her shuddering body in his embrace.

"I'm sorry, Ly," she sobbed. "I didn't mean to tell him, it just happened."

"Hush, little one," Lyaren smoothed her hair with his hand. "It's alright," he lulled. "It's alright." He looked over to Calin. "She told you everything?"

"I reckon so," he replied, awed sympathy playing over his features, "An' if you'll let me, I think I want to help."

"You have helped us enough, my friend." Lyaren reappraised the big man - this went beyond kindness. "This fight is ours, we cannot ask you to endanger yourself in our cause."

Calin laughed. "I'm not scared of a few Xyaky nuts! Look," he stood up straight with his hands on his hips, indicating that he meant business. "I'm a smith, just qualified and on my way home. I'd planned to be stopping off at Lower Gonfiels to see an acquaintance o' mine. The smith there, Samuel Youngwood, he was my mentor, like, when I was young, and, well, we've always kept in touch. Last few letters I've got off of him he's been telling me 'bout trouble in the village. Trouble with Xyakahan priests wanting to build a temple just outside of the village! Folks didn't mind at first, but then young'ns started to go missing. Well, Lower Gonfiels be a neighbourly sort o' place, so Samuel and a few other village men gets together to watch the priests and catches 'em red handed with a little girl. Well, that were that, they ran the bastards out o' town, pardon mi language Miss," he tipped his head towards Ela. "An' any Xyaky that comes near finds a hang man's noose waiting for 'em. Anyways, mi point is if your wants to come with me to Lower Gonfiels I'm sure the villagers will be only too happy to help shake off your pursuers. I mean permanent like."

Lyaren was astounded. He knew that Xyakah would send more priests, but if they could be rid of the one on their tail it would buy them a little time at least. At best it could even save their lives. Finally processing the information, realisation of the plan's simplistic surety finally struck home and Lyaren regained the power of speech. "Calin, I think your plan may work but there is just one thing you must know before you agree to help us." He swallowed hard and looked Calin straight in the eye - people around these parts were suspicious of magic. "The Xyakahan priest who follows us is a sorcerer."

Chewing his lip Calin nodded. "Figures, I always had 'em down as devils. Will that be a problem for the villagers?"

Lyaren smirked. "Not if he's dead before he gets a chance to cast a spell! An arrow through the heart will do it."

"Well we'd better get a move on then; Lower Gonfiels is about half a day's ride, if we hurry we'll be there by noon."

The sun was high in the sky by the time the little cart rambled over the cobbled lane which served as the main thoroughfare to the hamlet of Lower Gonfiels. A mixture of homely cottages and smaller shacks made up the small community which seemed to bustle with activity. Several people had stopped to watch the cart trundle through the hamlet, some even waved a welcome as they recognised Calin, and smiled curiously at the two figures huddled in the back of the cart. Towards the

44

centre of the village the remains of a market was hurriedly being packed away outside a large establishment, which had a painting of a fat journeyman drinking from a brimming tanker of ale hanging proudly above the door. After that the cart passed a number of small shops and a cooper's workshop, before Calin turned left down a side street which opened out into a small but well maintained courtyard. The cart had hardly pulled to a standstill before a large burly man in his mid-forties, wearing a smith's apron and covered in a gleaming sheen of sooty sweat, rushed from the smithy to the right of the courtyard and yanked Calin from his seat, enfolding him in a rough bear hug. Returning the embrace, Calin laughed a throaty chuckle and the two men separated patting each other on the back warmly.

"Oh Calin it's good to see ya," the smith smiled warmly. "And ya look good - built up some muscle I see."

"And you've not changed a bit, Samuel," Calin grinned back. "How's Dina?"

"All the better to know you're home. Come into the house and see for yourself." Samuel reached for Calin's arm, but Calin stayed his hand before he had a chance to pull him towards the house.

"I think the barn may be a better place for this reception," he nodded towards the two figures still waiting in the back of the cart. "I have made two new friends who I think you will want to meet."

Samuel raised an eyebrow and without a word went to open the large oak doors to the stable. Jumping up into the cart Calin took the reins and urged the ponies forward into the building.

Once inside, the doors were barred shut and a small oil lamp ignited to illuminate a clean and well-tended interior. Lyaren and Elayna clambered down from the cart, rubbing cramped muscles to return the

45

circulation. Calin jumped with practised ease from the driving seat and moved towards them, indicating towards the patient figure of Samuel waiting by the flickering oil lamp.

"These are my new friends," Calin began the introductions. "Elayna and Lyaren. They have a little problem I think you may enjoy helping them with."

"Any friend of Calin's is a friend of mine." He extended his hand towards Lyaren and Elayna shaking them warmly. "I have the strangest feeling that you have an interesting tale to tell, come..." He indicated a small, misshaped table and several stools in the shadows at the back of the barn. "Come and let me see what I can do to help."

Once settled around the table, Lyaren quickly recapped their predicament, omitting some of the details which may have caused Ela distress or which referred to his own talents. Samuel asked few questions. He listened intently and with empathy, particularly when mention was made to the Xyakahan priesthood. As the tale progressed his eyes hardened and even mention of the priest's magic did not seem to alter his manner. As Lyaren concluded his tale with their 'unexpected' encounter with Calin, Samuel nodded once and rose to his feet. "We can help." he said simply. Then, indicating that Calin should accompany him, he walked towards the door. "Wait here, we won't be long"

As the large oak door groaned to a close, Lyaren and Elayna finally found themselves alone. It seemed there was little to do but wait and so they made themselves comfortable. It was Elayna who eventually broke the silence with a question which had been haunting her since morning. "Why didn't you tell me the priest was a sorcerer?"

46

Taking her hand Lyaren smiled slightly. "I didn't seem to find the right time to tell you." He knew she had a right to know the whole truth, but that would be later. For now he needed her friendship... and her trust. "I will tell you everything, Ela," he promised. "In the forest you had enough to fear without me making it worse," his smile widened. "In retrospect I think I may have underestimated you. I'm very proud of you, Ela, you have proven yourself to be both brave and determined."

Ela returned his smile, "I don't feel brave, Ly. In fact I feel a total wreck, but I am not stupid. I know there is more going on here than I am aware of. I will need to know the truth sooner or later." arching her eyebrow she glared in his direction.

"Yes... I will tell you all I know, Ela. When this is sorted and we have a little time I will explain everything."

Calin and Samuel had been gone about an hour when at last the barn gates creaked open and Calin marched in, followed by Samuel and about another ten men, all dressed in loose cotton britches and leather jerkins. An elderly man, with a thick fur cloak draped over his shoulders, made his way purposefully towards the front of the group, leaning heavily on a stout stick for support.

"My name is Hayal; I am village elder. I wish you welcome to Lower Gonfiels."

Lyaren helped Ela to her feet where both bobbed a curt bow towards Hayal. "I am Lyaren and this is my charge, Elayna. Has Calin explained?"

"That he has, young man, and glad we are that we can help. We will not tolerate Xyakahan scum in our village. We will give you sanctuary and ensure that your

47

pursuers will not meet another morning." His eyes glinted with a steel edge.

"Has Calin told you about the sorcerer?"

Hayal nodded, "Will he bleed and die, like other men?"

"Yes, if he does not see you coming."

Now Hayal chuckled to himself. "Oh, no fear of that my friend, he will not see us coming. Kayel!" he called and a young man in woodsman's garb strode forwards. "Take three of your best archers out to the edge of Wentworthy field and hide in the thicket just beyond the bridge. As soon as you see them take out the priest." He turned back to Lyaren. "Will he be able to tell which one is the priest?"

"Oh yes, all the others wear mercenaries' gear, but the priest wears a full-length black robe, tied at the waist with a golden belt."

"That's what I thought!" Hayal confirmed, "Samuel," he turned towards the smith. "You take the rest of the men and wait by Hending's barn. Should the archers fail it will be your responsibility to deal with them, but should all go well there will only be those who don't flee to deal with."

Calin nodded solemnly and without a word the assembled men followed him out of the barn. As the last man exited, a short and plump yet affable looking woman strode purposefully to Hayal's side.

"I'm Dina," she smiled warmly. "Samuel's wife. I think you have spent long enough in our barn. Please come into the house. I have hot broth on the stove and tea ready in the pot." She took Ela by the arm. "By the looks of you you're ready for a decent meal, and perhaps a bath?"

Gratefully Elayna and Lyaren followed along with Hayal as they allowed Dina to lead them towards

48

the welcome glow of the little cottage adjacent to the barn.

A little bigger than the other houses in the village, the smith's house was built much along the same lines. Two stories high and with a thatched roof, the inside composed of a large kitchen with a friendly open fire roaring in the hearth, and a stout table which stretched almost the full length of the room. Flowers and herbs hung from the ceiling in large bundles and the smell of fresh baked bread hung in the air. To the left was a door, which led to a small and cheerful living area, with two large rocking chairs, and a long high-backed bench padded with large, intricately embroidered cushions. A narrow staircase ascended its irregular way towards the sleeping quarters above the house, but Dina led the company into the living area and ushered them towards a mismatched assortment of inviting cushioned chairs. Here, fed and comfortable, they awaited Calin and Samuel's return.

As it happened they did not have a long wait at all. The cottage door opened silently and in trekked Calin, Samuel and Kayel, each sporting a wolfish grin. Without ceremony Dina threw herself into Samuel's arms and hugged him warmly. "Thank the Earth mother." she sighed, "Did it go well Samuel? Did you get 'em?"

"We got 'em Dina," Samuel replied.

"It was easy really," Kayel jumped in. "They never suspected a thing. We got the priest no trouble, three arrows! He looked like a hedgehog as he fell off his horse."

Calin laughed. "That he did, Kayel, and the others ran like babies back to their mothers' aprons. We tracked 'em back to the forest; they'll not be back in a hurry."

Hayal stood. "A job well done then. Come on Kayel, we'll be letting these people be off to their beds."

"Thank you," Lyaren stood. "We can't tell you how grateful we are."

"No," Hayal spoke softly. "It is we who should be grateful. Those bastards killed my daughter and Kayel's sister. We have been waiting for a chance at our retribution."

"I'm sorry for your loss," Lyaren said. "You have done us a great service; we do appreciate it."

"I know, lad." Hayal smiled. "Get some rest - you look as if you need it." As Samuel and Calin saw Hayal and Kayel out, Dina turned to Lyaren and Elayna.

"I've moved the children in with us for the night, an' Calin will sleep in his old room in the smithy. You should both get a good night's sleep. There'll be a tub of hot water ready for you both in a jiffy, and I've dug out some clothes for y' both." With that she ushered them both up the stairs, fussing motherly as they went.

Lounging upon his huge throne in a lavish chamber of gleaming statues and rich fur-lined décor, deep within the bowels of Mount Tystar within the Eastern Desert, Xyakah detected a minor quiver on the power lines, which marked the passing of one of his brethren. Irked by the inconvenience he extended his consciousness across the universe, taking stock of his domain. Kizin was missing. Fool! Xyakah rumbled his discontent. He knew that fool was not up to such a crucial role in his scheme.

Sensing her master's irritation Kala slid from her perch by his side and wandered purposefully to Xyakah's throne. Straddling his knees invitingly she slipped her arms out of her scant shift, revealing more flesh for her Lord. Leaning provocatively towards him she rubbed her hand over his chest, teasing her way through his matted chest hair until her arms circled his neck. "What troubles you, oh mighty Xyakah?" she breathed, licking his scale- encrusted earlobes as the whisper escaped her lips. "May my services ease your disquiet?" Her voice purred like the plaything he liked her to be, though both knew she was far more than that.

"My glorious Kala," he crooned. "Your presence is all I need to calm my discontent, for when I look upon your pitifully vulnerable body, controlled by my whim; I know it will only be a matter of time before your sisters succumb to me also. I shall bend their will just as I did yours and as their bodies come to my bedchamber so will their spirits join with mine to enhance my power and ensure my ascendance to my birthright of ultimate power!" Catching her thick black hair in his talon-like grip he pulled back on her head, raising her exposed chest closer to his reptilian mouth. "It shall be only a matter of time before they shall all be mine, but I shall deal with them afterwards. First I shall deal with you!" In one motion he drew her into him, thrusting his manhood deep between her offered legs. As his lust grew he felt the need to feed; ripping what remained of her clothing away, he drew back his lips to reveal extended canine teeth which tore expertly into her flesh. Her desire turned to agony; holding her on the brink of death he devoured her spirit to nourish his soul then, just as he felt her life force waver, he pulled out from her, dropping her exhausted body to the ground where she would fight her own way back to life.

Invigorated he rose to his feet, renewed energy flowing through his every fibre. Silently he issued his summons and his minions began to file into the chamber.

When Elayna finally woke the sun was high in

51

the sky and the sound of children's laughter drifted up from the courtyard below. The fabric strung across the little window was old and frayed; meaning much of the sun's light filtered through and illuminated the little attic room. In the corner stood a small chest upon which someone had placed a bowl and pitcher of water. A stool stood to one side where Elayna had left her tattered riding gown the night before. The gown was gone, replaced by a simple cotton shift and woollen smock; typical of those worn by the women of the village who Ela had seen yesterday, when they had first arrived. The bed upon which she lay was the only other furniture in the room save a simple rag mat, which lay at the foot of the bed.

She struggled to rise, every muscle in her body aching like fury. Fighting the urge to roll over and reclaim the quickly receding - yet all too blissful - sleep, she forced herself to wakefulness. The combination of a chill wood floor and the ice-cold water splashing onto her face dispelled the last hints of sleepiness and she dressed quickly in the simple gown. Dina had also left a pair of leather boots which were a little on the big side but quite adequate. Last night's bath had sorted out most of the tangles in her hair so that a quick comb through saw away the frazzled edges. She pulled the locks into a neat plait which she tied with a thread she found hanging from the hem of her dress. Looking quite presentable, she slipped through the little door and headed tentatively downstairs.

The steep little steps lead straight down to the spice-scented kitchen, where Dina stooped over a large bowl of dough, and a pretty young girl with long, golden hair chopped vegetables for the broth already bubbling over the hearth. At the sound of her footfalls Dina turned with a welcoming smile. "There you are, we were beginning to grow concerned you may never wake."

"It has been some time since I had a decent night's rest. Your home is lovely, Dina, you have been so kind to us."

"Oh, that's nothing." She appraised Elayna with a satisfied nod. "And who'd have thought that filthy urchin from last night would scrub up to be such a beautiful young woman, It does my heart good to know you're safe from the Mother knows what!" Shaking her head she ushered Elayna to the large carver chair at the end of the table. "What will it be for breakfast? The bread is warm and the cheese better than any other in the dale. Sally," she turned to the girl who had stopped her chopping when Elayna arrived and who now regarded her with a sheepish smile. "Run to the cold store and bring eggs and milk... hurry girl, hurry."

"Yes mamma." Sally said, as she scuttled out of the front door into the courtyard.

The bustling atmosphere of the kitchen instantly helped Ela to relax and feel at home. The smells of baking, spices and sweet vegetables mingled with the delicious perfume of the tiny pink flowers which sat in an earthenware jug on the windowsill. Dina placed a whole host of simple but tasty produce before Elayna, who ate heartily. All the while Dina fussed around the kitchen with an air of confidence and contentment. This was her domain; it was where she belonged, her home. Elayna could not help but wonder where she belonged now. The sombre reflection brought with it thoughts of Ly. He had done more than his duty. He had brought her to safety, but what next? Surely he would not wish to burden himself with her for any longer? Without a chance to speak with him, Elayna was becoming more and more unsure of just where she stood.

Looking up from her thoughts, Elayna found Dina regarding her with compassionate eyes. "Was it alright dear? Would you like more milk?"

"No, thank you, everything was delicious." She pushed the empty plate to one side. "I was wondering where Lyaren may have got to?"

"Oh him," Dina laughed. "He was up with the lark. Went out for a walk after he ate enough for three men! I think I saw him go over to the barn with Calin and Samuel about a half-hour ago. We had some fresh horses brought in this morning. I think he went to look them over." She pointed through the window over to the barn at the opposite side of the yard. "Perhaps you could talk some sense into him? He's talking about setting out at first light tomorrow."

A chill ran down Elayna's spine. "Did he say why?"

"Didn't seem to want to talk about it," she shrugged.

"I'll go and see what I can find out." Elayna answered, getting up from her chair and heading purposefully out into the yard. Outside was awash with midday sunshine and several young children scampered around the otherwise orderly courtyard, involved in their game of kick ball. Skirting the edge of the yard to avoid the melee of the game, Elayna made her way to the large, open, wooden doors of the stable.

Lyaren felt the fetlock of the chestnut mare and nodded with satisfaction. He had no love of horses yet, if they were to reach the Silent Forest safely, speed would be their best ally. He had chosen the chestnut for himself and a more placid dapple grey for Ela. The farmer was a fair man and had asked a fair price, though it had dug deep into Lyaren's small purse and left just enough for a few supplies: a new hunting knife and twine for a longbow.

A light footfall announced Ela's approach and he turned with a cheerful smile. "Good morning my lady. I trust you slept well."

"Very well, thank you," she affirmed.

"Good. Come and meet our new companions." Taking her arm he led her up to the big chestnut. "I think I will call her Fire," he introduced, scratching behind the horse's ear as he spoke. "And this one..." he turned her to the dappled grey stallion. "Is for you. What would you have him named?"

Well that affirmed one thing at least - he planned to take her with him. But why the rush? "Oh he's beautiful!" she gasped, running her hands down his well-muscled neck and patting his shoulder. She thought for a moment before answering. "Well, only one thing can outrun fire," she announced. "So he shall be named Wind."

Calin and Samuel, who leaned against the stall door, gave a bark of laughter, both holding their sides like schoolboys trying to control an attack of the giggles. "Don't mind us," Calin gasped between chuckles. "It's just we had to name a horse 'Wind' once before; caused quite a stir, she did, till the old miller with no sense of smell took her on!" and both men dissolved into grunts of laughter.

Ela gave them a glare and turned back to the horse. "We'll show them to make fun of you," she mumbled, and then more loudly "Perhaps you are right. A horse like this one deserves more in his name. You shall be Hurricane, and childish men shall quiver in your wake."

"That we will." Samuel said, regaining his control. "A good name, it will be my privilege to shoe Hurricane and Fire as my gift, and," he smiled. "I am sorry if we caused offense."

"I think perhaps it was for the best," she said, relaxing under their friendly gaze.

Ly placed his hand on her shoulder affectionately.

"Now, I think that you may have come armed with

questions this morning?" he asked, as Calin and Samuel led the horses away.

"I was hoping for a few answers, yes."

Lyaren took her hands in his. "Come, we have a lot to discuss and I think we should find a more secluded place for the telling."

After a quick stop back at the house, from which Lyaren appeared with a small hamper of food and directions to a good picnic spot, they both set out in silence, each troubled with their own thoughts.

Ela desperately wanted to understand Lyaren and all the events of the past week or so. Lyaren searched his soul for guidance as to how he could explain something he only partly understood himself. He had only one option open to him. He must start at the beginning and hope she would accept her role as being crucial, even though he could offer her no assurance as to what that role would be.

Lyaren led the way through a narrow passageway at the back of the courtyard, which led out of the village and into pastures of soft spring grass. They followed a winding trail, which led through the countryside and came to an end on the bank of a cheerful little brook, which sparkled in the sunlight. They sat on the downy grass and let the warming sun's rays soak over them.

"I have much to explain to you, Ela" Lyaren broke the silence, "but in order for you to understand I must first share the history of my people with you."

Ela nodded slowly, she was beginning to suspect that Lyaren's people were not simply scholars from Sidmore.

Lyaren took a deep breath; slowly, deliberately, he began to chant the laws of his people, just as he had learnt them as a child from his father, who had learnt

56

them from his father before him and so on, back through the generations of their forefathers.

"Once there was no day, no night, no light, no dark, no sky, no sun, no moon, no good, no bad.

Once there was just it: energy, life force, God. Call it as you will, it just existed...

Slowly, without knowing why or how, the energy began to form a consciousness and that is how the Gods came into being.

At first it was a being without form, aware only of itself. Then it took on a form, though what it was I could not begin to describe, and it felt for the first time loneliness. So it created the heavens as a home and a playground. As the being played it grew and developed, but what it was became too much for its sanity and it began to battle with itself.

The agony was intense as the being felt its emotions, its needs and desires pulling it one way and then the other until, in one all-consuming explosion, the being shattered and from the whole came two mighty consciousnesses. Both beings took part of the whole and both were opposite to each other. One took on the form of a mighty warrior with the face of death. The other chose to take no form at all, though in later times it felt the need to take on an image and in each case the image changed.

At first the beings warred against each other but it was of no use as their powers were equally matched. Thus they chose isolation and both retreated to separate parts of the universe. Once the warring stopped they had a chance to look over their domain and that is when each became aware of a third presence. A being of lesser power also inhabited their world, but still this creature was like them. In fact the entity had not formed two full halves; a fraction of power had escaped and developed in

57

a third way. As the greater Gods had battled, this lesser God had been busy too. First it had taken on a form – the image of a beautiful young woman with long flowing hair. Then it had looked over the universe and chosen a world on which to live. This being was a flippant creature – taken to great acts of impulse – and so she had begun to create a home to suit her whims.

First she created the sky, then the sea and the land. In an instant plants were created and the being fed life into them so that they would grow and flourish. Next she created animals to live in her playground, and so came about the deer and the wolf, the horse and the ox, the owl and the eagle, the fish and the whale. And here she dwelt in paradise.

The greater Gods looked down on their little sister, for this is how they felt towards her, and both smiled at her minimal needs and foolish whims. They had nothing to fear from so simple a creature, and so they tolerated her presence and in time came to look upon her with affection, even naming her 'Mysta' from her nature, which in the language of my people means mischief-maker. She in turn named them Loquin – which she said meant constant unmoving law keeper – and Zuqule –, which she said, meant constant unmoving destroyer – and so their roles in the order of things were defined.

Zuqule by nature would destroy and create at whim, while Loquin would strive to maintain order and peace. Mysta would lead them both a merry dance in order to incite both Gods to carry out her will, and they in their arrogance fell straight into her traps.

It was by such an entrapment that man came into being, for Mysta was growing restless and wanted an intelligent pet to inhabit her paradise world. Her powers were too small to create such a creature yet the united powers of all three Gods could easily rise up to the task. So first Mysta enchanted Zuqule.

"Help me create a race of creatures and they will serve you as their God. They will create cities and temples in your honour, they will make music and art, and they will destroy this peace with war, and ever strive to follow your laws!"

Zuqule was seduced by the image of authority her manipulation lay before him and gladly gave her strands of his power with which to weave this creature that would destroy all it encountered and bow down before him as their God.

The creature she created was far from today's man, for it was savage and lived for war. Seeing the horror she had unleashed on the world Mysta hastily approached Loquin so that she could add strands of his power to her creation.

Persuading Loquin was a harder task, for his sure fast ways wanted nothing of the changes this creature would bring to his universe and the order he had created. Mischief knew she must take a very different tact to enlist his aid.

"Oh great and mighty brother" she beseeched him. "Please help me, for Zuqule has unleashed a horror beyond compare on my beautiful paradise." Looking down from the heavens Loquin spotted the warrior race and saw for himself the destruction they smote on the world. A rage surged up within him, so great that without thought he summoned up the power to strike down this abomination and wipe out its existence. Realising her mistake Mysta acted quickly, staying her brother's hand. "What a pity it is, brother, that by this act of destruction do you yourself become no better than the Destroyer. The Law Keeper should not need to degrade himself in such a way. If only," she swiftly continued, "It had been you who had brought this creature about,

59

for fair of face they are and wise and intelligent. If only their natures were not so destructive."

Loquin was overwhelmed with the thought that he, the law keeper, could so nearly have committed this act of destruction and instantly recalled his power. Looking knowingly at his sister he said, "I think it's time Zuqule learnt the full power of my Law." He hesitated. "You are right, Mysta, I must not drop to my brother's level. Instead I will use my true nature to bring order to the lives of these wretched creatures. I will give them a deeper intelligence in order that they may learn from their experiences and over time abandon their reckless nature in favour of a peaceful existence."

And so did Mysta achieve her ends. Her new creature was neither good nor evil, but had an independent intelligence so it could grow and develop into a free-spirited being, capable of creation and destruction as and where it felt fit. Mysta sat back to watch the race of man grow, and soon she began to look upon them as her children. For the most part they flourished well on their own but as the population grew Mysta realised her creatures could not be allowed to live forever or her beautiful world would be swamped under their masses.

Bringing about the wheel of life was a simple task, and Loquin all too readily agreed to the orderly system of life and death which Mischief proposed to him. Together they created a creature called The Spinner who would operate the wheel of life, reaping in the souls of the dead and directing them to be reborn within the next generation.

When man – the simple and primitive creature he was then – saw death for the first time, a bleak desperation over took him and the race entered an era of dark depression. Seeing their dread Mysta knew that they needed a system of belief to protect them from their fear and so did she appear to them in the form of a beautiful maiden. Thus the Mother Goddess came about; the Mother Goddess, who collected the souls of her beloved children to protect them in the afterlife. This, happily, the creatures believed. So as not to offend her brothers, should they look down on her tiny world, Mischief told the race of man about the warrior god and the law keeper god who resided in the heavens above. The men welcomed the teachings she gave them and constructed statues in the image of both Loquin and Zuqule. Temples became a meeting place and offerings were made by the warriors and peacemakers of Mysta's world. The women, instead, worshiped the Earth Mother Goddess who brought the passing of time, the birth of new life and gave comfort to all at the sadness of death. Now man had an understanding of the universe suitable for his intellect and in peace did he inhabit the world.

Content that her job was done, Mysta again sat back to wait for mankind to develop into the companions she yearned for but found she had gravely underestimated the time this would involve.

Years became decades, and decades became centuries, yet still mankind was in its infancy. Mysta realised it would take millennia for her children to develop enough for her to join with them, and it was with this realisation that Mysta admitted to herself her full desire. She didn't want a preoccupation, a diversion for her days. She wanted to belong. To have friends and a family who loved her for what she was. She had seen the families of man protect their own and she wanted to be a part of that. To belong.

After a long bout of melancholy, Mysta decided to approach her brothers and enlist their help in bringing about a second creature to inhabit her world, one more equal to her in intelligence and power. When, however, she looked in on her brothers she found them once again locked in a struggle of power and, try as she might, she could not attract their attention.

For several centuries she waited for their struggle to relent, but neither side seemed willing to give way. It was then that she had the idea to 'borrow' the power she needed and so it was, while neither brother was looking, that Mysta took strands of power from each of them back to her paradise world. Thus began the age of my people's masters."

Lyaren halted in his telling of the tale and smiled at Elayna. "This story is sacred to my people but I know it can be a lot to take in." He flashed her a half smile. "Have you heard enough? Should I stop for today?" he asked.

"No, Ly, please continue" she pleaded. "I wish to know the whole of the story." It was compulsive she found, yet a little voice in the back of her head was asking her if she really wanted to know more.

"Very well," he replied affirmatively, and continued with the telling. "The creature, which Mysta brought about this time, was far from simple. She had learnt her lesson well and was sure to weave into her magic the power of her own soul. So did the dragons appear: beautiful, powerful and majestic. They were the most noble of all the creatures, with an advanced intelligence to rival that of Mysta herself. They built their citadels in the high reaches of the mountains, far above the world of mankind. Their homes were the mountain crags, the high ridges and the skies themselves. They were more than animals, more than man. For they had magic and power and dominance over the world, and here at last Mysta found her family. A great and mighty civilization soon emerged from the seeds which Mysta had sown, and before long Mysta herself took on their form and lived amongst them. She found love, happiness and family, and before long bore four daughters: Shia, the silver dragon; Bora, the bronze dragon; Azura, the blue dragon and Scarla, the red dragon. They were her gift to the dragons for they would entwine her soul more deeply with their wonderful race. As their power grew the dragonkind looked around for servants to do their bidding, and this was when dragons had their first meeting with the lesser race of humans with whom they shared their world. Still mankind was savage and untamed, but the dragons had magic and so they chose a select few who they carefully and lovingly created into a more refined version of the species. These they called the elves, for they were more than human and, in themselves, held a simple magic, which aided their servitude to the dragons. The dragons made kindly masters and so the elvenkind thrived and developed into an industrious and thoughtful community of artisans, lovingly carving out their own culture as they coexisted with their masters.

And so it was amongst this magnificent empire that Maginus came about. As a youth he was a curious and studious dragon, spending much time in the study of magic, but as an adult he became greedy for power and hatched a plot to supersede the Gods Loquin and Zuqule so he could become the sole ruler of the universe. First he took the power of the sun and mixed it with the heat of battle to create the Sword of Death. Then he took the light of the moon and spun it into a working of dragon scales to make the Shield of Protection. He took the wisdom of the stars and wove them into the crystal of earth, giving birth to the Wisdom Stone whose council would protect him against any enemy. Finally he took a rotation of the wheel of life and turned it in the opposite direction; this he stirred into a stone cup to create the Cup of Life, which could bring one back from the arms of the spinner.

Armed with these tools, ignoring the beseeching of Mysta, he pitched himself against Loquin and Zuqule. At first the gods did not notice the intruder who hovered before them, but at last they broke off their battle and enquired as to the origin of this strange creature with mighty wings, who navigated their universe as if it was its own.

"I am Maginus," he declared to the Supreme Beings before him. "And I challenge you in the name of the dragonkind for dominion over all creation." So saying he released the power of the sword, shield and stone and – for a moment – the Gods were held in his power. But Maginus had vastly underestimated the power of the Gods and easily did they shatter his magic. Cowering before the enormity of his foolishness Maginus begged for mercy, but it was too late.

"You have no right to challenge us" the Gods boomed. "Who dared to bring such a presumptuous creature into being?"

And then did they look down on their little sister and detect for themselves her waywardness. The strands of their own power shone out from amongst the dragonkind announcing their theft and establishing Mischief as the perpetrator of the crime. For the first time since their creation, Loquin and Zuqule found themselves in complete agreement. This time she had gone too far; there was no room in the universe for creatures of such power and so the race of dragons was condemned.

Back in the Hall Of Dragons, a mighty conference was in progress as the dragons realised the fruitlessness of their situation. Amongst the younger dragons there was fear, but such was the nobility of the creatures that non thought of themselves. Instead they thought of their servants, the elves, and of Mysta, both of whom they loved, and they thought of their magic and knowledge and the great loss to the world its fading would be. So it was that they cast their greatest spell. Drawing the life force of all their kind together they channelled all their collective power and knowledge into Mysta's four young children, charging their souls with the legacy of their race. When the spell was done only faint echoes of the dragons were left and their kind had passed beyond the wheel of life for eternity.

Knowing she must act quickly Mysta said her farewells to her four daughters and called for Savarna, a young elfin girl who had always been a loyal and trusted servant. Then she called on the Spinner to come forth from the other worlds and aid her in her task. And so it was that Mysta took the lives of her own beloved daughters and set their spirits free to journey through the world of man and elf, within the spokes of life and death.

When Loquin and Zuqule released their fury on the dragons it was already too late. They found only Mysta, wrapped in a black cloak of misery and despair, her mind and sanity lost in her grief."

"What of Maginus?" Ela asked. "Did he perish with rest of his kind?"

"No" Lyaren shook his head. "Both Gods felt that would be too kind for his crime against them. Instead they took his sword, shield, stone and cup and flung them to the far edges of the Earth. Then they took back the strands of power, which Mischief had stolen, leaving him a crippled and powerless creature, wretched indeed. In doing so they cast him back down to Earth and to the mercy of mankind. Here he would have perished were it not for Xyakah, his Elvin servant. Xyakah found his master and nursed him. I am sure at first Xyakah wanted only to do good and to help his beloved master, but as he watched Maginus deteriorate before his eyes he became bitter and swore revenge on

65

the two Gods who had brought this upon the dragonkind. Finally Maginus passed away, giving in to the pain which warred within his body, and with his passing madness came over Xyakah. He pledged to spend each day of his existence in the retrieval of the four artefacts of power so he could challenge the gods in his master's stead."

"Is that why you are telling me this?" Ela interjected. "So I can understand who the Xyakah Priests are? So I know that it is the followers of this 'Xyakah' who are trying to kill us?"

"Not quite, Ela. You see I need you to understand who my people are and something of the power we have been entrusted with. My people safeguard the secrets our masters left behind. Secrets which could destroy our world if they were placed in the wrong hands; if they were placed in Xyakah's hands!"

"Surely you are being overly dramatic, Lyaren, this Xyakah is long dead – his worshipers could not possibly know what to do with these secrets." Elayna swatted a fly carelessly from her cheek as she spoke and so missed the terror which, for one fleeting moment, Lyaren allowed to show in his eyes. Controlling the emotion he answered her.

"If only that were true, Ela. You see, Xyakah did find one of the items of power – he found the cup of life, drank from it and has now achieved immortality! It is not the followers of Xyakah who are trying to kill you, it is Xyakah himself!"

The air seemed to reverberate with the weight of his statement. Ela swallowed hard, trying to make sense of Lyaren's words, but no matter how she arranged her thoughts the same fact always remained at the forefront: 'Xyakah was hundreds – no thousands – of years old and he wanted to kill her!... Why?'

66

"Would you like to go back to the village?" Lyaren asked, seeing her confusion. "I know it's a lot to take in."

Elayna shook her head forcefully. "No, no, really, Ly, this is fascinating," she laughed. "And terrifying, but I think I need to understand the whole story."

"I am glad you wish to know. You should know the whole story. But look, the hour is well past noon and my voice is growing thin with the telling of my people's history. Let us rest a while and enjoy the food Dina has provided." And with that he reached into the basket, his hand emerging with a large chunk of fresh bread and some succulent slices of salted beef. Gratefully Ela accepted the food and the two of them sat, on that bright sunny afternoon, once again relaxed in each other's company.

The clouds moved slowly over the sun-soaked sky and eventually Lyaren continued with his tale.

"Whilst Mysta and the dragons performed their last great magic my people returned to their city at the foot of Dragon Mount to discover their own fate. It is told that there was a mighty storm of unnatural colours and immense explosions, which shook the ground itself. Then an unnatural night-time descended over the world and my ancestors huddled together for comfort. It was in this darkness that a single figure emerged from the forest at the foot of the mountain, and as she came closer they realised it was Savarna, Mysta's maid. She was cut and bleeding in many places but, as they rushed forward to aid her, she seemed to draw on some strange power, reviving herself. Her eyes took on an unnatural indigo glow and her voice, when she spoke, crept into the very souls of my people, easing their disquiet and giving forth new strength, for she spoke with the voice of the dragons. "My children," she said. "Our time is short yet a mighty task I must bestow upon you." As one my ancestors dropped to their knees, anxious to serve the masters they loved one last time. "A mighty darkness has entered your world and as I speak it grows in power. The spirit of the dragons has passed into my four children, and is now beyond the wheel of life. It shall be reborn within my children's souls as four of your kind. I entrust you to protect them. Do not allow the legacy of the dragons to pass into the hands of evil, for that will herald the blackest of ends to the entire universe. There shall be one born to you who takes forth the form of a mighty white eagle. When this day comes, so the prophecy will begin. For a mighty battle shall ensue. Should evil be the victor mankind is doomed. Should the evil be banished the age of man will enter a new era, with the power and knowledge of the dragons to guide it.'

Then the light seemed to die from her eyes and the women gathered her to them and took her to the medicine house. It is said that many prophecies were spoken to the women in the dimness of the medicine house and after that day the women of my people kept the old laws, passing the knowledge down to their female children, but these are secrets which the women keep to themselves. By the sunrise Savarna was dead and the dragonkind had passed beyond the realms of death. My people were infants, left without parents to guide them, nursing the legacies of their masters.

The women emerged from the medicine house weeping. They told the men that in the end Savarna had become herself once again, and had died quietly, but it is said that her eyes held a horror, which foretold the end of the world. They told the men that Dragon Mount was to be a sacred place and that no elf should set foot on the hallowed ground; the wild spirit of the dragons still dwelt there, and any elf to encounter this untamed energy would be consumed by it and never again be the same."

"It's a sad story, Ly." Ela shuddered a little, as the wind seemed to pick up. "The destruction of a whole race."

"Sad it is. Yet I believe it was meant to be, for with their masters gone my people were forced to evolve and so they grew. Within the year, Savarna's younger sister gave birth to four beautiful daughters – unheard of in our people who enjoy a long life and seldom have more than one or two children in a lifetime. The children had unnatural eyes, slit like the dragon kind, and they grew more quickly than the others. After that a change came over my people. Children were born with powers, and the four dragon girls taught them how to develop these. Now it is common for our kind to be blessed with the gift. Sorcerers, your people would call us. But to us it is just the manipulation of the world around us. As you change things with your hands and strength, so we use our mind's eye and our desire. The strange girls were cherished by my people, and the love they seemed to emit gave a new strength to elvenkind who now understood that their dragon masters had indeed left them a great legacy. Their magic and much of their knowledge lived on within us.

When the wheel of life had spun its full rotation, the dragon girls passed beyond the walls of life. Yet, within a month of their death, four daughters were born to a young woman of the village. And so it has been ever since. With each birth the girls lost more of their dragon traits and took on more of those of my people. But they never lost their gift for magic, or their knowledge of natural laws, and they always seemed much older than their years.

For many generations my people grew in peace. All was well and the fear of the prophecies passed into folk law. That was until around two hundred years ago. We had forgotten about Xyakah but he had not forgotten about us! Over the years he had been busy scheming and plotting. His spies had been hard at work and somehow he had uncovered knowledge of the prophecies and of the four dragon daughters. Determined to take the dragon legacy for himself, he amassed a huge force on the edge of our forest. The war he waged was bloody indeed and many of my people perished, among them the four dragon daughters. But my people were not without skill and many of his foul army perished also.

In the end he retreated, accepting that he had underestimated just how much my people had grown and how strong we had become. Nursing our injured, the elvenkind began to rebuild the village and await the rebirth of the dragon daughters. For a great time there was much fear, for the period between their lives was always short – a matter of months – but this time the months gave way to years. Our strongest sages consulted the stars and the Spinner but could find no knowledge. At last, after around twenty-five years, a woman named Nia became pregnant and our midwives announced that she did indeed carry four heartbeats within her belly. With much celebration and light hearts my people awaited the birth and as the first child was delivered she was indeed a dragon daughter, so was the second and the third. But the fourth child was a boy. The four children were very close and it was obvious to the more powerful magic workers that the boy had great power, but he was not of the dragon kind. Something had gone terribly wrong, and a quarter of the dragon legacy had been stolen from my people. On his tenth birthday the boy was tested by the magic workers to find which aspect of the art he was strongest in. Few amongst my kind have been known to carry the power of shape-shifting and, so, part of the test was devised to see how easily the child could change his shape and, indeed, which shape he would take on. On this part of the test the boy excelled and, as the three dragon sisters watched, their brother began to transform into a giant white eagle. And so the prophecy begins."

Lyaren's eyes had misted over as he came to the end of his tale; his mouth twitched into a half smile. "There is one more thing I need to tell you." He smiled ruefully. "The boy. It's me." He paused, as if for effect. "I have been carefully schooled since my tenth year in the arts of magic. My sisters have taught me the laws of Earth, Water and Air. All my life I waited for a sign, something which would begin my destiny, and when it came it was a dream of a beautiful young girl in a strange human house far away from my home in the forest. My master, Kiam, believed you to be the fourth dragon daughter, disconnected from your siblings by some strange twist of fate, and so I journeyed to your home with the intention of returning you to your true people. When I found you I could see you were no dragon daughter but I knew I had to stay with you. You are part of my destiny, Elayna of Ladaston. Kiam agreed that I should protect you, and as it turned out my instincts were right. The Xyakahan priests want you, but I have no idea why. I don't know what part you play in this struggle between good and evil, but it would appear you are crucial to both. Perhaps Xyakah doesn't know your true role either; he, like me, could be acting on the instincts of a dream."

Dumbfounded, Ela tried to take in the implications of all Lyaren had told her. While images of gods and dragons danced in her imagination, the reality of being sought after by two opposing forces in a battle she knew nothing of; virtually overwhelmed her. "Well...well there must be some kind of mistake."

Lyaren shrugged and smiled. "I don't think the forces of prophecy make mistakes. Besides how else could I have seen you so clearly in my dreams, if I were not meant to come to you?"

"I don't know." She fell silent, allowing her thoughts to skim through the information reeling within her mind. "Did you know Gaylon, like you said when you first came to our home?"

He shook his head sadly. "No. I'm sorry, Ela, that was a lie, but I had to find a way to convince you to trust me, and I felt sure that your brother would not mind my deception, providing your safety was its intention." She nodded gravely. "So what happens now? You have rescued me from the Xyakahan priests – your destiny is fulfilled. You are free to return to your people."

"Yes I can now return home, but my destiny is far from complete. One of the dragon daughters is still missing; I fear Xyakah has her and her power and, just because we killed a few priests yesterday, I do not believe Xyakah will forget about you. I can't protect you in the open but I can protect you in our forest. I must take you home with me. The magic there is very strong – Xyakah cannot penetrate it, we have made sure of that! Will you let me take you home with me?"

"I don't seem to have any other options open to me right now."

"True, but I need to know you will come with me out of choice."

"I am not so fond of forests – so far I have had my bellyful – but your home sounds interesting." She smiled sheepishly. "Alright, I would be delighted to accompany you to your village." The playful lilt to her voice eased back the mental shadows, which had drawn around them, and Ela stood and curtsied grandly as a maiden would at her first formal ball.

Lyaren laughed despite himself. "Good! Then we will leave tomorrow and it would be good if we could get an early start, so let's get back to the house before the sun begins to set."

For the first time Ela noticed that the last rays of sunlight lay like fingertips across the horizon and that the day was almost at an end. Lyaren's tale had taken most of a day in its telling, but she could not help wondering if its implications would last for a lifetime.

Chapter 3
Tarrin

In the gloomy shadow of the smithy she sat on the tiny porch which overlooked the courtyard, listening to the symphony of the crickets. They accompanied the braying of the bullfrogs as they harmonised with the timbre of human activity from within the house. The crescent moon, high in the cloudless sky, cast its incandescent glow over a jubilant community and an anxious young woman. Confused thoughts grasped for the enticing notion of an attainable future ahead of her, but seemed to flitter to nothing as quickly as they formed. Lyaren won't abandon me." She repeated the thought like it was a mantra, anchoring her hopes to reality. They knew where they were going now and, without the priests breathing down their necks, a late spring journey north could be quite pleasant.

The tread of footsteps detached themselves from the melee of voices and laughter within the house, betraying someone's approach. As the door clicked open, the warm-fire glow from the kitchen hearth illuminated Lyaren's youthful features.

"They're asking about you, Ela, won't you come in and join the family?"

She smiled warmly. "I will in a minute. I'm just enjoying being a part of a night without fear."

Lyaren whistled under his breath. "A night without fear is indeed a precious gift. I am glad you feel safe here," he paused, then in a softer tone, "But you know we must leave soon."

"Yes." It was a whisper.

"Our enemy won't give in; they will be back and they may be more powerful next time. We can't put these good people in danger."

"I know," she smiled wryly. "There you go again!" she chided. "Bringing the fear back into my night."

"I'm sorry..." He came to sit at her side on the rough wooden bench. "I am aware of how much you've learned today." He paused, considering the truths she had been forced to face these past few days. Had it changed her? "I know it has overwhelmed you a little. I hope I didn't leave you more confused than before."

"No. I'm a little scared... and I fail to see what possible value I could be in matters of this magnitude." She forced humour into her voice. "But I'm not confused about what you told me, just a little in awe of it all!" Smiling, she sat back against the solid stone of the house and breathed in the chill, fresh night air. For a while they sat in silence, both aware of the happiness this place could bring them under different circumstances.

At last it was Elayna who broke the silence. "I think we are right to set out tomorrow, before I get too comfortable here."

"I agree." Lyaren put his arm around her, sensing how difficult this was for her.

"Besides; I don't want our presence here to put our new friends in any danger."

Lyaren was silent.

Ela spoke for him. Standing, she smoothed down the homespun smock Dina had given her. "Let's go and break the news." She gestured with her head in the direction of the house, an expression of resignation and determination etched on her face, and together they returned to the embracing warmth of the happy family home.

As Elayna had expected, Dina was horrified that her guests planned on leaving so soon. "But we're only just getting to know each other," she gasped, taking Ela by the hand. "Surely you can spare a few more days." After returning from her talk with Lyaren this afternoon, Ela and Dina had prepared the evening meal together and, as they worked and chatted, an affection had begun to grow between the two women. Ela knew Dina had felt it too, and that with a little time the two of them could become close friends. It had been such a long time since Elayna had felt the friendship of female companionship she would miss Dina.

"You are very kind, Dina." Lyaren spoke softly so as not to offend her after all her hospitality. "But we have a great journey ahead of us. My people are from the far North West, and it will be easier on us if we can get going before the summer sets in. In the mountains the summer heat can be overwhelming."

"Lyaren's right." Calin's voice was firm as he stood from his place at the large table, which had been erected in the centre of the small living room. Elayna and Dina had cleared away the plates from dinner a number of hours before but, still, everyone sat around the table, relaxed in each other's company. "My friends and I used to go hunting in the foothills years since. It was hot there in the summer months; we tended to hug the trees for shade." He coughed to clear his voice. "I think perhaps I'll be coming with y' anyways. I'm heading west too – it makes sense we go together."

"Oh, surely not Calin! We're just getting used to having you back; we see so little of you these days." Dina's exasperation multiplied; she was becoming more fretful by the second, though Ela suspected the rich red brandy they had drank with dinner was elevating her concern.

"The lad's right, woman!" Samuel snapped, though his warm smile betrayed the affection he held for her motherly fussing. "Besides, Sara will be beside herself waiting for Calin to get home. We can't be the ones keeping t' lad away from his mother."

"Dear lord you're right, and hasn't it been an age since your mother visited us here. We miss her herbs you know, Calin, you must tell her."

"I will, Dina, you can be sure of it. Although I think the travelling is becoming a little too much for her now, her joints have started to stiffen up an' she complains that riding mules jostle them about painfully."

Calin's mother was well known in the surrounding area and for many years had been midwife, herbs woman, and gossip distributor all rolled into one. Dina had been a good friend to Sara when she visited Lower Gonfiels and, indeed, it was through this friendship that Samuel had first agreed to take Calin on as his apprentice.

Dina sat with a sigh and dabbed slightly at the corner of her eye. "Well, I can see that your minds are made up and I'm sure there's wisdom in your choices. Though I'm blown if I can see what difference a few days will make" She turned to Samuel, a mischievous smile transforming her maturing features to those of a fresh-faced girl. "Fetch the good brandy, Samuel. The least we can do is send our guests off with a warm glow and a night they won't forget." The night progressed in affable comfort. It was good to be amongst friends and, as the night drew on and the strong liquor settled on the stomach, their worries about the future faded to whispers on the fringes of their memories.

Colonel Westlin paced agitatedly across the confined space of his office, forcing the other three officers to flatten their backs to the wall. All wore sombre expressions as they awaited their leader's orders. "Are you sure they knew who you were, Liftenl?" The colonel pleaded with his captain for the whole sorry mess to be some kind of mistake, although the man's – as yet untended – bruised and battered body confirmed the answer before it was spoken.

"Yes Sir," Liftenl shook his head sadly. "We spotted the Sandkind as they approached us and hailed them for news but, as we talked to the fellows, their companions circled around the back of us and took us by surprise. There was hardly time to draw swords and nowhere for us to run..." His eyes glazed a little as he relived the battle. "They fought like demons, slicing through the men as if they were blades of grass on the savannah. The few of us who managed to get away came straight back here, but they can't be far behind us!"

"How many did we lose?" He stopped his pacing and sat behind the paper battlements, which besieged his desk.

"Seventy four infantry and two captains, Sir. Jim and Sandy."

"Dear Gods!" He shook his head. Beads of sweat had begun to form on his brow. "How many men do we have left in the fort?"

"Only twenty six Sir," Liftenl replied. "Captain Heeks took a hundred men over to the Boarder for the talks, he's due back any day now; reinforcements can't be far away."

"Yes...yes that's right. What about the fort, can we survive a siege?" Torr-Arron Keep was little more than a token gesture; in a peaceful land of 500 years it had never seen battle and, as such, seldom received funding for its upkeep. It kept out the draft, and in warmer months could even be classed as comfortable, but as a defensible position it fared poorly.

The older of the four men shook his head. "The back wall is sadly in need of repairs and the wood of the west side gate has seen better days, but I think if we reinforce it, it may stand a day, perhaps two."

"Damn it! What choice do we..." The sound of a door being slammed open stopped him in mid-sentence as suddenly-angry voices exploded from the small reception room outside.

"The colonel is in conference, Sir. You can't just..." The young official had jumped to his feet but, in the shadow of the huge warrior striding through his office, he may as well have stayed sat down.

"Get out of my way, fool, before it's too late and we're all dead!" This appeared to do the trick, as the solider did not reply. A tall warrior with olive tanned skin and long black hair, slicked back against his head and tied in a scalp knot, stormed into the room. He wore black leather from head to toe, and had a blood stained broadsword at his hip. A straight, sharp nose gave him an almost hawk-like appearance, and keen ebony eyes surveyed the small room and its occupants critically. At last, settling on the colonel, he spoke, "I see you're waiting to die then?" he announced, his voice edged with disdain.

"Watch your mouth, Tarrin!" Colonel Westlin snapped. Your friendship has allowed you entry to my office in the past but you are out of order now."

"Fine!" The warrior turned his back and began to march out of the room, speaking as he left. "Heeks can tell you all about it when you meet him down in hell!"

"Stop!" Westlin sprung to his feet scattering documents from the desk in his hurry. "What do you mean by that, Tarrin?"

The warrior smiled without humour. "The border talks at the Peace Camp were interrupted by uninvited guests. They stormed our camp at night. No one was prepared; most of the humans died in their beds. My people are more agile but still many perished."

"Sandkind?" Westlin uttered.

"Sandkind." Tarrin confirmed. "They took the women; killed most of the men. I've tracked them to about a mile north of you, just beyond High Ridge Trail. They seem to be setting up camp for the night, but if you know what's good for you you'll pull your men out and head south."

"We can't just abandon our post, Tarrin. Torr-Arron Keep is the first line of defence!"

"Bollocks! If you stay you're dead. Do what you will but at least send a messenger south to your King. Your lands will need to prepare for war." Tarrin turned and began again to march out of the room.

"Now where are you going, man?" Westlin roared after him.

"South! A smaller band split off to the south with some Xyakahan priests. They took some of the women from our camp. They took my sister!"

Colonel Westlin looked, through desolate eyes, to his men. His voice faltered, and he shook his head in frustration. Swallowing hard he continued. "Split the men between you. Lionel, you head for Stagsonton. Daven, you go to Wezle and Liftenl, you make for Tormenton. Spread the word as you go, warn the villagers. And, for God's sake," his voice strengthened and returned to its usual boom, "Get the armies of Maldora mobilized. If the Sandkind are after a war they outnumber us at least seven to one and some of them have powers! Now hurry!"

All three men sprang into action, an automatic response to the command in his voice, then Liftenl stopped, tapping his companions to stay them. "But what about you, Sir?" Liftenl asked, which of us will you join?"

Colonel Westlin shuck his head sadly. "I'll hold the fort, lad, till you return. I'll not let it be said that my men fled their post and left it unmanned. Now go! And may the Gods go with you."

It would take well over an hour to mobilize the border legion and get under way. Tarrin didn't have that sort of time. His sister, Teah, was a strong woman, warrior trained, but the Sandkind had magic and she was unarmed. Tarrin had been hunting to the south when they attacked; he had rushed back to the camp as soon as he heard the sounds of battle but, by the time he returned; only a small unit of Sandkind remained to dispatch the last few bands of defenders. The Horse Clans were fierce warriors but, caught by surprise, they hadn't stood a chance. When he arrived, Tarrin was confronted by a scene of total devastation. Although temporary, the camp was sizable, made up of three long log cabins and several hundred canvas tents. Now, the place was unrecognisable. An unnatural fire had consumed the whole site and, as he neared the destruction, the acrid stench of smoke combined with the sweet, nauseating pungency of burnt flesh affronted his senses. Tarrin saw the scene for only a second before the battle anger came over him, clouding his peripheral vision and charging through the carnage in search of the fight. Like a berserker he had struck, his broadsword slicing through the Sandkind as though they were butter, cleaving his way through them to reach his kin. Only when silence fell did he stop to find himself standing amidst a bloody pier of decapitated body parts. He thought at first he was alone, then a whisper of breath on the wind betrayed the presence of someone close by. As his senses returned he realised the Horse Clan warriors he had been striving to reach had succumbed to their attackers. Just a few short strides away they lay, but it was from there the sound had come. Quickly Tarrin covered the distance and knelt by the young warrior. He wore the blue battle braids of the Wolf Moon Clan, Tarrin's own clan, but his face was a mask of blood and gore and Tarrin didn't recognise him. Slowly he opened his eyes, as Tarrin placed his arm around the man's shoulders and raised his head from the ground. "Tarrin" His voice was a choked whisper, and now Tarrin could see the man's throat was slashed open. Blood trickled through the wound, but by some wonder the main artery had not been severed and this had spared his life. Searching quickly for other injuries Tarrin spoke. "Lay still, I'll make you more comfortable."

The man raised his arm, resting his hand on Tarrin's chest. "Don't bother; I've got a knife between my shoulder blades."

Tarrin hardly heard, he was looking at the man's hand, his golden ring proclaiming for the entire world who he was. "Sardan?"

"Yes, it's me, brother."

"I... I didn't..." Tarrin was at a loss.

"There's no time, Tarrin, listen." Sardan's voice was failing fast and blood ran freely from his nose and mouth. "They took the women, Teah was with them, I have failed her..." A choked gurgle escaped his brother's throat and his eyes opened wide. He never got the chance to finish his sentence.

Tarrin hadn't buried Sardan, he had simply torched what remained of the Peace Camp and spoken a

83

silent prayer to the Earth Mother for his people's souls.

It had been easy to track the Sandkind through the mountain passes; he had seen the small band splinter south with the women, as the larger group set up camp just above Torr-Arron. Despite his impatience to rescue his sister Tarrin felt honour-bound to warn the humans. After all, they had traded fairly with his people for many hundreds of years. Even so, he'd played down the horror of the attack on the Peace Camp. He doubted the humans would get away; they didn't have the ability to shield themselves as he had and it was obvious the Sandkind intended to kill everyone in their path; they wanted no survivors to bear witness to their atrocities. Tarrin was not surprised by the humans' slow reaction to his warning. They had little contact with the Sandkind, unlike his people; they could not be expected to be prepared if his own people weren't.

The ceremonial fire surged and Juzuk looked upon the face of his master. "Mighty Xyakah, I am ever your servant." He chanted the formal greeting and prostrated himself on the ground before his God.

"What is your report, Juzuk?" Xyakah's voice echoed from within the flames.

Juzuk stood up to his full height, his pure white hair hung in oily ringlets around his sickly pale face, and he smiled with malevolent pleasure. "My Lord we are victorious. I led the raid on the Peace Camp myself! All are dead and the camp burned to the ground. It was a triumphant victory. Oh Mighty Xyakah, your fires of power burned bright crimson with the blood of our enemies." Juzuk's voice was smug, his confidence testimony to the truth of his words.

"Yes, I'm sure your attack on unsuspecting and unarmed idiots went well!' Sarcasm laced Xyakah's words, followed by a growl of mirthful laughter. "What about the humans? Did any escape to send out warning to the kingdom?"

"No my lord, we took them all. Most were at the Peace Camp but I have just returned from Torr-Arron Keep – its legion is no more. The fools tried to send out pigeons but we shot them all out of the sky and the Sandkind feasted on their flesh. Your minions are easily satisfied, Great Lord!"

Once again Xyakah's gravelly laugh leapt amongst the flames of the fire. "Yes, a most pliable people, the Sandkind, how goes your control of them?"

"They are compliant, My God. I had more Smyther moss thrown onto their night fires, it seems to still their fretting and focuses their minds on their responsibilities; they will play their part I'm sure."

"You please me, Juzuk. You are indeed worthy of your position in my priesthood. I have news I think may please you." Xyakah paused a moment to drink from his goblet. A rich thick liquid ran down his chin hinting menacingly at its identity. "Kizin is dead, he has failed me! The Ladaston girl escaped him. She is important. I want you to find her for me, Juzuk! Her blood is strong; I would have it feed me!!" Xyakah's face seemed to swell within the fire's flames filling, the tent with his presence. "Do you understand me, priest? Don't repeat Kizin's mistakes and you will replace him as first amongst my Second Tier Priesthood."

"You honour me, Mighty Xyakah. I will not fail you, My God, show me her image that I may begin my search." The flames of the fire twisted and merged, their colours melting and re-emerging into an image. A beautiful young woman with auburn hair and pale blue eyes stared out at him from the flames.

"She was last seen south of Lower Gonfiels. I believe she is making her way north. Be ready, Juzuk, do not let her get around you!"

Juzuk bowed low before his master. "May my success strengthen your power, may my failure bring the end to my life. I am your weapon, Master, my life is yours."

Xyakah nodded and the flames blinked out of existence.

Juzuk cursed, if he'd known about the girl he'd have gone south with the splinter group he had sent to subdue the outer villages. He didn't have the ability to send the detailed image he had received to the priests he had sent south – a verbal communication would have to do – but, then again, how many women with red hair could there be in the kingdom?

They had set out early the next morning, heads still a little sore from the previous night's celebrations but tummies full and a light-hearted optimism set the tone for the journey. The late spring weather had been kind for the first day and Ela enjoyed being back on a horse more than she expected. Hurricane was a joy to ride and Elayna experimented with his abilities. Despite her hesitancy she was an excellent horsewoman and, as she gave Hurricane his lead, he galloped happily out in front of Calin's wagon. Lyaren matched her for a while but Ela was lost in the ride, her full attention being on her and the horse. Just for a little while she would forget the horrors of the past few weeks and her apprehensions for the future. For now it was just her, the horse and the landscape she rode through. That night when they made camp she fussed happily over her new companion, searching through the food provisions to find him a large red juicy apple. Hurricane whinnied a happy thank you and nuzzled her shoulder affectionately. It had been a happy camp that night – Ela and Calin had chatted about their childhoods and families and Lyaren had even joined in a little, retelling a tale of a scrape he and a

86

friend had got into with a large mountain bear and an angry hive of honeybees. Ela noticed he was careful not to disclose too much of his heritage and, when Calin asked more about his village, Lyaren vaguely motioned towards the mountains. "Not really a village, just a few hunting lodges, very remote." And he quickly changed the subject. As night drew in they had rolled themselves up in their blankets and slept peacefully under the stars. To her joy the second day had been much the same as the first, Calin continued to be charming and even Lyaren joined in with the laughter. Elayna was actually enjoying herself. With good friends, warm sunshine and a beautiful horse to ride she realised this journey could become a pleasure.

It was on the fourth morning that the weather broke and menacing black clouds rolled in from the east rupturing their load in a miserable and persistent downpour. As if in sympathy, the winds began to surge and gusts battered the travellers heavily. Lyaren's horse whinnied and sidestepped to avoid yet another pool of mud in the waterlogged road. Lyaren tugged his cloak tighter around his shoulders – the only outward sign of his discomfort. After several hours of riding through the storm Ela had finally given up the effort and chose to sit under a waxed blanket in the wagon, close to Calin. The two of them had become very comfortable in each other's company and chatted light-heartedly, oblivious to the miserably dreary conditions.

"What will you do, Calin?" Elayna asked. "When you get home, I mean."

Calin shrugged. "Set up a smithy I suppose. There's money to be made in Waydonfield, it's the most northerly village of any size. There's only Riversway before the mountains and that's more of a hamlet than a village, so I'd get all the work from the legions up in the mountains and the hunters from the foothills, not to mention the farmers and village folk."

Ela nodded her agreement. "It sounds like a good life."

Calin grunted and winked theatrically. "I'll be wanting to make me fortune and find me a good wife." His wide smile betrayed his tormenting intent, but something in his expression suggested to Ela it wasn't merely a joke. "Want to give it a try? I'm quite a catch." He scratched his head and pulled his handsome features into a witless expression.

Elayna couldn't help but laugh at his antics. "You're incorrigible" she chided, landing him a hard slap on his arm, and the two of them dissolved into uncontrollable laughter again. "I noticed the boxes you carry in the wagon," Elayna queried after a while. "Are they the tools for your new business?"

"Some," Calin admitted. "But others are things I've made: horseshoes, bridles, bits and stirrups, tools to sell, daggers and rapiers; even a couple of broadswords. They should help me get the business going, and bring some coin in from the start."

"I should like to see" Ela answered. "Before we leave Waydonfield, that is. Only, I lost my dagger when I left home – I guess I should think of replacing it, if I can afford to."

Lyaren nudged his mount in closer; his voice was harsh and cut through their merriment. "There's a small thicket of trees on the horizon, I think it will be a good place to make an early camp, this weather is in for the night; we might as well sit it out."

Calin nodded. "Yes, we still have a good day's journey to go and there's no inn on this road. That place should give good shelter, and we can sleep in the wagon if the rain keeps up."

All agreed, they made their way steadily towards the trees. Lyaren, taking the opportunity to let Fire take his rein, reached the spot well in advance of the cart. Although too small to be considered a wood, the area was bigger than a copse and thickened considerably in the centre, providing the type of shelter from prying eyes that Lyaren preferred. There was enough clearance between the outer trees to bring the cart well into the grove and, with a little careful moving of shrubbery, conceal it from the road, which lay less than half a mile to the east. Luckily, this far north, the countryside was becoming rockier and so the tracks from the wagon's passage would be fairly simple to disguise once Calin and Elayna arrived. Efficiently, Lyaren began clearing a rough camp amongst the spreading vegetation below the tree canopy. To his disappointment he found the site to be quite saturated and dry wood for a fire in short supply, so instead he busied himself with cutting down branches for camouflage and then brushing down Fire and finding him the best shelter for a make-do corral. When he finally heard the cart making its way over the rise the area was prepared and camp could be set up quickly. Calin and Lyaren worked together, going back to the road to hide the tracks, while Elayna saw to settling Calin's large Shire horse, Greg, and Hurricane into the corral, which Lyaren had put together. She fished out apples for the three horses, who seemed content in each other's company and only mildly irritated by the rain. She then went through the packs in the wagon, selecting food for supper while she waited for the others to return. The rain continued its constant pounding while the wind lashed the branches above her head and whistled through the rough seams of the canvas wagon top. Despite this, the wagon held up well providing a warm, if somewhat cramped, shelter for the night, the dim light from Calin's small oil lamp adding a welcoming glow. Finding bread, cheese, cured ham and a flask of mead (a gift from Dina), Elayna set about preparing the meal in time for the men's return. She soon had the wagon shipshape and welcoming.

Lyaren and Calin worked quickly to brush out the tracks of the wagon's passage. Where the damp earth had been broken down by the heavy wheels Lyaren used a slight concealment spell, but luckily the shingle banking where the wagon had left the road was easily repaired and soon their trail was impossible to locate. Lyaren was pleased that Calin didn't question the considerable precautions and that he seemed to accept that there was more to Lyaren and Elayna's tale than they wanted to share. Satisfied with their work the two of them trekked back to the trees, an awkward silence between them. Lyaren couldn't come to terms with Calin being with them; he felt guilty for putting the lad in danger. Calin began to feel a little unnerved by Lyaren's lack of communication. Clearing his throat awkwardly, Calin finally hit on a topic of conversation. "Elayna mentioned she had lost her knife, back when we were talking in the wagon." He cast a glance at Lyaren whose eyes seemed to look through him as he continued to scout the surrounding countryside. "Only, I've a number in my supplies, do you think she'd be offended if I offered her one as a gift."

Lyaren's lips twitched with a smile. "You seem to like her a lot. That's a generous gift." His eyes went back to their scouting. "You know we have nothing to give you in return."

Calin nodded, still feeling the awkwardness like a weight sat around his shoulders. "I know, I...I only want to cheer the lass up, she's had a rough time and I thought it might help... I've got a few swords and knives and things for the business, you know."

90

Lyaren put his hand on the big man's shoulders, detecting his discomfort. "I am sorry Calin, you have been a good friend to us and I am sure Ela will take no offense. Come, I might even buy her a small sword if you've got one; perhaps you could adjust the weighting of one to suit her."

"Of course." Calin relaxed a little. "Back at home I've the forge, and I can make the changes before you get on your way." Calin smiled and was reassured when Lyaren smiled back. He had just started to tell Lyaren about the forge, which had been his father's when a horse whinnied nearby, and out of the gathering gloom Greg trotted towards them. "Hello boy, what are you doing out here?"

Lyaren at his side had stopped dead in his tracks, eyes focused ahead towards the trees. "The horses should be in the corral − it's sound, I made it myself."

Calin nodded. "Greg's not one to wander, especially in this kind of weather."

Sensing the danger together, Lyaren sprinted towards the trees as Calin threw himself onto Greg's broad back and dug his heals into the horse's side. Covering the ground to Lyaren quickly, he reached down and offered his hand. Lyaren accepted, leaping up behind him. The horse thundered over the rise, his hooves thudding through the mud almost as rapidly and Lyaren's heart pounded in his chest. Even as he sent out his silent plea, light exploded from amongst the trees confirming his worst fear. By the time they reached the wagon it was well ablaze. The remains of the packs lay sprawled over the ground, while the heavy boxes containing Calin's ironmongery had been smashed open, the weapons rifled through. The other two horses were also gone. As the two men jumped from Greg's back both drew their weapons and − instantly − a vicious cry went up from the surrounding trees, followed by the rush and clamour of men drawing weapons and intent on cutting them down before they had the chance to fight.

Luckily for Calin and Lyaren their combat skills had been greatly underestimated. Calin had fashioned his broadsword himself, and he knew how to use it. Bandits had set upon him once before and he was well aware that life only prevailed if you were prepared to fight for it. He took the first man diagonally through the shoulder, following through to cut down a second with a wide-arcing sweep to his chest.

At his side, Lyaren reappraised Calin; the large man handled himself with confident ease – he made a good companion in a fight. Six men flew at them and, as Calin took on the lead two, Lyaren levelled his throwing knife at the last, catching him in the neck. The man seemed to blink in surprise and then crumpled to the ground, dead. As the knife left his hand, Lyaren twisted and jumped into the air and, somersaulting, flew over the heads of the remaining assailants. Landing behind them he slashed true with his sword, delivering a deadly stab between one man's shoulder blades, straight into his heart. His fingers jabbed out towards the next assailant's throat, which gave him the time he needed to retract his weapon, whip it around in a wide arch and rip open the next man's chest. He veered to the man gasping for air at his knees and pushed the tip of his blade effortlessly into the spinal cord at the neck. He then turned to watch Calin draw his own sword from the chest of the final attacker. As the two men made eye contact the gulf between them vanished, its chasm filled with respect and companionship. Neither needed words as they turned to take in the remains of their campsite; it was obvious – Elayna was gone. Lyaren sprinted into the tree line where the attackers had emerged but returned instantly. "Some of your weapons are on the ground over there."

he told Calin. "They must have been the last of the group."

Calin was stood looking over the bodies of the fallen men. "What are they?" he asked Lyaren.

Lyaren looked at the dead creatures on the ground, their strange scale-patterned skin and elongated faces marking them clearly. "They're Sandkind" he answered. "And a long way from home!" He looked around the camp. "There's not much left but we should gather up everything worth taking. We can pack as much as possible on Greg, then we need to find a fresh camp; they'll come looking when this lot fail to return." Lyaren's voice was calm but his desperation was tightening his chest; he had to stay focused, keep calm.

"What about Ela?" Calin's voice cracked.

"She's alive!" Lyaren snapped. She had to be alive... she was too important...he needed her... she was his mission... she was... she was... she was his Ela! "There's no blood. They've taken her alive. When we are ready we will take her back." He turned to start collecting his gear. "And, by the Goddess, they will pay for what they have done!"

Chapter 4
Teah

The weeping finally dwindled to a whimpering sniffle and eventually gave way to silence. Teah breathed deeply relieved to find herself; once again, cloaked in the stillness of night. Now she could forget about the other prisoners, focus on her own situation, master her emotions and think! Her hands were bound behind her back, the flesh raw where the rope had bit deeply into it. The early onset of infection sent stinging tingles down into her arms – she would need to clean them soon or she could lose her hands. She was laid on her stomach, wedged between two other women, in a dark, wooden enclosure, the sound of their ragged breathing the only indication they were still alive. The roof above let through the rain, which ran over her back and collected in a puddle beneath her body. She cursed the damp dress which clung uncomfortably to her. If only she had worn her hunters' leathers, then she would have died with her tribe as a warrior, fighting for her own freedom. Instead, when the attack came, she and her friends had been caught by surprise in the women's tents. They had been quickly overpowered by the sheer number of attackers and herded with the other women into the forest. She hadn't given in meekly – that wasn't her way – but without a weapon and against so many she had been easily overpowered, and her resistance had cost her a considerable gap in her memory and a tender protrusion which was still throbbing on the back of her head. How long she had been unconscious she did not know; she was aware of being tended by other women of her tribe, who silently sent her healing which she was fairly sure had saved her life, but then she was moved away from them. Having had no food or drink she began to drift in and out of consciousness, but the sounds of despair kept her from sleep. A single bone-chilling scream had cut the night air from somewhere beyond her cramped prison, followed by the whimpers and tears of wretchedness from her fellow captives. Most of the women fell quiet a while ago but one had sobbed for what felt like an age. Clarity of thought had eluded Teah for a long time, her sanity lost in the desperation of her situation. More rain splashed onto her face and dripped down to her lips. Teah realised the rain had saved her; dehydration had weakened her but deep down in her consciousness her spirit was not diminished. She was Teah, Princess of the Northern Clans, Horse Mistress and warrior. She would not be beaten by these desert scums! The Sandkind had their magic, but she was not without her own. Her father's bloodline was thick with the magic of their ancestors. She would fight them, or die trying!

Footsteps approached and stopped outside. Lantern light filtered through gaps in the wooden walls and Teah could identify her prison as being an oversized wagon. Her eyes met those of a young girl with a large purple welt over much of her face. The girl smiled meekly and then the light moved on, returning the wagon to darkness. "What's your name?" Teah whispered. She didn't recognize the girl; she wasn't from the clans, she was a kingdom girl, Maldoran.

"Sally." It was barely a whisper.

"Do you know where we are?" Teah pressed. "I've been out of it for a while."

"They attacked our village this morning. I think most of 'em are dead. They separated out the young girls." She sniffed. It sounded loud in the surrounding silence, her voice cracking, "They killed the older women... Just stabbed 'em like they were nothing. Then they tied us up and put us in these wagons. You were here when they locked us in."

"I'm Teah. They attacked the clan gathering at the Peace Camp up in the mountains. Have you seen any other women from the clans?"

"No, but there were many wagons. Some had people in, I'm sure."

"What is the name of your village, Sally? I need to know where we are." Teah asked.

"We're in northern Maldora. I'm from Waydonfield; it's one of the most northern villages." The girl sounded so afraid. "What will they do with us?"

Teah considered for a moment. "I'm not sure, but I think we're spoils of war. We need to escape. Turn around and I'll work on your bonds."

"No!" There was terror in her voice. "Didn't you hear the screams? They took Jilly cos she'd undone her hands. They keep coming to check 'em." She paused. "She's my friend; do you think she's dead?"

Teah considered the scream that had awakened her. "Yes" she said. "Yes I do."

Teah expected Sally to cry but there was only silence. She began to work on her own bonds. If Jilly could get her hands untied so could Teah.

97

Juzuk's voice filled Galizund's head. He hated the mind-speech; it always left him feeling nauseated. "Can you hear me Galizund? Report."

Galizund steadied his breathing and focused his thoughts on his superior. He took hold of the thread of energy Juzuk held out to him and rode it swiftly back to its source. "I hear you Master Juzuk. The mission goes well, we easily took the outpost at Riversway, they were unsuspecting. Waydonfield was more challenging. The farmers spotted us and had time to take arms, but they were overpowered quickly. We killed all but the youngest women as you ordered. My men are scouting the surrounding countryside for travellers and a few have been found. We take the women and kill the men as you order, there are none left to give warning to the south."

"What of the women? Have you found any with red hair?"

"Yes, master, there were two amongst the village girls and a third was brought in yesterday. We keep them separate from the other prisoners and have given them a little extra food. They await your arrival."

"You have done well, Galizund. Do you sense power in any of the women?"

"No my lord."

"Very well. Hold your position; we will be with you soon."

As Juzuk abruptly cut of the contact Galizund's thought-string was shoved carelessly into the ether and sent reeling out of control on its haphazard journey back into his mind. Galizund collapsed to his knees, the world spiralling around him as he vomited, violently emptying the contents of his stomach onto the tent floor.

Tarrin lay flat against the wet ground, his breathing shallow, a concealment spell hung closely around his body. He was fairly sure he hadn't been spotted, but the magic the Sandkind had wrapped around their army made it difficult for him to see clearly into the camp. The hairs on the nape of his neck prickled slightly as a wave of subtle magic flowed over his own enchantment. Silently, he placed his hand on the hilt of his broadsword and with practised ease he sprang to his feet, twisting in mid-movement to face his unknown assailant, levelling his blade as he caught his balance. He assessed the threat, confident his magic would give him the edge on any attacker, but he felt his surety quickly dissolve as he met the emerald green eyes of a very powerful Elvin warlock, whose sword was held equally-prepared for a fight. Tarrin held back, waiting, every nerve and muscle taught and ready to respond. For a time no one moved, each man weighing up the other. Then Tarrin felt a sharp, hard, steel blade slip between the seam of his leather vest and push firmly against his ribs. He was a fool! He was so sure the elf was the threat that he never thought to look for a second man.

"Put up y're sword." the voice breathed into his ear. "We've no will to hurt y'. Do as we say and you might get through the night alive."

Tarrin flipped his sword to the ground and the man behind him reached around and removed his knives from their various straps. The elf retrieved his blade from the ground and motioned for them to follow him. The three men moved silently in the night; Tarrin could feel an enchantment around them, silencing their footsteps and keeping them safe from prying eyes. He would play this out and see where it took him. Besides, they hadn't found all his weapons! The silent march took several hours and led them to a small clearing within a dense crop of trees.

"Sit." the elf instructed, and Tarrin rested on the tree stump, which the elf had indicated. The elf brought over a second log and sat opposite him. All the while the other man stood silently by. Tarrin didn't think the man had taken his eyes off him once yet. In the dim light Tarrin could see little of his captors but he knew he was outmanned. The elf was a warlock and the other one was some kind of giant.

"Who are you?" the elf asked.

Tarrin answered truthfully, if they wanted him dead he wouldn't be here now. "I am Tarrin Strong Arm, Prince of the Wolf Moon Clan and son of Tarrin True Heart, King of the Grass Land and leader of the Horse Clan Warriors." He spoke softly, but the steel in his voice left no doubt as to the truth of his words.

"I am Lyaren of the Silent Forest elves, first warlock of the White Eagle. This is my friend Calin of Waydonfield. Why would a lord of the Grasslands be spying on a concealed army of Sandkind?" The elf's voice was light, almost friendly.

"They came through the Wayfinder forests seven moons past. My guess is they skirted the Grasslands, or my father's warriors would have seen them and cut them down. Their magic doesn't work on us; we have our own magic." Tarrin stopped, remembering the sight of the Peace Camp. "My people trade in the woodlands every spring; we call it the Peace Camp. Everyone is welcome there; it is a place of merriment and celebration."

Lyaren nodded, he had heard of the Peace Camp, representatives of his own people would often travel to the camps of the Horse Clan to trade, and the horse breeders of his people worked closely with the clansfolk whose horses were legendary for their speed, stamina and beauty. The clansmen were fierce and honourable warriors. "I know of the Peace Camp," Lyaren told him. "Go on with your tale."

"I was away hunting when the Sandkind attacked the camp. We have a weapons amnesty; no one was armed. My people fought bravely but they were caught by surprise and were cut down savagely. I was several leagues south, tracking an elk, but the sounds of battle travelled clearly through the woodlands. By the time I got back the fight was almost over. Most of their army had moved on; only a few remained behind to finish their bloody slaughter. I joined my brothers to help with the fight but I was too late, they were already dead. I am the only one to survive. My older brother, Sardan, died in my arms. He told me they had taken some of the women. One of them is my sister, Teah. I tracked the army and have been watching, waiting for my chance to get to the prisoners. I mean no harm to elf or human, my argument is with the desert scum who murdered my people and stole my sister." Anger and frustration spat the words from his mouth. "The cowards would never have achieved such a victory had they met us with weapons in hand and on equal terms!"

"Peace, friend." The elf said, passing Tarrin his sword back. Tarrin took the weapon graciously and lay it across his knees. The tension in the air seemed to relax a little. "I am sorry for the circumstances of our meeting," the elf went on. "But we mean you no harm either. We have a shared cause: the Sandkind took our companion, too – Lady Elayna, my young charge – and we also intend to get her back. I dare not offer you a warm fire, their scouts are everywhere, but if you will share our camp and food we can also share information and perhaps help each other." Lyaren held his arm out to Tarrin in an offer of friendship.

Tarrin took his arm warmly and offered a slight smile. "Allies would be warmly appreciated," he laughed without any hint of humour, "And I haven't eaten in days. I believe this may be a fortuitous meeting for all of us."

101

Lyaren had spotted the large Horse Lord warrior watching the Sandkind camp when he had flown over, earlier that day. He had sensed his energy and recognised it as the subtle magic of the Horse Lords. Their magic was a natural extension of their bodies, sort of like a sixth sense. They used it to cloak themselves and to communicate their emotions and thoughts to animals. This had allowed them to build up a close relationship with the horses they loved. They could feed energy to the sick and the wounded, but had no means of manipulating the magic in the way the elves did. The warrior seemed to be scouting the camp and, although the Horse Lords and Sandkind were neighbours, Lyaren knew theirs was a fragile peace and there was no love lost between the two tribes. Hoping the Horse Lord could help, Lyaren had enlisted Calin's help to intercept the potentially dangerous man and bring him peacefully back to their camp.

Lyaren had been distraught by Ela's abduction and out of desperation had revealed some of his magical ability to Calin. Calin had been surprised when Lyaren had revealed his magic, especially his ability to transform into the beautiful pure white eagle, but he was also surprisingly calm and accepting. Calin, too, had been deeply upset by Ela's abduction and more so at the realisation that the army may have come through Waydonfield. His growing anxiety meant he was only too happy to accept the situation and embrace the benefits of Lyaren's abilities. Unfortunately, finding Tarrin was all that came from their many days of surveillance. The Sandkind had their own magic, which hung, around their camp like a fog, and even Lyaren's eagle vision could not penetrate it. Whenever he had tried to land or get nearer the lizards fired arrows at him, as they did all birds that flew overhead to supplement their rations. It was when flying away from one such incident that Lyaren had noticed Tarrin's magic. The taste was so different to that of the Sandkind's that he had risked a closer investigation, and so he and Calin had come to ambush the clansman. They sincerely hoped that their new companion could help them locate Ela within the enemy camp.

The Horse Lord quickly devoured the food Calin had given him, and now sat quietly sipping a little of the warming liquor Samuel had given Calin as a gift back in Upper Gonfiels. As the silence of the night enveloped them Calin could hold back his impatience no longer and pressed, "How long have you been watching the camp?"

Tarrin regarded the huge man before him – he must be one of the largest humans he had ever encountered – but now he'd had the chance to look more closely he realised how young Calin was, barely a man at all. Still, he seemed to be able to use that enormous broadsword he carried around with him. "I followed the scum out of the northern woods and down through the pastures to Riversway. They burnt the hamlet to the ground then continued south. They came through Waydonfield a week back, that's where they took most of their prisoners, then carried on south for another two days and set up this camp. Since then they've been scouting the area. They come back occasionally with more prisoners but don't seem in any rush to move on yet. They've been here for about a week."

"Did they take all the villagers from Waydonfield prisoner?" Calin asked him, a rush of dread twisting a knot in his stomach.

"No." Tarrin noticed the concern in his voice and remembered the big man hailed from that village. "Why? Do you have family there?"

"You could say that, it's my home."

103

"Ah." Tarrin paused, nodded sadly and then continued. "I'm sorry my friend, they only took the young women. Everyone else they put to the sword."

"No!" Calin gasped, his breath turning the word into a moan. "Couldn't some have escaped?" He held back the nausea racing through his body and felt all the blood draining from his face.

Tarrin considered a moment. "It is possible, if they were able to get away early in the fight they could have got out. I kept my distance, tried to get to the prison wagons while the guards were distracted, but the bastards never let their guard down." This he spat out. "I saw no sign of survivors. I am truly sorry. These desert scum have much to answer for."

"Yes they do" Lyaren concurred, placing a strong sympathetic hand on Calin's shoulder. The big man had lowered his head and silent tears ran down his face. "We were taking Calin home to his mother." There was nothing more to say.

Tarrin nodded. "We both have family to avenge!" His voice cracked; the sound surprisingly tender for such a fierce looking warrior.

Lyaren split the silence. "Tell us all you know of the prisoners, start with your sister, we have much to plan."

"I think they have Teah in one of the rear wagons, they're the ones they have been guarding the longest. The camp is formed in a ring around them and they check on the prisoners about three times a day. There are about ten women in each cart; they get them out to check on them but their magic makes a shield that is hard for me to see through clearly. They pulled out a few dead women yesterday and I'm guessing there'll be more soon as I've only seen them take food to them a few times. The last three carts each have only one

woman in them, two from Waydonfield and the third –
well, she was brought in four days ago."

"That will be where they're keeping Ela then."
Lyaren interjected. "She was taken four days ago."

"Yes" Tarrin agreed. "She will be the one, but
that means she is in the cart furthest away from Teah
and that will make a rescue attempt more troublesome."

"True" Lyaren agreed. "Could you draw me a
rough plan of the position of the wagons?"

Tarrin picked up a small stick and began to draw
in the dirt on the ground. He made a rough circle on the
floor and then pointed to one side. Here the sun rises and
here it sets" he indicated, then returned to his drawing.
"They have set up an outer ring of defence made mostly
of lookouts and about two hundred men on guard duty.
Within this ring are their tents; they look set in for the
long haul – they seem to be making themselves
comfortable for now. The carts where the prisoners are
kept are right in the centre of the camp next to the corral
they have built for their ugly little ponies."

Lyaren studied the marks Tarrin had made in the
sand. "And which cart is our friend in?"

"This is the one I think Teah is in, by the horses,
and the most recent prisoners are in these far ones,
nearer to the tents."

"Mmm, and when did you say they checked on
the prisoners?"

"Three times a day: first light, midday and dusk.
I don't think they look through the night, but they double
the guards so it's harder to get into or out of the camp
then." Tarrin's face was strained with tension.

Lyaren sat back thinking through the problem.
He had only considered having to get Ela out, but now
Tarrin would want to rescue his people and he was sure
Calin would want his villagers set free as well. What to
do with so many people to help? He had enough magic

to shield a small group for a journey through the camp but not enough to shield all the prisoners and get them out. No, he needed to get the guards looking in the other direction. And then it hit him. If he could conjure an army, or at least an illusion of one, he could draw the guards away. It would take a lot of power but if he wove the spell beforehand he could conjure a small distraction for ten minutes or so, it might be enough. He would be exhausted afterwards but at least it was a chance. Then he needed to get weapons for the women, they would need to fight their way out of the camp; if surprise was on their side they just might do it! Lyaren looked up into Tarrin's eyes, then over to Calin. "Right" he announced. "We're getting them all out so listen carefully; we have got much to do!"

Calin's skin seemed to crawl, he wasn't sure if it was the rough wool cloak he had pulled around his shoulders (taken from the body of the dead lizard warrior) or the enchantment Lyaren had placed on him to make him look like one of the strange lizard men. He and Tarrin had set out together that morning. They had spent the last two days working out the fine details of their part of the plan and, in that time had, reached a friendly alliance. Lyaren had taken himself off to work on his conjuring of an illusionary army. Tarrin had taught Calin how to move silently through the rough terrain, so that his clumsy movements wouldn't jeopardize the magical camouflage, which he was able to enlarge so that it encompassed both men. They entered the camp together several hours ago but at that point had moved off in opposite directions. Calin had tried to spot Tarrin throughout the afternoon but cloaked in his own illusion, Tarrin was impossible to distinguish from any of the other lizard men. Calin reached out his hands to the brightly leaping flames of the blazing campfire in front of him, hoping his attempt at casual nonchalance was good enough not to attract attention. Just as Lyaren instructed, he'd wandered through the camp being careful to avoid eye contact with the Sandkind and moving frequently to avoid being drawn into conversation. The guttural grunting language of the Sandkind was like nothing Calin had heard before and he was sure that if he were to be approached he would be useless.

The Sandkind camp was a strange place. Not that Calin had ever been in an army encampment before, but he felt sure this place was nothing like a human army camp. The whole place was unnaturally quiet. The Sandkind moved slowly and quietly, grunting their language to each other only occasionally. Lyaren had explained that the desert men were affected by the sun's energy. When the sun was high and bright they were strong and fast, but here in the kingdom the late spring sun provided only a fraction of the energy they required. The Sandkind could also take energy from fire and store it, and so they kept all their activity to a minimum in order to have energy reserves left for battle. As Tarrin had said, the camp was a well-organised arrangement of perfectly made, dome-shaped leather tents, the entrances to which were thrown open to allow in the sunlight. Inside, Calin could see thick rugs and furs strewn across the floor. Opulent cushions and beautiful blankets of rich reds and golds were scattered over the rugs giving an inviting, comfortable appeal to the interiors. Weapons and tools were stored in an orderly fashion to one side and, in some; low-level tables and stools had been laid out. On the whole the tents were empty. The Sandkind mostly sat still in the sunlight or wandered slowly, as Calin did, through the camp. As the day had drawn on large campfires had burst into life and the lizard men gathered around them, working collectively to prepare food. Calin wandered away from the fire roughly in the direction of the prison wagons. So far so good, he told himself; he'd managed to keep his head down for most of the afternoon and, as evening closed in and the sun's light began to fade, staying inconspicuous should become easier. He looked casually in the direction of the prison wagons. He had been watching them all day, waiting for the women to be brought out. He was very close now and could hear the guards grunting to each other as they ordered the women out for inspection. He'd seen several wagons unloaded and the captives inspected by their captors. Most of the women looked terrified and filthy; Calin couldn't recognise anyone from his village. The women complied meekly as their bonds were checked and tightened. Each prisoner was given a drink from a large ladle of water but no food was given and many of the women seemed close to collapse. The women from Tarrin's tribe stood out from the others. Their clothes were much more fitted than the kingdom women's and physically they were in a far worse condition, all badly bruised and some with wicked cuts – many of which looked infected. Despite this they spat and swore at the guards throughout the exchange and received forceful slaps around their faces for their defiance. Calin couldn't see their eyes but he was sure that if he could they would burn with hatred. Calin had marked their wagons when the guards had passed, Tarrin would need to locate the women quickly.

The guards had moved on to the next wagon. The wooden bar which was shot across the rear door of the wagon was removed and the door thrown wide open. The guard grunted a word which resembled 'Out!' A single occupant cautiously emerged, but was roughly dragged down from the wagon and dropped unceremoniously onto the dusty hard ground where she awkwardly struggled to regain her feet, not easy with her hands tied behind her back. Just like the other women she was miserable, dirty and wearing only rags, but she held her head high. From his position he could clearly see the defiance which shone in her cool blue eyes and, beneath all the dirt, her beautiful auburn hair still shone through. *'Elayna!'* He'd found her.

Resisting the overwhelming urge to slaughter each and every murderous lizard man he passed, Tarrin had made his way straight to the corral just as Lyaren had instructed. He was overjoyed to find not only the ponies of the Sandkind but also a large number of young warhorses taken from the Peace Camp. The older horses had all died with their masters, but these ones were still too young to have developed a strong bond. Still, as his mind brushed gently at their consciousness, he felt their anger and regret. These horses were ashamed that they had not died with their masters. Tarrin began to work with these horses first, he sat in the shade of a small tent being used to house saddles and harnesses and began to show the beautiful creatures how they could help. He showed them how they could avenge their masters and, most importantly, still become warrior steeds of the Horse Lords. All afternoon he worked, touching the minds of all the horses and ponies in the corral. He was surprised to find how little the Sandkind's funny little ponies felt for their masters. They seemed to find the whole idea amusing and were only too happy to trick the creatures who saw them as nothing more than beasts of burden. The large carthorses used to pull the wagons were the most complicated to work with. They had been interested in the images Tarrin had been carefully placing into their minds but for a long time stayed disconnected from them. Their easy-going nature and reliance on their masters for all their needs was deep-rooted and difficult to override. Tarrin wasn't convinced they would play their part, but there wasn't much more he could do. One horse stood out from the rest. A young stallion. He welcomed Tarrin into his uncannily intelligent mind and told him firmly that he would stay with his mistress, who was one of the prisoners in the wagons. This Tarrin agreed to, after all, anyone who had such a firm bond with their horse deserved the respect of the Horse Lords. He would not override that bond and so instructed him to find his mistress when the time came. Horses taken care of, he now needed to play the part of thief. He would need weapons for the women, including his sister. Tarrin's thoughts went almost unwittingly to Teah; he saw her face, remembered her laugh, the way her hair looked when she plaited it with fresh flowers, the wicked look in her eye when they sparred together, the soft gentle tone to her voice, which she kept only for him. He could almost hear the way she said his name...

"Tarrin, Tarrin..."

Tarrin jumped. That wasn't his memory – he hadn't adjusted his thought patterns after communicating with the horses – he was still transmitting his thoughts and still open to receiving thoughts back. But that was no horse and this was unheard of! Calming his mind he focused all his energy on the voice in his head and projected towards it a clear focused question: *'Teah, is that you? Is this real? Can you hear me?"*

The response was beautiful; if thoughts could laugh with pleasure that was what he felt. *"Yes, Tarrin, it's me. I can hear you, how can this be?"*

"I don't know but this is wonderful. Teah, listen carefully, I need you to be ready, we are getting you out of here!" Quickly Tarrin outlined the plan to Teah, her mind growing more and more excited at the prospect of escape. She would be ready she assured him, she would get the women ready. This was going to work!

'Right' he told himself as he reluctantly let go of Teah's thoughts. 'Now we need weapons.'

Since she had woken Teah had managed to free her wrists from the painful ropes and had fashioned herself a convincing slipknot-based imitation, which she could pull on quickly when she heard the guards coming. Sally had been impressed and allowed her to do the same for her. Although quiet most of the time, Sally had chatted a little to Teah and the two had formed a cautious friendship. Watching her with their hollow, terrified eyes, the other women had been too locked in their silent terror to even attempt talking and pulled away quickly when she had offered to loosen their ropes. Poor fools, they would sooner face their fate willingly than strive for life and freedom!

Despite Sally's company the hours dragged by painfully slowly for Teah and so she took to stretching out her awareness to the wildlife around the camp. She spied on the strange alien images she found in the minds of a yappie young dog who scavenged around the fires of the Sandkind, and the silent patient cats who hunted the myriad of rats skulking around the camp. But it was melding with the minds of the horses that gave her the most pleasure. Even in their docile inactivity their minds were keen and intelligent and, what's more, they felt and acknowledged her presence, some even welcoming her into their thoughts and sharing their memories of the day willingly with her. It was through this communion that she discovered she wasn't the only Horse Lord communicating with the horses. The young filly she touched had eagerly shared the thoughts which someone had imprinted in her mind earlier in the afternoon. That someone had to be Tarrin! So few of the Horse Lords had the level of power which she and her bother held. Their line was so strong. If only she could reach him,

111

communicate with him as she did the horses. And so, widening her awareness, she searched for her brother, using images of the two of them as children together to help focus her mind. She cast out her thoughts like a fishing net, filtering out the small emotions of the little creatures before, to her amazement, he was there in her head and she was in his! Their time together had been short, the joy and amazement at their newfound ability overshadowed by their dire situation. Tarrin had shared his memories of his journey south as he had tracked the army. He showed her his meeting with Lyaren and Calin and then lay out their plan. It could work, she was sure of it! As his awareness slipped from her mind she felt the wrench – a loneliness like no other – but, fired with purpose, she knew what she had to do. First, she had shared her knowledge with Sally and the other women in her wagon. Even the most terrified had turned to listen as she quickly told them what she had just discovered she could do and what she had learned from her brother. Next she needed to spread the word to the other Horse Clan women. She knew they were here, just imprisoned elsewhere. She tried to find their minds, as she had Tarrin's, but to no avail. They weren't as talented as her, but they could touch the minds of the horses so Teah wondered if they could hear the whisperings of other creatures. Teah quickly found the little field mouse who inhabited the far back corner of their wagon. He curiously scuttled across the floor to her outstretched hand, causing screeches of concern from her cellmates. The little creature had only a delicate tiny mind but a huge capacity for adventure. She gave him only the simplest of thoughts: *'It's Teah, escape planned, be ready!'* Then she instructed the creature to find other women to hear its message, and he happily scuttled off on his mission. That was all Teah could do, now she just had to wait.

Ela rested her back against the rough wall of her makeshift prison. Her wrists throbbed with the pain of the ropes chaffing against them but at least they had removed the ropes from around her ankles. When they had attacked it had been sudden and brutal. She never heard or saw them coming, they had simply appeared and grabbed her. She had kicked and struggled and this had made them laugh. It took three of them to drag her into the trees where they had thrown her to the ground. One of them had rolled her onto her back and put his hand up under her skirt. She tried to scream but the others were ready and one put his hand over her mouth. The one on top of her had dragged her skirt up and savagely tugged at her small clothes. She could feel his fingers close to her – grabbing at her – and in one last attempt kicked her legs wildly, but this only made her attacker laugh more. Torchlight lit up the clearing as a fourth joined them. To Ela the light illuminated their inhuman appearance. The fourth creature had pulled the one on top of her off. He grabbed at her hair and pulled it close to the torchlight, grunting and growling in a strange alien language. The others stepped back subserviently and bowed respectfully. She expected the newcomer to do something, either continue her rape or perhaps help her up! Instead he kicked her in the head and she lost consciousness. When she woke she was alone and locked in this strange wagon. Her skirt and small clothes were torn but she was fairly sure they hadn't continued their rape attempt. The guards had kept checking on her, dragging her out and giving her water, but none had tried to assault her again.

After the initial shock of her capture an almost unnatural calm had befallen Elayna. She had felt fear and confusion ever since the night Lyaren had told her she was in danger; for now, at least, she didn't need to react. There was nowhere to run. And she still had faith that Lyaren would come for her. He wouldn't give up just like that.

A loud grating sound announced the opening of the rear door, which snapped back hard against the wagon. She pulled herself gingerly to her feet, her ankles were still so sore, but as she made it to the door the lizard creature grabbed her wrist and pulled her, head first, out and onto the ground. As she fell to the hard, dusty earth, Elayna couldn't help but notice the big white bird perched on one of the large posts which held secure the horses' corral fencing. She shivered, the thing seemed to be watching her with its spooky eyes and, as stupid a thought as it was, she was sure its presence was making her feel sick! Gods, it was a big thing! She hid a shiver and found her feet. The guard grabbed her roughly around the upper arm and pushed her back towards the wagon. Happy with her standing position he shoved the ladle of sour water into her face. She took a sip; the bitter taste hit her tongue but its coolness brought relief to her swollen, dry lips. She drank a little more, but as was his habit the guard moved the water out of reach just as she realised she was thirsty. "Please could I have some more water?" she asked him.

The guard just grunted, then turned the ladle over and let the remaining water soak into the earth at her feet. He grinned at her, at least that's what Ela thought he must be doing (it was hard to tell with their strange lizard faces). Elayna had read about the desert-dwelling Sandkind, although she had never met one before. She had been told they were a peaceful people, living isolated from other societies in the harshest most remote areas of the far northern deserts. Their skin wasn't exactly scaly but had a greeny-grey hue to it and a mottled patterning which made it appear so. They seemed to be a short people, the tallest being only her height, but they were stocky and strong. Their bone structure was different to humans also, at least the head was. They had an elongated face from the nose down to the chin and deep bony ridges both above and below the eyes which made them appear tiny. Up close, their eyes were deep and dark, with a green iris and a pupil split down the centre like a snake's eye. Elayna wasn't sure why she didn't fear these strange, warlike creatures. They had been cruel and without regard for her comfort or feelings, they'd even tried to rape her! They had given no indication that they cared whether she lived or died, and they were the most alien creatures she had ever seen in her life... but she could not fear them. She looked back to the bird – *that* frightened her!

The bird let out an ugly squawking sound and flew into the air. As it did so there was a loud crashing sound far to the north of the corral followed by the boom of a thousand horses' hooves. Both Ela and the guard whipped their heads in the direction of the sound. A huge section of the corral fencing had collapsed and hundreds of ponies and horses were charging out of the opening, their speed growing as they emerged into the main body of the army camp. Screams and chaos ensued. The guard almost forgot Ela as he set of running towards the commotion, but then shot a look back and nodded. Unobserved, the largest desert man Ela had ever seen in her life had crept up behind her and taken hold of her wrists. Suddenly horns started blowing from the outer rim of the encampment adding yet more anarchy to the clamour which erupted from all around the camp.

Ela looked back to her captor. He was enormous and held a gleaming, deadly-looking knife in his hand. Ela caught her breath and pulled back. Her captor giggled – a deep human sound, not the ugly grunting sound of the lizard men. It's all right, Ela, it's me,

115

Calin," He slipped the knife between the bonds at her wrists and her hands fell limply to her side.

"Calin?" She squinted at the creature in front of her. "How..." she stuttered.

"No time now!" The huge lizard man with Calin's voice turned as a large cart horse appeared at the front of the wagon and, in a most bizarre fashion, backed itself up into position ready to be attached to the collar and harness which a dark-skinned young woman had hurriedly thrown to the ground by the wagon before turning and running back in the direction from which she had come. Ela looked around; there were women at all the carts, hitching up the horses in a silent frenzy of activity. A horse whinnied nearby and she turned as Hurricane trotted over to her, nuzzling her shoulder affectionately. Everything seemed to be moving in slow motion around her – a beautiful orchestration of a chaos. Realisation dawned, she was being rescued! They all were! Amongst the clamour of activity Elayna could hear the soft tones of female voices, heartfelt *'thank you's'* and tears of relief. "They need to keep quiet" Calin commented nearby. "We're not out of this yet!"

The enormous bird squawked again. Both Calin and Elayna turned their heads to see a large group of over twenty fearsome-looking lizard men who had noticed their escape and were now charging back towards the wagons, evil curved swords drawn, and growling angry battle cries. The great white bird soared into the air. It hovered a moment then the light around it blazed and the bird seemed to shimmer and blur. A sound that wasn't a sound rippled through Elayna's body, touching her soul, the resulting sensation both nauseating and distorting. For a moment she looked away but, when she looked back to where the bird had been, she saw it had vanished and in its place stood

Lyaren. He was naked, his skin glimmering magically in the fading light making every contour of his athletic form seem even more perfect. Ela held her breath – he was beautiful! Lyaren stood confident in his own power, his hands held out in front of him, but without a weapon he looked woefully vulnerable as the terrifying group of warriors closed in on him. Screaming their battle cries, a fearsome group of women rushed up to Lyaren's position brandishing a rough assortment of weapons and tools. *'Too few!'* Ela thought.

"Get onto the wagon, Ela" Calin ordered. His Sandkind appearance was gone and she could see the concern in his young, handsome features. "Get ready to ride. Don't stop, just keep going!" A quick glance showed her the horse was harnessed and ready; he stamped his feet hard on the ground. Ela didn't move, Calin rushed past to join Lyaren and, as he did so, Hurricane whinnied insistently at her side. Still Ela didn't move. *'Too many!'*

A ball of pure white energy shot out from Lyaren's outstretched hands, hitting the first few lizard men and throwing their bodies like twigs to the ground. Ela's heart leapt with hope but, as she watched, Lyaren stumbled and her hope dissolved into fear. He turned her way and his eyes caught hers: *terror, regret, sorrow, love, exhaustion!*

"Too many, too many!" She was saying it out loud, speaking to the world, but no one listened. The strange sensation building in her gut was drumming up through her body now. ***"Too many. Too fast. Too angry. Stop! Stop! Stop!"***

Her arm shot up into the air almost involuntary but somewhere deep down she was in control. She spread her fingers wide, she had to stop this, but she couldn't hurt them! Not her lizard men! How could she stop them? What could she do? They needed to sleep...The growing sensation deep within her core throbbed and rippled, spurting up and up and out and **"Sleep! ..."** As she spoke the word she released the sensation burning through her body. An explosion of pure energy coursed through her veins washing her in an agonising pain which twisted and pulled the molecules of her fragile self and fractured her body into a thousand pieces. Ela's scream consumed everything, everywhere... and then everything went black.

Lyaren accepted the hopelessness of the situation. His plan had failed he had killed them all; Calin, Tarrin, Ela, the women. There was no way out of this. Recognising the front two warriors charging towards him as Xyakahan priests he had let loose a huge energy bolt instinctively, but it had been so foolish! The last of his energy shot out with the blast and, instantly, a crippling exhaustion grasped hold of his body and wrung him out. The overwhelming resignation of his mistake struck him instantly and Lyaren turned to look one last time into Elayna's beautiful blue eyes. His heart stopped. Power pulsed through her body uncontrollably, he could see the energy bouncing like mini lightning bolts along her skin, and the air around her sizzled with charged electricity. Her lips were moving, the sound lost in the pandemonium of battle. Lyaren watched as her arm shot up into the air. *'Goddess, so much power! Where did she get it? How did she get it?'* An explosion of blinding light shot up from her tiny body and out over the surrounding area. Wider and wider it grew, flowing harmlessly over the women and rescuers it radiated out hitting the first of the Sandkind in a billowing wave. As the power made contact with the lizard men they instantly crumpled to the ground. Lyaren watched in amazement as one after the other the enemy fell.

Lyaren turned to the woman at his side, her beautiful deep-brown eyes mirrored the confusion in his own and she whistled a long soft sound.

"Wow what was that?"

Tarrin ran up beside him, thrusting a pair of light britches into his hands. The normality of the action brought him back to reality and he pulled on the trousers hastily.

"You were fine as you were!" The woman at his side commented.

Tarrin scowled, "Lyaren this filthy-mouthed creature is my sister, Teah. Teah, this is the elf Lyaren." The smile turned to a grin as he threw his arm around Teah and pressed his head close to hers. "It's good to see you" he breathed into her ear.

Lyaren looked back towards Elayna. Calin had caught the crumpling woman in his arms and had gently placed her on the ground; he looked equally shocked and distraught. Lyaren managed a run with the last of his strength, joined Calin, and dropped to the ground at Ela's side. He felt for a pulse, it was faint but steady and her chest moved slightly. "She's alive but weak" he told Calin, relief washing over him.

Tarrin jogged up behind him and placed an arm on his shoulder. "They're asleep!" he reported, "All of them," he indicated the silent camp around them. "They're all fast asleep!"

"We need to get out of here!" Lyaren snapped back to his senses, he could deal with emotions later; now, logic was needed. "Get the women into the wagons. Can we take all the horses with us? It will slow them down when they wake."

Tarrin grinned. "Already done!" He pointed to where the ponies and horses stood patiently in a perfect line, waiting like children for a schoolmaster to instruct them.

119

Lyaren laughed. "Good work, Tarrin, come on, let's get out of here!" Hurricane whinnied nearby. Lyaren stood and rubbed the horse's neck reassuringly. "It's alright, boy, your mistress will be fine."

"A fine horses that one," Tarrin commented from Lyaren's side. "Your Ela must have a way with horses, he's loyal."

Lyaren looked back at Elayna; in her sleep she was perfectly beautiful. "Yes," he nodded. "She's quite extraordinary."

Chapter 5
The Crossroads

The ragtag convoy hurriedly rolled out of the lizard army camp, groans and creeks from the wagons and the clipping drum of the horses' hooves contrasting alarmingly with the deadly silence. Tarrin and the women of the Horse Clan had each claimed one of the beautiful horses stolen by the Sandkind from the Peace Camp. They rode out in front of the column, scouting ahead and – as they began to cover more ground – taking turns to double back and keep an eye on the situation at the enchanted enemy camp. Sally had joined the Horse Clan women in the rescue and upon seeing Calin had instantly recognised him. Together they had briefly explained the situation to the other women of Waydonfield, who had all remained cowering in their wagons throughout the fight. Calin and his mother were well known to the traumatised women but, even though his presence seemed to calm them, they were reluctant to leave their wagons, turning them into self-imposed prisons.

Lyaren sat in the back of the wagon which Calin drove. Greg, whom they had called to collect as they passed by their hidden camp, joined Hurricane and Fire and all three trotted along happily behind.

Lyaren held Elayna close to him. He couldn't help noticing the state of her torn and filthy clothing. An alarming swelling had come up angrily on her forehead and cuts and bruises covered her face and body. She had obviously been treated badly. He wiped the tears welling in his eyes. *How could he have let this happen to her? He was a fool! He'd let his guard down and Ela had paid for his stupidity!*

Ela still slept deeply; her breathing was slow but her face was relaxed and she seemed to be comfortable. "I'm so sorry, Ela." he whispered softly into her ear. He pulled her light frame even closer to his chest, careful of her injuries, and let his hair fall over her face as he took some comfort from her oh-so-familiar scent. The tears came faster and Lyaren was glad for their solitude in the back of this dark, covered wagon – he didn't want anyone to witness the truth of his feelings, a truth which, only now, he admitted to himself. He turned his head to the heavens and beseeched the Mother Goddess, Mysta, to help him protect this most precious of women from all her enemies! *'And Mother,'* he pleaded. *'Please, protect us both from the depth of my love. She can never know. I must never show her this truth. This is forbidden, but so help me Mysta I don't know if I can do this!'*

They drove straight through the night and well into the next morning before Tarrin finally called a halt. Feeling the wagon shudder to a stop Lyaren jumped down from the back and Calin joined him as they made their way to where Tarrin and Teah were organising a makeshift cook-fire and hospital. As Tarrin spotted the two men approaching, he and Teah walked over to meet them.

"We shouldn't stop for long," Lyaren warned. "They will come after us!"

"I agree" Tarrin concurred, "But the scouts have just returned from their camp and the lizards are still sleeping like babies. Tell me, how is your Lady Elayna?"

"Also still sleeping," Lyaren answered.

"Some of these women haven't eaten in days" Tarrin continued. "Teah and the other clanswomen have caught rabbit and game; we thought to make a stew, tend to the wounded and try to get a little rest. Then we shall get back under way."

"Sally tells us there is a large town to the South with its own army presence. Perhaps if we can get the women there, and in time to warn the regiment stationed there, they would be safe?" Teah stated her question quietly and it hung in the air for a while.

"Yes" Calin agreed breaking the silence. "That'll be Stagsonton. Lord Nunnington rules that Quarrel and he has a large keep there with a real big barracks." The land of Maldora was split into regions known as Quarrels and ruled over by lords, The Nunnington family held the largest of the Northern Quarrels. "Stagsonton is well fortified, it will be difficult for the Sandkind to attack and there should be enough warriors to protect the town."

"Then that's where we must go." Lyaren said. "What about Lower Gonfiels? They'll be vulnerable; we need to warn them."

"Yes." Calin agreed. "I was thinking to do that. You lot keep on the road, I'll split off and tell Samuel they'll need to leave, otherwise, if the Sandkind attack they'll be lost like Waydonfield."

"My horsewomen can carry the warning faster," Teah stated flatly. "The lizard men will have caught you and eaten you for dinner before you even get there in that crawling cart that you drive!"

"They don't know you!" Calin snapped indignantly. "They wouldn't take a group of women seriously! You'd be wasting your breath."

"How dare you!" Teah stepped up close to Calin, her fist curling around the dagger she had liberated from the lizard men's camp. "I am..."

"Stop!" Lyaren's voice was quiet but commanding. "We haven't gone to all the trouble of rescue for you two to kill each other here. I suggest that you find a horse, Calin. Go with a group of horsewomen and be careful. Oh, and try to get along with each other."

Calin nodded but his stomach lurched. He hated riding; he had spent all his life around horses but his huge size meant he either rode one of the heavy plodding carthorses or dwarfed the other poor creatures.

Teah smiled brightly. "I've got just the horse for you, I'll get it ready. We'll set out when we break camp."

Everyone agreed and the party broke up. Lyaren and Calin returned to the wagon to check on Ela. She was still asleep. "I think we should check on her wounds," Lyaren said quietly. "I'll carry her over to the campfire and get some hot water." Gently he lifted Ela's delicate frame out of the wagon and strode off, carrying her protectively towards the fire. As he approached, some of the women rushed over and indicated a makeshift bed of blankets upon which he should lay her. Calin followed silently behind. As Lyaren placed her on the rug three of the Waydonfield women, finally brave enough to leave their prisons came over with water and cloths. They knelt by Ela to begin the process of tending her battered form. Lyaren stayed them. "No...I'll see to it!" he said, taking the bowl of water and cloths out of their hands.

Calin stepped forward, irritation turning to anger at Lyaren's attitude towards the Waydonfield women.

124

"They only want to help!" he snapped. "And besides, that's not proper, Lyaren, she's a young lady, you shouldn't be doing that, it's not your place!"

"Don't interfere in this, Calin!" Lyaren's voice was a low growl. "She is my responsibility! I have let her down once; I don't intend to do so again. We don't know what they did to her; I need to use my skills to check for hidden injuries!" Lyaren glowered up at the bigger man, holding his ground firmly. It was a lie, he had checked her over in the wagon – her wounds were superficial and the sleep, although magically induced, was now normal and natural. The truth was he couldn't bear to be parted from her yet and this gave him the excuse he needed to stay close.

"It's not proper!" Calin repeated grumpily and strode off to a respectable distance, where he stood watching Lyaren, his face set in a scowl and his arms folded across his chest.

Lyaren ignored Calin; he knew he was watching and so was mindful of Elayna's dignity. He took a thin blanket and laid it over her delicate body, then carefully removed what was left of her clothes and gently washed the blood and grime from her body. He worked slowly and reverently, and all the while Ela slept. Once she was clean, he considered the deeper wounds. He could use magic to heal them, but following her magically induced sleep and with his lack of understanding around her condition he dare not risk it. Lyaren took needle and thread from his own supply bag and began to stitch the deeper wounds by hand. They would scar, he knew, but it would be better than the mess they would make if left. One of the women brought over a dress. It wasn't much better than the one he had removed, but at least it wasn't torn and would allow her more modesty. Besides he couldn't bear to see the torn dress – it announced the torment she had undergone as a result of his negligence; he might as well have done this to her himself!

Calin felt someone come to stand by him and looked down to see Tarrin's sister, Teah, at his side. Her eyes flashed a mischievous twinkle and she held a steaming bowl of broth out to him. "Peace offering," she smiled, passing him the bowl.

Calin took it. "Thank you," he grunted, his eyes returning to Lyaren and Elayna. He wasn't in the mood for her over-inflated opinion of herself.

Teah didn't move. "Why do you watch him?" she asked.

"Why do y' think!" he snapped back. *Was this woman really so stupid?*

"I don't know." she answered, exasperated.

For a while he was silent, tasting the surprisingly delicious stew. Finally he elaborated. "That young lass is a real lady, he's got no right to be doing that." He pointed as he spoke. "The women could do it, I'm watching 'em, she can't protect herself unconscious like that, if he puts one hand out o' place, if he crosses the line, I'll stop 'I'll…" He slammed another spoonful of stew into his mouth, managing to chew without smiling, and continued his brooding.

Still Teah didn't leave. "It seems to me," she continued conversationally, "That he crossed the line when he cut off her clothes."

Calin stopped, spoon halfway to his mouth and glowered at the horsewoman, who continued unperturbed, "Only he won't hurt her, will he?"

Calin looked at the woman; she had an uncanny ability to bring out the worst in him. He answered her angrily. "You've known the man two minutes and you're an expert are y'! How the hell do you know he won't hurt her, you've just admitted he's crossed a line!"

Teah ignored his anger and kept her tone even. "It's obvious. Look!"

"I am looking you idiot!" He almost bellowed at the woman. "What do y' think I'm doing?"

"Well," she went on, the soft mellow tone of her easy-going voice emphasising the anger of his. "I think you're sulking because he got what you want, but you see, he's not doing it for himself is he?"

"What are you jabbering on about woman?"

"Well, like I said, see how he holds her?" She paused; Calin had looked back towards Lyaren and Elayna. "See how he touches her? Now look at his face. He loves her, he would never hurt her. I can only hope and dream that one day a man looks at me that way, that he loves me enough to care for me as deeply as he cares for her. She is a very lucky young woman." She paused to give time for her words to sink in, then her face blossomed into a mischievous grin and she winked. "Yes, a very lucky girl! I've seen him naked!" And smiling she took the dish from the dumbstruck giant's hands and sauntered back to the campfire. She felt his eyes on her hips as she moved away. Job done, she told herself!

Tarrin smiled as Teah strolled briskly back to his small campfire. "What are you up to Little Sister?" he asked. "He's a good man; he doesn't deserve you teasing him."

Teah shrugged, ignoring the implication. "I'm going to get a group together for the Lower Gonfiels ride; I think I'll go too. I've had enough of kingdom women to last me a lifetime, they're weak and feeble, and their men are grumpy and pigheaded – but at least they are easy to torment!"

Tarrin laughed. "God you like him that much!"

"I don't know what you mean!"

127

"Yes you do." he smiled. "I've got a present for you."

"For me, really?"

"Yes, follow me." Tarrin lead his sister over to his small pile of gear and removed the makeshift package he had stored amongst his belongings. He placed the carefully folded bundle in his sister's outstretched arms.

Teah's eyes lit up with excitement and she threw her arms around her big brother's neck, "Thank you." she whispered, hugging him fiercely. "Don't die while I'm away."

Tarrin hugged her back. "I'll try not to, now go and get yourself ready. You are a true princess of the Clan's, Teah, you make me very proud."

Teah smiled up at her brother. "Thank you for coming to get me, Tarrin. I am happy to be alive." And with that she rushed away to prepare for her journey.

Teah had left Calin dumbstruck; it had never occurred to him that there could be something between Ela and Lyaren. He was her tutor, or so he had said, but then again he turned out to be an elf and a wizard, so perhaps none of the other stuff was true at all. Calin liked Elayna – she would have made a good wife – but it wasn't love, not yet. Still, at least she was pleasant unlike that unbearable Horse Clan woman! Selecting only limited items from his pack, Calin got ready for his ride back to Lower Gonfiels. He made a hurried farewell to Lyaren, his pride not quite allowing him to apologise, and he set out across the haphazard camp to where the Horse Clan women were waiting. Six of the Horse Clan women were already in their saddles, relaxed and confident. They smiled at Calin as he approached, but it was Teah who hailed him from behind.

"Glad you made it, Calin!" she called.

Calin turned to face her. Her voice was already grating... He stopped open mouthed. Teah lead the most beautiful chestnut stallion he had ever set eyes on; a powerful creature, this horse was a true giant and like nothing he had ever encountered before in the kingdom. Certainly he could never dream of owning such a creature. This was a warhorse, fit for a warrior and more than capable of bearing his weight. But it wasn't the horse that stopped him. Teah had pulled her long black hair back into a tight scalp knot, its deep, rich curls forming a ponytail down to the hollow of her back, appearing chestnut red as it caught the dying light of the sun's rays. With her hair pulled tightly back her features were transformed. Her dark brown eyes were larger and deeper, sitting perfectly within the exotic beauty of her well-defined but full face. Her confident smile seemed to give her a magical radiance which made Calin's heart skip a beat. She strode confidently towards him, dressed in fitted black leather vest and trousers, both of which hugged her figure so tightly as to leave nothing to the imagination. Calin felt his face flush crimson and averted his eyes. He was speechless.

"I said I'd the perfect horse for you, what do you think? He's one of my family's; we breed horses for size and strength. He should manage your weight easily."

Her words rattled around his head for a moment before he found comprehension and answered. "I...I...yes." Calin stammered, pulling his attention back to the horse. "He's the most magnificent horse I've ever seen, thank you. I will take good care of him for you while we are on this journey."

Teah smiled again, looked to the beautiful horse and rubbed its nose affectionately, then handed the reins to Calin. "He belongs to my family and, as you saved my life, I would have you keep him. Thank you." And without waiting for an answer she turned and strode over

129

to her own mount, jumping fluidly up into the saddle. She looked back over her shoulder and noticed Calin stood frozen in place holding the reins of the beautiful stallion, an unreadable expression on his face. "Come on then, Calin!" she ordered, with a friendly laugh. "We've a village to save!" Teah touched her heals gently to her horse, turned to the road and galloped away, the other women following in tight formation. It would take Calin a while to catch up but that was all part of the fun.

Juzuk opened his eyes and stood slowly, shielding his frustration from the five priests who stood around him, their bodies reflecting his own exhaustion. Since they had rode into the enchanted camp earlier that morning they had been trying to break the spell which hovered over the army, but the more they tried to grasp at the threads of power laced through the sleeping camp, the more they just seemed to slip away. It was as if the magic was invisible, or perhaps as if it just didn't fill the same place which their own magic did. No matter how hard he tried he just couldn't manipulate it. He couldn't even get it to sit still long enough for him to see it properly! It shimmered and glinted for a fraction of a moment and then it seemed to jump out of existence and reset itself.

"I believe I was able to neutralize the potency" he lied, "The spell will break soon. Get some rest."

"Yes master" the priests chanted in unison, and obediently filed out of the command tent. Juzuk looked down at the sleeping form of Galizund laid out on the floor. He had found his second-in-command sleeping like a baby, in the mud, over by the collapsed and empty corral. Wagon tracks led out of the village and away into the distance. So much for his promotion, Xyakah would be furious if he ever found out! At least he had held back on reporting the finding of three red-haired women; if he was clever he might still get out of this. He kicked the sleeping Galizund forcefully in the kidneys. The man didn't even twitch! Juzuk walked over to his own cot and lay down; he needed to build up his energy levels for when the idiot awoke.

Elayna had been aware of the swaying sensation for a while before she finally opened her eyes. She was still in the wagon but the door had been removed from the back now, allowing the early morning light to stream in and illuminate the inside of the wagon. She had been changed, another simple linen dress but perfectly serviceable and not as torn as the one Dina had given her. She looked down at her arms – they were clean and the ugly cut to her upper left arm had been stitched. It itched a little but didn't really hurt. She quickly put her hand to her abdomen – she had been cut there when she was grabbed – yes, that was stitched too. The pile of blankets at her side moved and Lyaren's head poked out from beneath them. Relief flooded his face. "Ela, you're awake."

"Yes, where are we?"

"Safe for now, what do you remember?"

Elayna thought for a moment, *what did she remember?* "Well I was a prisoner, they grabbed me while you and Calin hid the tracks...I remember this wagon, it's where they held me and then there was the big white bird, and the giant lizard man, but it was you and Calin..." She stopped and looked at Lyaren. "That was your magic, wasn't it?"

"Yes, Ela, it was. Do you remember anything else?"

"Yes, I remember the fight, there were hundreds of them, and you were naked and you had no sword, and there were some women and I wanted to help, but then I didn't feel well at all... and then... Well I must have

131

collapsed. How did you defeat them? Did you use more magic?"

Lyaren looked at her for a long time. For the seventh time he reached out his senses to her aura and felt through it for any hint of the magic she had wielded back at the camp, and for the seventh time he found nothing. Every trace of the magic had gone completely; she was totally unenchanted. He had no idea how she had done what she did – magic wasn't something you could just turn off – you were born with magic, it was a part of your soul, spun into the fabric of your body. Tarrin and Teah both had the beautiful purple haze of magic twining through their auras, just as Lyaren did, but Ela's aura was pure human, just as Calin's was. There was no trace of magic at all; it just didn't make any sense. Lyaren decided to tread cautiously. "Yes, the same magic that made you sleep made the lizard men sleep too."

Ela was astounded. "What, the whole army?"

"Yes, the whole army. We have scouts keeping an eye on things, last we heard they were still asleep. We're on our way to Stagsonton with the other women prisoners and Tarrin, our new friend. Calin has doubled back to Lower Gonfiels to warn them of the danger. The lizard army came through Waydonfield; the women we rescued are the only ones to survive."

Ela breathed deeply, striving to take in everything Lyaren had told her. Stagsonton was south of Lower Gonfiels so they were heading away from Lyaren's people. She knew the city well, it was to the north east of Ladaston and when she was younger her father had kept a small cavalry on the estate which he hired from Lord Nunnington. She remembered both Lord Nunnington and Daniel very well; they had visited her father's estate on many occasions before her mother had died and Daniel had always been one of the

132

prospective suitors her father had considered for her. Daniel and Gaylon had been good friends and their visits had always been a time of celebration. She knew they would help when they realised who she was.

"How far are we from Stagsonton?" she asked.

"Another two days' ride; you've been asleep for three days, Ela!"

Elayna nodded. "Yes, that would explain it" she replied.

"Explain what?" Lyaren looked puzzled.

"Explain why I'm starving! What's for breakfast?"

Their shared laughter shed light on their dismal situation and the two sat side by side as Ela ate a hearty meal of cold rabbit stew and a little dried fruit that Lyaren had stowed away for her. As the day went on, Lyaren recounted the events after she had been captured and Elayna avoided talking about her own experiences. Sensing her reluctance Lyaren didn't press the issue and the conversation was easy. It felt good to be with Lyaren again. They were like two peas in a pod, so comfortable in each other's company. Eventually the wagon rolled to a stop and Lyaren helped Ela down from the back. It felt strange to walk, her legs were weak and she felt as if the land was still rolling under her feet. Ela noticed that they were the last of a long trail of wagons, each driven by a woman and with more women climbing out from the backs – *there must be over three hundred,* she thought to herself. Most of the women were dressed in simple kingdom fashion, as she was, with full skirts which fell to the floor, but a few had shorter, ankle-length dresses in soft shades of green and brown, pleated at the front so as to look narrowly cut but still allow free movement. They must be the Horse Clan women, she thought to herself. As they walked down the line of wagons Ela felt the eyes of the other women following her. She smiled at

133

them as she went past but most of them turned away quickly. She let it go; they must all be terrified after their ordeal. As they reached the front of the column there were more of the horsewomen, this time holding their horses' reins and talking urgently to a fearsome looking man dressed in leathers and animal furs, who also held the reins of a beautiful stallion. Lyaren led her straight up to this group, who instantly turned respectfully to him. It was the warrior, who spoke first,

"Lady Elayna, it is good to see you awake and in good health, did you wake this morning."

"Yes," Lyaren answered for her. "As the sun rose."

"It would appear t he Sandkind also had their Wake-up call. Sahain just arrived back from her scouting and reports their camp is stirring."

Ela caught her breath. "Are we in danger? Can they catch us?"

"No" Tarrin reassured her. "We have three days' march on them and they don't have any horses; well, not until they round up their ponies, who I suspect may be enjoying their freedom far too much to come easily!" he smiled slyly.

"This is Tarrin," Lyaren introduced. "Without his help we would never have rescued you – Tarrin and his people have a special way with horses."

Lyaren had explained Tarrin's abilities as they had travelled. "Thank you." she said.

"My pleasure," his smile widened for a moment then vanished from his face. "We should not stop for long, however. I've suggested two hours to rest the horses then we ride through the night, if we are lucky we'll make Stagsonton by mid-morning. I was wondering about sending out an advanced party on horseback, if they know we are coming; they may send guards to escort the women back."

"A sound plan," Lyaren agreed. "Ela knows Lord Nunnington so perhaps the three of us should go on ahead?

Tarrin looked doubtfully at Elayna. "Perhaps My Lady is still too tired for the pace of such a ride. I understand you received a number of injuries?"

"I've slept for days," Ela replied. "And my injuries seem to be healing well. Besides, I'd love to ride Hurricane, I've missed him."

"Yes he's missed you too," Lyaren added. "Don't worry, Tarrin, Ela is an excellent horsewoman and more than capable of the ride. I think it will be for the best if she comes ahead with us; they will listen to her because of who she is. These Maldoran lords are suspicious of the northern tribes and, with the Sandkind being one of those very tribes; they may not be too hospitable to your people. Indeed, if they find out who I am I suspect they will feel the same way about me; I would appreciate it if you would keep my secret – here in the kingdom I pass for human."

"Humans can be easily fooled." Tarrin agreed. "Very well. Grab some food and get ready, we'll set out in the hour."

Calin and the Horse Clan women had ridden through the night and reached Lower Gonfiels just as the village market was closing down for the day. The people in the streets looked on in amazement at the sight of them riding through the market, horses' hooves clattering on the cobbles. They made straight to the smithy where Samuel emerged from his forge cursing and muttering at the commotion. He stopped abruptly at the sight of Calin on the huge war horse, his broadsword strapped to his back and surrounded by the outlandish women, one of whom rode at his side on an equally impressive horse and was dressed like nothing he had ever seen before! "Calin, what's this?"

"Samuel!" Calin shouted. "There is no time! You are all in grave danger! There's an army heading south, Waydonfield is destroyed, Lyaren and Elayna are taking the survivors to Stagsonton, you must call the town to a meeting and get the people to safety, there are too many, you'll be slaughtered!"

"Right." Samuel took Calin's words in without question as he took hold of the horse's bridle. "How long do we have?"

"We can't be sure." It was the young woman beside Calin who answered him.

"Samuel, this is Teah of the Horse Lord Clan. She and some of the other women of her people were captured by the army; they are our allies now."

"Powerful magic was used against the enemy army – that was why we were able to escape. It will delay them, but it won't hold them for long, you have little time to evacuate your town."

"Very well," Samuel nodded. "Calin, go and tell Dina everything, then come to the village hall. William!" Samuel called one of the lads in the yard. "Run to the meeting hall and ring the bell, call a meeting, lad!" He turned back to Teah. "Young Lady, you and your friends please leave your horses with my sons; they'll take good care of 'em for you, and come with me." With hurried efficiency everyone followed Samuel's instructions and, within minutes, the meeting bell sang out across the town.

By the time Calin arrived, the meeting hall was full. Teah and the other six horsewomen were sat on one of the long benches positioned on a slightly raised platform at the far end of the hall. Seeing him enter, Teah beckoned for Calin to join her. The woman had been blissfully silent for most of the ride and –

136

surprisingly – had been happy to let Calin take the lead once they had arrived at Lower Gonfiels. Her outfit still made him feel uncomfortable, but her relaxed manner made even these dire circumstances appear manageable and he found himself warming to her company a little. He smiled at her as he made his way across the room and she smiled back. *'Yes,'* he admitted to himself, *'She is beautiful, even in those ridiculous clothes.'* As he sat next to her she patted his thigh affectionately. Calin flinched, the woman was inappropriate, but he didn't frown quite so deeply as he removed her hand from his leg. He took her arm roughly at first but stopped as he noticed the deep, angry wound tearing around her wrist. "This needs treating." he told her sternly.

Teah sighed deeply. "It's been treated but it doesn't seem to want to heal." She shrugged. "I can still ride with a hook."

"Don't joke, Teah, I'll get Dina to look at it for you, before we leave."

Teah pulled her hand away from his, angry at herself for letting him see her vulnerable side. She looked sidelong at his youthful features, at least his face wasn't totally scarlet anymore, and especially as he was now sitting right next to her, that was a step in the right direction.

A loud voice cut across the clamour of the room. It was Samuel who addressed the crammed hall. "My friends!" he called. "I have gathered you all here at Calin's request. I have known this man since he was a child and trust him as one of my own. He comes to us today with dire news. Waydonfield has been attacked and destroyed, all but a handful murdered, and that very same army marches now against us!"

Samuel's words carved their way through the silence which seemed to quiver for a moment before pandemonium broke out across the room. Everyone spoke at once, some muttered angrily shouting and pointing towards Calin and the Horse Clan women. Others called out questions; no one was still and the room was in chaos. A heavy pounding sound cut through the commotion bringing the crowd once again to silence. It was Kayel, the young archer who had shot the Xyakahan priest. He had climbed up to the platform next to Samuel and brought down the huge ceremonial gavel onto the formal lectern (both of which were considered purely decorative by the town's folk). The effect of the metallic boom it created was instant and the room heeded the call to order.

"Listen!" Kayel called out to the startled crowed. "I know Calin too. Lots of us here do and even more of us know his mother, Sara. She saved my Mam when I was born and fixed up my Da's leg so he could still walk after he fell down that ravine in the woods. So I know he's no trouble causer. Now I want to know what's got him so rattled and I think we owe him a fair chance to say his piece. So I say stop y' yapping and let Calin speak!"

The room fell silent and all eyes turned towards Calin.

"C'mon then lad," Samuel urged. "Tell 'em what you know."

Calin could feel the colour rising in his cheeks as he stood to face his friends. He smiled feebly at Kayel, then coughed to clear his throat. "It's 'ard to know where to start. I left here just over a week ago, to go home to see mi Mam... but I never made it to Waydonfield. There was this army o' lizard men, see, thousands of 'em, and they took one of my companions from our camp, the young woman Elayna." Calin's mind was racing; he couldn't tell them the full story, magic was a thing not to be trusted in Lower Gonfiels, so he settled on a close second. "We thought she was lost but we met up with some people of the Horse Clans; he turned and indicated the women sat quietly behind him. We teamed up with 'em and together managed to rescue our friend and a load of other women too, turns out they were survivors from Waydonfield. That's how we know what's happened there. My Mam... well she's gone now, see they killed 'em all and now they're coming south and I don't want you to fall to 'em same way... and so, well..." He mumbled a little, feeling more uncomfortable under the glare of every eye in the room. Then he felt a hand on his shoulder and a collective gasp of shock rippled around the room.

Teah had been noticed by the villages but until she stood before them the full impact of her appearance had been overlooked. She stood with an easy confidence. The dignity and authority of her stance balancing the impact of her exterior. Her voice sang out strong and clear across the room. "I am Teah, Princess of the Grassland Clans. My people were attacked at our Peace Camp in the mountain forests. We were taken by surprise and many of us were captured. Calin and his friends are heroes, without them my people and I would still be prisoners to the lizard army. Calin rescued us and I know that he is a good, honest man. You and your families are in danger and that is why we have come. What you do with our warning is your choice, stay or go as you wish, but our warning is stated." She paused to let her words find their level in the room. "They will come! And they will put you to the sword! Their army is too mighty for one village! My brother, Prince Tarrin, bid me speak these words. Pack up your most precious belongings, take your families and flee. We are heading to Stagsonton tomorrow to meet up with my brother and the other refugees. Those of you who wish to do so are welcome to join us. My brother urges you to take what you can carry and burn whatever you leave behind! You are at war, People of Lower Gonfiels! Even if you leave you are not safe, for your city of Stagsonton faces a siege which may continue for many months." She turned to Calin whose face bore a mixture of admiration and horror, her arrogance and bluntness had cut to the heart of the matter and the whole room now stood in shocked silence. Smiling up at him she took his hand. "Come on, Calin," she said quietly. "Now they must make up their own minds." And she led him from the hall, the crowd parting before them as the other clanswomen fell into line behind.

They made their way back to Samuel's home where, predictably, Dina was well into the packing but somehow had still managed to put together a feast of meats and cheeses which the young women gratefully accepted. Calin relayed the events of the meeting to Dina who listened thoughtfully then returned to instructing the children in their sorting. He then looked for Teah but found her missing from the group. He wandered out into the courtyard and caught a glimpse of her over by the stable. She was sat quietly by herself on a small wooden bench looking down at something she held in her hands. As he drew closer he realised she gently cradled a tiny field mouse who munched happily on a grain of corn. She looked up as Calin approached and smiled warmly. "A new friend?" Calin enquired a little sarcastically.

"No." Teah replied, quite seriously. "A very dear little friend to whom I will be forever grateful and who I am happy to share my saddlebag with, while ever he wishes to stay with me."

Feeling a little uncomfortable Calin sat next to her and took her other hand in his, looking again at the wicked wound winding around her wrist. "Is it both wrists?" he asked cautiously.

She nodded once, carefully dropping the tiny mouse and his dinner back into her saddlebag and turning both arms upwards to show the damage. Although no black lines yet traced up her arms, the wounds were badly infected and Calin knew enough from his mother's teaching to know her jest about hooks could have some truth in it. He removed the lid from the small pot he had borrowed from Dina and gently began to apply the pungent ointment – one of his mother's. Just as he expected, Teah pulled away from him.

"Its fine," she dismissed him. "I can do it!"

"No," Calin smiled; his voice firm but warm. "Everyone should have somebody to care for them like this." And silently he tended her wounds.

The next morning Calin and the Horse Clan women led a wretched assortment of riders, wagons, carts, mules and barrows out of an unnaturally silent Upper Gonfiels. The entire town had voted to evacuate and strode out sadly towards Stagsonton. None looked back; all knew what they would see. The first amber licks of hungry flames enveloped the deserted town and its surrounding farmlands.

Juzuk sat back in the large chair and looked over the table of maps at the prostrate priest on the ground beyond. "Explain to me again, Galizund, how it is that when I ride into the camp of my mighty and victorious army, the one led by my most trusted acolyte, that I find everyone taking a nap and the prisoners vanished?"

Galizund dare not lift his head from the dirt. "There was an infiltration into the camp, Master. An Elvin warlock released this strange magic upon us, we were powerless against it."

"Mmm..." Juzuk leaned forward once again. "That's what I thought you said. So one elf got past all our defences without giving any warning and released a spell made from a mysterious magical source which put you to sleep so he could just stroll away with your prisoners?

"Yes Master."

"And how is it, if you were given no warning; that you were found with a sword in your hand laying on the ground by the side of the tracks left by the prisoners?"

"Master, I was inspecting the prisoners when I came upon the elf, I released my magic upon him but he was so strong I couldn't fight it." Galizund tried to spit out some of the mud which was working its way into his mouth, but the process just seemed to draw more of the stuff in.

"Yes...Yes you said he was strong. And what of these red-haired women, did any of them aid this powerful warlock in his magic?" Juzuk asked conversationally.

"No, my Master, the women were all locked in their cells; if it hadn't been for the magic we would easily have over powered him." Galizund held on to his bladder. He could feel the fear rising within him; if he wasn't on the ground he would have collapsed.

"So none of the red-haired women had power, thank Xyakah for small mercies! Had you allowed the Master's new chosen one to escape our clutches there would be no going back for you." Juzuk's voice was warmer now, back to its normal tone.

"Yes Master, I understand that, my mistake was unforgivable but the women were just ordinary humans, I inspected them all myself, they had nothing special about them." His breathing regulated, he would be punished but he would live.

"Well then, Galizund, no real harm done, get up, get up."

Galizund pushed himself up to his feet but kept his head bent low. "Thank you, Master."

"Oh, no need to thank me, Galizund, I always reward good service. You are dismissed."

Galizund turned slowly; a tingle of fear ran down his back. As he reached the entrance Juzuk called out to him. "Oh Galizund, just one more thing. Only, if the women had no power, why did the jailor tell me a red-haired prisoner released this spell?"

Their eyes met briefly, energy flared through the tent.

"Guard!" Juzuk called. A large lizard man guard entered the tent. "Galizund was just leaving, could you carry his ashes away please? Good man."

Even in the dark Ela felt totally relaxed as she rode Hurricane. The three riders galloped at a stunning pace, catching only glimpses of forest and field as they sped through the night. The horses, bred for speed, were more than ready for the exhilarating ride after the more restrictive pace of the convoy, and by morning's first light the impressive towers of Stagsonton Keep could be glimpsed on the horizon. Before the sun had reached its full height the three travellers were entering the south gate of a very impressive defensive wall and following the spiralling streets up to the Keep in the centre of the bustling city. The gates to the Keep stood wide open but, as the party approached, a guard strode into the roadway and purposefully barred their way. He beckoned for them to dismount but Lyaren motioned for Ela to stay on her horse while he and Tarrin talked to him. Quickly the party were allowed to pass through the archway of the portcullis and into the shadowy coolness of the courtyard within. A smartly-dressed steward waited to meet them and a trio of stable lads rushed over to take their horses. They were escorted to a small but comfortable reception room and asked politely to wait. Ela sat gratefully on the cushioned window seat, drinking in the familiar hustle and bustle of the busy Keep below her. Lyaren sat in a large, comfortable high-backed chair close to Ela, a strained look on his face, while Tarrin, looking outrageously out of place in the plush surroundings of the palatial waiting room, paced back and forth across the carpeted floor impatiently. They didn't need to wait long, the doors were thrown open and in walked a tall, fair-haired young man, dressed smartly but modestly in a plain deep-blue suit with pale beige hoes and high-cut shiny black boots. He scanned the room quickly; his eyes finally rested on Ela and he appraised her critically.

"Good Gods, Elayna! What the hell have you been up to?"

"Daniel," Ela smiled warmly, and stood as he walked towards her. "It's so good to see you again." She curtsied gracefully. "Daniel we need your help."

"Yes! Yes, that will be fine. Let me get you a room so you can clean yourself up, we can't have you wandering around the place looking like that! Not even my servants look as ragged as you!"

"Sir, we need to see Lord Nunnington immediately!" Tarrin's deep voice rumbled across the room, his annoyance obvious. "We bring dire news and need his urgent assistance."

"Do you indeed?" Daniel answered; his voice equally cold. "And who might you be?"

Tarrin pulled himself straight to his full height, an impressive if somewhat barbaric sight against the soft furnishings of the room. "I am Prince Tarrin of the Wolf Moon Clan, Son of Tarrin True Heart, King of the Grasslands and leader of the Horse Clan Warriors."

Daniel's eyebrows rose in surprise. "Then welcome to my home, my Lord." He nodded his head slightly, acknowledging Tarrin as an equal rather than as a prince. "I am Lord Daniel Nunnington. I am afraid my father is very ill; we do not expect him to see the summer through to its end. Until such time as I inherit the office officially I act on his behalf, and who are you?" he asked, turning to Lyaren who was still sat quietly in the high-backed chair.

Lyaren stood stiffly. "I am Lyaren, tutor to Lady Elayna."

Daniel shook Lyaren's out-stretched arm in the kingdom fashion. "I look forward, Lyaren, to hearing why the Lady Elayna is travelling alone with her tutor, looking half dead and abused, when her father is murdered and her home ransacked?"

"Later!" Tarrin cut in; he had ignored the slight but was very aware of it. "You have an army of ten-thousand Sandkind making its way down from the border; they have taken Torr-Arron Keep and put to the torch the outpost at Riversway and the village of Waydonfield. They are currently stationed two weeks' march north of your keep and it doesn't take a genius to work out that they may well be heading this way! We have a convoy of refugees a day behind us and, by now, with any luck, the villagers of Lower Gonfiels should be making their way here too. You need to prepare for a siege, man!" Tarrin slowed his voice as if talking to a simpleton. "Do you understand?"

Daniel's face blanched; he looked at Ela who nodded once to confirm the truth of Tarrin's words. "Guards!" Daniel called, and two smartly-dressed guardsmen rushed into the rooms. "Call a council meeting, urgently, I want General Griss now! Do you hear me?" He was shouting.

"Yes Sir!" Both guards jumped to attention and raced off to do his bidding.

Daniel turned back towards his guests. "Very well, we will hear your news in full but for now I will organise rooms for Lady Elayna and Prince Tarrin. Lyaren, you may present yourself to the kitchen workers

Who will find you quarters with my own staff; you and Prince Tarrin will both be shown to my office within the hour." His words were orders barked at the men, but as he turned to Ela he let a little tenderness into his voice. "You must make yourself comfortable while the men deal with all this talk of war, I will get you some ladies-in-waiting. Don't worry about all of this, Lady Elayna, you will accompany my mother south to Stronghold; we will get you out long before this army arrives."

Ela opened her mouth to object but, seeing Lyaren silently shake his head, instead said "Thank you Daniel, you are very kind."

"Lyaren will stay with me," Tarrin said. "He can act as my steward as I am alone."

"Very well." Daniel pulled a long velvet cord hanging from the ceiling in the corner of the room. Almost immediately two smartly dressed servants appeared at the door. Daniel snapped his instructions and the three were lead away to their respective rooms.

Elayna's suite was beautiful, larger even than her own suite back at Galloheart Keep. She felt too dirty to sit on the plush satin furnishings and so stood uncomfortably as the servants scuttled around busily, in and out of the annex room at the far side of the suite. Finally, a heavy-set young woman with very pink cheeks led her into the smaller room, where an enormous copper tub had been filled with steaming hot water. Elayna allowed the woman to remove her clothes (which were quickly disposed of) and help her into the steaming-hot tub of water. The heat was wonderful, scented with the dried petals of spring roses. The water eased her tired body – working its magic on the knots in her muscles and relaxing her whirring mind. The woman washed her hair and scrubbed her fingernails and Elayna took simple pleasure in the process. The young maid tutted and shook her head at the angry scars and bruises littering Ela's body and, taking care not to knock the stitches, tended gently to them. Once clean she was wrapped in a warm blanket and led back into the dressing room, where the woman brushed and dressed her hair before helping her into clean underwear and a beautiful green satin gown with golden embroidery around the neck and sleeves. She led her over to a large mirror and stood back examining her handiwork.

Ela smiled, she hadn't even asked the maid her name. "Thank you, it has been some time since I've looked anything like this."

"You're most welcome, My Lady" The maid curtsied.

"What's your name?"

"Tilly, My Lady."

"Well Tilly, you're good at making the most of a bad job."

"Oh don't say that, My Lady, I can see you've had things hard but you are still very beautiful." She curtsied. "If you don't mind me saying so, that is."

"Thank you, Tilly, could you get someone to show me the way to the council chambers? I should be at the meeting." Elayna asked.

"Oh no, My Lady!" Tilly replied. "We were instructed you weren't to leave your chambers, for your own safety, My Lady. There's an enemy army on its way here, My Lady, and Lord Daniel was very insistent. You have to stay here; he's sent guards to keep you safe."

Elayna looked sternly at Tilly, what was she to do? She couldn't stay locked in this room like a frightened rabbit, she was part of this whether Daniel liked it or not, but she had to tread carefully. Daniel was already suspicious of Lyaren; if she made too much fuss it could backfire. Carefully, she phrased her next question. "Tilly, when will I next see Daniel and my friends?"

147

"Oh at Dinner, My Lady, after the council meeting has finished." And with that Tilly curtsied and hurried out of the room.

The hours crept by painfully slowly. Tilly returned once to bring in a tray of delicious breads and fruits as well as a new embroidery hoop and threads for Ela's entertainment. This she decided against and chose instead to look out of her window over the bustling city below. She watched in frustration as the sun marched steadily across the crisp blue, spring sky and began its descent as evening drew closer. She scanned the horizon for signs of the caravan convoy but no sign of them appeared. Finally, a sharp knock at the door announced the end to her confinement. "Yes?" she called firmly and the door opened wide.

A smartly dressed castle guardsman stood in the open doorway. "I'm here to accompany you to dinner, My Lady." he bowed stiffly.

"Thank you." Ela replied and allowed the guard to guide her swiftly back along the warren of corridors, down a succession of stairways and finally into a large and radiant hall. Heavy plush tapestries hung from the deep wooden cladding which hugged the thick stonework of the castle walls. The room was lit with bright, cheery oil lamps which hung from the walls and a huge chandelier of flickering candles which hovered majestically above the table. Smells of roasting meats hung in the air enticingly. A large table occupied the centre of the room around which sat an assortment of lords and ladies, all in brightly coloured dress. Daniel sat at the head of the table and to his right, looking somewhat uncomfortable in a very tight but highly fashionable purple velvet jacket, sat Tarrin. The seat to Daniel's left was empty. Ela looked around for Lyaren but he was nowhere to be seen. Her guide announced in a clear, loud voice which cut across the chatter of the

148

room. "The Lady Elayna of Ladaston, ward of Stagsonton!"

Silence settled over the gathering and all eyes turned towards Ela as she made her way down to the only remaining seat at Daniel's left. As she drew closer, Daniel stood to greet her and took her hand to help her take her seat. "Elayna, welcome. You remember my mother, Lady Nunnington?"

An older lady to Ela's left smiled stiffly at her. "You are a sight for sore eyes young lady," she tutted, "I am glad you are found and returned to your liege lord where you belong."

Elayna coloured a little as she tried to think what to say. "It is good to see you too, My Lady, but my father never swore an oath to lord Nunnington; you and your son have no obligation towards me."

The woman smiled tightly. "Don't worry about that now, dear, we can sort out the details in order to keep you safe. My son, for one, will want to make certain that no more misfortune befalls you I'm sure!" She smiled sweetly at Daniel who looked affectionately back at her.

"Not now mother!" he laughed raising his eyebrows towards Ela. "Time for food!" he called clapping his hands and, as the servants brought in platters of steaming food, a happy chatter returned to the table. Ela was surprised to find her appetite was enormous and she ate as if she had never seen food. Tarrin also filled his plate and, although quiet, he answered Daniel's questions politely. Conversation turned to the past and Daniel began to recall stories from their childhood. Despite her concern for Lyaren the chance to remember happier times was a true treat for Elayna and she laughed affectionately at Daniel's recounts from their youth and some of Gaylon's hilarious antics. The evening rolled on merrily and

149

desserts were brought out: jellies, blancmange, tarts and pastries. Despite the warm, full sensation in her tummy Ela couldn't resist the sweet treats.

Ela had been introduced to the other guests, all of whom were visiting lords and ladies from surrounding estates. She wondered if they had been informed of the impending dangers to their lands but decided to leave this for the morning. By then, the other women would be arriving in the wagons and hopefully the villagers of Lower Gonfiels wouldn't be far behind; then she and Lyaren could be away and back on their own journey in the knowledge that their friends were safe and the kingdom warned of the approaching danger.

Tarrin caught her eye and looked purposefully towards her. "You look tired, My Lady. Perhaps I can escort you back to your chambers? I must confess that after the events of the previous week I find myself exhausted."

Ela wasn't tired at all, strangely she had woken from her mysterious sleep feeling more alert and invigorated than she could ever remember. However, taking her cue from Tarrin, she agreed. "Yes, I will sleep well tonight."

"Oh; how thoughtless of us!" Daniel stood. "Guards, please escort our guests to their chambers!" Two guards approached.

"I'm sure we can find our own way, Lord Daniel," Tarrin replied. "Lady Elayna will be quite safe with me." and before he had time to object Tarrin nimbly skipped around Daniel's chair and took Ela's arm, helping her stand and leading her into a brisk walk from the room. "Goodnight everyone." Tarrin added, and Ela flashed a happy smile as they left the room.

Tarrin increased his pace as they walked down the corridor. "Quickly," he whispered. "He will send the guards to make sure we go straight to our rooms."

Hearing the strain in his words Ela looked questioningly at Tarrin. "Where is Ly?"

"I don't know, Daniel made all the right moves in our meeting, he ordered troops out to all the surrounding villages and estates and sent messengers south to the king. He sent a regiment to escort the wagons and a second to Lower Gonfiels to assist in the evacuation. Then he called the meeting to an end but asked Lyaren to stay behind. He never returned to our rooms; when I asked about him over dinner Daniel made some flippant remark about Lyaren being his responsibility and nothing for me to worry about. Do you have any idea what's going on?"

Ela thought quickly. "Daniel has gone to great lengths to reinforce his authority over my father's lands, he was very protective. Do you think he could blame Lyaren for my father's death?"

"I don't know, did he have anything to do with it?"

"Of course not! My father was killed by Xyakahan priests who wanted to take me as a handmaiden; Lyaren saved my life."

"I didn't realise those maniacs had spread their diseased religion into Maldora. They tried to establish their faith in the Grasslands but my people are true to the Mother Goddess, we wouldn't tolerate their lies. Xyakah may have powerful magic but a God he is not and the dark rites they practise have nothing to do with worship. If you were to be turned over to them you were indeed in danger and Lyaren did save your life. I don't know you well, Ela, and know Lyaren only slightly better – but I trust you both. Don't worry we'll find him." Tarrin raised his voice slightly. "I believe your rooms are just down here, My Lady, just slightly further down the corridor than my own. I hope you sleep well."

151

"Thank you, Prince Tarrin," she replied clearly. "I hope you sleep well too." Then she added, in a whisper, "How can we find him?"

"Daniel will tell us." Tarrin twisted his arm slightly and the gleaming point of a slim but deadly-looking dagger caught the light then disappeared back into its hiding place. "Leave it with me, we will talk more tomorrow." He turned as footsteps approached their position. "Ah look, Lady Elayna, Lord Daniel sent his guards after all, I expect you are too precious to him to trust to a savage like me, even if I am a prince." Tarrin bowed stiffly. "I will see you in the morning." He turned and headed back down the corridor in the direction from which they had come.

Ela looked up at the smart castle guards who had positioned themselves either side of the door. "Goodnight." she muttered and retreated into the relative safety of her room.

"Master Juzuk, the agents have reported back." Juzuk didn't let his annoyance at the interruption show; after all, this was important.

"I will see them now, Bayzar, show them in." The young acolyte hurried from the tent returning immediately with two unremarkable looking human noblemen. As the men entered the tent both prostrated themselves on the ground.

"That will be all, Bayzar." The acolyte didn't need telling twice and scuttled from the tent. Juzuk drank in the young man's fear; he would love to feast on it. Juzuk wiped the spittle, which was running from the corner of his mouth and returned his attention to the figures at his feet. "Stand!" he commanded, and both men did. "Get on with it then, report!"

The men briefly looked at each other, then the taller of the two began. "My Master, preparations within the city are in place. The servants of Xyakah stand ready to welcome our God truly into our homes and stand ready to make the final sacrifice in his honour."

"Very good. Are our people active in their key positions?"

"Yes, My Master."

Juzuk smiled with a thin humourless expression. "Very good, you are dismissed." He watched the men leave his tent. These humans were weak fools, even easier than the Sandkind to manipulate. Their flesh would feed Xyakah for an eternity."

Chapter 6
Stagsonton

Despite the enveloping blackness of night, Ela hadn't been able to sleep at all. She still felt as fresh as if she had just awakened from a wonderful deep sleep and full of new energy to face the day. She went through the pretence of getting undressed and unbraided her hair but her mind was engulfed with worry for Lyaren.

Where could he be? Had he left her, thinking the danger to the north too great? More likely, could Daniel be to blame? After all, he had been accusatory towards Lyaren when they had first arrived yesterday.

She tried to push these worries to the back of her mind and instead watch the dots of flickering torchlight against the blackness of the city far below. From this lofty position they really did look like fireflies.

The night's hours crept by painfully slowly, a frustration of nothingness to Ela's over-alert mind, the absolute silence wrapping her in a prison of solitude. Just as the torture reached its zenith and with the sun not yet risen she caught sight of a trail of light out beyond the city wall. Elayna watched its steady progress towards the city gates and, through the stillness of the night,

155

could just distinguish the sound of wheels turning. As the lights drew nearer voices carried through the air: alarms risen, relief of recognition, messages sent. She watched as Daniel, Tarrin and a large group of men, both soldiers and servants, set out from the castle to meet the convoy. She saw the wagons were directed around the back of the keep, and the women being escorted to what must be an empty barracks block where the army was situated – a series of long, low-level buildings built within the east wall of the keep's fortifications. The activity filled the final hours of the night and, as the first rays of the sun's light expanded into the night sky, Daniel and Tarrin, escorted by two guards, returned to the keep, walked across the courtyard and disappeared out of view.

Slowly, the early morning sunlight strengthened and spread across the morning sky. Ela could no longer contain herself so, when the tentative knock announced the arrival of a fussy but friendly Tilly, armed with a tray of steaming tea and honey-dipped breakfast pastries, Ela was already dressed in one of the simple but elegant gowns she had found hanging in her dressing room. She had washed herself in the cold water from the previous night and dressed her hair in a plain but neat plait.

"Oh! My Lady!" Tilly exclaimed. "I had no idea you were such an early riser, the pastries are only just cooked but we can get them on sooner for you tomorrow! They might have been earlier today only," she took a deep breath then carried on with her commentary, "Lord Daniel had many of the kitchen staff up baking for the women; they arrived in the night, poor souls! They look the worse for their ordeal but they'll all be safe and sound here." Finding her stride Tilly recounted the morning gossip from the kitchens. Ela entertained herself by counting the number of sharp, rattling breaths the woman took to keep her narration going. As she chatted she collected up Ela's nightgown and disappeared into the dressing room, returning with the evening gown Ela had worn the previous night. "You know, My Lady, I would have helped you undress, you only have to call, Lord Daniel says I'm to be your lady-in-waiting now, anything you want. Can I help with your hair? Pin it up for you, perhaps?"

Ela had taken the tray of pastries over to the small table by her window seat and was sat, ravenously working her way through it. She knew she could get away with them, she'd lost so much weight over the past few weeks... almost a month, she told herself, a whole month since they had fled her home! Noticing the maid had stopped talking, Ela realised she was waiting for a reply.

"No, Tilly, really, this is how I like to wear my hair. I didn't have a lady-in-waiting at home so I'm used to getting myself ready. I'm quite happy with everything you have done for me, although perhaps you could find me some new riding boots, mine have grown thin and I should like to visit the women today and check on them."

"Right away Miss." Tilly headed hurriedly for the door.

"Oh Tilly," Ela called after her. "What time will Lord Daniel be up? I really must talk with him today."

"Oh, I don't think you can, My Lady, he's been up all night, poor soul, now he's with the old Lord and then he's in a meeting with the generals all day, getting ready for them lizard men – everyone's talking about 'em! If you don't mind me asking, My Lady, are they really like lizards? Will there be fighting?"

Ela's heart fell; if she couldn't see Daniel how was she to find out about Lyaren? The women were safe and Calin and Teah should be along soon, hopefully with Samuel and his family. Once she knew they were safe too she and Ly could get back on their way. She was excited now about seeing Lyaren's home, deep in the Silent Forest, and unpicking the mystery of how she was linked to the elves. She looked sadly at Tilly's overly-expressive look of alarm; she swore the woman had twice the number of muscles in her face than anyone else she had ever encountered. "Yes Tilly, I fear there will be. But Stagsonton is strong and well-armed, and I'm sure the King will send more soldiers. It will be fine."

"Yes Miss." Tilly curtsied awkwardly with the large bundle of clothes under her arm. "I'll be back soon for your tray, My Lady." And she turned and left the room.

Ela finished the whole tray of pastries and then marched across to the door, which swung open easily; perhaps she could see Daniel before he met with his generals? The first of the two guards stationed outside her room smiled easily at her. "Good morning, My Lady." He bowed stiffly. "Do you wish to go somewhere, the Solar perhaps?"

"I would very much like to see Lord Daniel, I believe he is with his father, could I visit him also?"

"Oh no, I'm sorry, My Lady, we have strict orders, Lord Daniel is not to be disturbed. You could see the head steward, Lord Tain; he deals with everything when Lord Daniel is indisposed." Ela remembered Lord Tain; her father had hated the man! No, he would be no help at all. "What about Prince Tarrin? Could I go and see him?"

The guard shook his head. "Sadly, no, My Lady. Prince Tarrin has left the keep to go and meet with his people who came back last night. He did leave a message for you though, in case you asked for him. He said he had preparations to make for his journey home, but that you weren't to worry, he would see you this afternoon."

Ela looked back at her bedroom door; she couldn't go back in there! "Very well, then, the Solar it is. Oh, and can you call Tilly to come and meet me there?"

"At once, My Lady!" He looked towards the second guard who rushed off in the direction of the servants' stairwell, then turned back to Ela and bowed once again. "This way please, My Lady."

Ela followed the man through a labyrinth of corridors and down numerous staircases until at last they arrived at a pair of large white doors. He opened them inwards to reveal the beautifully furnished room within. A marble fireplace was stacked high with fresh new logs and stood ready to be lit. Numerous chairs, benches and settees were positioned around the edges of the room with occasional tables close to each seat. A long, low coffee table stood in the centre of the room with a collection of delicate ornaments and two over-sized vases full of freshly-picked, fragrant blooms positioned neatly upon it. As they entered the room a small black cat jumped up from one of the sofas and made its way over to them, rubbing itself affectionately against their legs. The guard bent down and stroked it gently. "Lady Nunnington's cat, My Lady, I can take her away if you like?"

"No not at all," Ela smiled, picking the delicate little creature up. "I like cats."

"Would you like me to light the fire, My Lady?" The morning sun streamed through two enormous glass doors in the left-hand wall, pooling the room in glorious bright light.

"No thank you." Ela replied absently as she made her way over to the doors; she could see they led out onto a beautiful terrace which overlooked the river and countryside beyond.

"Very well, My Lady, I am just outside if you need me."

159

The guard left, closing the interior doors behind him. Ela opened the glass doors out onto the terrace and stepped into the sunlight. The cat leapt out of her arms and danced after a stray leaf rocking gently in the slight breeze. It was a beautiful morning. Spring was finally in full bloom. On the terrace was an array of baskets overflowing with rich, vibrant flowers. Ela breathed in the full fragrance and allowed the sun's light to bathe her in all its glory. Standing here, lost in this moment, she could tell herself everything was well in the world.

There was a clattering sound from inside which jerked Ela from her reverie. She turned to see Tilly entering the room, skilfully balancing the door, a tray of tea and an embroidery basket. She bustled over to a large chair by the window and sighed as she set the tray on the adjacent table and the basket on the floor.

"I thought you might enjoy a little more tea, Lady Elayna," Tilly smiled. "And I've brought you a few more of those breakfast pastries you enjoyed so much this morning. I thought you might also like to do some needlework, the light is very good in this room for embroidery."

Ela stepped back into the room. "Thank you, Tilly, the tea will be nice but I'm not one for needlework." She looked at the other woman, the only person who seemed to have any time for her; she had to take a chance. "Tilly, I'm very worried about my friend, do you think you could help me find him?"

"Oh, Prince Tarrin is off in the city shopping for supplies for his trip home, he left a message to say he'll be in to see you this afternoon." Tilly smiled, happy to be able to help.

"No Tilly, not Tarrin, I know where he is. I mean my other friend, my tutor, Lyaren."

Tilly's face looked stricken. "Do you mean the prisoner, Miss?"

"What do you mean 'prisoner'?" This was now making all too much sense.

"Well, Lord Daniel arrested the man who killed your father, My Lady, and tried to kidnap you, he will stand trial for his crime."

"Oh Tilly! Lyaren is not the one who killed my father, he is my friend and he has saved my life at least three times, not to mention rescuing me from the lizard men army. He is a hero not a criminal!" She could hear the desperation in her own voice.

Tilly drew in a sharp breath. "Then I'm very sorry, My Lady, Lord Daniel has had him thrown in the dungeons."

"I must see him, Tilly; can you take me to him?" Desperation pooled into her voice, breaking the words painfully.

Tilly shook her head. "I'm sorry, My Lady, the dungeon is forbidden to people like me, it's a place for only soldiers, jailers and prisoners. You would need to ask Lord Daniel to get permission to see him."

Ela sighed deeply and fell into the large chair by the tea tray. "Yes, I will have to do that." She turned her head and looked back out towards the terrace. "Thank you, Tilly that will be all."

Tilly left silently. The cat wandered back into the room and jumped into Ela's lap, purring happily. She scratched the little creature behind the ear, earning an increase in pace to the purr. What could she do? It was supposed to be Ly saving her, not the other way around. She just had to talk to Daniel. Tarrin could speak for Lyaren, too, and the women of the Horse Clan who had come in last night. When Calin arrived he could also support her. What was wrong with Lyaren? He was supposed to have magic, how could he let this happen? She felt a wave of despair begin to pull at her thoughts but shook it off, refusing to let it drag her into its

161

clutches. She would wait. At least she knew where Ly was, even if it wasn't the nicest of places.

Lyaren hadn't put up a fight to Daniel's accusations other than stating his innocence. Daniel seemed to have so much evidence collected together that even Ly had to agree he looked guilty. He had witness statements from the villagers and some of Gadon's household staff to place him directly in the frame for the murder. This was supported by statements from numerous lords and land owners, all associated with the Xyakahan priesthood, including several witness statements claiming he was seen firing the arrow. How could he defend himself? *'Sorry Lord Daniel, I didn't do it, I was actually flying in the sky shaped like a giant white eagle?"* At best they would laugh in his face, at worst they would burn him for witchcraft. Humans were seldom born with magic and those who were tended to join one of the organised churches where their talents were put to use helping the populace. Those wielding magic away from the church's control were mistrusted and feared by the majority. Declaring your talents was a death sentence for most. Lyaren wasn't afraid for himself; the dungeon was basic and he could easily release the locks, escape and be away before he was missed. He could even collect Ela and they could flee together. But there had to be a better way. They had to evade the Xyakahan priests and the lizard army. Avoiding Daniel's soldiers as well just exasperated their situation. Lyaren had considered that Daniel and the lizard army might be too busy dealing with each other to bother about him and Ela but the timing of this invasion seemed very suspicious and the presence of Xyakahan priests amongst the lizard army confirmed his suspicions – Xyakah was upping his game. As for Daniel, his eyes said it all. He obviously had feelings for Ela and so was certain to send men after them. Lyaren had thought through the situation fully; he either needed to deal with the accusation, prove his innocence and convince Daniel to let him take Ela away with him. Or he needed to leave Ela here and make his escape. This was the question, which brought him the most angst. Was this all his fault? Had he not found Ela in the first place would Xyakah even be interested in her? Perhaps the presence of an elfin warlock had acted as a beacon to the monster? Lyaren was torn. He loved her and yet he had almost got her killed twice, maybe even more. If he left her here Daniel would marry her, then she wouldn't be of any interest to Xyakah. Once married, she would be spoiled for him. But was she human? She had no magic now, none whatsoever, but how to explain what happened back at the lizard army camp? How could he ever explain that? Lyaren leaned back against the cold stone wall of his cell. He was thankful for the darkness and the solitude. He needed to think and, for now, he had a little time to do just that.

To Ela's overly-alert mind and body the morning dragged by. She even picked up the embroidery but, after a few pitifully poor stitches, she quickly put it back down again. She found herself back on the terrace followed by the cat who busied himself chasing the little insects, which scurried about on some crucial mission around the flowerpots. His lively little antics made her smile but couldn't distract her from her worries. Wandering over to the low wall which surrounded the terrace she found that she overlooked the river and docks area, just beyond the city walls. So she must be on the opposite side of the keep to where her rooms were situated. If her memory of the region's maps served her well it meant she was looking over to the south. There was a lot of activity down by the river and also along the

163

roadway leading out of town. It was bustling with carts and horsemen travelling in both directions. She sat and watched the activity below; everybody had a purpose – industrious cogs in a productive machine of human activity – but what was her purpose? What was her plan? What to do?

Once again the doors clattered open loudly and Lady Nunnington strode purposefully into the room. "Elayna, child! Are you out there?" Her voice was stern but not cold.

"Yes, Lady Nunnington, I'm here." Ela strode back into the room.

Lady Nunnington came over to greet her and hugged her fondly. "At last we can get a chance to chat. How are you, child? Have you got everything you need?"

Ela was a little taken aback by the woman's warmth; there had been little sign of it last night at dinner. "I'm very comfortable, thank you." *What else could she say? Could Lady Nunnington help her with Ly?*

"Good. Now I'm sorry I haven't been to see you properly before, my husband is very sick. I have been at his side most of the time but his doctors assure me he will live through the day, so I am entrusting his care to them in order to spend a little time with you. Come, child, come and sit with me. What are you doing out here?" She strode past Ela and back out onto the terrace to the bench where Ela had been standing. As she approached, Ela could see a sadness register in the woman's eyes. "They are preparing for war." she said quietly. "The barges bring in grain and supplies from the surrounding area; the roads are full of refugees – some seek refuge in the city, others flee from here before the gates close – there will be more arriving as the message spreads. Once the alarm is sounded the farmlands will be torched to leave nothing for the enemy. There is nothing nice about war." The woman shook her head sadly then sat down slowly on the stone bench, turning her back on the view. "Sit down, Elayna." Ela sat.

"Did you know your mother and I were friends?"

Surprised, Ela stumbled a little over her reply. "No no I didn't."

Lady Nunnington continued. "I suppose you could say we were rivals but we both liked each other. We were both sent here to Stagsonton when we were girls to catch the eye of Lord Nunnington and secure an alliance for our families. Rebecca was my only challenge; she was quite beautiful, you look a lot like her. Well, she caught the lord's eye right away. I was all ready to give up and go back home when your father rode into town, all handsome and exciting. He was a real warrior, not just some sickly lordling. Well, that was that, she rode off and married him and I got the lord...I was jealous for a while. Life here is far from exciting but it is safe and, looking back, I've been lucky. I was sorry to hear she died, it must have been hard for you."

"I had my brother... for a while, and then there was Lyaren."

Lady Nunnington raised her eyebrow. "The tutor?"

"Yes, he is very important to me."

"Mmm, I bet he is! Do you know you are in danger, Elayna?"

Ela felt angry, this woman had no idea! "Not from Lyaren!"

"Of course not, he's in the dungeons! No, from the Xyakahan priesthood."

For the second time today Lady Nunnington had caught her off guard. Ela kept quiet, better to find out what the woman knew.

165

"We heard about your father's death from neighbouring lords, both Eric and Mason sent word by bird. Daniel sent men to come and get you. Your father never bent a knee to my husband; wanting to rule his own Quarrel as his father had done before him, but Daniel wanted to offer you his protection. Your brother and he were close, he felt obliged to help you. Besides, a young woman alone is neither safe nor proper. The men returned with the news that you were gone. At the same time the priests turned up from the Xyakahan temple with papers to say your father had signed you over to their protection. We must tolerate the Xyakahan cult within our city walls, their followers are powerful men, but we do not trust them! No smoke without fire, I always say. Still you were gone, probably murdered by that tutor for all we knew, so that was that. Now we have a problem. You turn up on our doorstep and Daniel is bound to hand you over!" She paused to check she had Ela's attention but quickly continued before Ela had time to speak. "Now my Daniel, he's a smart boy. He knows that few remember the details and so, when you arrived, he had his own false papers drawn up to say your father did bow his knee and pledge his Quarrel and household to his liege lord as a young man. With no family members to state otherwise we can just about get away with it. That would bind you under the protection of the Nunnington family and so, for now, keep the priests at bay. You are safe for the time being but it's only a matter of time before the priests find out that you are here and, if anyone remembers the truth, those papers will be useless!" She looked Ela squarely in the eye.

Ela held her stare. "If the priests know I am here they will take me. They killed my father and they want me. Lyaren got me away before their mercenaries arrived to take me by force to their temple. They sent sorcerers after us and that army of lizard men marches with Xyakahan priests by its side. They will come for me, Lady Nunnington, and there is nothing you or your son can do to protect me. The only person who has any hope of helping me is currently sat in your son's dungeon!"

This time it was Lady Nunnington's turn to be surprised, indignation turned to alarm then disbelief. "The lizards are allied with the Xyakahan priesthood? Are you sure girl?"

"Quite sure, Lyaren saw them in the camp when he rescued me."

Lady Nunnington chuckled without humour. "That tutor of yours has you well taken in! Have you not considered these are his lies to keep you for himself?"

Ela kept her composure despite her annoyance. "Not for a moment, Lady Nunnington, Lyaren is my true friend. Besides, he is the one who brought me here. Would he do that if he wanted to take me away?"

Lady Nunnington didn't answer at once, considering carefully Ela's calm composure.

"You are a smart one, Lady Elayna, perhaps this tutor of yours is innocent after all, or maybe not. Still it is of no matter. He must die to keep the Xyakahan priests placated. We will help you because I liked your mother and because my son likes you. You will marry Daniel before the war begins and then the priests' claim to you will become void. You will be the next Lady Nunnington."

For a second Ela thought Lady Nunnington had understood her situation, but now it became clear she really didn't see the whole picture at all. "Lady Nunnington, it is very good of you to want to help me but you are in terrible danger!"

"I'm in danger?" she raised an eyebrow. "How so?"

167

"Don't you see?" Ela had to make her understand. "If there are Xyakahan priests in your city they will betray you. You must remove all of their followers from the city walls before the gates are closed."

"Impossible! The priesthood is made up of some of our most prominent citizens, it is our role to protect them from the threat of the lizard invasion, not kick them out of the city!"

"Lady Nunnington they *are* the threat! Please, I must speak to Daniel about this! Please!"

Lady Nunnington stood abruptly, her face panic stricken. "My poor child you are deluded! I will get you my physician at once! Guards Guards!" The doors flew open and the two guardsmen rushed into the room. The older woman didn't give Ela time to respond. "The Lady Elayna is feeling unwell, please escort her back to her rooms and make sure she stays there until I can see she is better!"

Gently the guards took hold of Ela's arms, her body stumbling along as they led her out, her mind screaming *'No Don't let this happen!'* "Please, Lady Nunnington, I must talk to Daniel! Please!" But her words fell on deaf ears; the Lady Nunnington had already left, rushing off in the opposite direction.

It had been a long time since Myllasanndia Nunnington had rushed anywhere but, the moment Ela was out of sight, rush is exactly what she did. Daniel had placed his most trusted guards to protect the young woman but if what she said was true the child was most certainly not safe here in the castle. No one was! As she approached the guards stationed outside of her husband's council rooms she slowed her pace to a more dignified walk and nodded authoritatively to the men. "I need to see my son, regarding his father."

"Right away, My Lady!" snapped one of the soldiers and opened the door promptly, announcing to the room beyond "Lady Nunnington to see Lord Daniel!"

Within, Daniel stood at a large wooden table positioned centrally in the room. Candles had been lit to provide extra illumination and the heavy oak chairs were pushed back to the walls. The council was in full attendance, the heads from members of all the prominent families stood sombrely around an array of maps, scrolls and reports. As she entered the room concerned expressions were hurriedly replaced with false smiles and an unnatural hush fell over the assembly.

Myllasanndia took a calming breath and was somewhat surprised by the lightness of tone she achieved in her voice. "Forgive an old woman this intrusion, Gentlemen. I appreciate the importance of your meeting today but my husband's condition is grave, if I could beg but a moment with my son?"

Daniel, a look of surprise on his face, turned to his council. "Gentlemen could you excuse me for just a moment, I'm sure my mother will be brief."

Myllasanndia smiled warmly. "Yes of course."

The council members responded with a variety of polite acknowledgements as Daniel walked over and gently took her by the arm. "This way, Mother," he invited as he led her across the room towards the shadowed doorway in the far corner. They entered her husband's private study and Daniel firmly closed and locked the door behind them. He turned instantly to his mother, a look of concerned confusion replacing his well-rehearsed, controlled face; very few people ever saw the true face of Daniel Nunnington. "This had better be important, Mother!" Then he hesitated. "Is it father?"

"No, your fathers condition is the same. Daniel, I talked with Ela as you asked. I think you need to talk to her. I think we have made a misjudgement."

Daniel raised his eyebrow slightly. "How so?"

"The tutor for one, but it's worse than that. She says the lizard army is allied with the Xyakahan priesthood; she believes their followers will betray us."

Daniel stopped in his tracks, his mind trying to process the information. He glanced at the thick wooden door then moved further into the room, motioning for his mother to do the same. "Don't be ridiculous, Mother, half of my council follow Xyakah but they are still good Maldoran lords and I am their liege lord – they will stand behind us."

"You need to talk to the girl, listen to what she has to say. She is distraught and very afraid; she believes there is true danger, Daniel, if the lords who follow Xyakah betray us..." She left the statement lying in the air.

"I must return to the meeting, they mustn't suspect we have any concerns."

"You are right. Dismiss me as a weak, grieving woman, conclude your meeting and then we must talk to your Lady Elayna and I think that tutor of hers also."

"You think he could be innocent?

"I don't know, but with your permission I would like to speak with him – you know how my gift works."

Daniel thought for a moment then nodded. "Very well, talk to him, but don't give anything away. If you sense he is innocent have the guards bring him here after dark, we will all meet then and hear the full story from their lips. But I warn you, Mother, I cannot release him purely on your say-so, if the council learn of your talents I will lose their support."

"I understand that well enough, Daniel!" Myllasanndia snapped. "I have counselled your father for all of our married life and never once led him wrongly. Now I counsel you and you would be a fool not to heed my advice! Only Rudley can be trusted. I will have the prisoner brought up; Ela and Tarrin should also be present. This is important, Daniel!"

Daniel seemed to wilt before her and an expression of sadness crossed his face; he hid the strain well but his mother could see the cracks. "I'm sorry, Mother, I will respect your counsel."

"Good." She reached up and kissed him gently on the cheek. "Your father taught you well. You are a wise man, Daniel, I know you are capable of this challenge."

Daniel wrapped his arms around his mother and held her tightly. "I hope so, Mother, I truly do." He stepped back slowly. "We shall meet at the seventh hour." He gave her a warm smile then smoothed his expression. Taking her arm gently, he pulled back the bolt silently and swung open the door, firmly marching her out into the room. In a stern but measured tone he addressed her as if speaking to a feeble old woman. "I know you're worried, Mother. Father is very ill but you can't keep interrupting me! The council has important work to do! I know you don't understand this but Father would. Now do as I tell you and get back to Father's bedside. He needs you with him now!" And then, gently but firmly, he as good as threw his mother out of the council chamber. Daniel turned back to his lords and raised his eyebrows. "Women!" he exclaimed. "Now Gentlemen, where were we?"

Myllasanndia Nunnington left her son swiftly and made her way over to the east tower. The guards and servants she encountered bowed respectfully as she passed but none questioned her presence. Myllasanndia made it her business to spend time in every area of the

171

castle, even the dungeons. She didn't pity the prisoners, they deserved punishment for their crimes, but she felt compelled to see that those whom her son or husband had sentenced to death were offered a last meal before their execution. The jailer, although used to her visits, looked up in surprise when she arrived. "My Ladyship, we have no executions scheduled for today."

"Yes I know, Horkins, but with war coming and my husband ill I wanted to make sure no one was missed. Are there any prisoners likely to receive the death sentence imminently?"

"Well yes, My Lady, we have a murderer in. Killed Lord Ladaston, he did, do you want to see him?" Myllasanndia feigned nonchalance. "Yes, yes I suppose I'd better see the man."

"Very well, My Lady, this way please." Horkins took the keys from his belt and opened the heavily-barred gate which stood at the top of a steep, spiralling stairwell descending deep into the dungeons below the castle. She followed him down, careful of the steep steps, using the handrail to help her in the dim light. At the bottom he opened a second gate which he locked behind them. Horkins took a torch from one of the wall sconces and led her down a dim passageway carved out of the solid rock of the mountain. The few cells they passed were all empty. Horkins stopped at the fifth cell and placed the torch in the sconce by the barred door. As its light flickered into the cell the occupant within raised his head and looked steadily at Myllasanndia.

"You are Lyaren, the tutor?" She asked.

For a heartbeat there was silence, and then the man answered. "Yes."

Myllasanndia turned to the guard. "Fetch me a stool, Horkins; I will sit with the prisoner for a while."

"At once, My Lady." The man scuttled off, returning momentarily with the stool.

172

"Thank you, Horkins, I will be fine for a while, give us ten minutes and then return for me."

Horkins was a little taken aback – this was not the usual custom. "Are you sure, My Lady? I can stay with you if you'd prefer."

"Quite sure," Myllasanndia said, smiling. "Lord Ladaston was a friend of mine; I have questions for this man."

"Oh, well, that's that then, very well My Lady." and nodding to himself the guard left.

Myllasanndia sat on the stool. "Do you know who I am?"

The man stood and walked closer to the cell door. "You are Lady Nunnington."

"Yes I am, and you are Lyaren the tutor. Tell me, did you like your employer Lord Ladaston?"

Lyaren was surprised by the question but not ruffled; he answered truthfully. "No, the man was a bully and a murderer. I know he had been a good person before his wife and son died, but the mixture of grief and Xyakah have a way of changing a man."

"This is true," Myllasanndia agreed. "But not a good case for your defence. Do you care for Lady Elayna?"

"Deeply, My Lady, I am sworn to protect her with my life."

"Again you fuel the argument for your guilt."

"That may be, but I will tell you only the truth: I did not kill Lord Ladaston. I am not a threat to Lady Elayna and I am not a threat to you. In fact quite the contrary – you and your son need me far more than I need you."

"You need us to pardon you and save your life!"

"And you need me to give you information about the enemy so you can save your city."

173

It was subtle, like a gentle breeze, but Lyaren felt the magical energy brush against his own and, as it did, Lady Nunnington let out a small sigh of surprise. Lyaren took his chance and looked the woman in the eye. "Have you found what you are looking for?"

If ruffled by the magical exchange Lady Nunnington didn't show it. She had quickly schooled her expression after her small exclamation of shock and looked coldly at Lyaren. "What are you?" Her voice was controlled but not unkind.

Now it was Lyaren's turn to look surprised. He shook his head in resignation, took a deep breath, which he released slowly, and allowed the glamour to slip away from his features.

This time Lady Nunnington didn't bother to hide her amazement, the face before her seemed to melt away as all the human features subtly adjusted. It became more angular – some may even say sharp; nose, chin and ears elongated, skin tone lightened, slight wrinkles smoothed and alarmingly intelligent almond-shaped eyes now shimmered with flecks of gold. The elf looked her firmly in the eye and smiled. "I am a friend, Lady Nunnington, and a powerful one. I have killed, true, but only to protect those I care about. And I did not kill Lord Ladaston. I am here to protect Lady Elayna from a grave danger and I am begging you for your help."

Trembling slightly, Myllasanndia stood and reached out to the bars of the cell before her. As she expected, the cell door swung silently open at her touch. "Why have you not escaped? You are far beyond our ability to imprison." Her voice was a whisper.

"I thought I should stay. There are friends of mine close by who might need my help."

Myllasanndia nodded. "Do we need your help?"

"Yes but I may not give it."

"We have misjudged you, Lyaren, but you have not been totally honest with us either; trust works both ways."

Lyaren raised a slight smile. "There I must agree." This woman was remarkably intelligent; Lyaren was impressed by the speed at which she had recovered from his transformation.

"I have spoken with my son and we are aware of the imminent danger from both the invading army and from the silent threat within our gates. Will you help us?" Her shoulders slumped and her eyes filled with tears, which she tenaciously refused to release. "My husband was a brilliant tactician, but his life has been blessed with peace. Daniel is young. He feels the weight of responsibility but needs guidance. How do we proceed when we could all be murdered in our beds before the invaders even arrive?"

"That may well be their plan, Lady Nunnington, but my first priority is Elayna. If I help you will you help me?"

"Yes I will do whatever I can. Will you be able to escape these cells at first dusk? I dare not be seen releasing you, it would tip our hand to the enemy."

Lyaren nodded. "Escape will not be a problem; you are wise to take such precautions. Where do I need to go?

Myllasanndia explained the location of her husband's private study and Lyaren assured her he was capable of getting there unseen. She believed him; she had never sensed anything like the power he had revealed to her. In fact, she marvelled that he had been able to shield so much magic in the first place. Loud footsteps announced Horkins' return and as, the guard came into view, Myllasanndia walked towards him. "Thank you, Horkins; everything seems to be in order with the prisoner. Please see he is well fed, we must maintain our standards even here in the jail."

"Yes, My Lady" Horkins bobbed his head. "Right away, My Lady." and he led her back towards the steps and out of the dungeons.

Tarrin listened sombrely to the clanswoman-scout's report. "The lizard army has received reinforcements and seems to be preparing to march. They're still sending out scouts to try and track their ponies but the horses have fled into the foothills and have made good distance – they won't serve the lizard men again. Nonetheless, they have brought in new wagons and horses with the reinforcements so they will be able to transport their provisions. All considered, for an army of that size, they are at least a good week away from mobilizing any type of attack on a city of this magnitude."

Joy for the small victory of the released ponies was overshadowed by concern for the impending attack. Although it had all the essentials to withstand a siege, from what Tarrin had seen Stagsonton was far from ready for battle. Truth be told, he doubted any Maldora citizen could ever be ready for war, tucked away from the world as they were in their comfortable stone houses, surrounded by their plump cushions and with their bellies stuffed full on over-rich food. Just like the fools up at Torr-Arron, and look what had happened there!

"What about Teah and Calin?"

"They are close, they have been intercepted by soldiers from the garrison here and should make the fortifications with time for us to evacuate before the city closes for the siege."

"Good. And the women are they comfortable?"

"I don't know!" the woman exclaimed. "These kingdom women are strange – they went from startled

176

hares to moaning monsters overnight! The moment they realised their lives weren't in imminent danger their moaning began, ungrateful..."

"Thank you, Tamira!" Tarrin cut her off. "Go and get some rest; make sure your warriors are provisioned and ready to go. As soon as Teah and her group return we will be leaving – we have been away from home too long at a time when I know our own people need us the most."

"It will be so." She held her right fist over her chest, a gesture of respect for Tarrin. With his brother dead he was warlord of the Wolf Moon Clan and, although not *her* clan leader, she would follow his orders until she returned to the Silent Sabre Clan. Tarrin returned the salute and the woman turned quickly and jogged away. Tarrin smiled; it had not taken his people long to recover. He was proud of his warriors.

The clans made no distinction between men and women; as children all were treated equally and trained as warriors. The Grasslands were dangerous for those without the ability to protect themselves. The giant Sabres came together in packs to mate and even the strongest warriors were hard-pressed to defend themselves against them when they attacked. Thankfully, that was only through the summer months, as the creatures roamed solitary for the remaining seasons of the year. Tarrin's people were taught as children to safeguard themselves from the beasts and so, as adults, all could hunt and all called themselves warriors. Tarrin admired the women of his people even more now he had met the kingdom women. Only the young girl Sally had shown any courage. These people were lambs compared to the lions of his people! The stink of lamb was firmly rotting his nostrils. Tarrin had had his fill of these kingdom people; he needed to fulfil

177

his obligation to Lyaren and get home as quickly as he could.

The loud, confident tread of boots announced the arrival of General Rudley. Tarrin had taken a liking to the man. He was in charge of Lord Nunnington's army and, unlike the lordling, seemed to have grasped some of the magnitude of their impending situation. The man had worked quietly and efficiently to mobilize his troops in order to inform and support the people of the surrounding countryside. At the age of around forty, Rudley showed some signs of the flesh sickness which afflicted so many of the kingdom men. An extra thick fat-layer covered his stomach but, unlike most that Tarrin had seen, Rudley was otherwise fit and Tarrin could tell by the man's well-muscled arms and legs that he could wield the large, no-nonsense sword which hung from his side. The man had a thick crop of reddish-brown hair speckled with grey which sprang unkempt from his head and face and gave him the appearance of an aging bear. Tarrin kept his expression neutral as he tried to remove the bear image from his mind. "Lord Rudley."

"Ah! Prince Tarrin, there you are, I was hoping we could talk; I've been in the council meeting with Lord Daniel for most of the day but have requested that I have a little time with you as you are the only one who has actually seen this army close up. I would like to go over the details with you, if you wouldn't mind?"

Inwardly Tarrin moaned, he needed to find Lyaren and get him and Elayna away from this place. But how could he not help? Thousands stood to suffer if this city wasn't ready."

"I am a tribesman, Rudley, I know little of cities and sieges, but I know your enemy and he is my enemy too. I will help you."

Rudley seemed to stoop before him, worry etched his face. "Prince Tarrin, our people have been at peace for a long time, I need to know what I am facing. No one alive has ever been involved in a battle let alone a siege and, although I've read my histories, I've got to admit this scares the hell out of me! I've a whole city and then some to keep safe, and that's a lot for one man to shoulder.

Tarrin was impressed this man knew his weaknesses and had identified the only person who could help him, Lyaren excluded.

"I suggest you talk to the women first, they can give you a sense of your enemy. Then I will talk you through what I have seen of their strategy, although my encounters with them were in both cases overt – in the first instance their attack on my people and in the second our rescue of the women. Then if you like we can go through your preparations."

"Thank you, that would be most appreciated."

Tarrin smiled; it was a hard determined expression and one which was echoed on Rudley's face. The afternoon marched on at pace for Tarrin. Rudley was an intelligent and personable man and, after they worked out the initial discomfort of their situation, both men efficiently turned to the business at hand. Tarrin was relieved that none of the women mentioned Elayna's part in their rescue, but still the decision whether or not to mention magic to Rudley weighed on Tarrin's conscience. Kingdom people didn't have magic – the mere mention of it would terrify them – but, without pre-warning, how could they protect themselves?

As evening fell the beginning of a firm friendship had formed between the two men. Tarrin admired the efficiency of Rudley, who acted quickly on his recommendations. Rudley's confidence grew as

Tarrin concurred with many of his decisions and, when the message came summoning both men to Lord Nunnington's office, both felt reassured that the city and its army were indeed up to the task in hand.

Myllasanndia left the dungeons and headed straight back to her apartments to check on her husband. She trusted the physicians implicitly with his care but still this was the longest she had left his bedside since his illness had begun. She sat by his bed while she ate a light lunch, chatting conversationally (as was her habit) to the unconscious man she had grown so fond of over the years they had been together. His breathing was laboured and the contours of his skeleton showed clearly against his tightly pulled skin. It wouldn't be long. She reached over and kissed his frail cheek gently. "I love you, Alex." she whispered and then, instructing her staff to fetch her if there was any change, she left and headed straight to Elayna's suit. As she approached she noted that the guards outside Elayna's door had been changed, but was relieved to see they were still members of Daniel's Elite Guard. These men had been selected because of their connection to the Nunnington family. They had been highly trained in an effective (although slightly unorthodox) manner but, most importantly, they had been discreetly scrutinised by Myllasanndia and, as such, their loyalty was without question. As she approached, both men stood stiffly to attention. "Good afternoon, Lady Nunnington." The taller of the two greeted her.

"Good afternoon, gentlemen, how fares our young guest?"

"I think the Lady Elayna is sleeping, My Lady. She was most distressed when she was brought back to her rooms but the physicians brought her a sleeping draft and since then the room has been silent."

"Good. The poor girl has been through so much. Stay vigilant, gentlemen, I fear this child has dangerous enemies and I owe it to her poor, dead parents to keep her safe."

"Yes, My Lady." both men clipped in response.

Myllasanndia smiled warmly and entered the chamber. She quickly took in the state of bedroom. Objects cluttered the floor and the bedding had been dragged off the bed and tied together to create a rope which had been tossed out of the window. Myllasanndia hurried over to the open window but, peering out, was reassured to see that the bedding reached less than a quarter of the dizzying expanse to the ground! Elayna had not gone out of the window.

A sniffle sounded behind her and, turning, she caught sight of the child curled in a ball and rocking silently in the far corner of the room. "Oh Elayna, my poor child." she comforted, rushing over and wrapping her arms around the girl. "Shush, shush now, my dear; there is no need for all this upset. It's all going to be well, child, I've spoken to your elf friend and I understand now; it's going to be all right." Carefully she guided the girl from her place on the floor and led her to the bed where she sat beside her, arms still holding her close.

Elayna hardly dare accept what she had heard. The guards had half-carried her back to her rooms from the Solar, and then the physicians had forced her to drink their potion. After that they had left her alone. The sedative hadn't touched her. Instead she had become more and more distraught. That was when she had started knotting up the bedding but it quickly became obvious that it wasn't going to work. At that point she had given in to her frustration, throwing the delicate bedside table and all its contents across the room. She felt so useless. Since this whole thing had started she had

181

relied totally on Lyaren and, on the two occasions she had been left alone, she had ended up incarcerated, this time getting Lyaren imprisoned as well. She struggled to put together what Lady Nunnington was saying; *perhaps the sedative had affected her after all?* "You talked to Lyaren?"

"Yes, my dear, I did, and he showed me who he really is. I have a little power myself; my magic is small and specific – I can feel a person's intentions and I can sense when they are honest, loyal and trustworthy or if they are deceitful. It is very accurate. However, a very strange thing happened when I tried to read your friend Lyaren, he felt my magic straight away. Thankfully he chose to trust me and I am glad he did. I understand now, Elayna: there is very real danger here for all of us. We are chicks in the viper's nest with little clue as to the viper's identity. We need to work together if we are to survive this."

Ela was stunned, "Lady Nunnington, thank you." She sagged against the older woman's embrace and, with heaving sobs, gave in to all the fear, uncertainty and frustration. As she cried, Lady Nunnington gently held her close and rocked her, giving her all the time she needed.

To Ela it seemed as though they'd sat together like that for hours. She had totally lost track of the time and wasn't even sure it was the same day. Finally, the tears stopped and her gasping breaths began to regulate. Feeling the change, Lady Nunnington pulled slightly away and looked into Elayna's eyes; she smiled reassuringly. "My dear girl, we need to get you cleaned up. Then you and I are to go to my husband's private study where Daniel, Lyaren and Prince Tarrin will meet us. When we are all together we will talk through the situation in full. Far too many of our wealthier citizens follow Xyakah. I have been aware for some time of a change in the commitment some of our oldest friends feel towards my family. At first I thought it was due to the changeover from Alex to Daniel, I thought Daniel just needed time to gain their respect, but now I'm not so sure. We need to work out just who we can trust, and I think the place to start is here. So, Elayna, I want you to tell me everything. Leave nothing out and start with your father's death. Let's get to the bottom of this.

The council room now deserted and tided away still held the odour of men, testimony to the day's work. The room was silent and shrouded in shadow. Myllasanndia and Elayna made their way across the gloom towards the hidden entrance to Daniel's study. A deep shadow detached itself from the wall and stepped out before them. Elayna's heart jumped into her mouth, flipped and exploded with recognition as Lyaren's features came into view. She threw herself into him, almost knocking the unflappable elf off his feet. He inhaled her scent and allowed himself the indulgence of the embrace. "Good to see you too." he whispered.

Lady Myllasanndia stepped towards them and Lyaren stepped back. "I am also glad to see you, Lyaren; I see that escaping our jail was no challenge to you."

"I have my talents, Lady Nunnington."

"Yes, so you do! Come, both of you, Daniel will be waiting." Myllasanndia led the way across the chamber and knocked lightly on the door before pushing it open. As they entered the room the warmth and light of the roaring fire engulfed them. Daniel sat at his desk, paperwork in his hand. General Griss stood behind him, arms folded and a deep frown on his face. Now it was Myllasanndia's turn to be caught by surprise, Griss was not on her list of most trusted. Hiding her concern she forced nonchalance into her voice, "Good evening

Daniel... Lord Griss, what a pleasure, I didn't expect you to be joining us tonight."

Daniel caught his mother's meaning and his eyes relayed his understanding. "Griss is the leader of our army, Mother; in a time of war he must be kept up to date on all developments." Daniel stood and smiled "Elayna, Lyaren, please come in and take a seat, we have much to discuss."

The study had been arranged for the meeting with one low settee and four straight-backed but comfortable armchairs positioned close to the fire. A low coffee table which was laid out with goblets and a jug of rich red wine occupied the centre of the arrangement. Myllasanndia took the chair directly opposite her son allowing her eyes to focus closely on Griss. He was a problem; they could not talk frankly with the man present. He had been of concern to Myllasanndia for some time; his loyalty to her husband had been unwavering, but the transition to Daniel's lordship had seen his ties to the family lessen and now she could only read the surface of his emotions, as if he had locked the door and blocked her from reading him fully.

Elayna sat on the settee besides Myllasanndia and Lyaren sat beside her. Before anyone else had a chance to comment there was a second knock at the door and in walked Tarrin and Rudley. Tarrin smiled warmly at Lyaren and Elayna. "Good," he said. "I see we finally have Lord Daniel's attention."

Rudley frowned at Tarrin's apparent rudeness but didn't comment.

"Prince Tarrin, I'm sorry I haven't been able to give you and your companions my time before this. Only I have been rather distracted by the large army of lizard men marching towards my city." Daniel's voice dripped a weary sarcasm.

"Perhaps a more experienced man would see the value in collecting all intelligence before moving forward with his plans." Tarrin flatly replied.

Daniel sighed and nodded, rubbing his hair from his eyes. "In truth, Prince Tarrin, you are right. I have no precedence for what is happening right now, no script or protocol to follow, and I admit I am unprepared. The kingdom has known peace for many years and we expected peace to remain. I suspect I have made several fundamental errors, and I can only hope it is not too late to repair the damage. Please, gentlemen, come in, close and lock the door, take a seat and let us begin."

Tarrin nodded. "Perhaps not too late." he acknowledged, his voice a low growl. "Apology accepted." He grinned and the tension in the room eased a little.

As the two men took their seats, Myllasanndia poured wine for everyone. Daniel sat back in his chair, his eyes returning to Lyaren. "Well master Lyaren, my mother suspects we have treated you unjustly. Perhaps you could start this evening by explaining your actions."

Lyaren felt the tension in Myllasanndia's bearing; her exchange with her son hadn't been lost on him. The woman didn't trust this General Griss and, however he answered, he must be guarded. "I have acted purely in the interests of Lady Elayna, My Lord." Lyaren began. "Following Lord Ladaston's departure from the house I went about my usual routine. However I was interrupted by intruders on the estate. The men looked like criminals and were well armed. They attacked the household staff and were looking for Lady Elayna. I rushed to her quarters and helped her escape the castle. We heard about her father's death from people in the village and so I escorted Lady Elayna here. On the way we encountered the lizard army and Elayna was taken prisoner. That was when we had the good fortune to

185

run into Prince Tarrin. And the rest you know." Lyaren sat back in his chair. He hoped he had threaded enough truth into the tale for it to be accepted. He could share the full story at a later date.

"I have spoken at length with Elayna, Daniel, and she corroborates this chain of events entirely. I can only assume the rumours of Lyaren's involvement in Gadon's death were misinformed. We appear to have narrowly averted a gross miscarriage of justice." Myllasanndia concluded.

"Yes, Mother, I feel you might be r..." Daniel was cut off by a torrent of frantic knocking at the door.

"My Lord... My Lord... are you there? We need to find Lady Myllasanndia! It is your father... please My Lord are you there?"

It was Lord Tain, the head steward. Myllasanndia didn't pause as the panic and concern for her husband overwhelmed all of her senses. She threw herself fluidly to the door, pulled back the bolt and flung it wide open only to find herself face to face with a crossbow. She heard the loud snap as the latch on the crossbow relaxed and watched in surprise as the blast seemed to throw Tain in an unnatural motion backwards across the room, while the crossbow bolt hovered unrealistically in the air – a hair's breadth from her skin – before falling harmlessly with a clatter to the ground.

Daniel groaned from behind her and an arc of silver light flashed in her peripheral vision, followed by a heavy thud.

The confusing jumble of events overrode her initial shock and Myllasanndia turned to see Daniel sprawled across his desk, a pool of blood spreading across the paperwork. As she rushed towards her son a hand stopped her. It was Rudley. "Wait, My Lady!"

Elayna fought down the nausea as she stared in horror at the scene. The man with the crossbow lay still on the council-room floor. Lyaren had blasted him off his feet! At the same time as Myllasanndia had opened the door Griss had plunged his dagger into Daniel's chest. Almost before the blade made contact Tarrin had thrown his own knife across the room, hitting Griss straight in the eye. The startled expression on the big man's face suggested that he hadn't realised that he had died. His body swayed slightly and then rocked backwards falling in a heap against the wall.

Lyaren seemed the only one in control. "Tarrin, Rudley, check the corridor; there may be more of them – don't let them escape!" Both men responded without question to the authority in his voice.

Myllasanndia's voice, in comparison, was a shaken whisper "Daniel?"

Chapter 7
The Elite

Lady Nunnington and Elayna both sprang towards Daniel, but it was Lyaren who got there first. Showing no sign of strain Lyaren gently lifted Daniel's limp form in his arms and carried the man over to the settee where he and Ela had been sitting. Laying him down cautiously, he placed his fingers to Daniel's neck and felt the feeble pulse deep within. "He's still with us," he stated. "But we need to act fast." He turned to the distraught Lady Nunnington. "I can use my magic to heal this wound, My Lady, but I will need your help. Are you up to that?"

The night held its breath as the seconds it took for Myllasanndia to process what Lyaren had said ticked by; worry and grief flowed over her face. "If you can save my son, I'm up to anything." Her voice cracked with anxiety.

"We need to remove the knife," Lyaren explained gently. "But as soon as we do so the heart will spasm and Daniel will die. I can control Daniel's body, steady his heart and keep him on this side of life, but to do so I need to touch the heart itself."

189

Myllasanndia looked in horror at Lyaren. "What do you want me to do?"

"I want you to hold this blade still while I cut open Daniel's chest; when I can hold his heart in my hand I can use my magic to repair the tissues and you can slowly pull out the knife. Once I open his chest the knife must be removed or else Daniel will die. If you don't think you can do this say so now, there will be no second chances once we begin!"

"Can I help?" Elayna ventured.

"Ela, I need you to sit down, this won't be easy for you."

"I'm not a child, Ly; I can handle a little blood." Ela felt a flush of anger at Lyaren's underestimation of her.

"It's not the blood, Ela, it's the magic. Sit down and I'll explain when I get Daniel safe!"

Ela glared at Lyaren and sat down petulantly, arms folded across her chest. As she watched the scene before her, grief replaced the anger; she was too exhausted to stay mad with Ly for more than a minute, and Daniel lay so vulnerable before her.

Lyaren looked at Lady Nunnington. "Are you ready?'

Myllasanndia nodded and carefully took hold of the knife impaled in her son's chest. Lyaren removed his own knife from its concealed sheaf. "Did you have that with you in your cell?" Myllasanndia asked.

Lyaren didn't answer. Instead, he touched the blade of the knife with his index finger and mouthed a silent incantation. A ripple of blue light ran down the blade. He then cut away the shirt from Daniel's chest, revealing the extent of the damage. Myllasanndia gasped in shock but remained still and focussed.

Elayna watched from the chair as Ly began to work. She saw his lips move as he began the incantation but suddenly her stomach heaved with sickness.

"This won't be pretty, Lady Nunnington." Lyaren warned.

"Call me Myllasanndia and, please, save my son."

Lyaren pushed his own blade into Daniel's chest and cut through the flesh. He chanted again and the muscle seemed to ripple and curl back, pulling apart the wound in Daniel's chest and spreading it wider and deeper, almost as if his body had opened itself up at Lyaren's command.

Elayna's ears began to hum, louder and louder, a silent buzzing drummed through her head.

Daniel's lungs and ribcage were now clearly visible and his heart could just be seen quivering lightly below. Dropping his knife, Lyaren placed his hand into the chest cavity and touched the ribs, which covered Daniel's heart. As he did so the ribs seemed to bend back on themselves, creating a space for Lyaren's hand to push in between. The lungs parted slightly at his touch. Lyaren placed his fingers around the heart and began to chant a little louder.

Her head was spinning now, or was it the room? The nausea intensified!

Despite her terror, Myllasanndia was enthralled. As Lyaren's fingers touched his heart she gently began to pull the blade out from its position and, as she did so, watched as his heart began to pick up its rhythm once again. The wound in the muscle closed, sealing itself, and as Lyaren let go of Daniel's heart it could clearly be seen to pump with a strong firm rhythm.

A change in the chant and Lyaren touched the ribs, which responded instantly, folding back to their natural position.

191

Her vision had all but failed and the buzzing was unbearable, she would scream if only she could gain some control over her own body!

The muscle knitted itself back together perfectly and the skin seemed to melt back in on itself, reconnecting seamlessly into place over the now-natural beating chest. Lyaren sat back, slapped the ground firmly three times and cut off his contact to the magic.

As suddenly as it had begun the attack stopped. The buzzing evaporated and the nausea lifted. Elayna realised she was curled tightly into a ball. She sighed deeply and struggled to sit upright in her chair.

Lyaren looked up into Myllasanndia's hope-filled eyes. Tears streamed down her face. "He needs to sleep off the effects of the magic but he will be fine."

Myllasanndia gasped. "I can never thank you for what you have done."

Lyaren smiled. "Yes you can, and I think before this night is over you will."

The soft tread of boots announced the return of Tarrin and Rudley. "Looks like it was just the two of them; there is no one else in this section of the castle." Tarrin reported.

"Good." Lyaren acknowledged. "Get that body in here and shut the door, lock it too."

Tarrin and Rudley dragged the dead castle-steward into the study and closed the door, bolting it in place. Then both men sank into two of the vacant chairs. Tarrin looked to Lyaren. "That was some magic trick you just pulled – I think they probably felt it all the way back to my village! Will the young lord live?"

Lyaren smiled. "We need Daniel alive if this city is to survive, but you are right – anyone with magic would have felt that..." Lyaren pinned Elayna with piercing eyes. "How do you feel, Ela?"

Elayna looked at Lyaren in stunned shock. "I...I...I don't know what you mean... I mean..." She grasped for words but stuttered in defeat. "What was that?"

Lyaren smiled. "That was my magic. But the real question is, why do you react so strongly to it? Mmm." He smiled reassuringly. "A riddle for another time I think." He looked back to the other men in the room. "We need to act quickly; the priests will have felt that. If we're lucky they won't figure out what's happened straight away, and before they have time to respond they'll have to secure the temple and round up all their followers." He looked down at the dead body of the head steward. "It appears the priesthood has infiltrated deeply into your household staff, Myllasanndia. Do you have anyone in the castle we can trust?"

Myllasanndia turned her head away from her son and looked up at Lyaren, who was now standing but relying heavily on the desk to support his weight. He looked drawn and was breathing heavily. "I trust the Elite Guard and no other." she replied. "But Lyaren, look at yourself, you need to rest."

Lyaren nodded. "Yes, I do need a little rest."

Myllasanndia looked to Rudley. "Simon, would you please check in on Alex for me? I need to know there was no truth in Tain ruse."

Rudley looked through heavy eyes. "Yes, My Lady, I will go now. What about Lord Daniel, should I call for the physicians?"

Myllasanndia looked to Lyaren, who shook his head. "Daniel will be fine, he responded well to the magic, the fewer people who know of this the better. If no alarm is raised we may have a little more time."

The initial exodus from Lower Gonfiels had been swift and orderly but as the villagers set out towards Stagsonton it became increasingly clear the journey would be a challenge. There were too few horses for everyone. Wagons were overloaded and many people were on foot. By mid-afternoon the gap between the front and rear of the cavalcade was vast, with the more vulnerable villagers, elderly and young making up the flank. Calin and Teah had led the way – the other Horse Clan women scouting ahead – but, as they sat around the fire with Samuel and the other village elders in the early evening, there was a considerable tension in the air. "We can't keep going at this pace!" Teah insisted. "You were vulnerable back in your village but out here, spread across the countryside like this, we are sitting ducks! It will take weeks if we let the slowest set the pace."

"I agree." Calin said. "We need to do something to speed things up."

Samuel shook his head. "I don't see what we can do. We've managed to get 'em to leave their homes; I doubt they'll abandon the few possessions they've brought with 'em."

"Could we split the group? Encourage the faster group to press on? At least that way we get some of the villagers to safety." Teah suggested.

"No!" Hayal stated flatly. "We are a community, a family. We set out together as one. We stay together as one!"

"Very well!" Teah snapped. "Then I suggest your family gets its act together. You have healthy strong men riding ahead on your best horses while the elderly and young walk behind. I for one don't want to look over my shoulder and watch the weakest die while those who could stand a chance against an attack are too far away to do anything about it."

"She's got a point, Hayal." Samuel said.

"I know" Hayal agreed. "But what can we do?" Hayal looked about twenty years older than he had last week, this had all hit him hard.

"We can go talk to some of the families," Calin suggested. "I bet most of the horses could carry a young 'un without too much trouble and that might make room in the carts for some of the old folk."

"Sounds good to me, Da." Kayel said, laying his hand on Hayal's shoulder. "Nobody will say no, not with so much at stake."

"Yes, it's worth a try." the older man agreed. "Can you organise this, Samuel?"

"Leave it to me, Hayal." the smith replied. "Come on, Calin, bring your new friends with you; we've a lot of folk to talk to and not much time to do it."

The reaction from the villagers was unanimous and, as the evening progressed, many of the younger men rode out to the back of the procession to carry in the slowest villagers on their horses. As night drew in the villagers reorganised their possessions, abandoning handcarts as neighbour helped neighbour.

Although still slow, on the second day of the journey the group made much better progress and, as they stopped for the second night, the rear of the column drew into camp considerably faster than they had the previous day.

It was on the third day of travel that the escort from Stagsonton met up with them and the extra security eased some of the tension in the camp. Just as well, as one of Teah's outriders brought in the news that the lizard army was once again on the move and heading in their direction. The news quickly spread and – with no order given – the whole company increased their pace, the urgency spurring them on.

Calin and Teah still lead the company. Both rode with a young child sat to the front of their saddles and

Calin had a huge chair strapped to the back of his pack. Teah looked on with laughter in her eyes, but she didn't laugh. She understood that to someone that chair was important and, as ridiculous as Calin looked; her opinion of him increased.

Daniel slept soundly, his mother sat beside him holding his hand. As soon as they had collected themselves Rudley had checked in on Lord Nunnington and found the man's condition had not changed. Tain had simply used the lie to get to Myllasanndia and this had been the trigger for Griss's attack on Daniel.

Lyaren had taken total control of the situation; Tarrin had reassured Rudley that his friend could be trusted and, still reeling from the shock of Griss's betrayal, Rudley complied. "We need soldiers who we can trust; we must deal with the enemy before they have time to regroup." Lyaren continued.

"I agree." Myllasanndia said, her eyes now back on her son. "Rudley, can you assemble the Elite Guard without alerting the rest of the army?"

"Yes, My Lady, where would you have them assemble?"

Myllasanndia turned to Lyaren. "The Elite are our most trusted soldiers; I have assessed every man myself. However, I would feel happier if I could check their loyalty again. There are five hundred men in the Elite Guard; it will take me some time to clear them all but if I have a few days..."

"We don't have days, Myllasanndia," Lyaren offered. "We have hours. I think I can help you check the men. Rudley, have your men assemble in the council room in two halves, I need you to be as discreet as you can."

Rudley grinned. He walked over to the wall beside the fireplace, reached over and pushed gently against the panelling. The wall silently swung inwards revealing a narrow, dark corridor. "The Elite Guard have their own ways of moving around the castle. Leave it with me!" He slipped into the hidden passageway and disappeared into the gloom.

Lyaren looked at Myllasanndia. "Can he be trusted?" he asked.

"Absolutely. Rudley is my second cousin, he came here as a baby with his parents when I first married Alex. He is a good man – loyal and honest."

"Good, I think I can help you with checking the loyalty of these men; you need to look at each one individually to know if someone is hiding something, is that right?"

"Yes." Myllasanndia agreed. "Really, I need to be touching them."

"What if you could look at a larger group and know the same thing?"

"That would be much faster, but how can it be done?"

Lyaren smiled. "With a little help from me."

"How are you thinking to deal with the threat Lyaren?" It was Tarrin; he stood by the door.

"We are going to attack the temple tonight and deal with the serpents in their lair. At the same time, we will arrest all the suspected traitors and put them in the cells for the night – Lady Myllasanndia can question them tomorrow. Once Lord Daniel is up and about he can decide what he wants to do with them, but the Xyakahan priests... Well, I will deal with them!" Lyaren looked over at Elayna. "They have a lot to answer for!"

He walked over and sat in the chair beside Elayna, a heavy weariness clearly in his eyes. "I need a little rest." he admitted.

"Sleep." Tarrin instructed. "I can keep watch, it will take some time for Rudley to mobilize the men and you will need your strength if you are to help Lady Nunnington."

Lyaren nodded, patted Ela's hand affectionately and closed his eyes. Sleep was instant.

Elayna shook Lyaren gently. "Ly, the soldiers and Lady Nunnington are ready for you."

Lyaren opened his eyes and stood stretching out his muscles. He could have taken a little more rest but his energy level was better and this next working was much more subtle and would require far less of him. Looking around the room he saw that he and Ela were alone with the sleeping Daniel.

"They are waiting for you in the council chamber." Ela told him. "I will stay and watch over Daniel." Ela looked pale, worry etched her features.

Lyaren stretched out his consciousness to Daniel. The magic was settling within his body and his sleep was deep and peaceful; he would feel wonderful when he woke. *'Considerably better than I do.'* Lyaren thought to himself. "Daniel is fine," Lyaren reassured her. "But I'm sure his mother will appreciate you watching over him."

Ela smiled but the worry still showed on her face. "I know you saved him... It's not that, it's just...well, me, the magic, will this hurt again?"

Lyaren smiled warmly and, risking the consequences, wrapped his arms around her comfortingly. To his surprise she moved closer into his embrace and pushed her body closely against him; she smelled of summer wind. "This will be fine, Ela," he whispered into her ear. "This is a softer magic, you may feel it brush against you but it shouldn't hurt this time."

"What's wrong with me?" she asked her voice distraught.

Lyaren pulled back to look her squarely in the face. "Nothing that can't be fixed." he reassured her.

"Ela, you are the strongest person I know; whatever this is we will work it out together."

"You'd better go." she said, moving back from his embrace.

Lyaren caught hold of her hand as she did. "I mean it, Ela, as soon as we deal with this threat we can start to unravel your mystery." He brought her hand to his lips and gently kissed it. "I have pledged to protect you with my life, Elayna, and I take my responsibilities very seriously."

Lyaren left Ela with Daniel and stepped out into the council room. Glancing at the windows he could see the moon was low in the sky, indicating the hour predawn. The room was packed full of smartly dressed household guards, all standing to attention before Myllasanndia. Lyaren walked to stand beside her.

"What do I do?" Myllasanndia asked him.

"You need to imagine that this group of men is one person, I will channel you a little extra magic to help with the reading, then do what you always do – look for indicators of deceit. If you see any, identify the general area within the room and we can look at that section in more detail."

Myllasanndia nodded, and then reached to the place deep inside herself where her gift lay; she connected her awareness to it and looked out to the room. As she did this Lyaren placed his hand gently on her shoulder and a warm pulse of power shot through her body, amplifying her awareness. She looked over the assembled men, filtering through the emotions, which tumbled out towards her: concern, confusion, loyalty, pride, sadness, joy, hunger, exhaustion, enthusiasm. The room positively glowed with the loyalty of these men. Myllasanndia relaxed and Lyaren removed his hand. She felt cold as his magic left her. Gradually her senses returned to normal. The men before her looked towards her, questions in their eyes. She turned to Lyaren. "The loyalty of these men is true." she stated. "Could I sit a little?"

Rudley rushed over to help her back towards the study but she shooed him away. "No, I mean sit here; I need to talk to the men."

Rudley bowed and brought over a chair and Myllasanndia gratefully sat. Then, with head held high, she spoke out to the assembled guard. "Gentlemen, we are in grave danger. Tonight an assassination attempt was made against my son." She waited as a collective intake of breath rumbled around the room. "My son is alive and recovering but only thanks to our new friends, Prince Tarrin and Master Lyaren. The assassins were – it saddens me to say – two of our most trusted citizens, General Griss and Lord Tain."

This time protocol was broken as exclamations of shock and disbelief rang out around the room.

"Gentlemen!" She raised her voice above the chatter which instantly stopped. "Lord Tain and General Griss were acting on behalf of the Xyakahan Priesthood; their actions are an open declaration of war and so, in my son's and husband's stead, I stand before you today and ask for your support."

For a moment the room was silent. Then, collectively, every member of the Elite Guard dropped to one knee before the Lady Nunnington.

Lyaren waited silently in the darkness of the riverside wharf. The shadows cast by the jumble of crates, carts and boxes creating the perfect location for concealment. Despite the high level of activity, which Lyaren knew unfolded around him, the night slipped by in silence. Daniel's Elite Guards were very good!

The screech of a cat's call split the stillness of his nocturnal surrounding, and with this the signal was given. Lyaren braced himself for the rush of magic as the night exploded with the clash of steal and the sounds of close-quarters combat. The Elite Guard had surrounded the temple and hit it simultaneously from three sides. Their orders were clear: 'Kill any who don't surrender, and leave an escape route to the rear of the temple for those with magic.' This was where Lyaren waited; if there were magic users in the building they would find the escape route and fall directly into his path. *Please Mother let his magic be strong enough to stop them!*

A soft padding of feet announced the arrival of the young officer, Grun, who had led the attack from the front of the building. "We're just finishing off the last part of the temple now, Sir," he reported. "The priests fought back at first but quickly surrendered. Half of them seem drunk! Only three fatalities so far."

"Ours or theirs?" Lyaren asked.

Grun seemed to stiffen but quickly shook off his offence.

"Theirs, Sir, the Elite Guard seldom take casualties, Sir."

Lyaren smiled. "I'll remember that, Lieutenant Grun. No one has exited from the back of the building, suggesting the higher-ranking priests have already left the city. It would make sense for them to return to their allies just prior to the final attack on Lord Daniel... Still, better safe than sorry, take me through the temple; if anyone is hiding I will sense them."

They entered the temple through the large wooden doors to the front of the building, which hung precariously from the few remaining hinges. Lyaren was sickened by the energy of the place. The air inside reeked of death and hummed with the dark, thick, perverted magic of Xyakah, but thankfully the

201

impression was stale and lacked potency. It was obvious the magic workers were long gone. The few priests remaining cowered in a corner of the largest of the assembly chambers, surrounded by Elite Guards and looking defeated and dejected. They wouldn't put up a fight.

So far this operation was proving to be less problematic than Lyaren had expected; it appeared the priests had been relying on their plan to work. Lyaren wondered how Tarrin and Rudley fared with their part of the operation, hoping they also met with little or no resistance. Quickly completing his search of the building, Lyaren left Grun and his men to escort the priests to the dungeons and hastened back to the castle to check on Daniel.

With Lyaren and Tarrin out with the Elite Guard to round up any potential enemies, and Myllasanndia fussing over Daniel, Ela found herself once again alone in her room. Tilly had made an excellent job of restoring order to her chamber, and Ela was pleased to see that a cold supper and jug of wine had been left out for her. Suddenly ravenous she sat on the bed with the plate of food in her lap and devoured every delicious morsel. Then, without bothering to change, she sank back onto the bed and fell into a deep and natural sleep.

It was some time before the pounding on the door penetrated her dreams and registered in her conscious mind. Fighting her way back to wakefulness Ela rose and cautiously opened the door. She was relieved to see her usual guard smiling brightly at her.

"Good morning, My Lady," the young man offered. "I'm sorry to disturb you, but My Lord Daniel is asking to see you."

Instinctively Ela's hand went to her hair, she must look a sight! Begging the guard's patience she hurriedly splashed a little cold water in her face and pulled the comb through her hair, catching it up in a loose braid. Then she followed the young man through the labyrinth of corridors to Daniel's chambers.

As the young guard opened the door Ela was warmly greeted by Lady Nunnington who ushered her inside. The door was quickly closed behind her and Ela found herself in a formal but cosy bedchamber, only slightly larger than her own. The centre of the room was taken up by a large four-poster bed upon which, propped up by a wall of pillars, sat a slightly pale but very alive Lord Daniel Nunnington. Daniel's smile vanished as Ela moved closer, propelled forward by an insistent Myllasanndia.

"Thank you so much for coming, my dear," Myllasanndia welcomed her. "Daniel and I have been talking and we have so much to say, so very much."

Ela found herself steered to a large, welcoming chair placed close to the bed. The cushions were warm, suggesting that Lady Nunnington had occupied the chair herself only moments before.

"Mother is right." Daniel added as she sat. "We both owe you a debt of thanks and a very big apology."

Ela smiled, a little uncomfortable under the attention. "No, really, there is no need."

"There is every need," Daniel responded firmly. "My mother and I both grossly underestimated you and misjudged your friend, Lyaren. Last night, were it not for your friend, we would both be dead and the enemy would have won a valuable victory in the war. Because of your actions and those of your friends, we have stopped their plans in their tracks and hopefully gained valuable information. With luck we may also now have the time necessary to pass this intelligence on to the king. You may have helped to save many lives tonight, Lady Elayna, not just mine, and I was a fool not to realise the truth of your situation sooner. I should have spoken with you as an equal when you first arrived and not dismissed you as I did. I am sorry."

"I appreciate your apology, My Lord, but really it is not necessary. Lyaren and I came here out of necessity – our lives were in danger and we needed sanctuary. We knew the danger when we came; we never expected you to welcome us with open arms. As it turns out we have now gained your trust and for this we are thankful. Let us help you gain control of your city and then we will be on our way. We have a long way to go and I for one am keen to get under way."

"Please, Elayna, call me Daniel, and will you tell us your story... In full, I mean. I know you shared a great deal with my mother, but I believe there is more. We will help you however we can."

"The situation as I explained to your mother is complicated. I don't really understand what is going on myself! It just seems that for some reason Lyaren thinks I'm important." Ela laughed. "I think it will come to nothing, I can't see what's so different about me. Nevertheless, I find myself in the centre of unusual events and, with everything so frightening and confusing, I have one constant in my life and that is Lyaren. I trust him completely." She looked Daniel straight in the eye and was gratified to see acceptance and genuine concern mirrored back. "I know he will only act in my best interests and that he will protect me with his life. I can't explain how I know this, but I do."

"I believe you are right, child," Lady Myllasanndia whispered, taking her hand comfortingly. "I must ask though, Elayna, are you sure this is what you want? You know Daniel could still marry you. We could offer you a safe life with us. No more running."

"I wish that was the case, but I know I would not be safe here. This is bigger, I think, than just my safety. I have this strange link to Lyaren's magic, I can't explain it; I feel like I should know something really important but I can't quite remember it. I have to find my answer and I think Lyaren is the only one who can help me do that." Ela smiled. "I know Ly and I belong together." She turned to Daniel, his eyes shone brightly and still held the acceptance but now also a sadness. "I'm sorry, Daniel, I do appreciate your proposal, but I cannot accept."

"Thank you for your honesty, Elayna, this answer I will take as the end of the matter. Now ladies, if you will both excuse me I will dress and get this day started. We have much to do and an army marching upon us! I suggest we have breakfast in my private office this morning. Mother, will it be all right if I ask Lieutenant Grun to join us? I suspect Rudley would want him there."

"A good choice, Daniel," Myllasanndia smiled. "He will always be loyal."

"Yes, I think so too." Daniel reached over and pulled the bell-rope hanging from beside his bed. Myllasanndia and Elayna both curtsied to the young lord and left the room.

Myllasanndia led Ela down the corridor in the opposite direction to her own room. This was Daniel's private wing of the castle. As such, it was warmly decorated with tapestries and rugs but it lacked the grand ostentation of the more pubic parts of the keep. The corridor ended with a small, nondescript door which Myllasanndia opened directly, revealing a large, airy dining room with a full-length glass window overlooking the city below. A family-sized table resided in the centre of the room, while a selection of adult and child-sized chairs were arranged in a mismatched array around a small fireplace. The walls of the rooms were lined with wooden shelves, most of which were taken up by books but some held an assortment of childhood objects.

"This was Daniel's nursery once," Myllasanndia confessed. "It's the room he feels most comfortable in and that's why he had it converted into his own private space. He doesn't spend much time here anymore, but that's a good thing. No one will think to look for us here and only the more trusted members of staff have access to this area of the castle. The door opened as she was talking and in glided a procession of servants, bearing an assortment of linen and utensils. They curtsied functionally to the two women and efficiently went about transforming the room for breakfast.

Ela and Myllasanndia sat quietly for a while. It was obvious that Myllasanndia was exhausted. Ela suspected the woman hadn't slept at all and using all that magic must be taking its toll on her as it had Lyaren. Ela listened as Myllasanndia's breathing slowed and the woman dozed in the chair. She allowed her own thoughts to wander.

What would their next move be? She and Lyaren had to find a way out of the city but the countryside was overrun with the lizard men, how could they ever get past them? Then there was Calin and the townsfolk of Lower Gonfiels, they should be arriving at any time. Could they have run into trouble? She hoped not! Finally her thoughts returned to her latest worry. What was wrong with her? Why did the magic affect her so? Thinking back she could remember feeling slightly nauseated when she had first met Lyaren, but over time it had passed. She had felt it in the woods too, as they had fled from her home, but at the time she put it down to her own fear. Suddenly it was as if she had become so much more sensitive. She could feel it now, the niggling pull of the magic nestled in Myllasanndia's chest. She let her senses take-in the area, feeling for the uncomfortable tightness in her stomach. Yes, it was there – a different taste this time – she could feel Lyaren's magic and it was moving closer to her.

On cue the door swung open and in marched a smartly-dressed Daniel followed by an exhausted and dishevelled Ly. Both men smiled as they saw her and came to join them on the sofas.

"Good morning." Ly grinned, and some of the exhaustion lessened around his eyes.

"Good morning, Lyaren." Myllasanndia welcomed, waking instantly.

Ela smiled back warmly. "I'm glad you are back safely. Is the temple taken care of?"

"Yes, all sorted and safe for the time being." Lyaren replied. "I came straight back to check on Lord Daniel, who incidentally has made a remarkable recovery. I was hoping to find Tarrin and Rudley back too."

"I believe both men have returned from their mission." Daniel interjected. "My men report our dungeons to be full of very disgruntled nobles and councilmen, but that can't be helped right now; if they're innocent they will be released soon enough. I've requested Rudley and Tarrin join us for breakfast and sent for Grun too. Shall we move to the table? I'm starving."

Tarrin arrived several minutes later looking none the worse for the night's escapades. Daniel insisted they ate first and reported back afterwards and so that is exactly what they did, devouring the eggs, ham and honey cakes as if they had never before seen food. Moments later, Rudley and Grun appeared; both seemed a little uncomfortable but after a few mouthfuls of food relaxed into the meal. Myllasanndia chatted light-heartedly, giving everyone a recount of her husband's condition. Lyaren asked Daniel a few questions about his own health, checking the wound was fully healed and no side effects were emerging from either the injury or the magic. Other than that the company was silent. As the last of the food was scraped from the plates, servers efficiently removed the wreckage of the meal and made their departure, leaving the group in private.

It was Daniel who brought the meeting to order, clearing his throat he addressed his guests. "I believe it would be appropriate to begin this meeting with an apology." He looked lovingly towards his mother. "I was warned not to trust General Griss, but to my own cost I thought I knew better. My judgment was off. Indeed, for a while I believe it has been off more than it has been on. I have grossly misjudged Master Lyaren, the man to whom I now owe my life; underestimated Lady Elayna, whose knowledge of the situation far outweighs my own, and been damn right rude to my guest Prince Tarrin of the Clans. Friends I am truly sorry, but the past is just that and now we must look to the future. Our scouts tell us the lizard army is on the march. Preparations for a siege are well underway and we can withstand years here in this fortress, however this will stand for naught if the enemy walk amongst us disguised as our friends. And so, gentlemen, with this in mind, now to your reports…Grun?"

Lieutenant Grun began to stand but Daniel motioned him back to his chair. "It has been a long night, Lieutenant, and rest will not be to hand for some time, I fear. Sit and give your report."

"Thank you, My Lord." Grun sat and began his report. "The operation at the temple was a success. The building has been burnt to the ground following a thorough search. The few remaining priests were arrested and are now locked in the dungeons. There was no sign of magic, and My Lord Lyaren made a thorough search of the area to confirm this. My men took no casualties in the operation."

"Good work, Grun." Daniel nodded then turned to Colonel Rudley. "Colonel, your report?"

"Yes, My Lord. I must also report a successful mission. We worked in silence, targeting each family-home simultaneously. When informed of the situation most recognised their duty and came willingly. These we have made comfortable in the dungeon as Lady Nunnington instructed. The family of General Griss was less cooperative. His sons were dressed and waiting; I believe they knew of their father's involvement. They put up a short struggle and two of my men received slight injuries. The operation, however, was a success as these men are now isolated in the dungeon and both under close guard. My men made a thorough search of the family property and the servants have also been apprehended, although I suspect they will be found innocent as they put up no resistance at all." Rudley nodded as he finished his report.

"Thank you, Rudley," Daniel responded quickly. "And well done on a successful night's work. But are we safe yet? Lyaren, what do you think?"

Lyaren measured his response. "It's impossible to say for sure, My Lord, but I believe there are a few more precautions we could put into place. The household staff must be checked soon, especially those who work closest to the family. Also, there are many guests staying in the castle. These, I believe, pose the greatest danger, as they have the run of the castle and come into close contact with all of you. Some even have small personal guards. The good news is that Lady Nunnington has met these people and should already be aware of any possible threats."

All eyes turned to Myllasanndia.

"Is that the case, Mother?" Daniel asked.

"Well I didn't sense that anyone wanted to kill us, although there are definitely secrets. But how do we move forwards? These people are our guests; they have shared our bread and drunk our wine. We can't just order them to a room for assessment like we did with the Elite Guard."

"I would suggest with respect, My Lady that this would be the best course of action. Once they are found innocent we can explain the need for our actions and hopefully they will appreciate the gesture." Lyaren smiled.

"Very well." Daniel agreed. "Can you check all these people alone, Lyaren? Or do you need my mother?"

"No, I'm sorry My Lord; your mother's gift is very unique. My magic can amplify it but I can't control the reading without your mother." Lyaren turned to Myllasanndia. "I'm sorry, Lady Nunnington, I know this must be taxing on you."

It was Daniel who replied. "My mother is very important to me, gentlemen, how do we go about doing this without exhausting her? You know she has not slept for over twenty four hours."

"I would suggest..." Lyaren was cut off mid-sentence by a heavy pounding at the door. Silence descended as each person remembered the last hasty knocking of a door only a few hours previously. This time, however, the door opened and two members of the Elite Guard marched into the room with one of Tarrin's Horse Clan riders.

"Sahain," Tarrin stood and began to move towards the exhausted woman but she proudly drew herself upright and motioned that she was well.

"I'm fine." she assured.

"I'm sorry for the interruption, My Lord, but I was assured by Lieutenant Grun that you would want to hear any news regarding the village of Lower Gonfiels straight away." the guardsman announced.

"You are correct." Daniel looked at the young woman – she was very young, he realised. "What news?"

"I have been sent ahead by Teah," Sahain looked directly at Tarrin. "The villagers are about half a day's march away but have been surrounded by a large group of lizard men. They have taken up defensive positions but they weaken and the lizards grow bolder. If they do not receive reinforcements all will be lost."

"I must go!" Tarrin was halfway to the door before anyone could stop him.

"Tarrin wait, please, just one moment." Tarrin stayed; his whole body strained to move but he waited.

"Take five hundred of the household cavalry and one hundred of the Elite. Kill those swine's and bring our people home safely."

Tarrin smiled though his eyes told a darker tale. "With pleasure, My Lord."

"Permission to assist?" Rudley asked.

"Granted. Grun, you will take command of the remaining Elite and act as General until Rudley returns. Rudley, when you get back you're my new General."

Grun looked dumbstruck. As Rudley and Tarrin marched from the room, he managed a feeble "Yes My Lord" and quickly retook his chair, his pallor a little green.

Ela looked to Lyaren. "We should go, Calin's out there."

"I know but I trust Tarrin and we are needed here." He turned back to Daniel. "I suggest we plan our order of examination, spacing each group to allow your mother time to recover and working through the most trusted first in order to strengthen our position."

"Very well," Daniel conceded. "Then we'll begin with the family staff, followed by the castle guests. Next, the noblemen in the dungeon and then we'll move onto household staff and palace guards. Griss's family can wait until last."

Calin watched the open land around them, every nerve of his body alert. The Sandkind had been attacking their group on and off for the last day. They were obviously members of a small scouting group, or they would have attacked more forcefully, however, they had underestimated the sheer tenacity and ingenuity of the people of Lower Gonfiels. What had begun as a small skirmish with a group of Horse Clan scouts had become more substantial and had finally taken its toll. They had lost about ten of the villagers now, mostly older members of the community who had bravely taken the brunt of the attack so that those more able could escape to the protection of the larger group. Now the convoy had formed a defensive ring with their ragtag assortment of objects and carts, sheltering the more vulnerable, while those able to fight met the attacks as they came. So far they had managed to hold the Sandkind back but they knew that if they got close enough to fire their wagons all would be lost. Thankfully this group seemed to have no archers in their company, while Lower Gonfiels on the contrary had plenty. This, along with the small regiment which had joined them from Stagsonton and the skills of the clanswomen meant that so far they were holding their own. Despite this Calin knew it was only a matter of time before the enemy's reinforcements arrived and they would be overrun. The camp was silent. Even the children knew not to make a sound. All ears and eyes scanned the terrain.

The drumming of hooves announced the arrival of a scout and Calin recognised Teah instantly as she rode into his line of vision. God, she rode that horse well. It was as if the two of them became one creature. She didn't seem to use her hands or legs to command the animal; rider and beast just responded to one another with pure fluidity. Teah's jet-black hair had worked itself out of its braid and flew wildly as she rode towards him. She was enlivened with energy and her eyes shone with a fire. As she reached the boundary of the camp a cart was pulled aside to allow her in and Teah leapt from the horse's back. The creature never slowed its pace, heading straight to its fellow beasts over by a makeshift water trough.

Calin, Samuel and Hayal greeted her hurriedly and she reported instantly. "They just attacked our perimeter again but they seem to be holding back now. I think we have inflicted significant damage to their ranks; it's obvious that they simply want to hold us pinned down for as long as it takes for their reinforcement to arrive. We have spotted large dust clouds to the west. I've sent out two scouts to investigate but they should have been back by now."

"What about casualties, have we lost any more of our own?"

"Not yet, the lizards are poor fighters they rely on numbers for victory and seem to care not for the deaths of their comrades. I will eat and rest for a while then take out the next group so that those patrolling can get some rest."

"I can take the next group out," Calin told her. "You need a proper rest too, especially if their reinforcement arrives."

Teah smiled. "I'm too alive to rest; I can do that when I'm dead."

"Well you're not dead yet and if we can help it you won't be for some time." Kayel chipped in. "I must thank you and your riders again for all you are doing. You have organized a group of hunters and farmers into an effective cavalry, and if we get through this it will be because of you and yours."

213

It was true – the passion of the women and their skill with their horses had inspired the villagers and within a matter of hours they had created a cavalry.

Calin followed Teah over to the small cooking fire which the women of the village had built and sat with her as she gratefully accepted a bowl of stew. At least the villagers had managed to bring a healthy supply of good food with them.

"I think you should take a couple of hours. Let's face it, we've no intelligence to suggest our reinforcements are even coming, we don't even know for sure that Sahain made it to Stagsonton, let alone that she enlisted extra support from Lord Nunnington. When that army of lizards gets here you need to be ready to fight."

Teah sat quietly for a moment considering his concern. "Very well..." she said. "You take out the next group, I'll take a short rest and we will be ready to kill those lowlifes together." She smiled and mischief flashed in her eyes.

Calin recognised that look; he was in for a jibe or about to be the butt of her joke. The joke never came. Instead, Teah reached over and placed her hand on his cheek. She gently ran her finger down the side of his face, feeling the definition of his bone structure. Her fingers traced the small scar by his chin, a gift from a lizard warrior. Calin froze, uncertain what this meant, but then all doubt fled as she reached in and kissed him, gently, tentatively but then – as he instinctively responded to her – with intensity and passion. A ripple of pure pleasure pulsed through his blood and then her lips were gone. He felt alone, almost as if he would cry with grief at the loss. He opened his eyes; he didn't remember closing them. Her eyes were there, waiting for his. They held no mischief; Calin saw something else, something he didn't recognise; something new.

"We both must live, I think." Teah said simply. "What do you think, Calin of Waydonfield?"

Calin took her hand and gently brought it to his lips kissing it softly. He wasn't used to sensitive – he was a smith – but in that moment she was the most delicate of flowers and he held her with the utmost of care. "Yes, I think you are right."

They sat in silence as Teah ate. Then Calin walked her to a makeshift sleep area and ensured she had blankets and a clear, dry place to rest. He knew she didn't need his help, but appreciated that she accepted it. Once she was settled he left; there were no words, they had already said all there was to say. He knew in his heart that he had just pledged himself to this amazing woman and, no matter what, there was no going back for him – not now, not ever.

Kayel had assembled the rested party of warriors, a mixture of clanswomen, villagers and members of the regiment from Stagsonton. They were all well armed, albeit in some cases with unorthodox weapons but nonetheless they were battle ready. They needed no rousing words; they all knew they fought for the lives of their loved ones. So, mounting his beautiful warrior's horse, Calin led his men out to battle.

Time slipped by painfully slowly. The scouts reported to Calin and Kayel every twenty minutes or so. A unit of enemy warriors around five hundred strong was making its way towards their position. Even with the arrival of Teah's half of their fighting force they were outnumbered two to one. Not impossible odds but an even larger force followed behind that one and the delay this battle created would open up the time the enemy needed to be upon them. Calin felt every passing moment. His eyes were on the landscape before him. His mind was on the families and children behind. He and the horse-warrior women could have left hours ago and may even be safe by now, but that was never an option. Teah had needed to order Sahain to take the plea for help to Stagsonton.

Noise erupted from behind him as Teah rode out with the remaining warriors. They were a formidable looking force and Calin knew they were all skilled with the weapons they carried. Lower Gonfiels was a border village and used to dangers from the north. Just not on this scale. Teah's horse drew up next to his. They could hear the distant sound of marching and the ungainly drum of horses trotting in a non-regimented formation.

"They draw near." Teah stated.

Calin looked back to the villagers behind them. Then again out towards the sound of the approaching army. "Yes." he agreed.

Off towards the horizon a bright flash of sunlight on steel blinked in and out of being, followed a moment later by more flashes. The flashes became more frequent; the drumming of feet and hooves more insistent. The very ground shook with the approaching army of horrors. Calin drew his sword with his right hand and ran his left hand over the assortment of knives he now wore around his torso. He heard the hiss of Teah's blade as it slipped from its sheath, a sound repeated as their companions did likewise. "Hold!" he shouted. The world held its breath...

Then the enemy were there. A collective intake of breath hissed around him as his companions set eyes on the monsters before them. The lizard men held a rough line just out of bow range. They began to growl a low, guttural animal sound. One of the larger lizards rode out on his shabby pony. The creature quivered under his weight. He wore slightly more armour than his fellows and carried a huge double-bladed axe, which he held aloft. The creature screeched in its nasal growl of a language, which Calin didn't understand, then rode forward until it stood only a short span away from him. "Relent now and we will show mercy to your women!" The creature grunted in broken Maldoran.

"You know nothing of mercy!" Teah threw back at him, hate and anger in her voice. "Know that this day you face the women whom once you terrorised and the warriors of Lower Gonfiels. We face you without fear and we will have revenge for our loved ones! Know that this day will be your last!" As her words flew to her target Teah launched forward and in one graceful motion removed the creature's head from its body. As the warm blood sprayed over her face and ran into her mouth chaos erupted around her and the battle was met.

For Calin the world narrowed down to the smallest portion of his vision. He noticed every detail before him: the hand each sword was held in, any weakness in muscle structure or posture, the ponies most skittish, the low-pointed blades of the infantry men rushing amongst the cavalry, the huge axes of the giant lizards, fear in the eyes of the dying, surprise as his blade removed an arm or slid through a chest. Teah had been by his side at first but now she was gone. He couldn't think of her, she knew what she was doing. He ducked as an enormous axe flew past his ear. The ground around him was littered with bodies and gore but his beautiful horse never once missed his tread as he bit and kicked at the enemy, breaking bones and weapons alike. For a moment Calin was alone, a pocket of calm in the midst of the battle. He took a moment to look around. The Sandkind army had taken losses but so too had their own. Human bodies lay amongst the dead of the enemy. Calin recognised faces, friends. They were still hopelessly outnumbered. Then the space crushed in on him and, once again, battle lust took over. More time passed, his movements were instinctive now. The lizard men looked terrifying and brutal but they had no control and his blade took many lives. He had been cut off from the remaining villagers. He could see Kayel – he had rallied his archers and taken position before the villagers' camp. Then in an instance Teah was there, by his side. "This way." she shouted and he followed her through the mass of the enemy, cutting a path to the now gravely depleted rally of the defenders. Samuel was there and one of his sons, though he couldn't see the older brother and many other faces he knew well were now missing.

"We can't hold them much longer," he shouted. "We should retreat behind the archers."

Teah nodded and turned her horse. The others followed. At their approach the archers ceased their fire until they passed through to safety. Then a barrage of arrows flew over their heads and the lizard men directly behind them fell. Safe for a moment, Calin rode up to Kayel. "How long can we hold them?" Kayel pointed to his quiver, it was almost empty. "This is hopeless! Goddess what can we do?"

Noise erupted from the south. The game was up, they were surrounded. He looked at Teah, her eyes welled a little as her thoughts echoed his. The ground shook and then there were horses all around them. Calin waited to die; but he didn't. The horses parted around their group pressing on past them and into the enemy lines. "They're human," he heard someone say. "Look!" And there it was, the banner of Stagsonton, flying high. The Goddess had heard them. They would live another day. His friends would live another day.

Chapter 8
Deception

Myllasanndia took a long sip of her sweetened lemon juice. Its tanginess seemed to chase away the taste of the magic from her mouth; it helped her to relax and she felt her body regain a little strength. She and Lyaren had scanned all of the family's palace staff and had been relieved to find that all were loyal. Myllasanndia had fretted over what she would do had one of them been found to be a traitor. Thankfully that had not been an issue. The process had taken several hours and they had planned to spend half an hour resting before beginning to assess the visiting castle guests. Lyaren had excused himself and gone to check on Daniel. The elf seemed not to tire as she did. She had heard stories about the elves as a girl – growing up in the northern territories, everyone did, but she had never met one and hadn't realised just how powerful they were. For the thousandth time she thanked the Gods for bringing Lyaren to them just when they needed him the most. Daniel was alive because of him; she was alive because of him.

The soft warmth of the sun's rays cut through the window and washed over her face but the light was too bright and she was forced to close her eyes. Exhaustion took her and she drifted into a light sleep.

When she woke, the light had left her eyes and instead shone high on the ceiling of the room. She had exceeded the half-hour nap she had planned to take. Lyaren sat in the chair to her left, his eyes also closed, but, as she moved so did he, instantly alert.

"Oh Lyaren, you should have woken me!" she chastised.

"That was not necessary," he assured her. "You are a valuable asset to your son right now, I have an obligation to protect you and keep you safe. You obviously needed the rest and now you will be better able to do what must be done."

She sighed deeply. "Yes, I suppose so. Do you know if the guests have been assembled ready for us?"

"Yes, in the formal audience chamber. They have been told Lord Daniel wishes to address them. However, your guards report a little animosity in the room. I believe they have been assembled for a good hour or so now, so if you feel ready I suggest we get started."

Myllasanndia stood and Lyaren took her arm. As they walked to the audience chamber they discussed their strategy. The nobles couldn't just be ordered to present themselves, as the servants were, they would require a fuller explanation. However, to tell them the truth risked warning anyone who may be disloyal of their intelligence and so giving them chance to escape the inspection. They decided they would update the guests on the situation regarding the approaching army and request that each party present their intent for the forthcoming siege. Lyaren would record their statements while Myllasanndia scanned the group.

As they entered the chamber the clamour of voices which rang around them instantly fell silent.

Lyaren was pleased to see a large contingency of Elite Guard posted around the room – if anyone did step out of line they would be ready for them. He followed Myllasanndia up onto the raised dais at one end of the formal room, where a table and two chairs had been placed.

Myllasanndia stood before the desk and calmly addressed the expectant room. "My Lords, Ladies and honoured guests; I beg your forgiveness for the delay and any inconvenience that this has caused. I also offer our thanks for your patience. Lord Daniel, my son, is tied up with urgent matters of state but he has asked that I deliver this message on his behalf." She paused for effect, as if collecting her thoughts. This was a ruse, she knew exactly what she was doing, but it was better if the guests saw her as a bumbling and unsure, elderly woman. "It is with great sadness that I must inform you that our worst concerns have now been confirmed. We are at war with the Sandkind – the lizard men of the northern dessert – and, as such, we must take action immediately." Myllasanndia waited for the news to settle on the assembled nobles and their staff. Rumour had been rife around the palace but this was the first official acknowledgement of the situation. "We have intelligence to confirm that an enemy legion, over ten-thousand strong, march this way and will be upon us within the week. This leaves us with no choice but to close and seal the city gates and prepare for a siege. In order to ensure you are all kept well informed; my son has asked that you register with us your intentions. Daniel bids me to offer you sanctuary with us here in the castle for as long as the siege may last. However, he is aware that many of you may wish to return to your own estates and families before the gates are closed for good. Master Lyaren here will record your statements so we can help you fully and ensure all preparations are moved along swiftly."

Myllasanndia turned to Lyaren and nodded. As she stepped back and sat in the large chair placed for her, Lyaren stepped forward quill in hand.

"Ladies and Gentlemen, we will give you a few moments to consult with your parties. Then, if you could make an orderly line I will speak with you party by party; please step forward as soon as your decision is made."

At first the room remained silent. These people were not used to being told what to do but neither were they used to being at war and the shock of the news had confused their aristocratic tendencies. Not for long. The hall erupted into a cacophony of loud and angry voices. Some groups moved hastily towards the doors, only to find them barred by the Elite. Thankfully the guests, and their entourages, had all been required to surrender weapons upon arrival to the castle and so the descent was quickly quashed. The volume level descended too; hushed stony mumbles and mutters rumbled around the room. The first party approached the table. A rotund little man with a balding head and huge eyebrows waddled forward, followed by an austere-looking woman dressed all in black and two younger women, equally austere, who were undoubtedly their daughters.

"Lady Nunnington," he stated, in a slightly high-pitched voice. "My family and I wish to thank you for your hospitality. However, we are already prepared and are keen to depart as quickly as possible."

"And I wish you every luck with your journey, Lord Trancmean. I hope when this is all over you will be able to spend a more pleasant stay with us here at Stagsonton." Myllasanndia looked over to the young guard just to her right. "This party are welcome to leave." she told him, and automatically a small group of Elite guard stepped forward and escorted the party out of the room.

Lyaren, his voice low so only she could hear, said "Gods Myllasanndia, he hates you!"

"True," she replied, her voice also low. "But he means us no personal harm. His hatred is fuelled by jealousy of our family position and the refusal of Daniel to meet his daughters, both of whom are of marriageable age. The man has a large but old estate three days ride southeast of here. He should be able to get home before the enemy army arrives. But, once there, he will not have the defences to resist an attack. I suspect that will be the last we see of the Trancmean family."

A rough queue had formed now and both Lyaren and Myllasanndia turned their full attention to the task at hand. Lyaren was shocked at the difference in attitude of these nobles in comparison to the palace staff. Although he didn't feel the full depths of emotion, which Myllasanndia felt, he got enough to realise just how hard it must be for Myllasanndia to function in her role with her gift constantly informing her of knowledge she may prefer not to have. He couldn't begin to imagine how hard it could be to socialise with people who emitted such emotions as jealousy, distain and dislike for you constantly. Despite the torrent of negativity, none of the guests made any attempt to hide their feelings and it was obvious their situation was nothing more than the normal bearing of aristocracy. Most of those who stepped forward thanked Lady Nunnington for her hospitality and requested that they be allowed to leave Stagsonton immediately. These the guards escorted out. Lyaren felt a distinctly different energy wash over him as the next group strode forward. A small party of five young men stepped forward and bowed respectfully. "My Lady," the eldest looking man began. "Our families are on their way and due to arrive any day; we would ask your permission to ride out to meet them and escort them into the city, we ask for sanctuary."

"And we will do anything we can, Jeremy, to help. I know Daniel will be pleased to have his friends close by."

"Thank you, My Lady. Might I ask how long we have? We are a little concerned; our families should be here by now."

"You are right to worry. The enemy roams all over the countryside but they are mainly to the north. Sergeant," She beckoned the guard closer. "Can you arrange a small unit of palace guards to ride out with Lord Jeremy and escort his family to safety?"

"At once, My Lady."

"Thank you, Lady Nunnington, your kindness is overwhelming."

"Daniel would want it this way and so do I. Let us hope the roads to the south east are still clear and you are reunited with your loved ones soon."

The young men bowed together and left.

"Daniel's closest friends," Myllasanndia explained. "He will be relieved to know they are so clearly loyal to him and the kingdom."

"And I am relieved to learn there are some pleasant aristocrats left in the kingdom," Lyaren smiled. "Your family excluded, of course, My Lady."

Myllasanndia chuckled quietly. "Of course." The hours dragged by. Three more parties presented themselves with warm and friendly intention – all requesting sanctuary – while, for the most part, the emotions of the groups were frosty at best and damn-right distasteful at worst. The last three groups remained. As the room became quieter, the emotions of its occupants became easier to read. Lyaren shared a knowing look with Myllasanndia, they had both felt it: *deceit, mistrust; someone was hiding something. No, several people were hiding something and there was also a hint of religious righteousness.*

The next party was large, made up mostly of a strong guard and a group of three young women. Lyaren looked again; no, not women at all but young girls and all were very well dressed. Their gowns were all of the finest silks and satins and coloured in the strongest, most expensive of shades. A heavy-set older man strode forward, obviously a soldier by his bearing.

"We will be leaving immediately!" the man snapped indignantly. "The ladies will visit briefly with their brother and then I will return them to the Summer Gardens."

"Captain Brighams, is it?" Myllasanndia asked.

"Yes!" the soldier replied.

"And which of our young General Grun's sisters do I have the pleasure of meeting today?" Myllasanndia kept her voice light, but Lyaren felt the energy-shift of the emotions like a knife between his ribs. None of the Elite Guard had missed the hand signal Myllasanndia had just given in warning.

The man's eyebrow rose in response to Grun's promotion and new title, but other than that his expression remained neutral. "This is hardly the place for pleasantries, woman! If your son is not here then the enemy is near and I need to get these women home. Get Grun and then we will take our leave. This performance has been a disgrace; I will be reporting back to the High Warden of Summer Garden and suggesting the King himself hears of this mistreatment!"

As one, the Elite Guard stepped forward and drew their weapons. The big soldier standing before Myllasanndia stared at her with open animosity in his eyes. His cheeks were flushed and sweat beaded his forehead; the man almost looked as if he was going to pop.

Myllasanndia didn't flinch. "Sergeant, please escort this party to a private reception room. These are the sisters of General Grun so ensure they are provided with a healthy guard.

"Is this how the nobles of the north treat their guests?" One of the young women stepped around Captain Brighams and drew nearer to the dais, ignoring the blades pointed at her. "I was under the impression that the Nunningtons of Stagsonton and the Highlords of Summer Garden were friends. Is this how Nunningtons treat their friends?"

"Only during war time." Lyaren offered. "I assure you, young lady, we have only your best interests in our sights. Now if you and your party will withdraw to a private room we will endeavour to get your brother as quickly as possible and this whole situation can be fully resolved." Lyaren knew he had said the wrong thing – he felt the hatred fired towards him from the furious young woman, and marvelled at the control she held over her features. There was no indication of her anger showing at all on her beautiful young face.

"And I assure you, scribe, much offense has been taken this day. My party and I will go nowhere under armed arrest. You will allow us to leave immediately." Her voice was crystal clear, authoritative and beautifully controlled.

The Elite Guard took a step closer to the group and the captain stepped forward and gently manoeuvred the young woman back behind him. "What is going on here?" he demanded. "This is war time; I must get my charges back to their family. You have no right to hold us here."

"We have every right, in war time, to protect the people of the kingdom from their enemies. And you and your party are hiding something from us, Captain Brighams! If you wish, your party may remain here while these other groups state their intentions, then we can discuss our concerns in private." Myllasanndia turned away from the Summer Garden delegation and looked over to where the two remaining groups waited. She scanned their faces as she let her gift sift through their emotions and her stomach rolled. Lyaren grabbed her arm, knowing she would need him to anchor her, for what they now faced was beyond anything they had met before. Lyaren cut off his flow off magic and heard Myllasanndia give a soft sigh of relief as she got control. He heard her whisper "I don't know who these men are!"

The remaining two groups were made up entirely of men and, as they walked forward, they formed into one unit. A tall, thin man with a long, pale face and a baldhead stood slightly to the front of the line, a thin smile drawn across his mouth. "A most entertaining afternoon, Lady Nunnington," he calmly stated, clapping his hands together sarcastically. "Tell me, have your son and husband left this mortal coil or do they still cling on yet to this life?" As he spoke he waved his hand out subtly in the air and a tiny pulse of magic rippled across the room. An illusion dropped and a subtle disguise slipped away revealing that each man was in fact armed and confident with their weapons. As one they drew their swords and, without warning, sprang out towards the Elite Guard, most of whom were still focused on the contingent from Summer Garden. The beautiful stately room was instantly plunged into a chaos of nightmares.

The attackers fought like berserkers, with no care for their own safety, and bloodlust shone in their eyes. The girls from Summer Garden screamed as one of their guards crumpled at their side; his head rolled across the floor and a jet of bright red blood pumped into the air, splattering them with its warm stickiness. More of their guards slumped dead along with the Elite Guard who stood by them. The room stank of death. Steel clashed on steel and frantic shouts rang out, amplified by the acoustics of the room.

Held in a pocket of calm within the midst of the confusion the warlock stood stock-still, eyes locked on Lyaren. Both attempted to gauge each other's power. Both were experienced enough to know that magic could be flung back at the caster. Both looked for weakness in the opposition. Lyaren stole a moment to take in the carnage around them. The Elite Guard were not faring well and soon would be overpowered. Only two of the enemy's number lie amongst the bodies which spewed the floor.

Myllasanndia's breathing was fast and sharp behind him. The warlock smiled and Lyaren felt his power building. The fool had mistaken Lyaren's calm for fear. Now he knew he had him. As the bolt of power shot towards him, Lyaren caught it and spun it straight back at the warlock, simultaneously releasing his own energy bolt, which he sent high above the warlock's head. Light flared around the room as the energy met its target. Recognition reflected in the eyes of the warlock, just at the moment that he was knocked off his feet by the power of his own spell blasting back into his body, followed a split-second afterwards by a loud creaking which cut across the clamour of the room. Everything seemed to freeze in an instant as the huge chandelier which Lyaren had targeted plummeted down on top of the warlock, splattering his body into a bloody pulp – a pooling contrast on the high polish of the marble floor.

The doors at the back of the room clanged open as more Elite Guard, led by Grun, burst into the room. As fast as it had begun the chaos was over. Lyaren rushed over to Myllasanndia, who had been knocked to the ground by the impact of the chandelier and lay on the floor. She smiled as he helped her back up to her feet.

"One to our side." she said meekly, eyeing the remains of the warlock suspiciously.

"So it would appear." Lyaren agreed. "Who were they?"

"I don't know; I hadn't noticed them until just now and when I looked at them I didn't recognise them."

"I think we just found the true Xyakahan priests, hiding in plain sight."

"Yes. I think you might be right."

"My Lady, Master Lyaren, we have the situation under control now." Grun reported. "May I check on my sisters?"

"Of course Grun, but please proceed with caution." Lyaren advised. "Something is not right with the energy of their group. They are hiding something!"

Grun gave him a concerned look. He had six sisters who often travelled to Stagsonton under the pretence of visiting their big brother; in truth they came to meet eligible young men at the northern court. The large, familiar figure of captain Brighams was helping the young ladies back to their feet. Their faces, hair and beautiful gowns were covered with dark splashes of blood and their faces were transfixed with revulsion and fear, but they appeared to be none the worse for their ordeal. "Brighams, what is occurring here?" Grun shouted, marching over to his father's guardsman, the man who had taught him to fight and who he had known and respected for all of his life. As the guardsman helped his final sister to her feet and she turned, Grun's eyes met those of the articulate young woman who had spoken out earlier. He stopped in his tracks and his jaw almost hit the ground. He instantly dropped to his knee and bowed his head before the young woman.

"Oh Grunny, it's so lovely to see you again." she said, forcing cheerfulness into a slightly strained voice. "Your sisters told me it would be an adventure to come and see you all the way up here in the wilderness but I had no idea it would be just so exhilarating. Does this sort of thing happen every day in the north? It's very exciting...Stand up you silly boy, it's only me."

"Your Highness..." Grun stuttered. He turned his head to Lady Nunnington. "My Lady, indeed my sisters are hiding a rather large secret! May I present Her Royal Highness the Princess Alexia, daughter and heir of our King, His Royal Highness Edric the Third of Maldora.

Elayna had considered spending the day with Ly but quickly discarded the idea when she realised it meant spending so much time around the magic. In retrospect she knew she'd made the right choice as her head had been pounding for the past two hours and had only just stopped, indicating that the servants must now all be checked and Ly and Myllasanndia must have taken a break. Ela had instead taken a walk, escorted by her now-permanent bodyguards, down to the stables to see Hurricane. The horse was decidedly frosty with her at first, leaving her in no doubt that he was angry at being ignored for days, but after half an hour of vigorous brushing and three red apples (liberated from the large fruit bowl on Daniel's breakfast table) she was well and truly forgiven. Elayna had enquired of her guard where she could exercise Hurricane and he escorted her to a large, private paddock adjacent to the palace gardens. There wasn't enough room for a full gallop but the horse was able to build up to a good trot and jump over the random objects, placed for that purpose, in the centre of the field. An hour later she felt significantly lighter of spirit and her mood had turned from frustration to almost enjoyment. When she returned Hurricane to the stable she declined the stable master's offer to settle her horse back into his stall and instead took another good hour rubbing the beautiful horse down and tending his tail and main. By the time she had finished he really did look splendid. Reluctantly she left his calming presence, checking quickly on Fire and Greg as she passed, and made her way back to the castle. On her way across the courtyard she caught sight of Sahain, the young Horse Clan woman, and called after her. "Sahain, I thought you would have left with Tarrin."

The other woman stopped and waited for her to approach. "Tarrin forbade it, he said I must rest and get this seen to." She indicated the bandage down her left arm. "I'm on my way to check on the women we freed from the lizards' camp, care to join me?"

Elayna felt a pang of guilt. She hadn't even considered her fellow prisoners, knowing they were safe she had removed them from her priority list, but she would feel better knowing they had settled into their temporary home for the time being. "That would be lovely, are they still housed in one of the empty barrack buildings?"

Sahain smiled. "Come and see." She led Elayna around the back of the fortress to the more practical area which housed the regiment. The complex was enormous, providing accommodation and training facilities for an army one hundred thousand strong. It had been a long time since the army had been so huge, these days it was home to a more modest army of twenty thousand infantry and a cavalry of around five thousand men. The women occupied several of the deserted barrack buildings furthest away from the regular army. They passed by several of the empty, low-level, rectangular structures which served for housing soldiers, before the sounds of life penetrated the stillness of this remote area of the castle. "The women chose to set up all together," Sahain explained. "So my people and the kingdom women are all mixed together; we felt it might help those suffering with trauma to see how the clanswomen

231

deal with it. My people are used to hardship and suffering. We set up as if we were at home, with a cooking and cleaning area, sleeping space, communal space and training area. Sure enough, the kingdom women followed suit and before long we had a properly-functioning little community. The kingdom women have even started work on a hospital wing; they had a lot of casualties following the escape but they are all well on the mend now." Sahain spoke proudly of the women's accomplishments and sure enough as they rounded a corner of the formally laid-out buildings they entered what could only be described as the commune of the women. Washing hung on lines between the buildings. The sounds of voices and laughter filled the air, but it mingled with the clash of steel on steel. Ela was surprised to see kingdom women sparring awkwardly alongside clanswomen. Noticing where her attention had gone Sahain explained. "Some of the women asked to learn how to fight. We have been teaching them for the past three days and they make steady progress. They wanted to be able to protect themselves, as all women should."

"Sahain, this is wonderful!" Ela exclaimed.

Sahain grinned back at her. "I know, I am very proud of my sisters who have stayed to work with these women. Come and talk with some of them."

She led Elayna into one of the buildings and her two escorts positioned themselves respectfully at the door. Elayna was surprised to find that, within; the buildings were light and airy. The women had spilt the space into living and sleeping accommodation and the hearth area had been made into a kitchen which hustled with activity as women chopped, peeled and mixed, chatting happily together. Elayna marvelled at the productivity of the women. For herself, the time spent in Stagsonton had been an imprisonment, an inconvenience; and she had plotted her and Ly's escape. For these women, it had been a rescue, a revelation and a new beginning. They had done a good thing bringing the women here. It had to be worth all the turmoil she had endured. Sahain led her over to where a small group of clanswomen sat, working on their swords and chatting quietly. As they noticed Sahain approach they all smiled and one stood, rushed forward and threw herself into Sahain's arms. Ela noticed the girl was little more than a child, perhaps fourteen, and her arm, which she held at an uncomfortable angle, was bandaged carefully. Sahain hugged her warmly. "This is my little sister, Dalhain." she introduced. "She suffered greatly at the hands of our enemy and my friend, Alyha, here has done a wonderful job of nursing her back to health." She introduced a tall blond-haired clanswoman who stood just behind Dalhain. "Look at her now" Sahain said proudly. "I think you will be ready to ride back home with us when Teah arrives with the others." she reassured the girl.

"She is mending well," Alyha agreed. "She has even been holding a sword with her left hand and joining the women in their training."

"Is that what you plan to do?" Ela asked. "Go home, I mean; it will be dangerous with the lizard army so close."

"True, but to us there is no choice." Sahain confessed. "We are worried about our families. If the lizards did come through the Grasslands there will be casualties and our people will need us. If they came around, as we suspect, they could now attack the Clans on two fronts and that will leave our people vulnerable. One way or another we need to get home. Plus, we have our magic. We know the lizard army will be looking for us so, with our magic in place, and moving in a small group, we should be able to avoid detection."

"You are very brave," Ela said. "Your people are lucky to have you."

"This is the way of our people. We live in a dangerous place. As babes we are taught to stand on our own two feet and sit on a horse. As children we learn to fight and protect ourselves. As adults we are warriors, men and women equally. We like to show our feminine side, to wear nice clothes, put ribbons in our hair, but that is for the peace camps. In the Grasslands we are warriors first and women second."

"I envy you, being able to protect yourselves, not counting on others." Ela confessed.

"You have it wrong." Sahain, told her. "We count on each other totally. One loose link could pull apart the whole chain, my mother would tell us. We stand together, it is in our union that we are strong."

"Yes, I see that, but to be equal in that role. Here in the kingdom women are weak; the men take up weapons to protect us while we must hide and be protected. I think these kingdom women have learned a great deal from your people; that they are taking training in arms is amazing. I wonder, though, what their fathers and husbands would say if they knew?" she laughed.

"They would be proud of us!" The voice was harsh and came from behind her. A Kingdom woman had just walked in through the low doorway. Sword in hand the woman marched over towards the group. "I am Jemima," she introduced herself, voice still harsh but respectful. "Back in Waydonfield I was a widow, my husband died from the winter sickness three years ago. He told me to do my best to raise our children, three boys. I cooked, mended, cleaned and provided for them. I traded for food with my neighbours and I thought I did well by them, but when the lizards came I could not save them. They killed my babies in front of me and I could do nothing to stop them. I failed my husband, my boys are with their father now. I will never be weak like that again. I will die with a sword in my hand before I will ever let those demons take another child's life." The woman's eyes were hollow, her frown firm and unyielding, but something shone through in her demeanour – a determination, a purpose. The women of Waydonfield had given up all hope of life after their capture, but now thanks to the clanswomen they had purpose again, Ela realised. They didn't care for themselves, they had already lost everything. Whether they lived or died meant nothing, but they would protect the innocent with their lives and that made them dangerous; at least to the lizards.

"You have my utmost respect." Ela bowed before the woman. "And I am sorry if I caused offense, none was meant. How old were your boys?"

"They were babes – five, seven and eight. Martin, David and Simon." Her voice cracked. "I can still feel them."

"They would be proud of you; you are right."

"I will avenge them at any cost and when I die I will find them once more and we will be a family again."

"Yes," Ela agreed. "I can see that."

"The kingdom women train very hard." Sahain stated the fact, leaving no room for doubt. "We are very proud of our Kingdom sisters. They will make fine warriors."

Ela realised Sahain was right. All the women had been spared by the lizards because of their youth and fitness. They were of an age to learn and were physically up to the demands of the training and, by the Goddess, they had the motivation. The next statement popped out of her mouth before the thought fully materialised. "Will you teach me? I have some basic ability, my brother taught me a little, but while I'm here will you teach me?"

Sahain smiled. "It would be my honour to train you myself."

"And I will partner you," Alyha offered. "But we do need to do something about your clothes."

Ela looked down at the formal riding gown she was wearing. Alyha was right. The wide skirts of the kingdom were fine for riding – they allowed her to sit on a horse like a man, rather than use a dainty side-saddle, covering her legs and maintaining her dignity – but it would get in her way when moving with a sword in her hand. As a child her brother had taught her the basics of sword fighting. He had dressed her in a set of his old clothes and disguised her as a boy so she could make her way down to the small private practice yard and spar with him. That had all come to a sudden halt when their father had discovered what they were up to and, although he had never said, she knew Gaylon had suffered considerably for his part. She looked at Jemima and Sahain and realised that the Waydonfield women had adopted the clanswomen's way of dressing. They had adjusted their skirts to create a loose-fitting pair of trousers, which was covered from the back and side by a loose skirt attached to one of the legs but cut away at the other side.

"I can sew, I'm sure I could make something like yours." Ela began.

"No need." It was the clanswoman, Alyha. She crossed over to a chest at the foot of the third bed along the row and removed a carefully wrapped bundle. "Because of you most of us escaped with our lives and for that we will be forever grateful. For three of our sisters the fight was a step too far. We tried to do everything we could but their injuries were too great. Vikkhi was my best friend. When we were attacked at the Peace Camp she had only just arrived. She was still wearing these when they took her. She was about your size."

Ela took the bundle and unwrapped a beautiful pair of soft, brown doeskin leggings and a tiny leather vest. Unlike the outfits she had seen the clanswomen wearing, there was no skirt attached. Her father would have been mortified! "I can't accept this." she said. "These should go to a clanswoman."

"For everything you did for us, you are a clanswoman." Sahain told her firmly. "Now go and try them on."

Ela changed behind a curtain screen in the sleeping portion of the room. The clothes fitted like a glove. Skin tight, they left nothing to the imagination, but so soft and flexible they moved with her. There was no mirror for her to see herself. Ela decided that may be for the best. As she strode out of the room she felt naked but the other women smiled and, with a satisfied nod, Sahain led the small party out to the practice area. Ela was glad she couldn't see the guards' expressions as she marched past, but the delay in their decision to follow and the quick rush as they followed on behind told its own story.

Sahain handed her a sword. The weapon was scaled to a woman's size but felt heavy and cumbersome in Ela's hand. "Some women choose to learn with practice swords but if you wish to learn fast this is the way." Sahain told her.

"Are you mad, we could get really hurt!"

"The sword is blunt," Sahain told her, and she took an apple from a barrel and pushed it onto the end. "And that takes care of the pointy bit! Now, let me show you our first basic practice exercise."

The routine Sahain showed Ela was more like a dance than fighting – a sequence of twists and turns with the sword. Her body ached with the unusual motions but as the session went on she began to settle into the routine and her stretches became easier and more fluid. They practised like this for well over an hour before Sahain stopped them and suggested a change. Ela faced Jemima and, before she knew it, they were sparring. Metal clashed on metal as each woman tried to push the other's blade away. Sahain watched silently for a while before stopping them. "You have some ability Elayna, but you must develop strength in you upper body if you are to..." Sahain's voice drifted off into the distance as the wave of magic flowed over her. Ela could hear a scream as the rush of nausea consumed her instantly. Then darkness.

Ela opened her eyes. The sun was still in the same position above her head but she lay on the ground, her sword dropped beside her. Jemima, Alyha and Sahain hovered anxiously by her side. "My Lady, are you alright?" Jemima asked, as Ela opened her eyes.

Ela slowly sat up. She felt fine, the sensation had totally left her. "Yes I'm fine, but Lyaren has just used a huge amount of magic." Instantly she knew what that meant. "They must have found traitors in the castle!"

The women helped her to stand but Elayna had already regained full control of herself. She decided it was better to change before she went to check on her friends, but was reassured by the soft pull of Lyaren's magic – still drumming deep in the pit of her stomach – that he was still alive.

Neither of her guards said a word as they rushed back to the castle and, for the time being, she hoped they would keep her activities to themselves (she wasn't sure how her decision to take up arms would be met by the others). It wasn't hard to find Lyaren. The sensation of his magic acted as something of a magnet, the pull of which she followed to the large formal reception chamber where the castle guests were being assessed by Myllasanndia. Entering the room Elayna froze at the scene of destruction before her. Dust still hovered in the air and the smell of blood assaulted the senses. Bodies lay in unnatural positions amongst the piles of wooden pillars, mortar and stonework which littered the floor of the once-grand room.

Lyaren turned as she entered the room. Ela realised he could feel her presence in the same way that she could feel him. He excused himself from the guard he had been talking to and rushed over to her.

"I see you've had some excitement." she stated sarcastically; then, more cautiously, "Is Myllasanndia alright? Has anyone been hurt?"

Lyaren indicated the chandelier now smashed to the ground in the centre of the room. "Most of the casualties are Xyakah's; Myllasanndia is fine, well physically at least. We've had a few... let's call them revelations. Come on, I'll explain on the way, we need to put on our best clothes, we're about to be introduced to royalty!"

And with that he led her out of the room. They made their way at pace back to their quarters, Lyaren hurriedly explaining the situation on the way. Both deep in conversation they practically crashed into a seriously preoccupied Daniel rushing in the opposite direction. The sickly pallor of his face said it all.

"I take it things didn't go well?" Lyaren asked.

"It couldn't have gone much worse!" Daniel confirmed. "The woman, if you can call her a woman, is threatening to have us all taken to trial for treason against the crown. She insists we hold a state ball in honour of her visit and has even requested that we take her on a tour of the deserted outlying villages. I'm not equipped to deal with this; I need to get on top of our own security without the added worry of playing nursemaid to the royal..." He stopped himself and looked away. "Forgive me, I forget myself."

239

Ela bit down hard on her bottom lip but Lyaren heartily laughed, lightening the mood considerably. "No, my friend, you are most certainly not equipped to deal with our visitor. However, you do have people around you who can help. Your mother for one will have sage advice, and I know a thing or two about dealing with spoilt aristocratic adolescents!"

Ela feigned disgust and elbowed him affectionately in the ribs. "Lyaren never had a problem with me." she announced impertinently.

"No," Lyaren agreed. "It's now that I'm having the problem!" And he rubbed his ribs theatrically. "Seriously, Daniel, I think if we handle the girl right and make her see the danger she is in we should still have a narrow window to get her out of here before that army arrives and the siege begins. After all, you do still plan to evacuate your mother to the south don't you?"

For a second Daniel looked desolate but as an idea occurred to him his expression brightened a little. "Mother refuses to leave me, especially with Father so poorly, but perhaps with a princess to escort she will agree and go to the capital after all. Yes, perhaps this may be a mixed blessing after all."

"That's the spirit." Lyaren agreed encouragingly.

"Yes, let's meet in my study and plan how to handle the, urmmmm... Situation."

Grun fixed Brighams with his sharp, grey eyes. What was wrong with the man! Had he lost his mind as he'd aged? Was he entering his dotage? Brighams had been Grun's first teacher of arms and a man he had always looked up to; respected. This whole situation was unbelievable.

"Well, Captain," Grun prompted sharply. "I think it's time you explain yourself! Why the hell are you escorting my sisters, not to mention Her Royal Highness, into the middle of a war zone?"

The man shook his head and rubbed his eyes heavily. "It's not as it looks, Grun." he said with a heavy heart.

Grun didn't give the man an inch. "I'm not interested in excuses, just the truth!"

"The Princess came up to the estate just over a month ago, unannounced. The rumour is that she quarrelled with the King and came up here out of her father's way. When news of war came, your father ordered the Princess and your sisters to be escorted south, back to Stronghold. I sent with them the largest escort I could spare and they went on their way. The next day two guards returned with distressing news. The Princess and two of your sisters had gone missing, along with their horses and some provisions. Your remaining sisters revealed that they were heading north to help with the war. Your father dispatched me and my men straightaway and we quickly picked up the trail, but by the time we intercepted them they were almost here. We decided to spend the night here in the keep and leave first thing in the morning, the hope being no one would be any the wiser and we would get the Princess home as quickly as possible. Next thing, the gates are closed and we're stuck here for another day. The King won't be happy with your father when he hears what's happened." The big guardsman shook his head sadly.

"It may be much worse than you think." Grun told his old friend. "Sit down Brighams. I'm going to tell you the true situation and let's see if you've got any solutions, because I'll be damned if I have."

Grun recounted the events of the past two days while Brighams listened intently. As he finished, the guardsman whistled loudly. "We got Lord Nunnington's message, warning of an army from the north but all this talk of magic and Gods takes some believing, Grun. Are you sure?"

Grun nodded sadly. "You saw the fight in the reception room. You must have noticed the illusion drop when those men attacked."

"No not really. I was too busy watching out for the Princess, but I know some of my men saw it. They are really spooked by the whole event, and I did see that Lyaren fellow do something I just can't explain." Brighams confessed.

"Lyaren is an Elf and a friend. Without him and his magic we would be at a serious disadvantage. You will meet him shortly..." Grun weighed up the situation. "Right, I must talk to the Princess and then report back to Lord Daniel. I suggest you get a little rest and wait for me to send for you. We need to get Alexia out of here and fast but we don't have the men to spare to protect her from this enemy. Gods this is a mess!"

Grun left the guardsman and made his way over to the royal suite. Thankfully Daniel kept the area clean and ready for visitors at all times. Grun had given the Princess a little over an hour to settle in but dare give her no more time. They had to get her out of here and his sisters too! As he rushed over to the royal apartment he discreetly checked all the Elite Guards he passed. He had handpicked those who watched over the Princess. His most trusted men had already been allocated to Lady Elayna but these men were equally trustworthy and would be discreet about their important visitor. At least all the Elite and most high-ranking palace staff had been checked by Lady Nunnington. Stopping before the ornate doors to the royal suite, Grun straightened his uniform and nodded to the guardsman to announce him. The door was thrown open and the guard's voice formally announced, "General Grun, Your Highness."

Grun marched into the room to find the Princess sat with his sisters drinking tea from dainty china cups. He bowed deeply and waited for the Princess to address him before standing. "Oh Grun, you are so tiresome!" the young Princess quipped. "Come and sit with us, will you have tea?"

Grun shook his head in disbelief. "No thank you, Your Highness. I am here on the issue of your safety." Bowing again he took the seat nearest to the Princess, acknowledging his sisters as he did so. "Layla, Lauren," he nodded. "It is good to see you both." His voice softened a little as Grun realised he truly was pleased to see his sisters, despite the situation. "You are both growing so."

The girls smiled brightly at their brother. "It's good to see you too, Grun, we thought Captain Brighams was going to bundle us off before we even had chance to say hello." Layla told him.

"Yes! And it's a shame he didn't!" Grun replied brusquely, burying his emotions. "So ladies, what is your business here in Stagsonton?"

"Why we've come to see you of course, Grun." The Princess cut in. "Your sisters were keen to make sure you were well and I wanted to see what this northern court was like. I had no idea it would be so exciting up here."

"Exciting is not the word I would use, Your Highness." Grun gave his sisters a disapproving look. "I am very disappointed in you both. "Your foolish actions have brought yourselves and the Princess into grave danger, not to mention placing Lord Nunnington in a terrible situation. Now, as well as protecting all the people flooding into this city for help, he must also keep the heir to the throne safe and out of enemy hands." Grun looked back at the Princess. "Your Highness, Lord Daniel Nunnington has called a meeting of his most trusted advisors to plan your safe return to your father. I have been sent to advise you of the meeting and will return to escort you there within the hour. Is there anything else I can get for you while you wait?"

"What a lot of trouble for little old Me." the Princess giggled teasingly.

Grun, face neutral, stood, bowed once again to the princess and left the room.

Daniel Nunnington paced the council-room floor. The stately old council chamber was cloaked with a rich gold and red tablecloth. The formal chairs were highly polished and everyone assembled wore their best clothes. Ela sat quietly by Lyaren's side. Myllasanndia sat to his other side and Daniel's chair, at the head of the table, was pulled back. Captain Brighams, his face weary with worry, sat across from Lyaren. The Elite Guard stood to attention by each door and the window shutters were closed tight on the approaching dusk. This meeting was to be kept as secret as possible. A rattling sound preceded the opening of the two large formal doors, and in marched Grun followed by the gliding figure of the young Princess and her two friends.

"My Lord Nunnington" Grun announced, in his most formal tone. "Please allow me to present, Her Royal Highness, Princess Alexia, accompanied by my sisters the Ladies Layla and Lauren Highlord."

Daniel marched forwards to meet the entering party of girls; Lyaren and Brighams stood and bowed, while Myllasanndia and Elayna curtsied respectfully. The young Princess waited momentarily in the doorway, taking in the scene, before walking up to Daniel and nodding curtly. "Lord Nunnington." she acknowledged.

Daniel bowed stiffly and held out his hand to the young woman, escorting her to a formal chair placed by his at the head of the table. As the young woman took her seat the others sat also – Grun and his sisters by Brighams, facing Ela, Ly and Myllasanndia. Alexia looked disdainfully over the intimate group. "I was under the impression, Lord Nunnington, that I was to be introduced to your council." She paused for effect. "Where are they?" she asked, her eyebrow raised.

"My council, Your Highness, is currently being reinstated, following an assassination attempt on myself by the General of my army and the keep's head steward." Daniel ignored the gasped intake of breath from Grun's sisters and continued with his explanation. "So far those gathered here – my Elite Guard and family servants along with the group of palace guests, which my mother assessed this morning – are the only trusted people in my castle. Unfortunately, Highness, you have arrived just as the enemy hidden within our walls reveals itself."

The Princess had schooled her face well. "I was informed there was to be war here in the north, My Lord. My friends and I have come to your aid in this difficult time. I'm sure my father would want his army to be represented by his bloodline while you deal with this threat."

Daniel ignored the ridiculous statement. "It is my duty, Your Highness, to see you are escorted safely back to your father in Stronghold. The threat we face here in Stagsonton is considerable and we have still not established who amongst us is friend and foe. This you saw for yourself this afternoon."

"Yes," the Princess agreed pleasantly. "My friends and I were somewhat shaken by the experience."

"Yes, Highness, I'm sure you were. Please let me introduce my most trusted advisors and friends. My mother, Lady Myllasanndia Nunnington." Myllasanndia stood and bowed, then regained her chair. "Lyaren the Elf." As he stood Lyaren allowed his illusion to drop.

Both the Highlord sisters gasped once again at the revelation, but the Princess simply smiled and nodded.

"Good to meet you, Lyaren. We have an Elvin ambassador who visits my father's court." she added.

Daniel continued with the introductions. "Lady Elayna Ladaston, Lyaren's ward, and of course you know Grun, my acting General, and Captain Brighams." Each stood appropriately as introduced. "Lady Layla; Lady Lauren." Daniel turned on his most charming smile. He had met the young ladies on numerous occasions over the last few years. "How lovely to see you again, please be welcome."

Daniel bowed and retook his seat. "Your Highness," he continued, his face trained with a neutral expression. "I can see you are a most intelligent individual and so I won't insult you with feeble excuses. I apologise for the situation upon your arrival and the ordeal of the past day. However, you join us in dire circumstances. As we prepare for a siege we have discovered that we have been infiltrated by the enemy and are now attempting to identify the foe within our walls. We are most lucky to have Master Lyaren here with us. He is most skilled in magic and is able to see into the hearts of people. The interviews he held with my mother this morning, although I appreciate that they were distressing for yourself and your company, were in fact critical for the security of your father's kingdom. With this in mind I offer my most sincere apologies for your ordeal. However, I cannot apologise for the process. Indeed, I advise you to see the identification of those vipers in our midst as a victory for you..." He smiled sweetly at the Princess, "And your father, Your Highness."

"In that case, Lord Nunnington; may I thank you in my father's name?"

246

The Princess offered an equally warm smile. Daniel ignored the platitude, from what Grun had told him Alexia was as astute and manipulative as she was naive and foolish. She would be easy to manipulate but only to a point. In the end he needed her to understand the seriousness of her situation, and he really didn't have time to waste on spoiled children.

"Thank you." Daniel replied, and continued with his commentary. "Highness, at this moment my men are scouting the land for the enemy. The guards at our gates are on high-alert and only essential travel is allowed. We wait for the last refugees from the north to reach us and the gates will be closed for the siege. The enemy we face is not of noblemen, knights and warriors, but an army of monsters! They are here to take our land and care not for us. Lady Elayna, could you share your experience with the Princess?"

Ela stood and dropped her third curtsy of the evening. She knew what to say; they had planned the contents of this meeting very carefully, their aim being to leave the Princess in no doubt as to the dangerous situation her foolish behaviour had placed them in, without undermining her authority. "Highness," she began. "I was captured by the lizard men and taken to their camp where I was held prisoner. I was abused and beaten by the creatures and, were it not for sheer luck, would have had my virtue stolen also as, following my escape, I discovered that other women had suffered far worse than I. Only because of my true friend, Lyaren, and his magic do I stand here today. As I know those creatures intended to sacrifice me to their God in the most brutal and barbaric of ceremonies. Highness, I worry greatly for your safety. As a Lady I was considered a great prize and I can only imagine what fate they would bestow upon a princess were you to fall into their hands."

247

Silence descended as Ela completed her statement. The two sisters had turned a sickly pallor and Alexia, her face still held in schooled control, had lost the expression of bemused entertainment, which she had worn since entering the room. Daniel, not giving the woman time to digest the implications of Ela's statement, turned to Grun. "General could you advise Her Highness of our strategic situation?" he asked casually.

Grun stood and began his address. "Highness, my men report one large force of one hundred thousand of these lizard men marching down towards our position. Where possible, the people have been evacuated here to Stagsonton or to the south. We believe the roads to the south to still be relatively safe. However, bands of lizard warriors have been spotted to the north, west and east and we have reports of bloody scenes of carnage encountered on the roads by our patrols. We can only wonder at the horror those poor souls encountered before their lives were ended. We await the arrival of a large unit of our men who set out this morning to help a large group of refugees from the village of Lower Gonfiels. We received notice this morning that they were under siege and that they faced dire odds. We can only pray our help arrives in time. Here in the city we are stocked and ready for the siege; with the force we currently hold here we are estimating the enemy outnumber us five to one so our odds in a battle are poor. However the citadel is in excellent order and is expected to easily deal with the threat. We estimate we can withstand attack for in-excess of a year." Grun nodded once again to the princess and again to Daniel before retaking his seat.

Daniel turned straight to Myllasanndia. "Mother, could you report on our internal security?"

Myllasanndia was his secret weapon. He had never yet met anyone who wasn't in awe of his mother.

He prayed her persona would have the desired effect on the Princess.

Myllasanndia pinned the Princess with one of her most piercing looks. "Young lady," she began. "I can't begin to express my concern for your safety!" Alexia looked the older woman squarely in the eye, the slight not lost on her. Myllasanndia returned the look calmly; she had been a highborn girl once, she had played these games, but never so stupidly! This girl was a fool and it was her role to make her see this for herself. "We have a dungeon full of possible murderers, the legion within our gates cannot be trusted and we have no way of knowing which members of the populace are our friends and which our foe. We cannot secure our own safety, your safety or the safety of your escort. The chances that we will all be murdered in our beds are high and if we do not die this way we may well die in the siege. You are unlikely to make it out of our city alive, let alone make it back to your father." Myllasanndia never let her eye contact drop. It was the Princess who looked away, her face now shaken."

"We have placed ourselves in terrible danger." Alexia stated, the first hint of doubt entering her voice.

Myllasanndia nodded slowly. "As first Lady of Stagsonton I have a city and its inhabitants to worry about. As a mother and wife I have my family to worry about. And now I have you, Your Highness, perhaps the most precious jewel of the kingdom. I will try, as will everyone here in this room to keep you safe, but you need to understand one thing. This is no indulgent entertainment for your diversion. This is war and in war you live or you die. Many are already dead. Do you want to be dead, Princess?"

Alexia took a deep quivering breath; despite her best efforts her lower lip trembled slightly. "No, Lady Nunnington, I don't want to die."

Daniel turned to face the Princess and offered his hand, which she took numbly. Gently, he helped the trembling girl to her feet and, once stood, he kneeled before her. "Your Royal Highness Princess Alexia," he announced formally. "My first loyalty is to the kingdom, its people and its lands. My second is to you. I and my trusted friends will do everything we can to keep you safe and return you to your father, but we cannot guarantee this safety – not from such an unsure footing. Please, Highness, we beg you, will you listen to our counsel? Will you act on our guidance?"

Clearly shaken, the Princess nodded slowly. "Yes, Lord Nunnington, I will do as I am told."

Myllasanndia walked round the table and placed her arm around the Princess in a way only a mother could. The girl turned into her and sobbed silently. "Shush now," Myllasanndia soothed. "We'll do all we can to keep you safe and now that you fully understand the situation our job will be all the easier.

"Trust only those in this room, Highness, and we will continue to keep your presence here secret until we can arrange for your journey home. Will that be acceptable to you?" Daniel asked.

"Yes, My Lord Nunnington, I can see what a difficult position my arrival has placed you in. Thank you for your honesty. We will be ready to leave as soon as you say we can. I can see you have enough to deal with without having me to worry about."

"You are wise, Highness. Thank you for your cooperation. I'll make arrangements for you and your friends to have a quiet meal in your apartments this evening. Then I will organise your guard from a carefully selected group and place Captain Brighams in charge of overseeing them. That way, should anyone not trusted appear in your entourage he will know instantly and be ready to act appropriately. Grun, can you send a coded message to your father? Perhaps if we let him know the supplies he sent with the Captain have arrived and are under our supervision."

"At once, My Lord." He jumped instantly but stayed as Daniel called him back.

"Oh and Grun, you may like to take an hour out to spend a little time with your sisters this evening." Grun turned to look at the two girls who now clung terrified onto each other.

"I will, My Lord. Thank you, My Lord."

Chapter 9
Siege

The reunion between Teah and Tarrin was emotional. Tears of joy streaked both their faces as the siblings rejoiced in being both alive and back together once more. Calin hung back, reluctant to intrude on the moment, but Teah beckoned him over and Tarrin greeted him warmly with a rough bear hug.

"It is good to see you alive my friend." Tarrin grinned.

"That's thanks to you." Calin grinned back. "You and this army may well have bought my friends the time they need to get to safety."

"All will be well, Calin, you'll see. Come, I want you to meet my friend Rudley and then we must get to work mobilising this band of desperadoes you have created and getting them safely behind Stagsonton's defensive walls."

A stout, older man in the formal uniform of the Stagsonton legion stepped forward with the confidence of authority and shook hands warmly with both Calin and Teah. "I've heard a lot about you both." he told them. "What you have done for these people is very brave. You are heroes."

"Is it far back to Stagsonton?" Calin asked, hastily changing the subject. "Will we all make it there before that larger force of lizards arrives?" He glanced worriedly over his shoulder to the scene of the recent battle.

"After Sahain delivered her report we rode briskly and got to you in just under a day." Rudley replied. "If we set out at first light we should make it back before bedtime!"

What remained of the day passed in a flurry of activity as the villagers reassembled the possessions they intended to take with them and discarded those no longer considered worth the effort. Calin was amazed at how the priorities of some of the fussier members of the community had changed. Everyone was focused purely on survival.

That evening they held a memorial for those who had perished in the battle. Many tears were shed as the survivors bid farewell to their loved ones. They were buried together, the mass grave marked out in pebbles with the sign of the Goddess, a crescent moon. Sombrely the evening came to an end and the night drew in.

Calin and Teah stayed close to one another throughout the service and as they helped with the preparations. Although neither said a word about their relationship, their partnership was visible to those who chose to look. Calin wondered if Teah might say something to her brother, but if she had he didn't give any indication. At night the two lay their blankets close and attempted to get some rest but, as was the case with everyone, adrenalin coursed through their bodies and sleep evaded them. Well before dawn the whole party was already mounted, possessions redistributed throughout the larger group, and the villagers of Lower

Gonfiels were finally able to continue their journey to safety.

The assessment of the general castle staff was considerably more manageable than that of the visiting nobles, a small mercy for which Lyaren thanked the Mother. There were hundreds of people employed in one way or another in and around the keep, and if they got through them all in a day it would be a miracle. He and Myllasanndia were seeing the staff in their department teams starting with those who had the widest access to the castle before working outwards to the grounds men, gardeners and grooms. Everyone would be checked, which made the whole process a logistical nightmare, but a detailed list of those employed in the castle had been drawn up and this allowed them to keep track of who had and hadn't been seen. They relied on the more senior members of staff to vouch for those under them and Myllasanndia's gift skimmed smoothly through the threads of their emotions and motivations. On the whole the process ran smoothly if not a little slowly.

Lyaren spared a moment's thought for Ela. He felt guilty for leaving her alone yet again, and the pressure to get back to their own journey and solve the riddle of her magic mounted in his mind. It couldn't be helped, he told himself. These people were desperate and over the last few days they had become their friends. He really liked Myllasanndia, with her shrewd mind and quick wit, and was even warming towards Daniel now he'd stopped swimming in his own self-importance. He knew how imperative it was for him to help here. He could feel it in his gut. If he could help Daniel and Stagsonton prepare a strong response for the enemy his actions could be the difference between defeat and victory for Maldora. Not to mention keeping the lizard army occupied and looking in the opposite direction to where he planned to take Ela. There was still time, he told himself. Just three or four more days here and they would be away, just before the enemy arrived. He estimated it would take a day and a half to finish with the palace staff then about the same to assess the higher-ranking officers of the legions. They had decided not to attempt to formally assess the lower ranks. Instead the officers would be given instruction on how to oversee their men to ensure any traitors were identified as effectively as possible. The nobles in the dungeons wouldn't take long to assess but would be the biggest issue. Those guilty would be executed, and the rest would be angry – very angry! But calming them down and getting them back on side would be Daniel's department. Yes, he thought to himself, as soon as we finish up here Ela and I will head directly east and skim the invaders before turning north and, with any luck, make it to the Silent Forest before the end of summer.

Ela winced as Tilly applied the ointment. "You must be more careful, My Lady," the maid exclaimed. "We are supposed to be keeping you safe here in the castle, not opening up all those nasty wounds you came here with."

"Yes, I know Tilly, I will be careful I promise. I was just so keen to go riding, I didn't wait for the stable boy to help and the saddle it just slipped." Ela lied; she had no intention of letting on what she had really been up to. This morning, after seeing Daniel's itinerary for her, she realised that if she wanted to continue with her fighting practice she would have to do so early, straight after breakfast. This afternoon she was to have an audience with the Princess. Daniel wanted her to have a long talk with the girl and ensure the young woman truly understood the danger of her situation. Then she was to meet quietly with Daniel, Myllasanndia and Lyaren to

256

evaluate their progress, before attending another meeting, this one with Grun and the heads of department amongst the palace staff to support Daniel while he addressed them. Finally she was to be present when the scouts reported back to Daniel on their day's work. Daniel had been true to his word when he had said he would include her in everything, and with a schedule like this she was starting to wish she could go back to being the vulnerable ward he locked in her room for her own protection. No, she told herself, those days were gone. For now she had become Lady Elayna of Ladaston, advisor and counsellor to Lord Daniel Nunnington of Stagsonton.

Tilly interrupted her thoughts as she heaved the heavy, overly ornate gown she was to wear for her visit with the Princess over Ela's head. Despite her best efforts she winced as the heavily-beaded fabric pinched against the developing bruise she had received in her training session this morning. Tilly raised an eyebrow and shook her head. "Well if you will go riding, My Lady!" and she continued to encase her in the torturous gown.

Ela was a little nervous about her visit to the Princess. It had been a long time since she had been in the presence of women of her own age and she knew she would appear provincial and unsophisticated to such a refined woman. No, not woman, but girl, she told herself; the Princess may seem older but she is only fourteen and that made her Ela's junior by four years. As for Grun's sisters, Layla was the eldest at sixteen while Lauren was also only fourteen. Every year counts, she told herself. She looked in the mirror at a woman she didn't really know. In her short life she had already played many roles. She had been Ela the child, Elayna the student, Ela the refugee, Ela the prisoner and now (if she had her way) she would be Ela the maker of her own destiny. This noblewoman looking back at her didn't really exist, although Ela was all too aware that this would have been the woman she should have been had life not been so cruel to her.

Calm down, she told herself. She needed to be relaxed, confident and friendly. She could do this! After all it wasn't as if she didn't have anything to talk about, just lots to hide.

The royal apartment at Stagsonton Keep was, as she had expected, quite beautiful. The wooden furniture gleamed to the highest sheen, while the soft furnishings and throws were plush, rich and luxurious. Ela elegantly curtsied to the young Princess who sat comfortably in an over-sized armchair close to the fireplace.

"Lady Elayna, thank you for your visit, please sit down." the Princess greeted her formally.

Ela sat in a smaller chair opposite the Princess with the fire to her left and Grun's sisters to her right. She waited patiently for the Princess to address her. The moment stretched into the silence and Ela felt the scrutiny of the younger girl, almost like a scientific scholar discovering a new species of insect to inspect. Finally the Princess spoke. "Tell me, Lady Elayna, what do these lizard people look like?"

Ela didn't need to feign a response; when she thought of her time with her captors the revulsion came naturally. "They are shorter than our warriors, Highness, though look human except for their faces, which are covered in green flaky skin which looks like scales. Their eyes are yellow, but the worst thing is their teeth. They have sharp fangs and their fingernails are long and sharp like claws. Their breath smells... Like...Well, like death."

Layla gave a little squeal at Elayna's description but quickly placed her hand over her mouth. Her sister

258

was more forthcoming. "Did they hurt you, My Lady? Were you scared?"

"Please call me Ela, my friends do. Yes, I was very scared. When they first took me they were rough with me, they hurt me. I think they wanted to hurt me more, I think they might have... Well I don't know what they might have done but then their superior saw me and he was angry with his men and stopped them. I don't remember the rest, they hit me hard. When I woke up I was imprisoned and there I stayed until Lyaren, Calin and Prince Tarrin rescued me and the other women."

"Who is this Prince Tarrin?" the Princess asked. "Where is he now?"

"Tarrin is a Prince of the Grasslands Clans. His sister, Teah, had also been taken by the lizard warriors and so he joined forces with my friends and they rescued us together."

"They can't be all that clever, these lizard men," the Princess concluded, "If three men were able to overcome their entire army."

"Oh it wasn't their entire army, Highness, just an advanced unit. And the men who rescued me were far from normal. Lyaren has powerful magic, while Prince Tarrin is a mighty warrior, and Calin is very skilled with a sword."

"Will this be enough to defeat their whole army when they arrive at our gates?"

"I'm afraid not, Highness, the lizards have magic too, as well as the dark power of Xyakah at their disposal. Lyaren's magic was effective because he was able to take them by surprise. I doubt they will let that happen again."

"That's a pity, Elayna. This Xyakah has followers in the south too. I know my father has been concerned by reports of the growing cult. I fear my father's kingdom is in grave danger."

259

"Yes, it could be. But the legion here is extensive and, when the King's army arrives to help, the lizards will be outnumbered." Ela reassured her.

"I'm not so sure, Ela." the Princess continued. "And please call me Alexia, no one is supposed to know I'm a princess and if you all keep calling me Highness the ruse will soon be up. No, I mean, my father's army is a long way to the south. It will take months to get help here, Grun and all his men will be dead before Father's men arrive and then these beasts will come south and we will all die." A small tear appeared in the corner of Alexia's eye but was quickly brushed away. Ela realised she was seeing the real Princess Alexia now, not the spoilt child she had met previously. This Princess was fully aware of both her own and the kingdom's situation. "This citadel was built to withstand a siege for in excess of a year, Prin... I mean, Alexia." Ela explained. "Before the enemy arrives the gates will be closed and it will be Daniel's responsibility to hold and distract the enemy here in order to give the King time to mobilise his armies. We are the kingdom's first line of defence."

"Oh I see," the Princess nodded, without the conviction of belief. "So we will leave before this battle begins?"

"Yes, that's what Daniel plans," Ela explained. "He wants to give Grun's father time to mobilise a unit to meet you as you flee to the south. He is also waiting for General Rudley to return, so he can release Grun from his duties here and allow him to escort you into the hands of his father's men. That way we can be sure you will be safe." She smiled reassuringly. "You can trust Daniel; he won't let anything bad happen to you."

"Mmm, I'm not so sure, the man seems awfully pompous to me, all puffed up and self-important. He doesn't look old enough to do what needs to be done. I think Daddy should send some of his generals up here to teach him how to run an army." There was the other Alexia again.

Ela stifled a laugh; she had acquired a similar attitude towards Daniel upon her arrival at his home. "Daniel is young and inexperienced, he has lost some of his long-term advisors because of their treachery and is doing the best he can under the circumstances, but don't underestimate him. He is learning, and he is learning fast."

"Yes, yes I'm sure you are right. Now enough of war! Come, Ela, tell us of life up here in the north. How do you come to be in Stagsonton? Where is Ladaston? We would know all about you."

Ela relaxed a little and even enjoyed her visit with the Princess in the end. She told the young women all about her home and her family, excluding the parts she and Lyaren had agreed to keep hidden. The Princess proved to be charming, if not a little mischievous, and the afternoon passed pleasantly. Before she knew it her escort had arrived to take her to her next meeting. She curtsied as she prepared to leave and was delighted when the young Princess jumped up and hugged her warmly.

"Thank you for your visit, Ela," the young girl said. "Please come and see us again, if you have time before we leave."

"I will, Alexia." she promised, and with a smile to Layla and Lauren she hurried to her next appointment. The rest of the day dragged a little after that and, although she could see the importance of each and every matter, she had very little to contribute to any of the points on the agenda, other than giving a brief feedback on the mood of their secret visitor. Lyaren talked about the assessments, which had uncovered several more threats, all of which had been smoothly dealt with. Myllasanndia discussed the running and staffing of the household and wider keep in preparation for the siege.

Then plans were made and responsibilities distributed for the remainder of the week and Ela found that her daily itinerary was to follow roughly the same pattern as today. The meeting with the heads of staff was brief but uplifting. Daniel thanked them all for their loyal service, informed them of the dangers ahead and outlined his expectations of them for the upcoming siege, ensuring all knew to pass on his words to their staff and their families. It was as this meeting came to an end that the bells began to ring-out across the city.

"That's Tarrin and Rudley," Daniel informed them. "I left orders that, on their return, the guards on the gates were to initiate the sealing of the outer citadel."

"Does that mean the enemy are here?" Ela asked anxiously.

"No, not yet but it wouldn't do for us to be caught by surprise so, as soon as the warriors and refugees are safely in, the main gates are to be sealed and all traffic will move through the smaller gates which are more easily defensible." Daniel smiled. "Shall we go and see how Tarrin and Rudley fared?"

A shiver ran through Ela's body. She had pushed thoughts of Tarrin and Calin to the back of her mind but, as her thoughts turned once again to them, images of Samuel and Dina surrounded by their wonderfully huge and loving family instantly came to the forefront of her mind. Please Goddess, please let them be alive. Lyaren placed a protective arm around her shoulders – he always knew when she needed him – and she leaned in, allowing him to take her weight for a moment.

"Come on," he urged gently. "Let us go and meet our friends."

By the time they reached the courtyard the whole square was engulfed by activity, in a scene similar to that of the arrival of the Waydonfield and clanswomen a matter of days ago but the chaos here was tenfold. The grooms and Elite Guard frantically tried to guide the villagers around to the available barracks buildings but the villagers were insistent upon first gathering into family groups, which then blocked the road to those coming up behind. A frenzy of activity was revolving around a small group of people not far from where they stood on the steps of the keep, and it was from there that the clear, firm sound of a familiar voice carried above the clamour and clatter of the mayhem. A cart was being pulled to that position and a man was hoisted onto the cart where he could be seen by all around him. Samuel came fully into view as he gave a loud shrill whistle, which cut effectively through the evening air. Ela smiled; as the space around Samuel opened up the faces around him became visible: Tarrin and Calin were the men who had lifted Samuel high and Dina stood close by him alongside a group of clanswomen.

"Friends," Samuel's voice called across the courtyard. The surrounding noise wavered and then broke, falling to a hush. Happy with the improvement Samuel's voice ploughed on through. "Friends! My friends, we are here and for now we are safe but I must ask for your cooperation. I know some of you have been split from your families over the course of the journey today but we are all here now, we have all arrived safely and this is our time to rest and regroup. These people are trying to show us to our accommodation and we will all be together. Please follow them and be at peace. All is well. I beg you let them take the horses, you will see them again I give you my word."

Another figure had approached Samuel, pushing his way through the throng to get to them. To her surprise Ela realised it was Daniel; she hadn't even noticed him leave her side. Words were exchanged and then Daniel was lifted up beside Samuel and the two men shook hands. The background noise dropped further as curiosity overcame the refugees.

"Be welcome to Stagsonton, my friends. I am Lord Nunnington, and I have heard from the Lady Elayna and Master Lyaren of your plight and bravery. You have my word that we will do everything in our power to keep you safe and comfortable while you are here with us. Do not be under any illusion. There will be hard times ahead of us and war is coming just as sure as the sun will rise, but the enemy are not here yet and now is our time for preparation and planning. We have accommodation for you all in the barracks and your livestock will be taken care of in the stables. Food and clothing rations will be distributed and tomorrow your skills assessed and work duties assigned. This is not charity, this is war. Today we stand together, shoulder-to-shoulder, brother-to-brother. When this enemy is defeated and you all return home you will do so as heroes and with whatever help Stagsonton is capable of providing for you to rebuild your lives. That is for the future and so, my friends please follow my men and take some rest; tomorrow our stand begins."

"Thank you My Lord!" a cry from the crowd.

"Blessed be Lord Nunnington!"

"May the Goddess watch over you!"

Thanks and platitudes rang out from around the crowd but began to lessen as the people of Lower Gonfiels were led to their new homes.

Rudley helped Daniel down from the cart and Tarrin slapped him affectionately on the back. "Well done, Lord Daniel. That was well timed, if you don't mind me saying."

"Good to see you back safely, Tarrin – you too, Rudley, I see your mission was a success."

"Indeed it was." Tarrin smiled. "Please let me present my sister Teah, daughter of the Wolf Moon Clan."

Daniel struggled to bring words forwards. The most beautiful woman he had ever seen stood before him. She didn't bow or curtsy as kingdom women would have done. Instead she stood smartly to attention at her brother's side, an air of regal confidence surrounding her, radiating her authority. His mother was the only other woman he had ever met who managed to carry that off so well. Not even Princess Alexia held such an air of power. "I am happy to see you returned safely to your brother, Princess Teah." he managed to articulate. "Please, I will have rooms ready for you in the main keep. Samuel, would you and your family take a room too?" Daniel had been hurriedly introduced to the smith upon the wagon and had realised he held authority over the refugees.

"Oh no, no, My Lord" the smith stammered, embarrassed by the offer. "My family and I will be happiest with our people, that's where we belong and where we'll be most useful. If it's alright to be saying, we ain't the type for castles and the likes, just an honest bed and a roof over our heads is all we need."

Dina stood by her husband's side, her expression matching his, and nodded encouragingly at his response. Her eyes widened in shock as a person appeared from nowhere, hurtling headlong into an embrace, then arms surrounded her, hugging her closely.

Ela had finally managed to escape the steps and make her way over to her friends, Lyaren following close behind. She couldn't help herself as relief for Samuel and Dina washed over her and tears welled in her eyes.

Dina regained her composure as she realised she wasn't under attack. Seeing Lyaren she realised the source of the affection and hugged back, pulling Ela tightly to her. "Well, just look at you young Ela. All dressed in your fancy clothes."

Ela laughed, realising she still wore the ridiculous formal gown, and pulled an uncomfortable expression. "The dresses you gave me beat this one hands-down Dina. I'm so glad you and your family are here and safe."

Sadness flittered over Dina's eyes. "Almost all, child. Yes, we're almost all here and safe."

"We lost Aaron in the battle," Samuel told them. "Our eldest."

Ela remembered the blond-haired youth who looked so like his father.

"He was very brave, our Aaron was," Dina added meekly. "He fought with the men, but he was still a boy and just not ready."

"We'll avenge him, Dina." It was Teah who spoke when no one else knew just what to say. "Those creatures are monsters but this place will be their end and justice will be done for all those who have fallen to their evil."

"Well spoken, Princess Teah." Daniel agreed. "I am very sorry for your loss lady; Samuel." Daniel opened his arms wide. "Come, friends, you have had much hardship but now you all need rest and we too are weary after a long, hard day. Let's all take our leave."

Samuel and Dina gave their thanks and followed the remaining villagers around to the barracks blocks. Tarrin placed his arm affectionately around Teah's waist and escorted her towards the castle. Daniel, Myllasanndia and Rudley followed. The courtyard was much quieter now; the horses had been led to their stables, the last of the carts were being guided out of sight and only a few of the older villagers still made their way, at a slower pace, to their beds. Calin stood uncomfortably as all went their separate ways. Teah never looked back, Samuel and Dina had not asked if he intended to join them, and now stood before him were his friends but he hardly recognised them. Lyaren looked every part the lord and Ela... Well, she looked like a princess. *What should he say? Where should he go?* He couldn't even bring himself to look them in the face.

"Calin?" It was Lyaren. "Are you alright? Are you hurt?"

"No."

Soft fingers wrapped around his; Ela took his hand. "We've been so worried about you and the villagers. It's such a relief to have you back with us again." She threw her arms around him and hugged him closely.

Calin relaxed a little and smiled at her. "It's good to see you awake, Sleepyhead!" he teased. "I was worried you might not wake up."

"Oh, she's awake alright!" Lyaren laughed and took hold of the giant man in a rough bear hug. "We've got lots to tell you, my friend. Come, let's eat together, I've made preparations for you to share a room with me; Ela is nearby, and Tarrin too."

"No, I couldn't sleep in the castle, no, I don't belong."

"Calin." A woman called from the direction of the castle. Calin jolted at her voice, his head lifted and their eyes locked. "Are you joining us or do you intend to go with the villagers?" Teah asked.

"You are one of us," Lyaren told him firmly. "You have earned your place with us and will continue to do so, just you wait and see."

"Lyaren's right." Ela told him. "Please, Calin, we've missed you so much, you must join us."

Teah had walked briskly over to them and stood hands on hips, eyebrow raised. "Well?" she asked, a hint of anger in her tone. "I thought we had an understanding."

"I wasn't sure." Calin said softly. "You are a princess but I don't belong..."

Teah ignored him. She ignored Lyaren and Ela too. Facing Calin her head reached only his shoulder but she still had a way of making him look smaller than her. Reaching up on her tiptoes she wrapped her arms around his neck and kissed him with every ounce of passion she possessed. "You belong with me." she told him. Then, more softly "Or did I make a mistake?"

Calin slid his arms around her waist and brought her body closer into his, he kissed her once lightly but his eyes sang with the joy of being close to her. "No, Princess," he smiled. "You didn't get it wrong."

"Good." she smiled back. "And, by the way, we don't have princesses in the Grasslands, just warriors."

"That's all right then." Calin laughed but then caught himself, remembering Ly and Ela's presence.
The two stood dumbstruck but Lyaren quickly regained his composure. "So, I take it you're sleeping in the castle tonight Calin?"

Teah answered for him. "Yes, master Elf, he's sleeping in the castle." And she led the gentle giant inside.

Ela grinned at Lyaren. There were so many reasons that relationship couldn't work, so many warnings Calin should know, but something about the purity of what they had just witnessed washed them all away and Lyaren smiled back, filled with hope to know that such joy could grow from so much hardship.

That night was a night of celebration. Music and laughter sang through the air around the newly-occupied barracks buildings. In the castle Daniel hosted a far-from-formal dinner in his private dining room where

Teah and Calin recounted their journey and Lyaren and Daniel explained what had been happening in the castle. The mood was one of concern and fear for the future but happiness too for the reunion of good friends, and a warm sense of camaraderie overrode all. Daniel and Rudley took their leave a little early, Lyaren knew they were discussing the Princess and preparing for Grun's departure. They would leave quietly at dawn, and there would be no reason for anyone else to know of her royal presence in Stagsonton. Myllasanndia also took her leave to spend a little quiet time with her husband before catching up on her own much-needed sleep. Lyaren looked around at his friends. These were people he truly trusted and took comfort in their presence. "So," he finally asked. "What now?"

"Teah and I will lead our people home." Tarrin replied. "The lizards must have come through our lands; our people will need help either to fight or rebuild, we will face that when it comes." He looked at each of the friends as he continued. "We of the clans are open and honest. We will always give shelter and friendship to those who earn our respect. There is a place for all of you in the Grasslands, if you will join us?"

"That is kind, Tarrin," Lyaren answered. "But Ela and I have our own journey to take. Our work here is almost complete and, as soon as it is, we plan to continue what we originally set out to do."

"Which is?" Teah asked, intrigued.

Lyaren didn't answer straight away as he weighed up how much to share. Then he let his illusion slip and his Elvin features rippled into place. He had no reason to wear his disguise here amongst friends. "I'm taking Ela to my people. We don't know why the priests of Xyakah want her so badly. I think it is to do with her strange magic, but as I have never seen anything like it and don't have a clue how to explain it I can't say for

269

sure. One thing I do know is that amongst my people we have the means to unravel the mystery and keep Ela safe. Xyakah will not enter our lands."

"That is a dangerous journey, Lyaren, and with the lizards roaming the countryside even more so. Are you sure this is the wisest course?"

"Yes, I'm sure. Travelling just the two of us I can ensure we are not seen. We will head east and travel up the coastline as far as we can, before entering the northern mountains. Once there the Elves have their own ways to negotiate the dangers."

"Very well." Tarrin accepted. "And what of you, Calin?" Tarrin caught the young smith in a fierce glare. "Do you plan to stay here and fight for your kingdom?"

A week ago Calin would have been intimidated by that look. A week ago he would have done everything he could to avoid confrontation. Two weeks ago he would have done everything he could to avoid Tarrin altogether! What a difference a few days could make. He looked across the room to where Teah sat. Still wearing her clanswoman leathers she sat cross-legged in a large plush armchair. He smiled confidently, then returned Tarrin's glare. "My mother is dead. I have no family here in the kingdom. No one to fight for, no one to protect, no one to care for."

"You could take a kingdom wife, raise your own family." Tarrin pointed out.

"I don't want a kingdom wife." He paused a moment, measuring the mood. Teah was worth the risk. "I thought I might come back with you. Travel and learn a little of the Grasslands. Perhaps meet a clanswoman and make her my wife."

"Clanswomen make bad wives," Tarrin laughed. "They never do as they are told and only the strongest of warriors can earn the right to take one as a wife. The higher the woman's rank the worse it is for the warrior."

Calin considered Tarrin's words for a moment then calmly replied, "Just as well I know nothing of kingdom women then, I guess it means I'll have nothing to compare it to."

The room held its breath. Then Tarrin laughed a deep, throaty guffaw of pure delight. "Good for you, my friend." he chortled. "You'll need to keep that sense of humour if you hope to stand a chance in hell with any clanswoman, especially my sister." He calmed a little. "You've made the right choice. The clans will need to regroup and grow strong. We will need good warriors and you have proven yourself worthy. You will be very welcome to join us." He looked at Teah. "What do you say, sister?"

She smiled without humour. "I say nothing, brother." she replied. "Calin is a smart man. He will do just fine." She unfurled her long legs and crossed the room with a catlike grace. As she passed her brother she made a pretence of straightening his shirt then continued on to where Calin was sat. Taking the empty chair by his side she re-crossed her legs. "Only the bravest and strongest warriors can hope to win the hand of a clanswoman; it's such fun watching them try." She patted Calin's cheek. "This will be such fun, my love, I'm glad you are taking the challenge. Now you just have to prove you're up to it and fight off the other suitors."

Calin laughed nervously. "Are there many?"

"No not many, only one or two." She smiled sweetly.

"That's right." Tarrin agreed. "Just one or two...War leaders, but my money's on you."

It was Ela who came to Calin's aid and changed the subject. "I wonder how Daniel will proceed with the siege after we leave? He has a huge responsibility here;

271

if he can't distract the lizards and hold them here, locked in battle, the kingdom will be overrun in no time."

"If the reports from my scouts are accurate it may still be," Tarrin agreed. "There are hundreds of thousands of the reprobates teaming down from the north, I dread to think what we will find when we get back to the clans."

The evening passed in idle chat and speculation, until finally they all took their leave and for the first time in many days all five slept soundly and restfully the whole night through.

"What time is this anyway?" Alexia grumbled as Grun led her and his sisters quietly through the secret paths of Stagsonton Keep. All three girls wore the uniform of the Elite Guard and to the untrained eye passed as young guards. If only he could get them to stop talking Grun might stand a chance of this crazy plan working.

"It's the hour before dawn." Grun told her. "It's the quietest time for the castle staff as the night staff are just abed while the morning staff are yet to begin their chores. Only the guards are alert at this hour. Not much further now, we are able to take this secret corridor all the way to the stables. The keep is a maze of hidden tunnels, corridors and rooms. I only know a handful but Lord Daniel and General Rudley must be hard-pressed to remember all the ones they know of."

"This castle is a very exciting place, Grun," Layla exclaimed. "Has it always had a history of secrets and espionage?"

"I have no idea, Layla, you would have to ask Daniel about that. His family have lived here for generations and I'm sure there are many family stories passed down from generation to generation."

272

"I wish we had time to stay and find out about it all." Lauren said. "That was just the kind of idea that made us want to come here in the first place."

"I'm sure that once the battles are won and the war is over Daniel will be only too delighted to welcome you back officially, ladies. I might even enjoy a dance with you all at the ball."

"We'll hold you to that, Grun." Alexia promised.

"Hold him to what?" Daniel stepped out from behind a corridor which intersected the one they trod. "I've been waiting for you, come on, it's this way."

"Oh goodie, a new secret path." Alexia beamed.

"Yes this one is new to me too." Grun told her.

Daniel led them down a steep, narrow corridor. As they descended the light became dimmer and the air cooler. The corridor seemed to wind and turn from one direction to another, twisting for what felt like miles. They walked for a good half-hour before the pathway began once again to rise upwards and the air became less damp and chill. Finally the tunnel ended in a dead end, a solid stone wall barred the way.

"Right this is it," Daniel told them. "This is the city's outer defensive wall. At the other side is open countryside. We are about half a mile from the main road but this pathway leads to the same place, only more discreetly."

"That's wonderful, Lord Daniel, but how exactly are we to get through to the other side of the wall?" Alexia couldn't help slipping back into her condescending princess tone with Daniel. She knew it was unwarranted but she just couldn't stand the man."

"That's the easy bit." Daniel said, fixing his torch into a sconce on the wall. Daniel was a tall man, over six foot, but even he needed to stretch to reach the secret catch. His fingers skimmed the rough stone work until he located the smooth patch and the channel just below it, which led to the indentation where the catch was located. There was a soft clicking sound and then the wall swung outwards and the amber rays of early morning light crept in through the gap. Rudley waited patiently beyond the wall with a unit of twenty men. Anymore and they would draw undue attention. Any less and they would put the girls at unnecessary risk. There were four horses waiting for Grun and the girls. Everyone was swiftly mounted and the Elite drew their horses close with the girls in the centre. Everyone knew that, at the same time, Captain Brighams was leading a second group out through the south gate, a distraction to draw the eye of any enemy scouts in the area. If all went well the two groups would rendezvous at a junction a half-day's ride to the south where hopefully the roads would be much safer. If Grun's father had made good time the handover would be smoothly completed shortly after, allowing Grun and his unit to return to Stagsonton. "A safe journey to you all." Daniel spoke respectfully. "I am truly sorry for the unfortunate circumstances of your visit. I hope we have an opportunity to welcome you back to Stagsonton in more peaceful times."

"We will look forward to that, Lord Nunnington, thank you for your aid, I will be sure to tell my father of everything you have done for us."

"Keep your eyes and ears open, Grun." Rudley told him. "We have no idea how far south their scouting groups have gone, but that group that pinned down the Gonfiels villagers was big and angry."

"We will do, Sir, thank you." Grun turned to the ladies. "Alright, everyone ready?" and with a nod from the girls the group set out on their journey.

Ela took breakfast with Lyaren, Tarrin, Teah and Calin but, when Ly went to start work with Myllasanndia, she excused herself and headed straight down to continue her training. With the Princess away she now had a much easier morning and was able to give a little more time to her practice. By the time she returned to the castle, midday had been and gone and she hurried to change in time for Daniel's council meeting. It was a relief to find the council chamber almost half full, in comparison to just the four or five of them she had been accustomed to. Tarrin, Teah, Calin, Rudley, several other officers of the Stagsonton legion, two members of the Elite Guard, Hayal, Kayel and Samuel, all sat around the large table with Daniel and Myllasanndia at the head. Daniel addressed the group formally, reemphasising the need for heightened awareness and security, thanking those who had only recently been cleared for their patience and succinctly bringing everybody up to speed. Reports were given and then the discussion turned to the planning. Although Daniel planned to engage the enemy throughout the siege he did have a number of surprises up his sleeve and planned a host of assaults, ambushes and booby traps for the enemy. Poisoned food had been strategically stashed amongst the almost desolate remains of the surrounding farmlands. Explosives were stockpiled and attack groups organised to be released through the secret passages in the defensive walls. Of the fortifications themselves, the forest provided some cover to the south although it was also problematic to their defence. With so little time there was nothing more to be done about it. The earthworks to the north had been widened, bridges raised and masonry stockpiled to replace and repair any weaknesses which may develop once the siege was underway. The populace were all briefed now as to the many alarms and signals, which may be raised, and food and provisions were now officially rationed and controlled. Tarrin agreed to give Daniel one more week before leaving with Calin and the clanswomen. Teah agreed she and the other clanswomen would continue scouting until then, while Tarrin and Calin would work alongside Rudley and Grun when he returned. Lyaren, on the other hand, promised only two more days of working alongside Myllasanndia, and Daniel grudgingly agreed to release him and Ela to continue their journey. Samuel gave a brief report on the organisation of work duties for his people, and Hayal and his archers were assigned their own position atop the keep walls. The meeting was all but over when the knock came and a note passed to Daniel. He read it briefly and those closer noted the colour drain from his face. Daniel hurriedly closed the meeting asking his mother, Rudley, Ela and Lyaren to spare him a minute. As the others left he ordered the guard who had handed him the note to show in two men.

Ela hadn't seen them before. Both were about her age, perhaps a little older, and wore high-quality travelling clothes. Daniel greeted them warmly but the lines of concern hadn't left his face.

"These are two of Daniel's friends." Lyaren whispered. "They left two days ago to escort their families back to the city."

"What happened?" Daniel asked simply. The taller of the two men broke down, Myllasanndia was there quickly bringing him a chair. The second man took up the telling.

"We rode out on the south road then cut off to the east to meet and escort our families back here; they were late, as we explained to your mother."

"Yes, Lyndon, Mother told me." Daniel acknowledged.

"We rode for over a day and there was no sign of them anywhere. The roads were deserted, not a soul.

That night we camped off the highway in the woods; we heard a scream but there were only ten of us in the party and we dare not risk revealing ourselves, so we snuck up quietly. .. It was awful. There must have been a hundred of them, perhaps more, they're monsters!"

"Go on."

They had a big fire going in the centre of their camp, and off to the side of the fire were a group of women and children. They were just...just throwing them on the fire, just throwing them on like they were logs to burn...just throwing...just throwing." He looked up in desperation. His mouth moved but no more sound came out.

"It was them," the other man cried. "They killed them all, Kitty, Emily, Martha, the children, the baby. They killed them all....."

Lyndon had regained some control. "We didn't know what to do, James and some soldiers tried to attack, but there were too many of them. They cut our men down before they even had a chance. We hid, Ronald and I, we didn't know what else to do. We're no fighters, we're scholars... We wanted to do something but we didn't want to die." The man crumpled as he gave way to the inconsolable grief.

"Are you sure it was your families?" Myllasanndia asked gently. "After all, it was dark. There are other travellers on the roads."

"We hid all night. When they left the next morning we found the remains." He held out a beautiful silver locket. "This was Kitty's; it has a painting of the twins inside. They just killed them. Just like they were nothing." He looked helplessly at Daniel.

The room felt ten degrees cooler. "Where did they go?" Daniel asked. "Which road did they take?"

"They headed south cross-country. I'd say they will intersect with the main south highway."

277

Daniel looked over to where his mother stood with Ly and Ela. "Oh Goddess no!" He didn't need to say anything else.

Chapter 10
Concealment

Daniel grabbed a large map from a side table and threw it onto the heavy council table before the two distraught men. "Lyndon, Ronald, I know you have had a terrible ordeal, and that you really need to go and see the physicians immediately and get some rest, but it is very important that we know where those lizard soldiers went. Please, I will get you the help you need in just one moment but can you first show me on the map where you last saw the enemy?"

By this point Lyndon was hopelessly lost to his grief, but Ronald nodded and pulled a pair of slightly bent magnifying spectacles out of his jacket pocket. Placing them on the end of his nose he studied the map for a moment before pointing to a location on it.

"And you say they moved out this morning?" Daniel asked him.

"Yes," he confirmed shakily. "A little after sunrise."

"Did they have horses or were they on foot?"

"They had some pack animals but the lizards marched on foot... Although they set a good pace."

279

Daniel motioned for Lyaren to come closer; he traced a road with his finger. "This is the road Grun and his group took this morning. Here is the main south highway, which Brighams took, and this is the rendezvous point for the handover with Baron Highlord, which is scheduled to occur this evening. Ronald places the lizard warriors here and describes this as their direction of travel..." Daniel scraped his fingers through his thick curling hair, pulling it away from his face. He sighed deeply. "Please tell me I'm wrong."

Lyaren studied the map intently. He looked at the scale and roughly calculated the speeds at which the parties travelled. His stomach twisted. "The Sandkind will get there before Grun and Brighams, but we also expect Grun's father to have arrived earlier..." He considered the situation for a moment. "This could be a blood bath. Do we know how many men Baron Highlord travels with?"

"Grun and Brighams have around seventy men altogether; we are assuming Baron Highlord will have around fifty men with him, but we don't know for sure. They should be able to put up a fight." Daniel pointed out.

"They should, but the two groups will definitely arrive at different intervals and there is one more thing we haven't considered." Lyaren cautioned. Everyone looked at him. "If there is one band of lizard warriors wandering the countryside south of Stagsonton, then could there be more?"

Silence stole the room for a heartbeat. It was Myllasanndia, with her ever-practical mind, which moved the thought process on. "We can't be sure either way, but we have placed a very important package in potential danger and so we must act quickly. Think everyone... What can we do?"

"We could send a large unit of men south to retrieve our package and destroy any enemies we encounter." Daniel suggested.

"We could do that, but it will alert every Sandkind in the area to the importance of that package. Also, we reduce our numbers here which places the city at greater risk." Lyaren advised. "As I have said before, stealth may be a more appropriate course of action."

"Go on." Myllasanndia urged.

"Well, two well-trained men with the ability to conceal themselves from enemy eyes could travel quite quickly through the woods and may reach their position by nightfall. If there are survivors it may be possible for these men to remove the package and conceal it until the danger has passed, returning it to Stagsonton for safe keeping." he theorised.

"Will you go, Lyaren?" Daniel asked.

"If you want me to," Lyaren offered. "Although I can't help your mother tomorrow with your guests in the dungeons if I'm roaming around the countryside. There are others with the abilities I'm referring to."

"You mean the clanswomen. I can't put them back into that kind of danger."

"It's no more dangerous than the scouting exercises they've been running through the whole process, but I wasn't thinking of the women either, I was thinking of Tarrin and Calin."

"Calin has no magic!" Ela was shocked that Ly had suggested placing their friend in such danger.

"Calin is an excellent woodsman, Elayna, and he learnt a lot working with Tarrin and I when we worked on your rescue. By all accounts he's picked up even more on the journey to Stagsonton with the villagers. Tarrin has enough magic to conceal three people, and Calin has the ability not to jeopardise his illusion. They both have the fighting abilities we need and they've

281

fought the Sandkind before so they won't be shocked or intimidated. I know that they plan to set out soon for the Grasslands but I think they will agree to help us before they leave and, most importantly of all, they can be trusted with a secret."

Daniel weighed up Lyaren's words for a moment. "Does anyone have any further advice or suggestions?"

All shook their heads.

"Guards!" Daniel called. The door opened and an Elite Guard entered the room, standing smartly to attention. "I need Prince Tarrin and Master Calin now. Have them brought to my office!" he snapped. Then, more softly, "And then would you please escort Lord Ronald and Duke Lyndon to a guest suite and arrange for a physician to see them both as quickly as possible." Suddenly remembering his friends Daniel added, "Wait! What of Jeremy and Jarrod? Mother said they set out with you."

"We don't know," Ronald answered sadly. "We haven't seen them since they left us."

"Right..." Daniel pushed the worry from his mind; there was nothing to be done right now to help them. "Thank you, my friends; let's hope they are both safe and well." With that Daniel led his friends to the doors and the guards escorted them to their rooms.

"I don't like this." Grun confessed to Brighams, as they made their way down the main south highway. The woodland lane had ended in a narrow trail, at which point his smaller party had made their way out onto the main highway and met up with Brigham's larger group.

"What don't you like?" the older soldier asked gruffly.

"I don't know..." Grun surveyed the road. "It's quiet, no birds – which is odd for such a lovely day, but it's more than that. I thought Father would have sent a forward scout; we should have heard something by now."

Brighams considered for a moment. "Yes I would have expected that also. What do you want to do?"

Grun spoke his thoughts out loud. "By my assessment we've got a few hours' ride to reach the meeting place. I think caution would be prudent... Let's get off the road and send out a scouting party. In the worst case we'll lose an hour, but at least we'll know we're not walking into some kind of a trap."

The escort party was brought to a quick halt and they all carefully made their way off the main highway and into the heavy wood, which hugged the road to the east. Once off the highway, some men were put to work setting up a temporary camp and making the ladies comfortable while others concealed the signs of their presence from the road. Grun was impressed by the women. All three had proved to be excellent horsewomen and none had complained or questioned his decisions since they set out this morning. They were happy to comply with the unexpected rest stop and Alexia agreed with Grun when he explained his concerns. Grun had first thought to scout ahead himself but then thought better of it. As much as he trusted Brighams he felt he should stay with the girls; if need be he would protect them with his life. Instead he sent three of the men from his original twenty. They were all Elite Guard and their skills more refined than those of the legion men. As an added precaution he stationed a guard and positioned three far-seeing lookouts, one to the north, one south and a third he sent high into the branches of a huge oak. Then all sat tight to wait for news.

News found them in the form of the alert whistle from the treetop lookout. The whistle was clear and shrill: trouble from the south. Grun virtually flew to the foot of the tree where he found the man descending at a death-defying rate. His face was red from the exertion as he struggled to regain enough breath to speak. "Lizards!" the lookout announced. "Lots of them, coming from the south."

"How far?" Grun asked.

"They'll be here within the hour." The man still gulped air into his lungs between statements. "There's hundreds of them, Sir."

Grun looked at Brighams. The big man had crept up quietly beside him. "We can't risk engaging them. Not with our cargo."

Grun nodded his agreement. "No. As much as I want to spill their stinking blood, this is not the time." He thought for a moment. "Hide all signs of the camp, split into smaller units and pull the girls further back into the woods. We keep quiet and hope they move straight past. If they do notice our tracks and come after us they will have to enter the woods in small groups; we can be ready to ambush them, keep them distracted and lead them away from the Princess."

His orders were carried out quickly and efficiently. Grun gave a moment's thought for the scouts he'd sent out earlier – with any luck they, too, were hid up somewhere safe. The ladies waited by their horses, concern written on all three faces.

"We'll need to leave the horses." Grun told them.

"Don't be ridiculous." Alexia snapped back.

"How can we hope to get away from them without the horses? Surely you don't expect us to walk!"

"No, Highness, I expect you to run!" he shot back, perhaps a little too shortly as the colour leached from Alexia's face. "My men will give the lizards something to keep them busy while we get you as deep and as thick into this woodland as we can. The lizards are from the desert; their eyes won't function so well in the gloom of these trees, especially as night falls, but if what Tarrin tells me is true they have an excellent sense of smell so I suggest we waste no more time and get ourselves moving." With that he strode off towards a small dear track which wound its way into the depths of the woods. Grun intentionally didn't look back, but his shoulders relaxed significantly as he heard the women hastily following behind.

Teah stood with growing impatience, arms folded defensively, as she waited for her brother and Calin to emerge from their meeting with Daniel. She had no intention of hiding her irritation at being excluded from the meeting. The two guards posted outside Daniel's office eyed her nervously. Silently, she enjoyed the unease her appearance spread amongst these Maldoran men. Some of the solders she had observed had made lewd comments but these Elite Guard, in their smart green and black uniform, recognised her ability from her posture and, if there was any uncertainty, one look at the array of weaponry on display left them in no doubt. Tarrin had told her that in peacetime weapons were not allowed in the castle but Daniel had dropped the rule so that everyone could protect themselves. Just as well, she had thought. He wouldn't have taken her knives from her – no one would ever do that again.

A half-hour crawled by, frustratingly slowly, before finally Tarrin and Calin emerged from the office. Daniel remained inside – *perhaps he knew she was ready to rip his throat out?*

"Well?" she asked of the two men, sharply. Calin's eyes said it all; he was under instruction to talk to no one. That wasn't a problem; she could have the information out of him in no time. Tarrin, on the other hand, was willing to tell all but had no intention of doing so here. Following his lead she waited for the explanation.

"We need to take a couple of days to do a favour for Lord Daniel." Tarrin stated calmly. "I'm going to need you to take care of a few things here while we are away. Let's talk as we walk." Tarrin's eyes promised a fuller explanation and so she waited.

Teah held her temper until the door to Tarrin's room was closed behind them. "Well?" she demanded.

It was her brother who explained the situation and Calin appeared relieved that he didn't have to be the one who disclosed their mission.

Teah processed the information for a moment before reaching her furious conclusion. "You are both a pair of fools!" she snapped. "You are going to risk your lives for some snivelling little princess! Do you really think it wise to waste more time here when our people need us at home?"

"These people have been good to us, Teah; it's only been one day since they saved our lives." Calin pointed out.

"Yes but they only needed to do that because we were saving the lives of their people in the first place."

"My people." Calin said calmly.

"Enough, Teah!" Tarrin cut in. "Daniel has asked this of us because he knows we can accomplish what others cannot. We will be back within two days and that is about the time it will take to get everyone ready to leave. You can take over the preparations and have everything ready for when we get back. You don't have to worry, Teah, I won't let anything happen to Calin."

Teah scowled hard at her brother. "Like you would make a difference! Calin can look after himself. I'm not needed to oversee packing, I'm coming too."

"No." It was Calin. Teah was somewhat taken aback by his tone. "No. This is a stealth mission and two is all it will take. I will return you to your people, Teah; I will not risk you on this mission. If anything happens to Tarrin you must live on to carry on your father's line." Teah opened her mouth to answer but when no words came she closed it again.

"He's got a good point, Teah. You are my sister and I know you are more than up to this mission but you need to get a little rest before we set out home. Stay here where you are needed and take some time for yourself, the journey north will be unimaginably taxing."

"Yes, on Calin too."

"I'm a smith, Teah. I'm used to hard work day in, day out. I'm up to this and I'll be ready to travel with you to your home." He smiled and kissed her softly on the lips. "I'll go get my gear." he told her, then left the room.

"He's a good man." Tarrin stated.

"Yes."

"Have you told him?"

"Not now Tarrin. Don't you dare do this now!"

"Yes now Teah. You have to tell him. I can   see in your eyes how much you care for him but he needs to know he has no chance. He needs to know he can't have a future with you."

"I won't tell him that. I can't!" Now she really was angry, *what right had Tarrin!*

"You have to... Look, we don't know what we will find when we get home but building strong links between the tribes will be essential." He took her hand gently in his. "The bond must be made; your husband is not your choice."

Teah snatched her hand away from him. She could feel tears welling in her eyes but pushed them deep down, just as her big brother had always taught her to do. "And what if the bond is already formed?"

"How can it be? I'm the only clansman here and you can't bond with a sibling. Humans have no magic. Calin has no magic."

Teah took a long, deep breath then slowly let it go. "The bond must be won, but a woman can only bond with one she truly chooses – every daughter of the clans knows this. To win a bond a man must prove himself the strongest but first prove himself worthy of love, then the magic from both people will merge." Teah held out her bare arm for her brother to see. "Look with your magic, Tarrin."

He did. Clanspeople wore their magic like a skin – it rippled over them – but once a couple had bonded the magic would pucker and make connecting strands which would join to the strands of their partner, allowing a two-way sharing of the magic. As he looked at Teah's arm he saw the strands waving proudly into the air.

"When he's here they just wrap around him." she whispered softly.

Tarrin stared incredulously. "Have you told him, Teah?"

"No."

Then, more softly, "You need to tell him."

"Why? He can never understand the significance."

"You underestimate him, sister. You need to tell him. If nothing else he needs to know what awaits him back in the clans."

Teah fought down the frantic panic building inside her. "I can't! What if he chooses not to come?"

"Then you will know the bond is false and we will face that together. Tell him! Tell him as soon as we get back."

She nodded, then reached up and hugged him close. "Take care, Tarrin, I'll miss you." He hugged her back, then he opened the door and she left the room. Once alone Teah reached into her pocket and found mouse in his usual ball, fast asleep. She pushed the image of Tarrin and Calin into the little creature's mind. *'Follow them.'* she instructed and left the tiny creature on the ground by the door.

Teah felt the mouse's thoughts enter her head. Her brother and Calin had taken a complex network of tunnels, which led them deep below the city and out into the woods to the southeast of the citadel. As they made their way on foot mouse had no problems following and relayed their journey as a sequence of visual impressions into Teah's head. She watched as they left the city through a concealed gate in the outer wall, the gloom of late evening aiding their camouflage. She saw, just as mouse did; the vale, which Tarrin dropped over the two of them with his magic and, although mouse could still see them, Teah found it almost impossible to focus on them. She considered going after them but knew it wasn't necessary. They would only face danger if they were found and Tarrin would not let them be found. She called mouse back. If she needed to go after them she now knew how.

Daniel, Myllasanndia and Lyaren stood in the small guard chamber of the dungeons, wary and tense in their mood. Elite Guards lined the walls of the little room with more stood on the narrow stairway and yet more waiting beyond the door. Daniel was taking no chances with his traitorous council members. "So, how are our guests?" Daniel enquired of the jailer.

Horkins looked uncomfortably at his feet. Never in his lifetime had he known such strange goings on. "Well mi Lord. I've kept 'em well fed, and they've all got blankets and such, but they're not 'appy, mi Lord, not 'appy, any of 'em."

Daniel nodded. "I suppose that's to be expected." His mother placed a comforting hand on his shoulder. "If they are loyal they will understand in time. If not, they are where they need to be. Come on, let's get on with this." She looked at Lyaren who nodded encouragingly. "Fetch the first man out, Horkins, and be careful."

They had made up a list of all their high-ranking prisoners, sorting them in order from most trusted to most worrisome based on Myllasanndia's instincts. The first to be seen was – in everyone's opinion – innocent, and so everyone was a little concerned as to how the man would react.

Horkins nodded and made his shuffling way to the iron gate which marked the entry into Stagsonton's dungeons. Two Elite Guard followed him through the gate. The sounds of metal rattling and scraping travelled through the air, followed by the return of Horkins who now escorted out his chained prisoner. A short middle-aged man of slight build, with steel-grey hair and what had once been a well-trimmed beard, was led over to the waiting chair where he was instructed to sit. His hands and legs were shackled and the man's eyes held a terrified quality, flickering nervously from side to side. As he saw Daniel, the man threw himself to the ground before him. His voice was high-pitched and hoarse, both from his imprisonment and through fear. "Mercy, My Lord, I beg mercy."

"Stand up, Master Grimsore." Daniel instructed the man, and gestured for the guards to help him up. Once on his feet Myllasanndia took the man back to the chair and, as he sat, placed her hand on his arm. "Do you know why you are here, Sir?" Daniel asked.

The man was shaking now, his pupils wide and deep, his teeth chewing fretfully at his lower lip. He looked from the floor to the faces of those around him as if searching for an answer. When none was found he stammered "I am sss... sorry, My Lord, I ddd...do not."

"Master Grimsore is a trader of medicinal herbs and consultant to our physicians here in the castle. He has access to a number of poisons and narcotics which means he is potentially a highly dangerous man to know." Daniel explained to Lyaren. "Master Grimsore is a wealthy and well respected member of our community and has backed many charitable events in the past, which is how he came to our notice and was offered his position on my council. When my life was threatened by the assassination attempt he was the first person I identified as a potential threat. I do not fancy being poisoned."

Lyaren caught Myllasanndia's eye; her face was relaxed and her eyes open wide – the signal all was well.

"Tell me, Master Grimsore, have you ever traded with the Xyakahan priesthood?"

"No Sir! No, my family and I are loyal to the Gods. My mother was a herbwoman, and her mother before her. I follow her teaching even to this day. The Goddess is our mother, the Gods our father."

Without acknowledging the man's answer Lyaren continued. "Tell me, Master Grimsore, are you loyal to Lord Daniel Nunnington?"

"Yes Sir, and his father before him."

"And Master Grimsore, did you ever collaborate in an attempt to murder Lord Daniel Nunnington and his mother Myllasanndia Nunnington?"

The man's eyes grew even wider. "No Sir! No, no... I would never, Sir. He looked away, his face a mask of fear.

Myllasanndia smiled at Lyaren, who returned the smile.

"All is well, Dominic." Myllasanndia advised the distraught man. "We can see you are telling the truth. Mister Horkins, if you could remove Master Grimsore's chains and bring him a small tot of spirit for his nerves."

"I'm sorry for your ordeal, Dominic." Daniel attempted to relax the unsettled man. "Please accept my apology for your imprisonment, I beg your forgiveness, but if you will please hear me out I am sure you will see the necessity for our rather heavy-handed actions."

The man took the drink which Horkins offered and sipped slowly, taking deep breaths as he attempted to calm himself.

"I was so afraid." the man admitted. "I thought I was wrongly accused."

"We don't know who is friend and who is enemy," Daniel explained. "But both my mother and I would be very dead were it not for our new friend Master Lyaren. My two most trusted counsellors, General Griss and Lord Tain, were the perpetrators of a plot to kill me; with the stakes so high and so alarming we dare do nothing else than suspect the whole council. We have held you and your fellow council members here because we did not know who was involved and now we face the task of sorting the loyal from the traitors. Do you understand?"

The man nodded, mouth agape and eyes still wide. "I can't believe it, Marcus Tain, General Griss... My Lord are you sure?"

"Sadly, yes. I witnessed the attack with my own eyes; both had affiliated themselves with the Xyakahan cult and subsequently betrayed both the kingdom and my family. We have spent the last few days interviewing the household staff, Elite Guard, official visitors and most senior officers of our army to ensure there were no more traitors and are as sure as we can be that those who remain are loyal. Today we are interviewing all members

292

of my council. I had hoped to find you loyal, Dominic, and am delighted you are. Your position on the council will be reinstated if you so wish and I will personally make amends to both you and your family for the concern this situation has caused. If, however, you prefer to resign from your position I will understand and give you my word you will be treated with the respect you are due."

The little man sat in silence a moment. "This is all so much to take in; may I please see my family?"

"Of course, I will have some guards escort you home immediately and give you a day to discuss things with your family. However, I must request that you give me your decision tomorrow. The enemy are almost upon us; I need people I can trust."

"Yes, My Lord. I understand." A little confidence had returned to the man's voice. "Of course, My Lord."

Dominic Grimsore was led out of the dungeon respectfully by the two guards who had escorted him out of his cell.

"That seemed to go well." Daniel suggested.

"Time will tell." his mother cautioned. "He is confused and shocked, not quite sure what to believe and eager to talk to his fellow council members to verify what you have just told him. He doesn't know, himself, what he thinks and so that makes him impossible to read, but he is not loyal to Xyakah and will not betray the kingdom."

"I agree," Lyaren added. "I hope he chooses to support you. He is a good man at heart." He paused and took a deep breath. "Right, who's next?"

Daniel looked down at his list. One more man he trusted then the real work would begin.

Calin and Tarrin set out at speed, the horses covering ground quickly. As night set in, the trees became blurred shadows in their peripheral vision. Calin could feel the strange tingling sensation on his skin which he felt whenever one of his friends practised their magic. He knew that Tarrin had pushed his aura out into the surrounding woodlands and shrouded them both in a shadowy camouflage. The horses moved surprisingly quietly in the dark; with their hooves wrapped to muffle the sound, only a well-trained ear would have warning of their approach. It was about five hours into their journey when Tarrin called a sudden halt. His voice was a whisper in Calin's ear. "There are many people in the trees up ahead. I think both human and Sandkind. We should walk from here." The two men dismounted and Tarrin communicated with the horses, instructing them to return to Stagsonton. Then he and Calin made their way cautiously on foot, weapons close to hand.

On foot the going became much slower; several times they hid to avoid small groups of lizard soldiers who were stumbling around awkwardly in the thick woodland vegetation. The creatures were noisy and ungainly and, even without magic; Calin could have avoided them in this environment. He and Tarrin, however, were silent and, with Tarrin's magic drawn close, they continued invisibly through the woods. They had travelled for around another hour before they met up with the first human group – six legion men, who were following the trail of a group of lizard soldiers that had passed by a little earlier. Tarrin dropped the enchantment and snapped a twig deliberately. Then the two stepped out into the path of the soldiers. They hurriedly swapped information, learning that Grun's party had never reached the rendezvous point and that Grun had taken the ladies deeper into the woods while instructing his men to wage a wave of guerrilla attacks on the less-adept enemy. The men were a little disorientated in the dark, so their directions were vague, but at least it gave them something to go on. They decided to head straight for the position from which Grun had split his team and track the girls from that point. As they neared their destination, their progress became slower still as they hid to avoid group upon group of lizard soldiers. Most travelled in bands of around twelve. These the two men avoided easily, they made so much noise – so obviously out of place in the forest as to appear almost comical. Some, however, travelled in smaller groups, and these Calin and Tarrin targeted themselves. Waiting until the last man had passed their position; they would silently slip through the predawn gloom and dispatch the unsuspecting lizards with deadly precision. Something had changed in Calin since the battle with the villagers. He still cared that he took a life, still felt that pain deep within his chest, but he wore that pain now with the surety that he killed so others would live. He killed for his friends, his countrymen and his homeland and so he would carry the pain of his actions with the knowledge that his sacrifice was for all the right reasons. Tarrin demonstrated none of Calin's regard. On the contrary, the warrior easily slipped into the role of assassin. "The more we kill today," Tarrin observed as he kicked the decapitated torso of his latest victim, "The fewer for us to kill tomorrow." Leaving the dead where they lie, they returned to the shadows searching out their next targets, be it more enemies to dispatch or a princess to rescue. There was an easy alliance between the two men. They had barely known each other long enough to consider themselves friends but both knew that, with time, there was already a bond of trust between them which would easily foster and grow. Calin had been overwhelmed by Tarrin's acceptance of his relationship with his sister, but the more he saw of the siblings together, the more he was beginning to see the mutual respect and bond of unconditional love between the two of them. He was in awe of Tarrin's skills as a warrior and the depth of loyalty which had ensured he hadn't given up when Teah had been taken. Tarrin was a man who always accomplished what he set out to do.

Tarrin, on the other hand, had known Calin for who and what he was at first glance. The giant man wore his heart on his sleeve for any with eyes to see. His humble and self-diminishing demeanour sat in stark contrast to his sharp intellect and physical ability. For a man of his size, he was agile and light on his feet, dexterous and surprisingly flexible, and his ability with the huge broadswords he crafted was admirable. This man may have been brought up to be a smith but he was born to be a warrior.

As dawn probed thin shafts of light through the thickening late-spring canopy, Tarrin and Calin found a dense patch of vegetation and carefully made their way into its depth. Calin took first watch while Tarrin took an hour's rest, then the two swapped. The environment offered little in the way of comfort or space, but they were happy to sacrifice both for the protection of the cover. They ate a light breakfast of biscuits and dried meat and returned to the task at hand.

The day became a monotonous process of hide, strike, avoid and search. They encountered several more groups of Grun's men and each time stopped to share information. The guerrilla tactics they were employing appeared to be working well; as they searched the terrain they encountered more and more dead lizards and fewer living ones. What's more, lizard men seemed now to be retreating from the woods, as more and more of their number met with a mysterious end. Some of the human soldiers they encountered confessed to enjoying their task, finding the disadvantaged desert dwellers easy to locate and ambush under the gloomy shadow of the trees. The last group of humans they had encountered had been most adept and inventive in their pursuit of the enemy, warning the two of a number of traps they had constructed in the forest ahead. It turned out they were one of the last groups to see Grun before he had headed deeper into the forest with the ladies. They had stayed near to that position, forming a rear defence for Grun and striking at any of the lizards who had stumbled close. Tarrin instructed them to retreat, as he had done with the other groups he had encountered, while sanctioning a continuation of the guerrilla tactics upon any of the enemy they met. It wouldn't do to let such efficient methods go to waste. They scouted the area and located a subtle trail, through the undergrowth. Grun had headed off track, through thick vegetation. He had done a reasonable job of concealing their tracks, but a trained eye was able to spot the subtle signs: indentations in the moss, a broken grass head, mud pulled by a shoe heel. With their target now in their sights the two men set off with renewed vigour.

The deeper they moved into the forest the fewer signs they saw of the enemy. Tarrin touched Calin on the shoulder and motioned for the two of them to sit on a fallen log. "There is no one within a mile of us, and I don't sense any of the enemy ahead of us at all. I think taking the Princess deeper into the woods may have been the best option, given Grun's situation. I also think I'm sensing a small group of people up ahead of us. They're stationary right now. I can't be sure it's them but I think it is. I suggest we go a little faster, catch them up and take it from there."

"That sounds good to me," Calin agreed. "Might even make it home for breakfast."

"Make it lunch and I might even agree."

Jogging through the undergrowth was hard going but, for the ground they covered, worth the exertion. Tarrin dropped the camouflage and focussed his energy on scanning the terrain. He risked them being picked up by enemy magicians but so deep into the forest he felt the risk minimal. As they approached the group ahead Tarrin confirmed four individuals. He worried as to why they had been stationary for such a long time but pushed the worry to the back of his mind.

Grun looked again at Layla's ankle. His sister had slipped and tumbled down a small but treacherous ravine, resulting in a badly broken bone. She wouldn't be walking any time soon. "Stay strong, Layla." he comforted the girl. "We'll have to make some kind of litter but we'll get you out of this yet."

Silent tears fell down his sister's face. Her pain was obvious but the girl was trying to be brave. "No, Grun, you must leave me. It's Alexia who is important, not me."

"Nonsense." the Princess whispered. "I refuse to go anywhere without my best friend."

Layla looked at her brother and smiled courageously through her pain. "I will slow you down and there is no way you can move quietly with me on a litter. Hide me and leave me with a knife. Get Lauren and Alexia to safety and then come back for me if you can. I'll be fine."

Grun thought through the situation. Layla was right – their protection was in their stealth and there was nothing quiet about transporting someone on a litter. He looked around; they had travelled deep into the woods. He had planned on turning north soon and beginning the slow journey back towards Stagsonton, discarding the idea of heading south without knowledge of the enemy position. There was plenty of vegetation capable of concealing his sister, but he hated the idea of leaving her. Still if he could get the others to safety he could come back with reinforcements, and perhaps with some rest her ankle may be able to take a little weight. He pulled his medical supplies from his pack and rummaged through for the small flask of brandy he carried for emergencies. "I'll need a length of fabric and a piece of wood to make a splint." he told the girls. "We'll fix this leg as good as we can. Then we'll get you hidden nice and safe, and then I'll come back for you, Layla. Do you hear me? I'll come back for you."

Grun was impressed with Layla's level of self-control. As he'd pulled the ankle into place the pain must have been excruciating but the girl simply bit into her own fist as fresh tears tumbled down her face. Focused on his work, Grun had failed to notice the approaching sound until it was too late. Footsteps were upon them; he heard a sharp intake of breath from Layla as she looked over his shoulder and knew he couldn't pull his weapon from this position. When the voice cut the air he could have wept with relief.

"So, General Grun, fancied a dalliance in the woods with the ladies did you?"

Trying to steal back some self-respect, Grun slowly straightened and made a show of cleaning his hands on part of the rag he had used to strap Layla's leg. Grun had met Prince Tarrin briefly on a number of occasions over the past week and once he had become accustomed to his somewhat barbaric appearance he had decided he rather liked the man. Grun smiled widely. "Yes, that's right, Prince Tarrin," He bowed a little theatrically. "Good of you to join us, the woods in spring time are quite exhilarating."

"Quite so," Tarrin was enjoying the banter after the enforced silence of the previous day. "Lord Daniel thought you might like a little company."

Grun reined in his humour. "We shouldn't be complacent, I don't know how far away the enemy are."

Tarrin looked out over the area, sending his senses into the surrounding forest. "Not a living soul within an hour of this position," he confirmed. "Although back the way we've just come it's all gone to hell. Some bloody fool set a league of deadly assassins on a witless group of desert dwellers and they're chopping their way through lizard guts like they were bloody trees!"

"Good." Grun smiled. "Are you sure about the enemy position?"

"He's sure." Calin offered, he wiggled his fingers in front of his face. "He uses his clansman's witchy powers."

Tarrin laughed. "I like to think of it more as warlock than witchy. This is Calin." he introduced.

Grun took Calin's hand. "Glad to meet you, Lyaren speaks very highly of you." He turned to the ladies and formally, for the sake of the Princess, introduced them. "My Lady, may I introduce Master Calin and Prince Tarrin of the Grassland clans. My Lords, these are my sisters, Lady Lauren and Lady Layla, and this is our Esteemed Royal Highness, The Princess Alexia."

The women weren't at all what Tarrin had expected. All three were dressed as men and carried short daggers in their belts. Layla had obviously broken her ankle and that accounted for the delay in their progress.

Tarrin bowed formally. "Delighted to make your acquaintance." he smiled. "As beautiful as the flora is in this part of the forest, I think it would be wise to get further under cover and then we can plan our journey back."

Calin lifted Layla easily and the group relocated to a denser area of the forest, a secluded thicket where a tree had previously fallen and now provided a handy natural seating area. Once settled, Grun quickly outlined his intended plan and Tarrin shared their information on the enemy position. Calin explained how Tarrin had been able to use his abilities to conceal them from the enemy, which had in turn enabled their rapid progress through the woods.

"I can shield two people easily, three at a push." Tarrin continued. "The plan is for me and Calin to get the Princess back to safety so that you and your sisters can follow at a slower pace." He looked at Layla's ankle. "That is no longer an option. I suggest we travel north through the woodlands, just as you originally planned. Calin can help with Layla and I can try to get us a horse. I'll put my energy into detection, rather than protection, and we'll go around the enemy. It will mean a slower journey home but you will be safer with our help, Princess."

"Sounds good to me." Grun agreed.

"No, wait..." Alexia said. The Princess had been uncharacteristically quiet since Calin and Tarrin's arrival. Grun had put it down to shock at the sight of the enormous and fearsome-looking pair, but he was wrong. "Have I understood this fully, Prince Tarrin, you are the son of Tarrin True Heart, King of the Grasslands clans, and you have the ability to know where our enemy is and, what's more, hide yourself and others from their sight."

"I cannot make people invisible but my magic will make us harder to find."

"Yes, as I understood. Gentlemen, I've got another idea." Alexia ploughed on with her thoughts. "I could go to Stagsonton and sit out the war to its end, but my father and our army need to understand the danger

301

this threat poses to our kingdom. I'm pretty sure, gentlemen that my father has no idea how big a threat this is. I need to warn him, we need to mobilise the whole army! I have to get home! Prince Tarrin, you will escort me south while Calin will aid Grun in getting Layla and Lauren to safety in Stagsonton."

"I am sorry, My Lady, I am here simply to return you to Stagsonton. Then I must return to my own home; I am needed there."

"Oh yes, I agree." Alexia countered quickly. "But if you can get me to my father I can ensure that you return home with an army to retake your home from the Sandkind and help your people."

Tarrin stopped, words and thoughts forming and dissolving in his brain. As insane an idea as this was, it did have its merit. "How far is it to the King's palace?" he asked Grun.

"Stronghold is three weeks' ride on horseback. But you can triple that time on foot." Grun replied.

"We would only need to travel on foot until we got a little further south. The lizards don't know about the Princess so they won't be looking for her. Once we get beyond their lines we are just two travellers and, dressed as she is, she will not call unwanted attention." He sat for a moment mulling over the idea. "Calin, how do you feel about getting Grun and the ladies back without me?"

"Seems to me Grun is capable of getting them back on his own, but I can help with Layla. We can deal with the lizards as and when." He tapped his hand on the pommel of his broadsword to reinforce his meaning.

"There are no lizards nearby at all." Tarrin told them. "We know as you get nearer to Stagsonton that will change, but if you travel north through the thickest part of the forest I think you should be fine. What's more, I can sense a cavalry horse close by and it's making its way here now. You can get moving as soon as it gets here and, with any luck, be back behind the walls of Stagsonton within a couple of days. I'll get the Princess to her father then set out to the Grasslands with the extra men. If you, Teah and the warriors set out as soon as you get back, you will have the reassurance that I will follow after you with reinforcements. That way, if things are too difficult for a small group to resolve... well, we will have options."

Calin pulled his mouth shut. "You're serious?"

Tarrin nodded soberly. "I don't make this choice easily, I need to get home, but an offer of help and support from the kingdom must not be turned down. I have responsibilities as my father's son also."

"So you want me to go tell your sister you'll be late home for tea?" Calin stated.

"Yes I suppose I do." Tarrin grinned back. "But if anyone can tell her, you can."

Calin shivered theatrically. "Great!" he sighed.

"Just do me one small favour will you?" Tarrin carried on. "Don't get killed on the way home. That would make her really mad, and we don't want that to happen!"

Calin laughed. "No," he agreed. "Teah mad is not something I want to see!"

As the door closed and the last member of her husband's former council was led from the room, Myllasanndia collapsed against Daniel's chest. Twelve of the original fifteen had been found guilty of treason and had been sentenced to execution, as had the two sons of General Griss. Tonight they would enjoy their last meal; tomorrow they would be beheaded in a private courtyard outside of the dungeons. Their families would be informed and given an option to attend; other than that the executions would be private. Myllasanndia and

Daniel would both attend. The remaining, innocent men had all been freed and invited to re-join the council though Myllasanndia doubted that they would. The shock of their ordeal was too much for them, but it was nothing at the side of what she had just experienced. As she had scanned the guilty men, she saw and felt first-hand a litany of hard, black deeds, with no other motivation than that of pure evil. It was as if the men they had once been had been washed away by a deluge of depravity and malice. She could still feel the evil – a smell without smell, a taste without taste, just a toxicity within her sensors. "What can do such a thing to men?" she sobbed into her son's shoulder. She felt Lyaren lay a comforting hand on her back.

"Xyakah can do such a thing. He has done it many times over! What we have witnessed this day is the true enemy Maldora faces. As you have experienced for yourselves, this enemy hides in plain sight and has infiltrated positions of extreme power. The lords of every city will need to evaluate who they can and cannot trust."

"We must warn the King." Daniel told them both. "I'll prepare a message for the birds." He hugged his mother warmly. "Thank you, Mother. I don't know where I would be without you. Come; let's get you to your bed." And with that he led the exhausted woman from the dungeon.

Lyaren made his way over towards Ela's chambers but realised before he reached her room that she wasn't there. He felt her presence outside and so changed his direction. It would be good to surprise her and shake off some of the horror of the dungeons. It had taken much of the day to assess the men and each individual had brought his own challenges. Some had smouldered quietly whilst others were lost in a fever of religious fanaticism. Whilst some had awaited their fate

304

quietly, others had tried to attack in an attempt to finish off what Griss and Tain had failed to accomplish. Lyaren had found the experience exhausting but for Myllasanndia it had been so much worse. She felt the full weight of the emotions those men had directed towards her and her son. She personally was their target and facing that with the dignity and strength which she had shown was commendable. Indeed, Myllasanndia Nunnington was truly remarkable. Lost to his thoughts he almost missed Ela. As he walked purposefully in the direction of the stables, Ela and her guards emerged from the opposite direction and it was only the movement from the corner of his eye which rallied his thoughts enough to feel the pull of her presence. He stopped and turned to find her marching at speed back towards the castle. Hailing her he hurried over to her side. "I was on my way to find you." he confessed. "I thought you might like some company. A ride perhaps?"

Ela screwed up a very red face and shook her head. "No thank you, Ly. If you don't mind I'm a bit tired."

"Are you well, Elayna? You are very red; you don't have a fever do you?"

Ela smiled. "No, I've been helping down with the villagers and the clanswomen, just worked up a bit of a... well; I'm just a bit hot. Perhaps we could take tea together?"

"That would be a lovely idea." Lyaren took the opportunity to move a little closer and placed a comforting arm around her waist. Ela moved closer into him and placed her own arm affectionately around him. "Let's go and sit in Daniel's sitting room, the light in there is lovely in the evenings and we can talk a bit. I've had quite a day, and I'm guessing you have too."

Ela's smile hid her true thoughts. She had no intention of telling him about her day, well at least not about the past four and a half hours she had spent training. Nor did she have any intention of mentioning the large bruise she was hiding beneath her second rib on the left side of her body, slightly above where he currently had his hand – the pressure of which sent a stinging sensation up into her chest. She lay her head against his shoulder and bit her lip. It was worth a little pain to have her Lyaren back with her again.

The tea was hot and delicious. Ela let the steam from her cup wash over her face. "I knew you were looking for me." she told Lyaren.

"I know." he replied. "I think that something is changing in you but I'm not sure what. You still respond to magic but not quite so strongly as you did, as if you are acclimatising to the presence of the magic, but I still can't see why. You are a conundrum, Elayna Ladaston."

They both laughed, then Ela asked, "Do you think I have some magic inside me somewhere? Could that be why I did what I did and why I react like I do to your magic?"

Lyaren considered for a moment. "If you had no magic you could not have enchanted that camp of Sandkind and you would not feel the magic of others so strongly. Calin says he feels a prickly sensation on his skin but if he didn't know I was using magic he would just shake the feeling off as his imagination. He doesn't get sick like you do. No, I think you must have some magic but I can't sense it and neither could the Sandkind, which means your magic is different to ours. My master may know more; we need to get back to our own journey and then, when I get you to my people, we can untangle this mystery once and for all."

Lyaren and Elayna enjoyed the rest of the evening in each other's company. Lyaren filled her in on his day while she talked about the people she had seen from Lower Gonfiels, being careful to avoid the subject of her training. They ate a simple meal and chatted happily about the new friends they had made since this whole thing had begun. They sat late into the night, neither willing to leave the other. It was a little before midnight when the death bell tolled its mournful notes over the castle and the citadel beyond. Lord Alex Nunnington had finally passed away, lost to the sleep which had consumed him many days previously.

The council members' executions were carried out at dawn and, following that, Daniel proclaimed a day of mourning for his father's passing. Myllasanndia never left her suite, while Daniel requested he be left alone to his work. The whole city seemed to hold its breath and time stood still within Stagsonton. Beyond its walls time felt no such restraints and, as the sun set on that saddest of days, an enemy army of two hundred thousand warriors arrived uninvited at the city gates.

Chapter 11
The Enemy at the Gate

The whole city seemed to hold its breath. From the heights of the outer city's defensive wall the enemy army could be seen stretching out over the surrounding fields like a layer of venom on the landscape. The Sandkind made no attempt at communication with Stagsonton. They simply occupied the space beyond the north wall for as far as the eye could see. The first five days were an agonising waiting game for the inhabitants of the city. The new council worked tirelessly to ensure every man; woman and child knew their part and had the correct equipment necessary for the battle to come. Daniel liaised with the council and his armies while continuing his daily role as Lord of Stagsonton, jumping from one task to the next so quickly as to seem to be in two places at once. On the evening of the second day a simple, intimate funeral service was held for Alex Nunnington where his family said their last goodbyes. There was little time to dwell on their loss; grief would be a luxury for peacetime and they were in no doubt they would mourn the loss of many more if that day should ever arrive.

Lyaren had taken the appearance of the Sandkind army with his ever-calm pragmatism. He was angry with himself, for miscalculating the time they had, and all too aware that his mistake had placed Ela and himself firmly trapped within the city walls for the foreseeable future. But, if experience had taught him anything, it was to quickly adjust to your errors and recalculate the plans. He decided that for now he would take each day as it came and wait for his opportunity. He was beginning to feel that, although contrary to his wishes, events were panning out just the way they were supposed to. His and Ela's arrival in Stagsonton had been a significant advantage for the city; without them Daniel would be dead, the preparations for war would not be underway and the whole province would be at the mercy of the enemy. He would get Ela out of this one way or another and accept that, for now, things were just what they had to be.

Ela on the other hand was quietly happy with the situation, at least in the short term. As Lyaren was otherwise occupied, she was now free to concentrate fully on her sword training and was finally beginning to feel she was making a little progress. There was a tension amongst the clanswomen, many of whom had planned to return home with Tarrin and Teah, and the intensity of their emotions was reflected in the aggression and energy of their training sessions. Ela noticed that the Maldoran women also now placed even more focus on their fighting skills and an air of anticipation hung around the women as they waited for an opportunity to reap their revenge.

Teah had taken an interest in Elayna's progress, watching as she trained and annotating her practice sessions with a tirade of criticism, a hint of sarcasm and a splattering of constructive wisdom. The commentary spurred Ella on to try harder and Teah's occasional word

310

of praise gave her a true sense of achievement.

This morning Teah was different; agitated. She had been quiet while the women trained, watching from a distance as she sharpened her own blade. After an hour or so she hung her sword belt up on the pegs intended for that purpose and took up an older practice blade, she then systematically went to work on the women, sparring with each in turn. Some lasted for several minutes against her attack, but for most it was closer to seconds. Ela felt her nerves rising as Teah approached her position. Alyha, who she sparred with, pulled back and called a halt, turning respectfully to her princess.

"You go too easy on your student, Alyha. In the Grasslands you would not be so forgiving." Teah's manner was beyond its usual light-hearted arrogance; Calin and Tarrin should have returned from finding the Princess by now and her concern at their absence was beginning to show.

"I do not need to be treated differently." Ela stood up for herself. "The Sandkind will not go easy on me, I must learn to fight for myself."

"Good! Take a rest, Alyha. I will work with Elayna for a while."

Alyha nodded respectfully to Teah, then turned towards Ela and mouthed a clear 'Good luck,' followed by a rueful smile.

Ela concentrated on not letting her fear show. She stood lightly on her feet, balancing her weight and the weight of her sword as she had been shown. She didn't have the confidence to attack and so she waited for Teah to make her move. When it came, it literally knocked her off her feet. One minute she was waiting to spar, the next Teah's leg spun, hooking her own at the back of the knee and rendering her breathless in the dirt.

Teah looked down at her. "You are dead, Elayna! Get up." she said without humour.

Teah offered no hand to help her regain her feet. Ela stood shakily, trying to recover her breathing and ignore the new cluster of bruises she could feel erupting down the right hand side of her body. She retook her stance and waited again, watching, this time, for movement from Teah's legs as well as her sword arm. Again the attack was unexpected, Teah moved in quickly, under her defences, knocking her sword up into the air and following through with a punch into Ela's stomach. She knew the woman had held back, but still the force was enough to knock her off her feet.

Yet again Teah looked down at her. "You are dead again, Elayna! Get up." she told her.

Teah was relentless. Ela spent most of the following hour regaining her feet and wondering what on earth Tilly would say when she saw the state of her. Try as she might she couldn't get a single swing of her sword in before Teah had disarmed her. Just at the point where Ela knew she could go on no longer Teah called a halt.

"That's enough for today." Teah told her. "You need to go through your sword dance routine before you cool down. If I am still here tomorrow I will help you again." Teah didn't wait for a reply, which was fine with Elayna who wasn't sure she was up to a repeat session tomorrow. Teah quickly collected her own weapons and set off back towards the castle.

Ela scrambled to her feet. "Teah!" she called after the formidable woman.

Teah turned.

"Thank you." Ela said simply.

Teah nodded and her mouth turned up into a dry smile. "You'll do, Lady Elayna..." she nodded, "And...

you are welcome." Then she turned on her heels and strode quickly away.

Teah marched through the city streets, making her way to the stairs, which led to the upper levels of the city wall. She had spent hours here over the last few days. While most eyes were to the north and the enemy camp, Teah looked southwards, scanning the tree line for any sign of Calin or Tarrin's return. Her magic allowed her to scan the area for around a mile in all directions and she was sure that, should either of the men come into range, she would be aware of their presence. Worry nagged at her, they should have been long back. A boot shuffled a little way along the wall. Teah turned expecting to see one of the sentries; the full measure of the wall was manned now and there was activity at all points, as arrows and other ammunitions were stockpiled and catapults were moved into their positions and carefully checked over by the engineers.

The footstep on this occasion was not that of a sentry. Teah saw Lyaren walking along the wall and making his way towards her position. The elf wore his human face again but nothing about him said human. He walked slowly, one hand pressed to the outer wall. His mouth moved silently, as he worked through incantation after incantation. Occasionally he stopped, placing both hands on the stone, and his body stiffened with concentration. Teah watched him approach, considering whether or not to hail him. She was still angry with Lyaren, as Daniel had told her it had been the elf's suggestion to send Tarrin and Calin out on this damn fool's mission. Part of her wanted to turn away and leave the area whilst, simultaneously, she wanted to spill the elf's guts. She settled for stepping back into the shadows and waiting to see if he noticed her. She thought she had avoided his detection as she stood with her illusion pulled tightly around her. Lyaren had stepped past her

313

position, intent on his examination of the stones, and appeared not to have noticed her at all, but after completing this incantation he straightened to his full height and, without turning to face her, spoke.

"Good morning, Princess Teah. Do you watch for your brother's return?" Lyaren's tone was conversational.

Teah stiffened at his casual manner. "My brother and I should have left this wretched place well before that foul army arrived. Were it not for you and your plotting we would be long gone!" She spat the words back at him.

Lyaren considered for a moment. He had been so focused on helping Daniel that he had neglected to consider Teah in his decisions. If truth be told, he wasn't sure why he'd chosen his friends for the task of rescuing Alexia in the first place. The idea had come to him with the certainty of prophecy and so he had suggested it without a second thought.

"I must admit I had thought we would have more time but had you left when you planned you would have found yourself trapped in the open by that army out there, so perhaps your delay was well timed." He turned to look at her, maintaining a dignified expression. "Do you search with your magic?"

"Yes." Teah dropped her cloak and stepped out from the shadows, there was no point in hiding now. "I have been casting my power as far as I can but there is no sign of either of them."

"Yes I know. I've been keeping a watch too. Something is troubling me. I too expected them to be back by now." Lyaren admitted.

"Yes but you are the man who said we had another week. Perhaps you are not always right, elf."

"I don't profess to be right all the time." he sighed deeply. "I'm sorry, Teah, I know you are angry with me and you have every right to be. I sent them out into the path of danger, but something told me it had to be that way. My magic, like yours, is a part of me, but it is more than simply a tool as yours is. Sometimes I feel that I am merely the tool for the magic...Whatever the explanation, my instincts told me that Calin and Tarrin had to go on that mission and my instincts tell me now that they will both return to you."

Lyaren looked out over the wall towards the expanse of woodland before them.

"What are you doing with the wall?" Teah asked. Her tone was a little less angry now. She wasn't sure she believed his explanation but at least he had offered one.

"Daniel asked me to check our fortifications. I thought I would take the precaution of setting some magical wards into the stonework, but it seems someone has beaten me to it. I forgot that magic was once common amongst the humans. Some time in history these walls were imprinted with powerful magic and that power still remains today. I am simply waking the magic with a little of my own and checking there are no parts left unprotected. So far my work has been most promising. It will take powerful magic to break these walls, which means the Sandkind have lost their advantage and it also means I will not feel so bad for leaving the city without a magic worker when Ela and I leave."

"You still plan to leave even with that army camped outside our front door?"

"Yes, we will leave soon. I'm just not sure of the details yet." Lyaren looked at her and smiled then he looked back out towards the trees. "Do you feel them?"

She knew what he meant; she had been aware of their growing presence for the last few days. "You mean the men in the woods?"

"Yes. I think they are our soldiers, the ones who set out with Grun and Brighams." Lyaren could sense maybe two dozen or so men hidden amongst the trees, just waiting.

"They are wise to stay hidden if they are ours. The Sandkind ride the perimeter of the city every half hour or so, if they make a run for our backdoor they may give away its position and leave the whole city vulnerable." Teah stated.

"Yes you are right, but we do need to work out a way to get them back into the city safety. Then when Tarrin and Calin do return with Grun and the Princess we can get them back in safely too." Lyaren pointed out.

"Tarrin can use his magic, he will be able to get the others to the gate..." Teah stopped as a thought hit her. "My people can help," she said. "The clanswomen can all wear the cloak of concealment and would be able to get beyond the wall without being seen. Once in the woods, each one could return cloaking at least one human each."

Lyaren smiled. "Now that; Lady Teah; is a very good idea."

Lyaren stood in the narrow tunnel with the fifteen clanswomen and two guardsmen. Behind the concealed doorway, he cast out his far-sight. There was a lizard patrol approaching their position. He motioned to the group to remain silent and followed the progress of the patrol. When they moved beyond their position and out of sight of the door he cast out his own web of illusion. The women could handle themselves and the stranded soldiers but he would need to keep the secret gateway concealed. The natural contours of the land meant that the door was only visible when you were close to the wall, and the excellent workmanship of the secret exit camouflaged it perfectly with the wall. If you didn't know it was there you would never see it. Though, of course, if the doorway stood wide open, its presence would be announced to all who passed by. Once satisfied the patrol was out of sight he opened his eyes and nodded to the guards, who silently slid open the door. The first clanswomen became shadow and slipped out of sight, before the rest followed suit. With their soft tread they became ghosts in the evening light, the slight movement of air the only sign of their passing. Teah turned to Lyaren. "Replace the concealment in one hour and then again one hour after that. We will all be back by then."

"Very well." Lyaren told her. As she went to pass he reached his hand out to her arm and stopped her. "And Teah... Don't go getting any silly ideas; I don't want to have to explain to Tarrin or Calin why you are not here when they return."

Teah smiled wickedly. "Perhaps that will be your penance for initiating this mess in the first place!" And then she too was gone.

Lyaren waited in the gloom of the tunnel. The hour stretched slowly by and he was aware of two more patrols of enemy soldiers passing by beyond the wall. As the second passed by, he repositioned the enchantment and the guards opened the door. He held the enchantment for ten minutes, it was as long as he dare, and was relieved when six of the women returned each sheltering a member of the unit sent out to escort the Princess. The men were in good spirit and he sent them straight to report to Daniel. The women reported to Lyaren and then returned to their quarters. Teah was not amongst them. The second hour seemed to pass in no time at all. Once again Lyaren waited until a patrol had passed their position before casting out his illusion.

Sahain touched Teah gently on the arm. "The enchantment is up," she whispered. "It's time to get back."

Teah stared stubbornly out into the forest. "We know they passed these men, travelling in the opposite direction on their way to find the Princess. That means they will be a little longer before they return. You go back, tell Lyaren I will stay out here for the night and ask him to reopen the gate at the forth hour after sunrise. I will come back then, even if they are not with me. I promise."

Sahain rolled her eyes. "Be careful, Teah, there are lizards all over and they have magic too."

"I will! Now get back before Lyaren drops that cloak."

Sahain nodded and returned to the group of Clan's women and ten human soldiers, who waited for her. "Come on," she told them. "Let's get back and explain our crazy princess's death wish to the elf!"

Juzuk bowed low before the leaping flames of his enchanted fire and awaited the arrival of his master. The wait was agonising. Juzuk had learned over the years that nothing about Xyakah was predictable and, so far, this philosophy had kept him alive and allowed him to progress through the ranks to his current position. Now all he needed to do was stay calm, hide his fear and firmly lay the blame for any failure at someone else's door. His wait came to a sudden halt as his master's presence flooded the vicinity, fuelling the flames which leapt higher within the confines of the grate, threatening to engulf his small tent.

"Report!" His master's voice echoed through his mind. It was emotionless, offering no clues as to his frame of mind.

"I have completed my initial task, Master." Juzuk answered cautiously, his mind striving for a way to put a positive spin on their situation. "Your army stand in readiness outside the gates of their northern city. We are ready to strike as soon as my brothers arrive."

A rumble of irritation escaped the flames; Xyakah was angry. Juzuk had feared that he would be, he had to deflect that anger elsewhere. "The city still stands?" Xyakah demanded.

"Not for much longer, Master. I have awaited my brothers' arrival so that our victory will be absolute, but their advent is badly timed. We stand ready, yet they are not arrived."

"So you stand behind their inaptitude in order to hide that of your own?" Again the flames surged, pushing out with an unnatural intensity of heat. The flames formed into fingers which spun out from the main body of the fire and snaked around his arm, pulling Juzuk closer to the furnace. Juzuk smelled death; it lingered in the flames waiting for him. He fought down the nausea rising in his gullet and employed every ounce of his control to stay calm and hide his fear. It was essential that he didn't show weakness here.

"Master, I simply hoped for your blessing before we met the battle without those who have failed you. My men and I have everything we need to bring you victory this day."

The features in the flames curled into a snarl. "I like you, Juzuk," There was no warmth in his voice. "And so I will oversee your delay this one time." The flames tightened their hold on him, biting down into his left arm, melting away his flesh on contact. "But this will be your only chance at redemption. Do not fail me, Juzuk! I want every inhabitant of their pitiful city screaming in the flames of my fires and I want it done quickly."

319

Juzuk pulled his thoughts away from the agony encasing his arm. Blocking out the distraction, he focussed all his thoughts on his master. "So it shall be, oh mighty Xyakah." Juzuk made the formal supplication. As suddenly as he had arrived Xyakah was gone.

Juzuk collapsed in agony to the ground, breathing deeply. He pulled magic from the earth beneath him to fuel his incantation, and the pain lessened enough for him to pull himself back up into a sitting position. He looked in horror at the blackened remains of his arm. He would be able to repair much of the damage but it would never regain its previous shape and strength. The stench of cooking meat assailed his senses and he retched, his stomach rolled and he emptied its contents onto the ground. Once done he shakily regained his feet and made his way over to his chair where he collapsed. Time slipped by but slowly his wits returned. *He must move, the men were waiting for his inspection.* Pulling his sleeve down to hide the damage, he mastered his body and strode out of the tent into the sunlight. His captains stood to attention as he approached. He decided to take a leaf out of his master's book. "Report!" he instructed.

"Sir, all is in readiness, we can proceed on your order."

"Good." he acknowledged. "What of the scouting groups?"

"They report the city to be open to all fronts, Sir; we have ridden around it many times now. Only the woodlands have given us trouble. We believe the humans have men hidden amongst the trees, when our patrols enter they are ambushed and they do not return." Damn the Sandkind, their ineptitude in dim light was more than frustrating. "Take three patrols together with one of the magicians and burn the trees to the ground. Let's see how they fare amongst the ashes of their precious forest." He brought his focus back to the task at hand. "We attack at first light, they must all burn!"

He turned on his heels and marched back to the sanctuary of his tent. Once back, Juzuk poured himself a glass of wine and drank deeply. "Bayzar!" he called and within moments the younger priest entered his tent. "I need one of the prisoners, Bayzar, a child – make it a girl – and bring me the Dragath and some antidote. I will not require anything else for the next few hours."

Bayzar bowed respectfully and rushed off to do his master's bidding. Juzuk breathed deeply, soon he would feel better; he would hold the child on the edge of death for as long as it took and when he finally let the soul slip away he would be mended.

Calin cursed under his breath. The undergrowth in this part of the forest was thick and wild with the supple young shoots of brambles, which snagged at clothes and cut into flesh indiscriminately. The horse they had found to carry the injured girl whinnied loudly in protest to the conditions, announcing their position to any enemy in earshot. *What the hell did Tarrin think he was doing, taking off with the Princess?* Grun and he had been taking it in turns to scout ahead but as they moved further north the lizards they encountered moved in larger groups and, working alone, there was nothing they could do to neutralise the threat. They were forced, therefore, to rely on stealth and this meant moving more slowly and in a far-from-direct route. Layla had shown extreme courage throughout the journey; obviously in considerable pain, the young woman hadn't made a sound or protested once as they made their steady way back towards Stagsonton. Her sister Lauren, on the other hand, had grumbled continuously, despite her brother's chastisements and Calin found himself wondering what the witless girl would have to say should her jabbering

321

bring them to the attention of the enemy. His thoughts, as ever, returned to Teah. Not for the first time he wished Tarrin had let his sister accompany them; were she here they would have made considerably more progress, not to mention the fact that she would never have let Tarrin go rushing off across the countryside with the heir to Maldora's throne.

Grun stepped out from behind a tree just ahead and hurried over. "The woodland ahead is teaming with lizards; the trees thin out, letting in more light. We need to double back and go around that gully we cut across earlier this morning. That should take us around them and I think it's a denser patch of forest."

Calin frowned. "This is taking too long, we need to get your sister to a doctor and I need to get back. Are you sure you and me couldn't just leave the girls and slip off to deal with them together?"

Grun considered for a moment. "We could," he agreed. "But we would need to be really quiet. If one group called out, there are others close enough to hear and we could find ourselves surrounded. I can't say I'm happy about taking such a risk with my sisters stranded out here."

"I'm glad you haven't forgotten us altogether!" Lauren snapped at her brother. "I can't believe you are expecting Layla and I to continue in these conditions."

"Lauren, I have considered nothing but you and Layla. I am sorry for your hardship, but the alternative is death at the hands of those lizard creatures. I will leave the choice in your hands." He looked her straight in the eye.

Lauren glared at her brother but said nothing.

They spent the next half hour retracing their tracks and then cut north-east following the line of a natural gorge, which ran through the landscape. Calin had to admit this seemed to be a better path and their scouting revealed fewer signs of the enemy. On a number of occasions, he and Grun left the girls and reduced the lizards' ranks by several more, only to return and continue their steady trek to the north. As night fell they made a small, secure camp. Calin estimated they were only a few miles from Stagsonton but in such dim light and with no knowledge of the land they dare not press on. If all went well, he told himself, they should be safely back behind the walls in time for a late breakfast.

Daniel and the new council of Stagsonton listened to the report of the final soldier rescued by the clanswomen earlier today. The man efficiently recounted his actions since beginning his mission with Grun to take the Princess to safety and, just as with all the other men, his tale was one of hope. It appeared Grun had got the girls off to safety and his inspired action to use these stealth tactics against the Sandkind had been extremely effective. The man had finished his recount and now waited patiently for instructions. Daniel coughed to clear his voice. "Thank you, Guardsman Riley, for your full and detailed report, and on behalf of Maldora for your bravery and service. It is to our benefit that you are returned safely to serve Stagsonton in these troubled times. Please take some rest and eat a good meal, visit your family briefly and then return to your post." He nodded formally to the man. "You are dismissed."

"Thank you, My Lord." The man saluted and, turning on his heels, marched formally from the council chamber.

Daniel looked around the table at the assembled men and women. To his left sat Dominic Grimsore and James Rothenburg – the only two men from his father's original council. Both had chosen to retake their seats and had presented themselves to Daniel when the enemy army had arrived at the city gates. Daniel's friends,

Lyndon and Ronald sat next to them, both highly educated men who knew first-hand the evil this army posed. Next came Sahain, who represented the clanswomen, and Sally, who represented the Waydonfield women. Hayal and Samuel also sat at the table, then General Rudley and Captain Lions, who sat in Grun's stead. To his left sat Lyaren and Ela, followed by an empty chair which was his mother's seat. Myllasanndia hadn't yet left her rooms since his father's funeral, although Daniel knew it had been the strain of reading so many people which had really incapacitated her. Lyaren had counselled rest and Myllasanndia for once had taken his advice.

"Right then," Daniel continued, drawing the room's attention. "Captain Lions, could you report on our preparations?"

"Yes Sir." the young officer replied. "I am pleased to report that both the north and south gates are now secure and stone masons have erected extra fortifications behind them. The walls are fully manned and all of our weapons and supplies are stored effectively. The engineers report all of the machinery to be in working order and the men are trained in their operation. Master Lyaren has also used his gifts to fortify the walls and nothing more can be done now until the battle begins."

"Is this right, Rudley?" Daniel asked. "Would it not be prudent for us to make the first move? After all, sitting at our walls like this is an open act of aggression."

"I don't think that would be wise, My Lord." Rudley advised. "They are sitting out of bow range so arrows will not work. We could use some of the war engines but it would be a random strike. We have no way of knowing where the best place to hit them is. Also, it would reveal our strengths to the enemy and may have repercussions further into the fight. I feel it would be better to wait until they attack us. I have far-seers watching the movement of the enemy; with a bit of luck we will be able to identify the command tents and aim the main thrust of our attacks at them."

"Very well, does anyone have anything else to add?" Daniel asked.

"On behalf of my people," Sahain spoke. "We had hoped to be making our way home by now but as circumstances have not gone our way we wish to offer our services. If Master Lyaren will assist us we can continue with the stealth missions targeting small patrols from the safety of the trees. We could work with your men, or Sally has another suggestion..."

All eyes turned to the young woman from Waydonfield. "Yes." Her voice was young but confident. "My sisters and I have been working with the clanswomen, they have taught us how to fight and we would like to work alongside them. That way you wouldn't need to release men who are needed on the wall."

"Thank you for your offer, Sally, I will note that for later." Daniel began to brush the idea aside.

Ela spoke up in Sally's defence. "I think they would make a very effective team, Daniel, the clanswomen have worked very closely with the Waydonfield women; they are ready now to put their skills into action and I know they are keen to repay your generosity and avenge their families."

Both Daniel and Lyaren looked a little shocked by Ela's support of the women, but neither tried to argue. "Thank you." Daniel told her, then, turning back to Sally, "I will give that matter serious consideration; we just need to ensure safe passage is possible through the back door." Everyone now referred to the concealed doorway as the back door; Daniel found it reassuring to know they had a way out should they need it. "Any other matters before I call this meeting to a close?"

"I wondered if there was any news from the King." Lyndon asked.

"Sadly not." It was Rudley who replied. "The damned creatures shoot our birds and eat them, I can't even be sure our messages have got through to the King. We have to assume we are on our own."

"Unfortunately I have to agree," Lyaren added. "We must plan as if there will be no help then, should help arrive, it will be a bonus."

A loud knock came from the door and an Elite guardsman entered the room. "My Lord, forgive the interruption but there is a rather colourful gentleman insisting that he see you urgently. The man has been waiting for an audience now for two days and..." The guardsman looked a little embarrassed. "Well, he is becoming difficult to subdue. My men have asked if they can place him under arrest."

"Has the man committed any crime? Do we know what this urgent matter is about?"

"No Sir, on both accounts, My Lord. He says he can only speak to you and it must be in private. Some of my men think they know of the man and they don't have any good things to say about him but... Well, to the best of our knowledge, he has committed no crime."

"Then what is the problem with making him wait his turn, just like everyone else? Daniel was getting sick of the small population of his city who refused to see the bigger picture and were still insisting on complaining about the inconvenience this war was having on their lives.

"It's just... He is... Well, he is singing, My Lord, rather inappropriate drinking songs, and very loudly, in the anti-chambers, and it's becoming rather... Annoying."

"Come on, man! Surely you can ignore the fellow! Is he a halfwit?"

"No, Sir, he's been singing now for ten hours straight and seems to be showing no signs of stopping." Daniel laughed, "Well, it's good to have something other than war to think about for a moment. What is the man's name?"

"He claims he is the Lord of Safehelm." the guard answered.

"Never heard of it. I think, perhaps, you should make this man comfortable in a private room for the night and tell him I will see him as soon as I have a minute. He'll just have to wait like everyone else. But guardsman, no, you may not throw a man in the dungeons for singing, even if it is a little on the impolite side."

A ripple of laughter passed around the tense council members but it was short lived as a loud shout went up from beyond the room and a warning bell tolled across the city. Every member of the council simultaneously shot to their feet. A second soldier darted into the room, not bothering this time to knock. "Fire!" the man announced, puffing and out of breath. "It's the woods, they've set fire to the woods; the trees are all alight!"

Teah pressed her back into the trunk of the oak tree. She could feel the heat of the approaching flames but she dare not move; she kept her breathing shallow and held her enchantment as tightly to her body as she could. She was lucky the magic user seemed to be inexperienced; he was relying on his guard of thirty or so lizard warriors to protect him and so he didn't bother to use his power to feel for the presence of other magic around him. Teah had been forced to leave her cover when the flames had threatened her position; she had

327

fled deeper into the woods and ran straight into the path of this large group of Sandkind with their magic user priest. It was pure luck that had saved her; she would have run straight into them if it wasn't for the sound of a snapping twig. She had frozen as she heard the sound and the lizard had missed her in the gloom. Retreat wasn't an option; the woodlands burned fiercely behind her but the way ahead was most certainly blocked. She was under no illusion; alone she didn't stand a chance against so many, even in the dark. Perhaps, if she could take out the priest, she could make a little trouble for the lizards and then slip back into the night before they had a chance to catch her, but it would be a huge risk. Calin would be furious with her for trying it, although Tarrin would understand. Movement at the far side of the enemy group, deeper into the woodland, caught her eye. There were men over there, perhaps more of the soldiers from Grun's regiment? She held her breath, if she had seen them then surely the enemy had too. But, *no,* it appeared the priest had his head turned in the other direction and the Sandkind were as short sighted in the dark as she had been told. Seconds slipped by, surely there would be an attack. Then it happened. Figures charged out of the forest – shadows in the night. She could see they had covered themselves in mud and leaves to blend in with their environment. A shout of alarm went up from the enemy and several crumpled immediately to the ground, taken by the element of surprise. Then the attack was met. Still Teah remained frozen to the spot. There weren't enough attackers to take this whole group, these men were obviously desperate. She counted nine of the lizards lying dead on the floor, but the desperate men were surrounded and were quickly overwhelmed. Teah recalculated her chances; twenty one lizards and one warlock priest – the odds were not in her favour. She ran her finger along the blade of her best throwing knife. The priest was crossing over to the now-restrained men; *if he was only a little closer she might get her chance.* Teah waited, weighing her options. She did not want to watch these men die, she had been working to rescue their comrades all day, but she saw no value in dying alongside them.

The priest was talking to his prisoners, she could just make out his voice and he spoke in the common tongue. "Where are the rest of your men?" he challenged. The men remained silent and the priest seemed to anger at their defiance. "You will answer me or die." the man told them. He raised his hand, pointing to the man closest to him, and red hot flames flew from his fingertips. Hitting their target dead in the chest the flames instantly took hold and, within seconds, had engulfed the whole of the man's body. The lizards holding him leapt back from the burning man who writhed in a macabre dance, the scream he fought to utter engulfed by the flames as completely as his body. It took only moments for the man to die but the horror of it lingered long after his lifeless body had slumped to the ground. The priest raised his hand again and pointed to the chest of the second man. "Are you alone or are there others?" he demanded.

This time the man answered, though the hate in his eyes was visible even in the darkness. "Our brothers will bide their time; you will never be safe here in our forest." Flames hit the second man, just as they had done with the first. Teah fought the nausea back down. Not again. This time the man seemed to die more slowly – the priest was doing something to prolong the agony. Teah closed her eyes. *She had to kill that priest, she had to, or he would continue and kill the other two in front of her...* The skin on her arms began to tingle with an ever-so-familiar sensation. It took her only a second to register the tug of the bond. *Calin was here.* Again she

329

searched the trees; she felt his presence over to the left of her position but she couldn't see him. She risked using a little magic – the priest was occupied with his torture; she felt out for Tarrin, but he wasn't there. There was another man, though, Calin wasn't alone. She waited, anticipation growing. The priest had moved over towards the third man, he was raising his arm, and then it happened. Two men burst from the trees, swords swinging in the dance of death. It was beautiful to watch the precision of their movement as they cut down the enemy with deadly accuracy. The priest had seen them; he began to cross towards Calin and the other man and that brought him closer to Teah's position. She didn't stop to think. She sprang from her concealment into the thick of the chaos, cutting down three lizards as she silently leapt through the air. Turning effortlessly she spun over the heads of the bewildered lizard warriors, kicking one with a deathly blow to his face as she came down closer to the priest who had now turned to face her. It was too late; her blade already arced through the air with deadly accuracy, planting itself firmly into his eye. The man's face took on a startled expression but he was dead before he had the chance to comprehend what had happened. Teah didn't pause in her movements; she replaced her throwing knife with her second sword and carved her path through the astounded lizards, to Calin's side.

The battle ended almost as soon as it began. The two remaining soldiers from the initial attack had used the distraction to escape their captors and that swung the balance in their favour. As the last of the enemy was dispatched, silence settled over the clearing. Teah bent forward breathing deeply; she had a long deep cut to her left arm but other than that was unhurt. Her eyes rose from the ground and found his waiting for her. The bond surged like a wild energy swirling through her. She let a smile touch her lips and then he was there and she was in his arms and, as it always did, the anger and blood-lust fled; overshadowed by the deepest sense of peace she had ever known. Her heart swelled with absolute devotion to this man, who she had known for so short a time but who she knew she would love for eternity.

Although laced with sarcasm and urgency there was an amusement to Grun's voice. "I hate to interrupt this little reunion but we need to get out of here!"

Both Teah and Calin snapped back to their situation and took in the scene. Grun was right, the flames had taken hold and raged through the woodlands, only metres from their position. If they didn't move now they would find themselves trapped. Teah had just watched men die at the hands of fire; it was far from pleasant.

"This way." Calin told her, and they all set out in the direction he and Grun had approached from. They ran for half an hour over the rough terrain of the forest. Thankfully the light wind was against them and so they were able to outrun the flaming trees, but any slight change in the weather and the fire would be upon them. Calin led them to a sheltered glade which he had concealed with well-placed foliage. Within the shelter sat two young women and a beautiful white stallion. The group collapsed to the ground, all breathing heavily, and silence settled as they recovered from their exertion.

Calin looked at Teah, his eyes a turmoil of questions, confusion and gratitude. "What were you doing there?" he finally gasped.

Teah grappled to gain control of her breathing but her voice was still hoarse from the exertion. "I came to look for you, of course, what did you think I'd do? Where's Tarrin?"

"It's a long story," Calin told her. "But he's safe for now and so is the Princess. I was on my way back to you with Grun and his sisters but these damn woods are

331

teeming with lizards and it's taken a bit longer than we hoped."

"It's a miracle we found you!" Grun stated.

"Well I for one am glad you did." It was Brighams; he smiled broadly at the small group. "We thought we were dead for sure; how did you all know we were there?"

"We didn't." Grun told him. "We settled up for the night, planning to head for the city in the morning. Then Calin starts getting all edgy, says he thinks Teah's looking for him!"

"We all thought he'd gone mad!" Layla butted in.

"Next thing," Grun carried on, smiling at Calin. "This idiot's running headlong through the night and leading us straight to the biggest, ugliest group of lizards we've seen so far and, to top it all off, they've got a bloody priest! I'm all ready to pull him out of there forcefully when we see them kill your man and that's when I realised it was you, Brighams. Well, we couldn't just leave you there could we? So we thought we'd try an insane rescue attempt. It should have been a disaster, only... well, seems this idiot is not so stupid after all cos, well, he was right, Teah was there and that knife of hers just saved all our necks!"

"I'll second that!" Brighams agreed. "You certainly can throw a blade, girl, and handle a sword too, I'll take you on my team any day." He smiled warmly. "Thank you. Jimmy here and me thought we were goners for sure."

"But how did you know, Calin?" Lauren asked. "How did you know Teah was there?"

Calin shook his head. "I've no idea. It must be being around all this magic, might have rubbed off on me I suppose." He looked at Teah and placed his huge arm around her shoulder, drawing her close. "I'm glad I was right though, just sorry we weren't in time for the poor souls that monster killed with his magic."

"They were good men," Jimmy told them. "They didn't deserve to die like that, but they were loyal to the end and we'll make sure their families know how brave they were."

"That we will, lad." Brighams patted the man on his back. "Well, we will if anyone's got any idea how the hell we're going to get back into that city."

"You are right," Teah told them. "The city is sealed and the siege has begun. Lyaren let me and some of my people out of the back door this afternoon; we picked up a lot of your men and got them to safety. I'd stayed behind to look for Calin and arranged for Lyaren to open the door four hours after sun up for us to get back in, only that part of the forest is an inferno right now and we can't risk moving across the open – there are enemy patrols circling the wall at half hour intervals."

Calin looked at Grun. "You know the city best, are there any other ways in?"

Grun shook his head. "No, we sealed all the lesser gates with stone work. North gate, south gate and concealed door – that's it! Unless we can fly I'd say we've had it."

"We can't just give up," Teah said. "I say we take our chances with the flames, make our way as near as we dare and hope the wind changes direction. I know Lyaren will open that gate, we just have to be there!"

333

Chapter 12
The Deluge

The members of the council of Stagsonton looked out in horror over the inferno that was the southern forest. Elayna stood closely beside Lyaren, his hand clutched in hers. "Our friends are somewhere trapped in that!" she murmured for his ears only.

"I know." he said soberly.

Daniel's face was desperate; he had sent out Alexia into the chaos of this war, and then he had sent men to bring her back only for them to be met by a firestorm. "Lyaren, is there anything you can do?" he asked of the elf.

"I don't have the power to stop a blaze of this size. It doesn't threaten the city – the wards on the walls will dampen it – but anybody out in those woods will be at its mercy."

"Then we pray to the Gods for a late spring deluge!" Rudley sighed.

Lyaren looked at Rudley sharply. This region was famous for the deluge. Most of the year the region's weather was fairly uniform – it got warmer in the summer and colder in the winter. It was too far south to experience the two suns working in conjunction and thus avoided the sweltering heat that those living north of Maldora had to put up with. Similarly, it was too northerly to escape the freezing conditions of the south. One thing this region did know was rain. It was the reason its lands produced such abundant crops and why so many farms scattered the landscape. Weather magic was dangerous; one miscalculation and whole ecosystems could be wiped out, it was the first thing young Elvin warlocks were taught. But, if all he was to do was increase the pace of a natural weather phenomenon it wouldn't be so deadly. "I've got an idea," he told the startled group around him. "But it will be costly."

"Costly how?" Daniel asked.

"I mean it will be costly to me. I can enhance a natural weather pattern, like the deluge, make it happen faster than it naturally would, but this is powerful magic. After it is finished I won't be able to work more magic for days; I won't be able to shield the back door while we get our people back in."

"Then we open it without a shield; we have to get the Princess and our people back to safety." Daniel stated.

"That's out of the question!" Rudley argued. "We can't risk leaving ourselves so vulnerable, even for the life of a Princess."

"We've got to save them, Rudley." Daniel said. "Tarrin, Calin, Teah and Alexia. They are too valuable, but they are also our friends. Lyaren, do what you need to do. Rudley, take a team of stonemasons down into the tunnels. Get our friends back behind these walls and then close that door for good. I will not let my friends die. Now, ladies and gentlemen," He looked to the other members of the council. "I suggest the rest of you get to your beds and get some rest, who knows what tomorrow may bring."

Ela went with Lyaren to his chamber; he stopped at the door and looked deeply into her eyes. "You need to get as far away from me as you can, Ela. This is going to be very unpleasant for you, I'm about to unleash a lot of magic."

"No," she replied flatly. "I'm going to stay right here with you. I know I will feel sick and dizzy, I might even pass out, but who knows what this will do to you, Ly. What if you are ill afterwards? I will stay and watch over you then, when you finish; I will be here to make sure you have everything you need to make a full recovery."

"That's kind, Ela, but not necessary. This will be the most magic you have ever encountered."

"More than at the lizard camp?"

Lyaren stopped himself before answering; back at the lizard camp she had released more magic than he had ever experienced in his life. "The most magic you have ever felt me use." he answered cautiously.

"Stop trying to protect me, Lyaren. I'm not a child anymore and I will not allow you to do this thing alone. Now stop delaying and let's get our friends back into the city."

Lyaren shook his head and, despite his better judgment, opened the door to his and Calin's room. As they entered he lit a small candle which stood on a table to the left of the door then used it to light several more, pooling luminosity into the modest room. Just as she had expected the room was neat and orderly. Lyaren had only a few possessions, but they were all laid out in a neat little row on a tiny table under the window. The room was much smaller than hers and the furnishings more homely and simple in their design. Two functional beds occupied the centre of the room. There was a large chest, two stools, a writing desk and two small tables. A hearty fire burned in the grate and a thick tapestry concealed the entrance to a water closet.

"It will be best if you sit on Calin's bed," Lyaren told her dryly. "That will be more comfortable than the stool when you pass out."

She ignored the sarcasm in his tone and made herself comfortable on the bed Lyaren had indicated. He took the other bed and sat cross legged in the centre, his open palms face-up on his knees. He looked over to Ela. "You ready?" he asked her.

Ela hid her fear. *She had to face this and, besides, she needed to know what effect strong magic would have on her.* "Get on with it!" she told him.

Lyaren nodded once and closed his eyes. At first Ela felt nothing – just the usual tingling sensation which Lyaren's magic caused – but as she waited she began to feel the drumming building in her ears; next came the nausea and then the cramps. She felt her body react and, somewhere under the pain, recognised how lucky she was to have the bed beneath her. She pulled her thoughts away from the mounting pain and told herself it wouldn't last much longer. Throwing logic at her situation she found she could control the instinctive panic which had always consumed her before and wait for the pain to pass. The pain didn't pass. The drumming in her ears just built up and up, the cramping twisting and tearing inside her. She gave in to the misery and let go of her consciousness, knowing the oblivion of sleep would bring her relief. Ela felt a rushing sensation as the world slipped away from her; her body falling beneath her, she found herself suspended in some sort of bubble. Realising she could still see, she took in her surroundings. The room looked different – her perspective had changed. Panic thundered through her – she could see her own body, there lying on the bed

338

below! *Sweet Goddess, she was dead!* She looked around for the Spinner; he would be coming for her... But what she found wasn't the spinner, it was Ly! Ela couldn't explain how she knew it was Lyaren, he appeared simply as a ball of light-blue energy and, although he had no human features in what she assumed was his magical form, she knew he saw her. "How is this possible?" he asked her. It was as if the words and the sound of his voice had just appeared in her head. *Only she had no head,* she reminded herself.

"I don't know," she told him. "I thought you had done something."

"No, you did this all yourself, look." He moved closer and, as he did, she saw a thin trail of purple light which linked his magical self to his real body below. The light split, however, and formed an offshoot, which she realised connected her to him. "We call this the anchor," he explained. "It must always remain connected to our bodies, but somehow you have linked our anchors together; it looks like you are coming too."

"Where are we going?" Ela asked.

"To bring the rain. Come, I'll show you." The light which was Lyaren shot through the air at a dizzying speed and Ela found herself pulled along. They flew through the darkness of the night, the world chasing by beneath them at speeds beyond comprehension. Lyaren swooped through the vastness out towards the land's end and still onwards over the water. Here he finally stopped.

If she'd had breath Ela would be catching it. Instead, she looked out at the monstrous cloud which hung before them. "What is it?" she asked.

"For now it's just a result of hot water and cold water meeting in this location. But, as the spring sun warms the water more, it will become more and then this cloud will bring the deluge."

"Then we have failed, it is not enough yet."

"Not yet, but we have not failed, watch." The energy ball that was Lyaren began to glitter and crackle. Tiny lightning bolts exploded over the surface and energy built up, expanding outwards. Just as Ela thought he would explode, a surge of energy shot from the orb and crashed headlong into the partially-formed cloud. Heat built over the ocean and, before her eyes, the waters boiled and turned to steam and the cloud swelled.

"That's amazing!" she told Lyaren.

"Might be, but I don't think it's enough." Lyaren replied. His voice sounded weak now and strained. Ela brought herself closer to him. She could still feel the energy he had created; she could feel the same energy inside of her. Instinctively, she began to pull the energy up and bring it to the surface. "Take it easy," Lyaren cautioned. "Not so much or you will exhaust yourself."

She stopped herself and pushed some of the energy back down. Then she focused on the cloud and sent a streak of power out just as Lyaren had done. Once again the seas boiled and the steam rushed into the cloud which had now doubled in size. "Is that enough?" she asked him.

"Yes," he replied. "Now we just need to get it over the southern forest. Lyaren sent out another jolt of energy; this time it encircled the monstrous cloud, tethering it to him. Ela looked from the cloud to Lyaren. She could see from the waning of his orb that he was tiring, his energy almost depleted. "Let me." she told him and, without waiting, she shot back in the direction from which they had come, her speed easily equal to that of the outward journey. Her spirit rang with the joy of this freedom, the exhilaration of the speed, the sense of oneness with all around her. Stagsonton appeared before her; she sped over the occupying army then over the city and out towards the flames enveloping the woodland.

She had worried the heat would be too much but, in this ethereal form, she could not feel it at all.

"Thank you," Lyaren told her. "That helped." He removed his tether from the cloud which now hung menacingly over the trees. "Now for the rain, do you think you can help?"

"Yes, just tell me what to do." Ela was enjoying herself; this was intoxicating.

"We need to rattle the cloud, make it release the rain, and to do that we are going to create thunder. Look at the air around you; do you see all the colours?"
Ela looked around her; the sky was made up of a myriad of colours. "Yes I see them."

"The colours are different temperatures. This cloud is still hot, charged with energy, all we need to do is throw cold air into it; where they clash we will get the lightening and that will release the rain."

"Which colour do we need?"

"Blue, icy blue, do you see some?"

"Yes over to the north, away from the flames, but it's a long way from here."

"Look up, Ela."

She did. Up above, the sky stretched on forever. Ela sensed a rumble of amusement from Lyaren. "It's beautiful!"

"Yes, it is. Come on, let's pull down that cold air." And this time Lyaren was pulling her straight up into the universe, higher than she had ever imagined existed. When he stopped she could sense the cold air all around her, but she didn't feel the cold. She helped him secure the air and then they plummeted back down; at breakneck speed they descended deep into the heart of the cloud, pulling the freezing sky in with them. Lightening flared all around them; the noise was deafening. "Time to go." she heard Lyaren say and felt the pull on her tether. He brought her back up and out of the cloud and then they were over the city and back through the little window to Lyaren's room.

Looking down, Ela saw both their bodies laid peacefully as if asleep. "How do we get back?" she asked.

"Just let yourself drop, your tether will pull you back when you get close enough. Are you ready?"

"Yes." She felt Lyaren separate their tethers from one another and, as he did, felt the pull of her own body below. Letting that natural pull guide her she gently descended before experiencing a sudden overwhelming pull and rush. She hit her body like a crossbow bolt and pain engulfed her, followed almost instantly by oblivion.

The small desperate party made their slow way through the darkness of the forest. As they approached the tree line, they could just make out the looming structure of Stagsonton's outer walls through the gloom and smog. Grun recognised their location; they had come out about half a mile to the east of the concealed entrance and would need to hug the trees as they made their way towards it. The open expanse of grassland between the city and the woods teemed with activity, as parties of lizard warriors organised and grouped themselves in what appeared to be an unstructured, haphazard formation.

"They look like they're getting ready to make their move." Calin observed.

"Yes, I think you're right." Brighams agreed. "So what do we do now? We can't stay in the trees, we'll be walking into the mouth of hell, and we can't make a dash through that – look at 'em, they're like locusts, there's so many of the damn creatures!"

342

"We've got to risk the trees," Teah suggested. "If we tie cloths over our mouths and noses for the smoke and stay low..."

"That's easy for you to say," Lauren interrupted. "How do you expect Layla to do that?"

"Don't worry," Calin reassured the distressed young woman. "I'll carry Layla; we can let the horse go, she won't want to get any nearer to those flames."

"I'll send her back into the woods," Teah offered. "We've got to try, otherwise we might as well head south right now and that would be ridiculous when we are so near."

In agreement the party tied cloths around their noses and mouths for the smoke. Calin repositioned his sword so he could still get to it if needed and placed Layla on his back. The girl was still a child and her weight wasn't a problem for him. Staying low with her on his back was more difficult – nothing he couldn't deal with but he might just need a hot bath in the morning to unknot the muscles.

They stayed as close to the tree line as they could, making their steady way west. As they drew nearer to the inferno the smoke thickened and they could feel the intensity of the heat. It became difficult to breathe and the need for silence was soon secondary to the need to cough and clear their lungs. It didn't matter too much. The forest was alive with the sizzle and snap of the burning trees and there were less lizards in this section of land, perhaps also discouraged by the thick clouds of smoke which blew over from the woods. Calin tried to talk, his voice dry and weak. "We can't keep going, this isn't going to work."

Teah looked distraught. "What else can we do?"

"We could rush the lizards; we'd catch 'em off guard and there's not so many here, we could deal with them and creep along the outer wall."

343

"What then?" Grun asked. "Knock on the door and hope someone is passing by. The lizards would soon work out what had happened and probably catch us sat by the door, we'd put the whole city in even more danger."

"We'll have to retreat, wait it out in the woods." Jimmy suggested.

"Perhaps the lad's right, we know there are places where we can hide." Brighams offered.

"Not if their new tactic is to burn the trees. They only stopped because we killed that magic user, I'm fairly sure they will send more when they realise he didn't finish his job. I don't fancy being trapped in the centre of a blazing forest." Teah still remembered the horror of running from the intensity of the flames earlier that night. "We can't give up, let's just try and get a little bit closer."

"We'll try, but I'm not risking my sisters' lives on a damn fool's errand." Grun told her. "We will get as near as we can then make the decision, but I think we might be wasting our time. I'm a soldier, I won't die in a bloody fire!"

"Agreed." Teah said, and she led them closer to the flaming section of forest ahead of them.

It really was like walking into the jaws of hell. Above their heads the canopy raged and embers of red-hot debris rained down on them. They could hardly breathe at all now, all gasping to get enough air into their lungs, and the heat was agonising. Teah looked in frustration out towards the wall; even in the thickening smoke she knew they were close, but it wasn't close enough. There was an unspoken agreement made within the party and, with heavy hearts, they turned to retrace their steps.

A thunderous crack shattered the night and lightning ripped through the sky up above them. They all froze as the area all around them was suddenly illuminated. There were shouts and calls from the Sandkind and, instinctively, everyone drew their swords. A second bolt of lightning clattered through the night, followed immediately by a deep ground-shaking rumble. Then, without warning, the heavens opened as a surge of torrential rain hammered down all around them.

Everyone looked at each other in surprise, the rain was the most intense Teah had ever experienced and it had literally come from nowhere. They could hear pandemonium breaking out from the nearby Sandkind, apparently they had never experienced weather like this either.

"It's the deluge!" Grun explained, it usually comes in the last week of spring but it's early! It's a miracle."

The rain wasn't showing any sign of stopping; if anything it was picking up momentum. As it flooded down on the woodland it snuffed out the flames and broke apart the smoke, cooling the night and bringing clean air to breathe.

"This is not your usual miracle!" Calin laughed. "This is Lyaren's doing. I say we make a run for that door and we do it now!"

There was no argument, the path ahead had opened up and they dived straight through. The ground was quickly becoming thick and slippery with mud as the persistent water flowed from the sky, but this was little concern after the horror of the forest fire. It took only moments to reach the patch of forest across from the backdoor. The expanse of grass before them was clear, although there were lizard soldiers within sight in both directions.

"Do you think they could see us in this rain?" Grun asked, knowing how poor the creatures' vision was.

"I'm not sure they're even trying to see," Calin answered. "I don't think they've ever known rain, let alone rain like this, look at 'em!" It was true – the lizards seemed to be wandering aimlessly. Some were holding cloths and shields above their heads to provide some shelter; all appeared distracted and it might well be possible that they could make the dash without being seen.

"I'll go first," Teah offered. "With Lauren. I can shield us as we cross and there is a small mound just to the left of the door where Lauren can stay out of sight while I try to get someone's attention. If this rain is what we think it is they'll be expecting us. The rest of you stay here until I give the signal, there may be more clanswomen waiting to shield you as you cross."

The others agreed but in the end didn't need to wait long. The gate was thrown open as Teah and Lauren drew near, and shadows scuttled out into the night. Within minutes the rescue was over and, as everyone regained their breath in the narrow tunnel, the stonemasons went to work sealing off the backdoor for good.

Juzuk and his fellow priests stood before the gates of Stagsonton. They jointly cast a spell which held an invisible shield above their heads to deflect the relentless rain, whilst at the same time levitating their feet above the deepening mud. For the remainder of their army there was no such luxury. Indeed, the Sandkind army was getting its first taste of rain and it was not to their liking. Nevertheless they were here to do a job and, as Juzuk's master had bid him, they would begin today. Drawing strength from his brothers around him he amplified his voice so he could be heard by every member of the army. He spoke in their tongue of the Sandkind and laced his words with a spell of compulsion

346

which would act on all who heard his words. "Sandkind of the Blood-Red Desert! Children of Xyakah! Your God has spoken. We must bring death to these heretics! In the service of your God, I command you... Attack!"

Dropping his amplification, he turned to the initiates who surrounded him. "My brothers, we will give the lizards one day to weaken these walls; tomorrow, we will shatter them. Drink the blood of our enemies, make your rituals and strengthen your powers. For your God demands the souls of those who dwell within these walls, and we will bring them to him screaming!" He returned the amplification and began the chant "Xyakah!"

"Xyakah! Xyakah! Xyakah!" As the chant repeated it picked up momentum, growing and swelling. The attack had begun.

It took Ela a moment or two to realise she was in her own bed and not the simple cot from Lyaren's room.

"Glad to see you are finally awake." Lyaren said dryly, from the stool where he sat at her bedside. "We thought you might be planning to sleep through the siege."

She ignored him. "My head hurts." she murmured. Her voice was hoarse and as she tried to sit up her muscles resisted and she slumped back down. "I feel like Teah has just used me for target practice!"

"Here, let me help you." this time Ly allowed his compassion to show in his voice. He placed his arm around her back and gently helped her to sit, then took a small cup of steaming tea from the table and passed it to her. "I made this just as I realised you were coming round. Drink it, it will help."

She took a sip and pulled a face. "That's revolting, what is it?"

"Drink it all down," he told her. "It's my own recipe: calamine, mint and a secret restorative I carry for those more-taxing magical tasks. You will start to feel more like yourself when you've drunk it."

She screwed up her nose but still drank deeply and began to feel some of the weakness leave her. As her head cleared everything came back into focus in a rush. "Teah! Did they get back? Did she find Tarrin and Calin and the Princess?"

"Teah is back and safe, as are Calin, Grun and his sisters along with two of his father's men. Tarrin has set off cross country with Alexia to try and get her back to her father – Calin said he was going to use his magic to shield them both from sight and intended to pick up horses on the way. We think they stand a good chance if they avoid the roads and don't trust anyone they meet."

"Tarrin's no fool, he'll keep her safe." she smiled. "We did it, Ly, it was wonderful. See, I knew I must have some magic."

"Yes... Well it seems you do, but just how it works is a mystery to me. The moment I woke I checked you over and, just like before, there was no sign of any magic at all. You are an enigma that is taking considerable solving, Elayna."

Ela smiled, a little distracted by the persistent noise from outside. "What is all that noise?" she asked.

"Well, some silly fool brought about an early deluge so some of that sound is the persistent rain (they tell me it can last for up to two weeks and they have never known it to be quite this torrential). The pounding you can hear alongside the rain, that's the Sandkind trying to break down our walls."

"It's begun?"

"Sadly, yes. It started yesterday morning; so far they haven't caused much damage. In fact they seem to have inflicted more casualties on themselves than they have on us. The knock-on bonus of the rain is that conditions are pretty miserable for those outside the walls, but I'm sure they will have more to offer in the way of a fight before this war is over."

"You said 'yesterday;' have I slept all that time?"

"Yes, apparently you are the warlock of sleep!" Lyaren laughed at Ela's outraged face and was rewarded with a pillow thrown into his. "Get out of here!" she growled at him, I need to get dressed!"

"Don't worry, I'm going!" He made a show of running to the door, laughing heartily as he did so. Then he stopped as if something had just occurred to him. "Oh by the way, Teah called by – she said to tell you there was no time to sleep; she would be waiting to continue your training as usual?" The question in his statement was undeniable.

"Oh thanks," she said, her manner as nonchalant as she could manage. "She's just been showing me a few bits and bobs."

"Good. That means she's saved me a job! I might drop by and watch you train later, see what other... bits and bobs, you might need to work on." And with that he left.

Lyaren was impressed by Ela's initiative. He had planned to train her in basic swordsmanship but hadn't had chance; events had overtaken him and there just hadn't been the time. He knew she could hold a sword – her brother had taught her – so, if Teah had given her some useful strategies, she might be able to protect herself a little at a push. He made his way straight from Ela's room to Daniel's office only to find that Daniel had already left for the wall. After making a few enquires as to the specifics, he rushed off to join him. Lyaren was fast and, after his own prolonged sleep followed by the wait for Ela to waken, he was ready to use his body and so chose to run through the city. The exertion woke his muscles and sharpened his mind. As he reached the wall he could see Daniel and his party mounting the steps and he had caught them up by the time they had reached the top.

"Glad you made it, Lyaren." Daniel smiled, but there was no joy in his eyes. "This goes badly for the attackers, what are they playing at?"

Lyaren looked out over the surrounding fields. The land at the foot of the wall was littered with the dead bodies of lizard warriors.

"Do you think they plan to pile their dead up so high they can climb their bodies to the top?" Rudley offered.

"The priests are the ones running this show," Lyaren told him. "They will have no concern for the number of dead on either side. They are simply testing our defences; when they find a weakness they will use magic to attack."

"Will the walls hold? You said they had magical wards of their own."

"I think they'll hold at first; it depends how many priests they have and how powerful they are. If they start to fail we will pull back to the inner bailey. The wards up there are much stronger and by that time their priests will be weakened. With any luck we will be able to eliminate a few of them at that point."

"If we get chance we'll eliminate them sooner." Rudley growled.

Lyaren pointed out into the field. "Do you see them?" he said. "The black cloaked figures up on that ridge?"

The other men looked out to where he pointed; his Elvin eyesight was exceptional but at a push they could just make out what he was showing them. "Will they stay so far away?" Daniel asked. "They are well out of range up there."

"It's hard to say, and will depend on how much power they can create. It is harder to throw magic over a long distance – like throwing a ball it loses momentum but if you throw enough balls you are bound to get in a few good strikes."

Just as Lyaren finished speaking a streak of yellow light flashed outwards from the position of the mass of black-clad men. The bolt hit, crashing into the wall with an audible sizzle. There was a deep rumbling sound followed by a soft ping and the light scattered across the walls and dissipated into the air. All eyes turned to Lyaren.

"It seems their magical attack has now begun too." he told them sombrely. "That was a practice shot; I suspect they can see us and thought they might get lucky. I suggest we move a little further back and make sure we keep our clothes neutral whenever we come up here. Amongst the guards uniforms our clothes will stick out like a sore thumb."

"At least the wall did its job!" Daniel said.

"Yes it did!" Rudley grinned. "Bet they had a surprise then!"

"Maybe," Lyaren was more cautious. "But that was a half-hearted shot. They will have a lot more than that up their sleeves!"

Ela made her way straight to Teah's rooms but found them empty. She hadn't bothered with her usual subterfuge, the cat was out of the bag and Lyaren didn't seem to mind that she had been learning to fight so there seemed no point in hiding her intentions. Besides, they were really at war now and she needed to be ready to fight as soon as the need arose. She wore her clanswoman clothes proudly and had the sword and the

351

knives she had been given secured in their respective places. It felt strange to wear these clothes in the opulence of the castle but she brushed off her discomfort and pushed her shoulders back. *She had earned the right to wear these clothes,* she told herself, *and if anyone had a problem with that she would be happy to prove herself.* Her usual guards followed her down through the castle and round to the women's compound. Neither appeared surprised and both treated her with their usual courtesy and respect.

Sahain and Alyha saw her approach and both rushed over to meet her. "Lyaren told us you helped him with the rain," Sahain said. "Are you alright?"

"Yes I'm fine," Ela smiled. "I've come to train but I was hoping I might see Teah."

"She and Calin are down in the common room. Come on, they'll be glad to see you. Your timing is good – the stew's almost finished, you can eat with us before we put you through your paces." Alyha looped her arm through Ela's and the three women made their way over to the low-level home of the women.

Ela expected a warm welcome from Calin, but was taken by surprise at the warmth of Teah's greeting.

"I'm glad you both made it back." she told them. Calin beamed. "We heard that we owed that to you and Ly; we were about to give up when the rains came."

"It was Daniel who insisted we do everything to get you back, I'm just glad we could help." Ela smiled.

"Well I don't know how much time I will have, but we (that's Calin and I) were hoping we could help you with your training, our way of saying thank you, if that's what you would like?"

Ela looked to Alyha and Sahain, a little concerned she might offend the women who had begun her lessons.

"Its fine, Ela, I couldn't begin to give you what Teah can. She has been trained by our best warriors since she was a child. You must accept this offer, you have much promise and, with Teah's help, you could become very skilled."

"Then I will be honoured," Ela accepted. "Thank you."

They chatted happily together as they ate but the drumming of the Sandkind's attack never relented and the reality of war was firmly in everyone's minds. With the importance of this at the forefront and, under Teah's firm guidance, Ela put all her effort into her work.

In the rain it was a little miserable at first, but the beautiful leather of her clanswoman suit was sufficiently waterproof to keep most of the rain from reaching her skin. Ela couldn't help but wonder how uncomfortable this would have been in the heavy woollen skirts of the Maldoran women; she guessed they would weigh a ton with so much liquid soaked in. Despite the rain, sweat beaded her body and her muscles pumped with the exertion. She found she had more control today and, although Teah brought her to the ground many times, she seemed to get more blows of her own in and her tumbles were less frequent. Two hours into the training session something changed. Teah pulled back a bit, letting Ela have more room to practise her movements before countering them. Something had been nagging at the edge of her awareness for some time but she was too focused on the fight to pay it any attention. It was only when she landed with a thump in a rather large puddle and heard Lyaren's hearty laughter that she realised it was his presence she had felt and been ignoring for the past half-hour. Suddenly it all made sense – Teah had held back to give her a chance to show Lyaren what she could do.

"I'm impressed." Ly said, offering her a hand.

Ela ignored it and pulled herself to her feet. There was a little more water inside the leathers of her clothes now. "Thank you," she said wearily. "Though I fail to see why you should be impressed, Teah can disarm me in less than a minute."

Lyaren looked at Teah and smiled broadly. "I suspect there are very few people in this city that could last more than a minute with Teah, Elayna. You have picked up some good habits and sound basics. Those are impressive 'bits and bobs!' I'm not so sure about the outfit though, Daniel will have a fit."

"Well Daniel will just have to deal with it!" she snapped. Something about his personal lack of interest irritated her immensely. "We are at war; would he have me fight in skirts?"

"I would have you not fight at all, but we may not have that luxury. Do you plan to wear it for dinner or could I escort you up to your rooms to change?"

Ela turned to Teah. "Are we finished for today?" she asked simply.

"You have done well, Elayna." Teah smiled. "You are not quite so dead today. Keep that fire in your belly and we will resume tomorrow."

"You did well, Ela." Calin added. "I never expected you would have learned so much so quickly."

Ela grinned at the huge smith. She still found him ridiculously handsome, but something about his relationship with Teah had removed the girlish attraction she had felt when they first met and now she knew she would always see him as the dearest of friends, and that sat so much better with her. "Thank you Calin," she said. "It helps to have people see my progress." She reached up on her tiptoes and planted a gentle kiss on his cheek. I'm so glad you and Teah found each other." she said.

Then turned and bowed before Teah in the fashion of the clanswomen.

"We'll see you later." Teah said casually. "Go and get out of those wet clothes before Daniel or Myllasanndia sees you and has that fit."

She could hear Teah's joyous laughter as she and Lyaren made their way back up to the castle. "What news from the wall?" Elayna asked after an awkward silence.

"The enemy are not really trying yet, they are testing us I think."

"Will the walls hold, Ly? Are we safe here?"

"I don't think so. I think we have a little while, but there is a lot of power building up amongst those priests out there and the wards are old. I'm going to work on the inner defences tomorrow, see if I can strengthen them more so that if need be we can move everyone into the inner bailey."

"I could get the women preparing more of the empty buildings in case they are needed to house the people."

"Yes I think that would be a good idea. I might even suggest Daniel begin to move some of the women and children from the homes nearest to the walls; it could take some time to evacuate everyone and it won't hurt to be prepared."

They were both quiet for the rest of the walk. Ly left Ela at her door and said he would return for her within the hour. Daniel had asked them to join him for a meal and Ly had the funniest feeling that this would be the last chance he and his new friends would have to break bread together for some time.

When he returned an hour later, Lyaren was relieved to see Ela in more conservative attire. It had taken considerable control to shield his emotions and his usual tactic of making fun either of her or himself was not going to work in this situation. Ela looked magnificent in the clanswoman leathers and, as her body worked through the rigorous training session, he had been mesmerised. He couldn't bring himself to insult her and was too witless to insult himself so instead he deflected the attention to Daniel and decided to avoid watching her training from now on. Teah had it all in hand. His situation was hard enough as it was. He was hopelessly in love with the one person on the planet he could never love, the one person he spent the most time with and who he was tasked to protect at all costs. He couldn't add desire to the situation! *No, this wouldn't do at all.*

As Rudley marched into the courtyard, Grun hailed him and ran over. "Are you on the way to Daniel's dinner?" he asked his friend.

"Yes, are you going too?"

Grun nodded. "Daniel said he wanted a chance to see us all together before the world turns completely crazy."

"From where I'm standing he's too late!" Rudley grumbled. "But it will be nice to hide behind the pretence of normality for an hour or so."

The two men chatted light-heartedly as they entered the castle, taking an opportunity to share some of the less-essential elements of their day. As they crossed the formal entrance hallway they both stopped in their tracks; a raucous tirade of obscene expletives boomed from behind one of the closed doors to an antechamber, which was used to house the petitioners who waited to see Daniel on a daily basis. They both stopped in shock and turned to look directly at the household guard who stood smartly to attention, unresponsive to the commotion.

It was Grun who enquired; the guard was Elite and, as such, directly under his authority. "Guardsman!"

Grun addressed the man. "Report on this situation. What is the meaning of this? We are in the Keep of Stagsonton, not at some dockside brothel!"

The man stood even smarter to attention and saluted formally. "Sir, we are carrying out Lord Nunnington's orders, Sir. He hasn't had time to see this man and says we must keep him comfortable until he has time to see him, Sir!"

"Oh it must be the singing man." Rudley remembered the guard from two nights back and quickly filled Grun in on the situation.

Grun frowned deeply; keeping the peace in the castle was his main responsibility and this was not appropriate. "Open the door!" he ordered. "I will see this fellow for myself."

The guard opened the door and the two officers walked in to find a smartly dressed fellow sat sideways in the chair, his feet resting across the arm and his head thrown back, eyes closed.

He was in full voice as he reached the midway point in 'The Ditty of Fanny's Nursemaid', the chorus of which brought a red glow to Rudley's cheeks. When the song came to an end the man opened his eyes and, noticing his audience, quickly jumped to his feet. He was a slight fellow with long, spindly legs and a huge mop of deep, rusty hair. It was hard to guess an age but almost certainly older than Grun and younger than Rudley. He wore plain brown trousers and a garish flouncy yellow shirt covered by a faded but smart red velvet jacket. Although he appeared to be very clean and smart, to the eye of those accustomed to gentry, it was clear the clothes were very old, verging on antiquated, and here and there a very carefully inserted patch could just be seen.

The man bowed with a flamboyant waving of his hand. "Why, at last!" he announced. "Gentlemen of

357

quality. I see I have hit the jackpot: General Rudley and the newly appointed Lieutenant General Grun, I believe."

"You have us at a disadvantage, Sir." Rudley said. "Who might you be?"

"I am known by many names, General – some of them you may well know – but today I am here on family business and so today I am Lord Safehelm."

"Ah yes, my men mentioned this. It seems to me, Sir, that men with more than one name have much to hide, and there is no Lord Safehelm, which means you, Sir, are a liar and, judging from your knowledge of unsavoury vocabulary, quite probably a villain. Lord Daniel advised that singing was not a crime, but impersonation of a Lord may just be. I will give you one opportunity to leave this place of your own free will or I will have you taken to the dungeons until I have time to investigate your crimes which, by my current calculation, I would say will be in about five years..."

The strange man smiled dryly. "You are wise to be wary of me, General. I may well be your worst nightmare but I am indeed Lord Safehelm and I have the paperwork to prove it, if I may?" The man pointed to a small chest placed on the table by his chair.

Rudley nodded and the man opened the chest and pulled out a scroll. He handed the paper to Rudley solemnly. "I will be happy to leave now if you can promise me that you will place this directly into the hands of Daniel Nunnington and no other."

Rudley looked at the scroll and then at the strange man in front of him. "I can pass this on to Lord Nunnington for you. We are on our way to meet with him now, in fact."

"Oh excellent," the man beamed. "Please tell your Lord that if he wants my help I will return to his beautiful home in two days' time for his convenience.

However, if he is not in need of my services I will not tarry. I wish you every success with your siege, gentlemen." Smiling pleasantly the man picked up his little chest, bowed politely and meekly left the room.

Grun could control himself no longer and burst out laughing almost as soon as the man was through the door. "What in the seven hells was that?" he asked.

Rudley shook his head perplexed, a strange expression on his face. "I don't know," he confessed. "But look at this seal, Grun."

Grun looked at the scroll Rudley held and whistled in amazement. He knew that seal well enough. It was that of the House of Nunnington and only two people alive had access to it, namely Daniel and Myllasanndia Nunnington.

"I'm going to get this to Daniel." Rudley said. "Either that man's a major criminal or he is connected to the family and, with everything that's going on, we need all the help we can get."

"Tread softly, Rudley." Grun advised. "Help, in my opinion, seldom comes without a price."

The two men shared a concerned look before continuing on their way to Daniel's private dining room.

Chapter 13
The Lord of Safehelm

"At last... We were worried you couldn't get away from the wall!" Daniel said as Grun and Rudley entered his private dining room.

The room was full of Daniel's family and friends, in the main the council members, with the addition of Dina and Kayel, Alyha and the three doctors who had previously been working with Daniel's father. A number of other women were also present, who were obviously the wives of the other council members. The little room was very full but there was a happy, cosy atmosphere about the place.

As the last guests entered, Daniel picked up his glass and addressed the room. "My friends... Thank you for joining my mother and I tonight. It may seem a strange time to host a party, when our enemies are at our door; the momentum of their attack builds and we have no idea how we are going to face the horror in front of us." He paused as the weight of his words settled in the room. "However we wanted you to know that, despite the desperate nature of our situation, we are not afraid. We stand ready to face that which is ahead of us, with the sure knowledge that we stand shoulder to shoulder

361

with you our advisors, our experts, our friends. Were it not for those gathered here tonight we would have lost this battle before it began; lost our courage, lost our control, lost our family and lost our lives. But instead we are alive and we have hope. Tonight we wanted to remind you all of the reason why we do what we do; why we put ourselves on the front line, why we place ourselves in the path of danger. Some of us may not live out this war, perhaps all of us, but we fight for our freedom, we fight for our families and those we love. And so, tonight, we will enjoy our freedom, enjoy our families and be amongst our friends and loved ones, and it is with the memory of this night in our hearts that tomorrow we will face our enemy."

Daniel's words hung in the room for a while as their importance registered on the assembled guests. It was Lyaren who regained his wits first and, holding his glass high, announced "A toast, to Stagsonton and to victory."

The guests repeated his words and, as they drank the rich wine that was the specialty of the region, the evening settled into the rhythm of a pleasant family gathering.

No one stayed late. Those with children were keen to get back to them, while others had responsibilities to attend to. Lyaren and Elayna spoke to James Rothenburg and Dominic Grimsore about their idea to begin the evacuation of the city into the inner bailey. The two loyal townsmen were happy to oversee the work and agreed whole-heartedly with the plan. Daniel had already moved all his council members into the castle so they were to hand at short notice. These honest men had felt a weight of guilt about accepting the extra security which their friends and neighbours were denied; this would redress the balance. Alyha, Sally and Sahain agreed to organise the living spaces as people began to arrive, starting with the spare barrack buildings and then moving on to any and all available spaces. Myllasanndia agreed to look at the castle accommodation and readily agreed that formal rooms and function rooms could house some of the families.

As the evening progressed and the guests bid their goodnight, Rudley hung back. He knew he had duties which he should attend to but the scroll in his pocket had pricked his interest and something told him it was important. He deployed Grun to carry out his tasks and Grun readily agreed, under the understanding that Rudley fill him in on the outcome of the mysterious scroll.

As Myllasanndia began to take her leave he bid her stay for a moment. Only Lyaren, Elayna, Calin and Teah remained and Rudley knew that, other than himself and Grun, these were the ones Daniel confided in the most. All eyes looked to the soldier with interest.

"You may remember, My Lord, the night of the fire. Before we knew of the blaze, one of my men asked you about an unusual petitioner who was causing some commotion?"

Daniel thought for a moment before the memory returned. "Oh yes, the singer, has he returned?"

"No, My Lord, the man never left. As we made our way here tonight Grun and I encountered the colourful individual for ourselves and, if I'm honest, I threatened to throw the man in the dungeons if he didn't leave immediately."

Daniel laughed. "And did he leave?" he asked.

"Yes he did, and we thought he must have been some kind of simpleton or something, claiming to be the Lord of Safehelm, or some such place, but then he took this out of a small metal chest and asked if we would pass it on to you." Rudley drew the scroll out of his inside pocket where he had kept it safe all evening. "I had intended to read the contents myself and put my findings into my daily report but, well, see for yourself, My Lord, I felt you would want to look at this yourself."

Daniel took the offered document while the others looked on with interest. It was obviously old; the parchment was thin and discoloured with age. Two ornate caps protected the ends and gave it the appearance of an official document, but it was as Daniel looked at the seal that its true importance hit home. Daniel scowled, his face betraying his anger. "Where is this man now, Rudley? I want to know how he got his hands on my family seal, theft of a seal is treason!"

"Calm down Daniel." Myllasanndia told him. "May I look?"

He passed the document to his mother who looked closely at the pattern pressed into the rich red wax. "It's our family seal, but it's old, this mark was made hundreds of years ago, look at the outer ring."

As she passed the scroll back, Daniel looked closer. His mother was right; each member of the Nunnington family had a ring which held the family seal. They wore it always and took the ring with them to their grave, which for most was the crypt deep in the bowels of the keep. When each new ring was made the owner's initials were inscribed into the outer edge of the design. Daniel's ring held the letters D. A. A. N., signifying him as Daniel son of Alex, son of Alistair with the N being for Nunnington, while his mother's held the letters M. A. N. n., which stood for Myllasanndia Alex Nunnington with the lowercase 'n' representing her birth family, Nightburry.

The letters on this seal were A. S. S. B. N. B. "This Seal has too many letters." Daniel said thoughtfully. "Either it is a forgery or it is the seal of one of the very first Nunningtons. For the first six or seven generations the initials of every forefather were used in the rings; they changed it to signify only father and son when it became obvious they would run out of space. But this ring ends in B. N. – Bordin Nunnington. He was the only one of that name and the only Nunnington to have B as their initial. He was also the first of the Nunningtons to take the seat at Stagsonton, which makes this the seal of his great grandson and means this document must be over four hundred years old."

Myllasanndia looked to Lyaren. "Could you use magic to check its authenticity?"

Ly considered the question. "No, but I can tell you that the colour and texture of the parchment is correct for that period in history." He thought for a moment. "Perhaps we could use your gift, Myllasanndia?"

"I can't read objects, Lyaren, only people."

"Yes but I might be able to lift the impressions of the people who have held this scroll. If I channel those impressions into you, perhaps you could sense something of their emotions at the time."

"It's worth a try." Myllasanndia agreed, handing the scroll over to Lyaren.

Ly held the scroll in one hand and, with the other, took hold of Myllasanndia's. He flicked through the impressions, quickly tracking back until he found the oldest which he then passed through.

The image of a large, heavyset man rushed into her head. He was aging but had retained his handsome features well and bore a close resemblance to her late husband, Alex. His eyes were heavy and Myllasanndia felt an overwhelming sense of sadness and loss. The man vanished, replaced by a youth who held a striking resemblance to the first man. He also radiated sadness but something more, the weight of responsibility and nobility. There followed a succession of images of people, men and a few women, each retaining some features from the previous and each reflecting the exact same emotions: honour, commitment, responsibility. Finally the image came to rest on Rudley and Lyaren removed his hand from hers.

"I could only see their faces," she told Daniel. "But they were obviously father to son or daughter and there were certainly enough for this to be over 400 years old."

Myllasanndia's emotions still rung with the depth of what she had just experienced. Tears welled in her eyes. "Daniel these people, whoever they are, have carried the weight of a huge responsibility for many generations and I think they have done that for us. Daniel this is no forgery, we need to open it and we need to find that man – he has something very important on his mind and he is very worried about letting his family down. They have held this scroll for generation after generation and they have held it for you."

There was silence as they all took in the sincerity of Myllasanndia's words.

Rudley said quietly. "This Lord Safehelm said he would return in two days' time."

"Right." Daniel said. "I suppose I should open this now."

Everyone waited as Daniel took a knife and carefully opened the seal then removed the end caps. As he unrolled the scroll he found the contents had been carefully rolled to hold two documents – one being the scroll itself and, the second, a smaller piece of parchment which Daniel read out first:

'I pass unto my most beloved son the birthright of his soul family.

I task you this day and all those of your line,

Conceal that which must never be found,

Take up the watch and guardianship of Safehelm,
Pass on only through your line the knowledge,
Until such time as it's needed by the line of your
brother,
When you shall return it to the lord of your family name
and Stagsonton shall be once more the seat of the Goddess.'
Alextrallion Nunnington

"What does that mean?" Ela asked.

"I'm not sure." Daniel told her.

"I think it was written by the first man I saw, he was so sad but so full of honour and so proud. As if he was losing something of huge importance but he did it of his own free will and for a greater good." Myllasanndia advised.

"This man was Alextrallion Nunnington." Daniel said. He had unrolled the other scroll and was looking at its contents. He held it out so that everyone could see. "I recognised this straight away," he told his friends. "Father and I would spend hours looking at one nearly identical to this when I was a child. I used to love following the branches and working my way up to the one where my name sat." He smiled. "Only on this family tree my branch hasn't been born yet; this is the family tree of Alextallion Nunnington and therefore different to the one I've got in my office."

Myllasanndia ordered one of the stewards to fetch Daniel's family tree from the office and within a few minutes both documents were laid out together. Daniel quickly found Alextallion's branch of his much bigger tree. "You see on my family tree Alextallion married Daska of Beenburg and they had one son, Warren. Then it shows an offshoot, which represents a bastard, and the name Daniel Stagsonton is registered. The line of the bastard children of noble families are never followed on these charts, they are usually married off or sent into the regiments. But look at this version of the tree. Here is Alextallion, Danska and Warren, but then Danska dies and Alextallion marries again... It says he marries..." Daniel looked again, his eyes not truly registering what he was seeing. "It says he marries Myllasanndia Nightburry! Mother that must be one of your ancestors. And they have a second legitimate son and – you are not going to believe this – he's recorded as Daniel Nunnington! It seems I may have a very distant ancestor who carried my name and whose mother carried the same name as you."

Lyaren looked closer at where Daniel was looking on the ancient document. "There is some tiny writing under the second son's name but it's hard to make out, even for me. Calin, could you pass me that candle please."

Lyaren placed the extra light near to the parchment and got as close as he could without getting in his own light. "It's a bequest," he told them. "It says: 'I bestow upon you Daniel Nunnington, the Lordship and Guardianship of Safehelm.'" The small company of friends all looked at each other, waiting for someone to break the silence. Finally it was Calin who did.

"Well I'm no scholar or expert, but what I do know is sense, and my sense tells me we've got a right riddle here to solve, but we also have a war to fight and no amount of standing around looking at each other will win that war or solve that riddle. I say we wait for the two days that fellow said and in the meantime put all our effort into keeping this city safe. That way, one way or another, we will all still be here to get some answers."

"That, Calin, is the most scholarly thing that I have ever heard." Daniel smiled. "There's nothing like going to bed on a mystery, let's all get some sleep."

Rudley came over to where Grun was stood watching the enemy from the top of the wall. The lizards had continued to throw themselves at the wall all night and through much of the morning. They had made little impact on the fortifications and the Stagsonton archers had picked them off effectively. They tried to position scaling ladders to get over the wall but, again, the people of Stagsonton were ready and so far not one lizard soldier had made it up to the battlements. The black-clad warlock priests had kept up a steady barrage of attacks which shook the wall and made impressive light displays but again had made little impact. Then suddenly, about an hour ago, everything had stopped and, at that point, Grun had sent for Rudley. He watched as their warriors withdrew and began to construct what looked like a huge bonfire.

"You say they've been at this for the last hour?" Rudley asked.

"I'd say so." Grun told him. "It's giving me the creeps; do you think they're going to burn their dead?"

"They might be, at least that way the stench will stop wafting up here."

Rudley had a good point. The rain had stopped late last night and then as the wind had picked up it brought with it the stench of death from the numerous, decaying Sandkind bodies littering the mud-encrusted battlefields.

"I think we should get Lyaren up here, see if he's got any ideas. Is there anything else to report?"

"Only that they seem to have been joined by another regiment of lizard warriors. They arrived last night in a convoy." Grun pointed to where a line of wagons had been positioned over to the left of the enemy camp.

"Any idea what might be in those wagons?" Rudley asked.

"No, but we're keeping a watch on them."

Lyaren was working on the fortification of the inner bailey when he got the message that Rudley and Grun wanted his help on the outer wall. He quickly made his way over and joined them on the wall, listening to their concerns and watching for himself the peculiar activities of their enemies.

"This is what I was worried would happen." he said. "We will need to prepare ourselves; this won't be nice."

"Why?" Rudley asked. "We were hoping they were going to burn their dead."

"That won't be on their agenda, they will want the stench of the dead to make life unpleasant for us and they will not worry about how it affects their own men. No, that fire is for something very different, and I think it will be very painful for anyone on the wall who witnesses it." Lyaren took a breath as he tried to find the best words to explain this horror. "Those priests have been using their power for days now to try and break this wall but they haven't made any visible progress. They need more power to throw more energy into their magic. They can get this from a number of places. Those with magic can combine their magic, like Ela and I did with the deluge. That's no good to them, they already have all their number contributing. They could draw magic from the land, everything around us contains natural magic, but to take from the earth is a slow process and these priests don't appear to be the patient type. There is a

370

third way to raise power, the practice is forbidden by my people but these abominations justify it through their sick religion. My people call your people The Magicless, meaning those without magic. In fact this is not true. You have magic, just like the rest of us, but your magic is tethered to your soul so tightly that you are unable to use it at all. In fact, the only way to release it is to set your soul free and move it on to the Spinner. At that point the magic is released and can be claimed by strong magic users. That fire will be the means by which this is achieved and, if I'm not mistaken, those wagons will hold the souls they intend to harvest their magic from."

"Are you trying to say they intend to burn people to death in that fire?" Grun exclaimed in horror.

"Sadly yes, I think they do." Lyaren replied.

"Why burn them?" Rudley asked. "It seems a bit drawn out, why not just cut their throats? Dead is dead isn't it?"

"The fire ensures a slow death, as the body fights to hang on to life it builds up fear and fights for survival; this act draws the magic up and to the surface. Few humans can access this power, but by this point even those who can are seldom capable of using it. As death claims them, they have no choice but to hand over their power to the priest."

Rudley and Grun looked at Lyaren in horror.

"So," Grun said. "We've got to stand here and watch those monsters torture and kill people, and while they grow more powerful we have to stand by helplessly and watch?"

Lyaren nodded. "As I said, this won't be nice. It is what I had feared and when their power is built up; then we will begin the real battle for the wall."

"Should we mount some sort of attack? Send some of our men out to draw them into battle while a second group try to rescue those poor souls?"

"I think that's what they'd love us to do; we are grossly outnumbered, we wouldn't stand a chance. And if they took any of our men alive..." Lyaren left the thought for them to complete.

"By the Goddess, Lyaren, what demons are these?" Rudley asked.

"Demons they are not, they are men like us, even the Sandkind are just men, but their souls have been darkened by the blackest of evils and, when men become so lost in the dark, their deeds plunge to the deepest of depravities."

"Then promise me one thing." Rudley asked his friends. "If those bastards ever get me... one of you put an arrow through my heart."

Stagsonton was a hive of frenzied activity as the populace prepared to leave their dwellings and move up to the keep. Most followed the advice they were given although some did refuse to leave their homes, claiming they would fight for their survival when the time came. With all the activity the day passed quickly and then the second day arrived, that which Daniel and his friends had been waiting for. Rudley had left Grun in command of the wall so he could wait at the petitioners' door and watch the castle gates for the return of the strange man he and Grun had encountered two days previous. Daniel had hoped the man would present himself early in the day so that his mystery could be uncovered, but in actual fact it was almost midday before Lord Safehelm came to the petitioners' door. He wore the same outlandish clothes he had worn previously and still carried the small metal chest from which he had taken the scroll.

"Will Lord Nunnington see me now?" the man asked innocently.

"He is waiting for you in his private office." Rudley told him. "This way." And he led the man through the keep to Daniel's rooms.

Daniel stood as the peculiar man stepped into the room. He held out his hand which the man took and shook warmly. "You have given us a true mystery, Sir." Daniel told him. "May I present my mother, Myllasanndia."

Myllasanndia also shook the man's hand and, as she did, opened her powers up to him. She was instantly engulfed by his emotions, all of which he offered like an open book: fear, frustration, anger, betrayal, resentment, murder, survival, duty and honour – over everything was honour.

"Have you felt enough, Myllasanndia?" the man asked. "I am not a good man, as you have seen. It is hard to survive in this world without the fortune of family connections. My family has made its own way in this world, ruling the shadows. I am the lord of thieves and assassins, I am the honour that stands in the darkness. I am the master of secrets and the creator of deception. This was my birthright, a gift from my father as it was to his father before him and back to the first of my name. I am Daniel Nunnington Lord of Safehelm, descendent of Alextrallion Nunnington Lord of Stagsonton and Myllasanndia Nightburry his mistress of spies and secrets, of which my family line is one." The man bowed respectfully to Myllasanndia who still held his hand.

Myllasanndia looked at her son with wonder in her eyes. "He's telling the truth." Her voice was a gasp restrained by her surprise, "Daniel he is telling the truth, this man is also named Daniel Nunnington and he is a direct descendent of ours. He could feel my power and knew exactly what I was doing and, what's more, he helped me read him by opening his emotions in a way I have never felt before."

373

"Don't be so shocked cousin," the other Daniel said. "Our family has always had strong magic running through it; my line of the family in particular has worked hard to keep the laws of the Nightburry mages safe over the generations; we have always welcomed those with power into our fellowship."

Daniel looked at the man in amazement. "I think you need to take a seat," Daniel told him. "And tell us your tale from start to finish, ending with why you chose to reveal your existence to us just when our full attention is required at our city walls. Oh, and we need another name for you; I can't allow you into my home with the same name as me, it would be far too confusing for everyone. What else can we call you?"

The strange man sat in the chair Daniel indicated and smiled. "My friends call me Danny." he said. "Is that acceptable to you?"

Daniel nodded. "Yes I have always been Daniel, so Danny is fine, go on..."

"My family live in the docks in a modest home, but we have always been well-respected in that area of town."

"That is a place of criminals and brigands." Daniel explained to those who were not so familiar with the city. "He is telling us that his family business is far from legal."

"Some might say that," Danny agreed. "However, that business has always carried the Nunnington name even before Bordin took his seat at Stagsonton. My father told me that Bordin himself was a pirate who did a good deed for the King and was given Stagsonton in thanks for that service. But I digress. On my sixteenth birthday my father took me on a most unusual walk through the alleyways of Stagsonton and led me to a small doorway which stood between two buildings. Behind the door were steps which were cut into the rock and led deep down into the mountain below us. The steps ended in a solid stone wall, but when we reached the wall my father placed his hand upon it and the stone disappeared. I was shocked, for at this stage I knew nothing of my birthright, but behind that door my father showed me what his father had shown him – a wonder beyond my belief, for he showed me the city below. He showed me Safehelm."

"Are you talking about the tunnels, boy?" Rudley snapped. "Because if you are you are wasting your time, we have long known of their presence."

"Then you know of the citadel?" Danny said, sarcasm laced his voice. "You won't need my services then, for you already know the secret of the magic embedded in the walls of this keep, you know of the secret home waiting below to keep you and your people safe from attack and hidden from the enemy. You know of the magical weapons stockpiled beneath your feet and the magical volumes of the Nightburrys, and you know of the circle of Safehelm and their oath to stand firm behind the Nunnington name and in the name of the Goddess Mysta. We went to great lengths to keep all this hidden, but here you are all along knowing all of it." He waited for a response.

Daniel looked gravely at the man. "We know nothing of these things as you well know, but we are not children to be toyed with. You are the warden of an ancient history which your family have watched over on our behalf for generations. Don't trivialise the importance of your role. You are here because we believe you, we want to know what you have to say and then we want to bring you back into the family from which you have been outcast for so long. We believe you may have answers as to how we can win this war. Please, our questions are because of our bewilderment not disbelief."

Danny nodded slowly. "Forgive me, on my last visit to your home I was incarcerated in a room and treated with scorn by all I met. I have been trying to help for days but none would pay me the courtesy of a fair hearing, including you, Lord Daniel. For this I am still angry. As I say, my family is well-respected in the docks; the Lord of Safeguard is not left waiting, I have never known such treatment."

Daniel smiled. "Spoken like a true Lord. Go on Danny, your father took you down this magical passageway."

"Yes." Danny picked up his story. "He took me into a huge room which was full of books and scrolls, a collection of histories and magical books. Then he tested me with a magical tool and that is when I discovered that I had inherited the gift from my family. The Nightburrys were powerful sorcerers, but Myllasanndia, that is the first Myllasanndia, pledged that power to the Nunnington name. She was the most powerful Nightburry there has ever been and she was very much in love with Lord Nunnington. She used her talents in his name and built up a secret organisation which he used to keep ahead of his contemporaries. When his first wife died he married her and she gave him a second son, my ancestor and the first of our name, Daniel. We have passed the name from father to son from that time. Anyway I digress. On that day I was initiated into the circle of Safehelm, a small group of gifted individuals who keep the secrets which Myllasanndia had amassed, and when my father passed away last year I became the Lord of Safehelm, as he had been before me. Myllasanndia the First was a truly powerful sorceress and a devout follower of the teachings of the Mother Goddess in the form of Mysta the mischief-maker. It is said that this Goddess blessed her with a terrible vision of an evil that would rise many years in the future, in a time when all the knowledge that would be needed to defeat it would have been lost. The vision was a gift as it allowed Myllasanndia the First to put a plan in motion that would protect against that evil, and it is in service of this plan that my line of the family was tasked to keep the secrets safe, so that when a Lord Nunnington arose who would have need of them, he would have them. Two weeks ago I also had a vision. A beautiful woman appeared before me and said she was my grandmother of ancient times. I knew a spell had been triggered and that the woman before me was Myllasanndia the First. She told me it was time and that Lord Nunnington needed me, and so I set about trying to get your attention. Finally I see I have it."

"Have I got this right, young man?" Lyaren asked him solemnly. "You are telling us that there is a hidden city beneath our feet which will offer protection from this army and has magical items to help us defeat it?"

"Does my cousin know an elf hides amongst his advisors?" Danny asked, accusation lacing his question. Lyaren dropped his glamour and smiled broadly at the youth. "I am Lyaren, Lord Daniel's friend, and well done, few ever see through my disguise."

"You have interesting friends, cousin." Danny said. "Yes, Lyaren, that is sort of what I'm saying only it's so much better than that." And he sat back in his chair smiling broadly at his astonished audience.

"I'm not sure you can do better than that!" Daniel said in wonderment.

"I'll show you." Danny said, reaching for his small chest. He touched a plate on the top of the box and the lid popped up. Reverently he placed his hand into the chest and lifted out a beautiful crafted ruby. As he took it from the box Ela swooned and Lyaren only just caught her as she plummeted to the floor. Danny raised an eyebrow. "The sleeper is mentioned in the prophecy; she will be out cold until I get these away."

Lyaren didn't question him; he just carried Ela over and laid her on one of the couches.

Danny took six rubies from the box each identical to the other. "There are niches in the walls of this citadel where these stones should sit. They work with the magical fortifications of the walls and when this citadel is attacked by dark magic the spell will be triggered and the citadel will be saved."

"What do you mean 'saved'? What will it do?" Teah asked.

"You are the animage?" he addressed Teah.

"I am Teah of the Clans." she replied.

"You have power over animals?" Something about Danny's eyes was quite unnerving – he seemed to see straight into your soul.

"Yes, I can talk with some of them." Teah confessed.

Danny nodded as if he were putting pieces successfully into place. "And your friend is the beast; I can see you are bonded." He didn't bother waiting for an answer, he knew he was right. These people were all supposed to be here and he could trust them, although he still didn't like the general. "It will save it, the whole citadel shall be moved – magically relocated to its natural home, my home, the cavern below your feet known as Safehelm."

"Is this possible?" Daniel looked from his mother to Lyaren.

Myllasanndia shook her head in wonder. It was Lyaren who answered. "I know that humans once wielded powerful magic, it was said amongst my people that they were the strongest of all the races but that a mighty spell was cast back in history which trapped that magic within them so they could never access it. There have always been some, like your mother, who could

378

reach some of their power but I have not heard of any strong human mages in my lifetime. This being said, the wards which protect these walls are old and impressive and I can only just stand to be this close to those stones. I don't doubt why Ela is reacting as she is; if she was awake she would be in agony. So I suspect yes, as amazing and far-fetched as it sounds, I'm inclined to believe Danny of Safehelm."

"Very well, as much as I am fascinated by all this we are in a situation which calls for urgency. Danny, I hope we will have the luxury of many hours together when we get everyone to Safehelm in one piece and, at this time, I look forward to learning all about you and your people. For now, I would like you to go with Lyaren and my mother and place your stones where they need to be. Calin and Teah, when Ela wakes I want you to get every single person into the citadel as quickly as you can. Rudley, keep the walls manned until Calin gives the signal that the city is evacuated. At that point I want a token presence on the outer wall and the rest of your men up here with us. Make sure those who stand on the wall know to make a dash for the keep as soon as the wall is breached, if they get trapped outside we won't be able to help them. Now, if it's alright with you all, I have other duties to attend to."

Everyone in the room stood, bowed to Lord Nunnington and left to their tasks.

Ela woke as soon as the stones were out of her presence and Calin helped her find her feet, explaining what she had missed as they rushed to carry out their tasks.

Once alone, Daniel walked into the council chamber and cast his eye over the many plans and maps littering the desk. If this outrageous story proved to be true, all this paperwork was unnecessary. His people were about to be saved, whisked away from danger by powerful magic. He shook his head, still trying to comprehend it all. A sound by the door drew his attention, Rudley had returned. "Daniel, there has been a message from the wall." he said sadly. "You need to see this for yourself before we decide what to do."

Evening had drawn in but the light was still strong enough to see the garish scene before them. The enemy army stood to attention, positioned around the huge fire which burned behind the assembled, black-clad figures of the Xyakahan priests. The Sandkind chanted repeatedly, 'Xyakah, Xyakah,' the chant creating a beat like drumming. The flames of the immense fire danced their mesmerising flicker through the crisp air, casting a red glow over the scene. To the side of the priests stretched a line of people all in single file, swaying to the chanting as if in some kind of a trance. Each one was naked and each one was a young human woman. One of the priests took the hand of the first young woman in line; she was beautiful. He led her forward, closer to the wall, closer to where Daniel stood but careful to stay out of bowshot range. Then he addressed those stood on the wall. His voice was loud and clear, obviously magically enhanced. "People of Stagsonton, we grow tired of this game. Our armies are in need of refreshment." He lifted the girl's arm out to the side, making a show of fondling her breast as he did so. Then, with practised precision, made a cut of his knife which slit the girl's wrist. A second priest approached holding a silver goblet which he held beneath the girl's arm, collecting the deep sticky blood, which flowed, freely from her vein. Still the girl remained in place as if oblivious to her plight. The first priest raised her second arm, repeating the process, and another cup was brought over. The young girl swayed as her lifeblood pumped into the waiting goblets. The priest pointed to her wrists and the blood stopped pumping.

380

Then the two priests with the goblets drank deeply from them before carrying them over to the waiting lizard warriors, who in turn drank and passed the cups along. The priest had his knife in hand again but this time he used it to flay slithers of the skin from the girl's body, just as if carving a finely-cured piece of meat. He passed the flesh over to another priest who held a large silver plate. Still the girl did not move. The priest continued his grisly act until the girl began to sway uncontrollably. Once again his voice carried over to the wall. "This shall be the fate of all your women! As for you, men, we will make you watch before we kill you!" The priest pulled on the cord which held his robes and they fell to the floor. Naked he approached the girl and with one finger pushed her body to the ground. More priests approached, this time they poured a liquid into the girl's mouth; the effect was instant, a scream of agony whipped from her throat and she tossed her body about in an uncontrollable spasm. The priests held her down while their naked leader entered her and took his perverse pleasure.

Daniel could endure it no longer. He turned away from the exhibition below. All around him he could hear the outpouring of anger and disgust from his men on the wall. "Do we have anyone who can shoot that far?" he asked Grun.

"No Sir." Grun answered sadly.

"What about the catapults, will they reach?" he asked.

"Yes Sir," Grun told him. "But they are not accurate, we may hit the women."

"I know." Daniel looked at his friends; tears ran silently down his face. "It's the women I want you to target." He didn't look back, he knew he was leaving his men to do what he could not do himself, giving the order was all he could bear. As he reached the bottom of the stairs he heard the twang of the first catapult snapping into action, followed by the boom of the impact. The voices of the Sandkind's chant didn't even dwindle. Daniel hunched his shoulders and fled from the wall.

It had taken Danny some time to locate the exact position for each of the rubies, but finally they had found them and were now at the point in the walls intended for the sixth stone. Danny repeated his ritual for the final time. He held the jewel in his open palm and pushed a little magic out into it. Then in a clear voice he simply whispered, "Return to whence you came." The stone pulsed slightly in his hand and then began to rise through the air as if pulled up the wall by an invisible force. Finally it settled in a tiny recess high above their heads, which they never would have noticed, were they not aware of its presence.

Danny smiled at Myllasanndia and Lyaren. "Well, my friends, it is done. And by the sound of that army it may be just in time."

They had tried to ignore the sounds from beyond the city but they could all feel the mounting of the dark power beyond the walls. Daniel had returned from the scene a little while earlier, and rumours of what was happening out on the fields had already circulated around the city.

Lyaren was in no doubt that the rumours were true. He knew there was nothing they could do to stop the atrocity or help those poor women, and when he heard of Daniel's course of action he was in sad agreement that it was the only way they could help.

In an odd way the horror of those scenes was helping the evacuation process in the city, as a new urgency motivated the people of Stagsonton to move up into the safer position offered by the citadel. All they could do was hope it would all be enough. They had chosen not to mention the magical protections to the populace; their only experience of magic would be those monsters beyond their walls and they couldn't risk scaring people away.

"You must be hungry, Danny." Myllasanndia said, moving thoughts away from matters they were powerless to address.

"A little" Danny confessed. "Food is in short supply these days, we have limited stocks."

"We too," Myllasanndia told him. "But I think we will be able to find a little something." They all made their way downstairs and Myllasanndia led them to a small room off the main kitchen which housed a simple wooden table and chairs. "I often eat here when I'm working," she confessed. "I love the smells which our chef creates as he works."

Lyaren could see what she meant, a mixture of freshly baked bread and some herby stew flavoured the air. "Tell us a little more about Safehelm." Lyaren pressed. "Once we are there how do we leave? Will we be trapped by the magic?"

"No, there are ways out but many of them require travel of great distance underground. There is one shorter exit through a cavern system which comes out in the southern forest. This will be the means by which we will bring fresh produce into Safehelm and, should Daniel see fit, the way we can launch attacks against the enemy. I believe from the prophecy that Daniel may choose to take such action.

"I would like to see the prophecy." Lyaren said. "I am especially interested in what it says about Elayna. I have been trying to work out why she has such strong reactions to magic."

"The prophecy simply says the sleeping woman will be one of the markers which confirm it is the right time. There is no other explanation. Apart from where it says she will sleep in the presence of powerful magic. I wonder how she is dealing with that black stuff out there."

"I don't know, but I think perhaps I should go and see." Lyaren said, just as a woman entered the room carrying three bowls of steaming hot soup. It smelt delicious. "Right after I fill my empty belly."

The others laughed as they too tucked into their meal.

"Would you like to stay in the castle, Danny?" Myllasanndia enquired. "We can accommodate you and your family."

"It's just me, the circle are awaiting your arrival in Safehelm. I will stay for the spell to run its cause."

"Then I will find you a room and, if it doesn't offend, perhaps a change of clothes and a hot bath, should time oblige of course."

Danny smiled. "No offence taken, I hate these rags but they belonged to the first Lord Daniel and have been handed down and kept as free from moths as possible just for this time. I suggested acquiring new but my colleagues wouldn't hear of it."

Teah and Calin sank into a large soft sofa in Daniel's private dining room. The castle's many quiet rooms had become home to the townspeople, and almost the entire castle was bursting at the seams, but Myllasanndia had managed to keep this one space free for the use of Daniel's council members and close friends. The couple had expected to find others taking advantage of the cosy little room but, as it happened, the room was empty and so, for the first time in days, they were actually alone. Teah laid her back against Calin's chest and he enclosed her with his arms. For a moment they sat in silence both enjoying the contact and stillness of the moment. It was Calin who broke the silence.

"You're worried about all this magic business, aren't you?" he asked, his voice a whisper at her ear. He kissed her softly on the cheek – a reassurance that he was there for her, no matter what.

"I'm relieved for the people of the city that they have the power available to them to stand up to those abominations out there. But I cannot help thinking about my own people back home, and how they fared when that army marched through the Grasslands. I just wish I could find a way to get out of this place and get home. I need to know what became of my family and my friends. I just can't stop thinking that they might need help and no one is there to help them. Me and the other women of our clan, we could make the difference."

"I would help too." Calin told her.

She squeezed his arm gently. "Yes, I know you would. Calin, I want to talk to Daniel about leaving. I'm not sure how but I don't want to be stuck in some underground vault for the Mother knows how long. I need to get my people out of here."

"I think that is a good idea. Perhaps this Danny will know of a way out, he seems to know things about this city that no other person does." Calin suggested. "Yes I was thinking the same thing but, Calin, I think there is something I need to talk to you about first." She paused a moment, choosing her words. "Tarrin wanted me to tell you sooner but I was afraid." Her voice was so soft, it caught in her throat.

Worried he was the problem he hugged her closer to him, again kissing her as he tenderly laid his head against hers. "You will never need to fear me, Teah. I am yours, you know that."

She returned the gentle affection but then pulled away, turning in his arms to face him. "I need to explain to you about the clans, about our traditions and laws. If you are to come back there with me you must know what you are getting yourself into."

He smiled at her. "Too late, whatever it is I'm already committed." he said.

"Stop it Calin!" she snapped. "This is serious, I'm trying to save you a lot of hardship and you are fooling about."

He pulled back a little, the hurt showing on his open face. "I'm sorry Teah; I thought you wanted to be with me, I thought we wanted the same thing."

"I do want to be with you, we do want the same thing. I want you to come back with me and become my husband and I want to spend the rest of our days together."

"Then we have nothing to worry about because that is exactly what we are going to do."

"But Calin, this is not about what I want. Nor is it about what you want. This is about how it is in the clans. Oh Goddess this is hard." She took his hands in hers and looked into his beautiful, honest face. "I'm sorry; I'm saying this all wrong. Let me try to explain." She took another deep breath. "You know all the clanspeople have magic. It is part of us, who we are and our way of life. Everything we do is a little bit different to your people's ways because it has magic involved. Humans have no magic, well at least most of them. You have no magic." She waited for him to nod, a confirmation that her words made sense, and then she continued. "When a warrior of my people wants to marry he is expected to prove he is worthy of the woman. The more important the woman, the more is required of the suitor. For daughters of chiefs there is often more than one interested warrior and so they fight for the right to take her as their bride. The fight is not to the death but they must prove themselves by defeating all others. This does not worry me. You have saved my life more than once and are by far the strongest warrior I have ever met, you would triumph without a doubt. But the warriors must also win the woman's magic, and this they do by creating the bond. It's hard to explain to someone who has no magic, but imagine I had ribbons flowing from my arms. To win the bond the warrior would have to take those ribbons and tie them to himself, and then he must hold on to them so that no other can pull them away." She took his arm and placed hers next to it. "I know you can't see it but my bonds are wound around you so tightly, I can feel your presence whenever you are near me, and when you are not near it is as if I have been torn in two. I am afraid, Calin, because you have no magic. What if someone breaks my bond to you? How can you hold on to it with no magic of your own? My father will know this when he sees you. He will forbid me to marry you and he will try to cast you out. My people will turn against you and men will come from all of the clans to fight you. Only if you are strong enough to stay the course will we win a chance to fight our case. I will never remove my bond from you but if you are weakened it may be forcibly snapped."

There was silence as Calin thought through her words. "I never expected your people to welcome me with open arms; I never expected it would be easy. I'll admit I didn't think it would be quite as difficult as you describe but if that is how it has to be so be it. Teah, I might not have any magic but I will hold on to you for always and forever. I don't know a thing about magic, but since I met you I do know about love. I think that bond might be the strongest of all."

She kissed him then, throwing herself into his arms she kissed him and he kissed her back. When they drew apart she smiled. "Will you come back to the Grassland clans with me?"

"Yes."

"Will you fight for me?"

"Yes."

Teah stopped as a thought hit her. "Calin, I've just had a very wicked idea. It won't remove the obstacles we face but it will make them more difficult for people to lay them in our paths and it will make my father very angry."

"From what you've just said I'd say he's going to be pretty mad anyway, what's your idea?"

"Calin, we need a priest. We're getting married."

Chapter 14
A City in Ruin

Seeing Daniel and Danny walking side by side down the staircase was one of the oddest sights Myllasanndia had ever witnessed. Danny was a head taller than Daniel, who was more heavily muscled and had that distinct bearing of nobility in contrast to Danny's gangly gait, but the similarity between the two men was uncanny. Danny had cut his hair short, and it now fell in exactly the same fashion as Daniel's did. He was also now clean-shaven, revealing the fact that both men had the exact same jaw line. Danny wore the new clothing Myllasanndia had found out for him and had a sword hung at his hip. The two men were making their way down the stairs and out towards the courtyard. They both stopped and called out when they saw her.

"I thought for a moment I was seeing double." she exclaimed. "I'm not sure how we are ever going to explain this."

"I'm not sure we ever will." Daniel smiled.

Bringing her thoughts back to the present she asked. "What's the situation now? I've just come from

389

the ballroom, we've converted it into a hospital for the time being."

"Things are moving as planned." Daniel told her. "They're bringing the last of the patients from the chapel infirmary up now. That should be the last of our people who are choosing to join us up here."

"Are there many staying behind?" Myllasanndia asked.

"More than we would have liked." Danny told her. "My people have tried to get the message out but some people are too pig-headed for their own good."

"There have been some pretty big bangs down on the wall," Daniel told her. "I'm about to signal the retreat." He beckoned to an Elite officer who acted as his security detail. "Marcus, send the runner, it's time to get them off that wall!"

"Yes Sir!" the man snapped and sprang off to start the retreat.

"Good, I don't like the idea of those men being stuck down there, and poor Ela is having palpitations." Myllasanndia shook her head at the thought of the poor girl, she really had no idea how obvious her feelings towards Lyaren were to everyone else and seemed to be totally oblivious to them herself. "Are the defences up here all in place?"

"Everything is ready," Danny told her. "We just need to hold the lizards back while we wait for the priests. As soon as they throw any kind of destructive spell at the wall our enchantment spell will ignite and the citadel will" – he made a flicking motion with his fingers – "Vanish. I've got to say, I'm really looking forward to experiencing it."

Both Daniel and Myllasanndia gave him a disapproving glare.

"I'm worried about the people." Myllasanndia said. "We dare not warn them, if word of the spell got out we could ruin everything, but they will be in shock. Most will be very afraid when it happens and there are a lot of us crammed in here to have wide-spread panic."

"But they will all be alive and they will all be safe." Danny told her. "Besides, it is about time they started accepting that magic is real and that, in the right hands, it can be a good thing!"

Daniel cut in, changing the subject; he could see Danny and Myllasanndia were going to have very different view on how to handle the people of Stagsonton. "I heard Calin and Teah were looking for me, do you know what it's about?"

"No." his mother said. "Although I think it is to do with getting back to the Grasslands. They both seemed to realise this is most definitely not the time and I believe have taken their swords outside to defend the main gate."

"That's where we are heading now. Start to prepare the people, Mother. It won't hurt to tell them now. Make sure they understand it is magic from the Goddess and is something the citadel was always meant to do when attacked by evil. Tell them it is a miracle and not to be afraid."

Myllasanndia smiled warmly at her son. "Thank you, Daniel. That will go a long way towards helping with the transition."

Lyaren sprinted along the fortifications. He had been working with the company holding the east section of wall through the night. The assaults had been steady and they had lost a few men but, on the whole, the enemy's strike was a little half-hearted. That was until dawn when things had stepped up a notch and was when the losses had occurred. A scaling ladder went unnoticed by his men and half a dozen lizard warriors had made the wall. The skirmish which followed had been brutal but short lived; no repeat of the incident occurred. About an hour ago things had gone quiet and the enemy had withdrawn and relocated to support the massing hoard at the north gate, where the main force of the attack was now focussed. Lyaren had ordered all but the skeleton crew of his section of the wall back up to the safety of the citadel and was now making his way as quickly as he could to the main focus of the attack, from where Rudley was overseeing the battle. He could make out the figures of Grun and Rudley atop the city's ramparts, which meant the situation to the west, mirrored that of the east. Here by the north gate was a very different story. The whole wall swarmed with activity.

Ever since they had interrupted the priests in their grotesque ritual the enemy's push at the north gate had stepped up. The numbers they threw at this section of the barricade was increased tenfold and shouts went up from all directions as lizard warriors found their foothold and the legion's soldiers sped to defend the position.

The outer city was almost evacuated now and most of the troops had been recalled to the upper citadel, leaving only limited reserves to hold the wall. Daniel had asked these men to hold their position as long as they could to allow time to move the last of the populace to safety; at this point every minute was crucial.

As Ly reached Rudley's side, the wall heaved and shook beneath their feet and everyone threw out their hands to balance until the trembling had finished. Lyaren looked over to the Xyakahan priests; still they hung back, never risking themselves. He considered sending them a little blast of his own but thought better of it; if any one of them was waiting for a magical attack they would simply repel it straight back at him.

"The wall's weakening!" Grun shouted as he engaged yet another lizard warrior who had made it onto the top. We need to pull back."

Lyaren shot an arrow above Grun's head, taking a second creature in the eye. The lizard swayed slightly a little before pitching right and plummeting off the edge.

"Lyaren, behind you!" Rudley shouted.

Lyaren span without hesitation, his second arrow taking yet another of the creatures through the throat. Thick red blood sprayed out in all directions. More men rushed in to confront the enemy as they attempted to make the wall. This was followed seconds later by the sound of screams, which wove through the general bedlam of the battle sounds, as their ladder was hurled back to the ground throwing them off wildly in all directions.

"General! General!" A red-faced soldier raced up the steps puffing and panting as he made the top. "Lord Nunnington says to pull back, the evacuation is complete."

"About bloody time!" Rudley bellowed. "Get back up to the citadel, lad." Another blast hit the wall, which groaned and pitched dangerously. "I think we need to get everyone back, this wall will go any minute!" He reached for the torch which would light the beacon and signal to all his troops that it was time for them to retreat. The town of Stagsonton was about to fall. The beacon flared into life and along the wall other lights sprang into being. Instantly men began to withdraw. Lyaren stayed with Grun and Rudley, attempting to hold off as many of the enemy as possible while their men made their dash for the upper citadel. Every sword ran with fresh blood while arrows whizzed perilously through the air. The smell of smoke mingled with the stench of blood and sweat.

Below the wall the enemy had finally decided to burn their dead, just where they lay. The red-hot flames, which leapt from the fires, were inflicting yet more pressure on the now precariously-weak wall.

"All clear!" Grun shouted. "Let's get off this thing!" Immediately they began to withdraw, just as yet another magically-charged blast hit the wall, followed by a deafening boom. The stone beneath their feet seemed to pull itself apart and a huge section of the wall to their left crumpled to the ground. Plumes of smoke and dust clouded the scene. Not waiting for the dust to settle the lizard warriors swarmed over the broken masonry and into the undefended city.

"Quickly," Rudley yelled. "The steps are giving way!" Without hesitation the three men threw themselves down the hazardous staircase.

The scene was one of nightmares, the enemy had already begun to torch the building and sounds of the battle rang out from all sides.

"I hope our lads make it back." Rudley thought out loud. They didn't stop to think, or attempt to engage the enemy, this was when they ran! Lyaren brought up the rear, his bow providing cover as they negotiated the streets now teaming with lizards. They'd planned their route back up to the citadel, just as everyone else had. As they rounded the corner by the bakers square an ear-splitting boom, this one the loudest so far, sounded behind them. They didn't need to look back to know that the rest of the wall had just fallen.

Ela waited with the clanswomen by the portcullis. The last of their soldiers had begun to arrive back from the wall, breathless from the exertion of the steep climb to the top of the citadel. There was no sign of Ly yet, but she knew he would be one of the last; he just had to get up here before the Xyakahan priests

394

triggered the spell. She had wanted to stay with him on the wall but everyone had forbidden it on the grounds that if the magic made her pass-out they would have to carry her back. She didn't think for a moment she could argue that and so had given in.

"Stop worrying Ela," Calin told her. "He'll make it back."

"I know." she forced a smile.

Calin and Teah had been on their way to speak to Daniel when word had come that the wall was about to fall. Their plans would have to wait until they were all out of danger; leaving was not an option right now.

Another group of soldiers came chasing into view, a group of lizard warriors hot on their heels. Arrows rained down from above, cutting the enemy down before they got close to the gate and allowing the men time to get into the relative safety of the citadel.

"That's Hayal's men," Calin grinned; he's had 'em practising for this since we got here."

More lizard warriors came into view; appearing from a side street over to the right, they swarmed into the square before the gates. Another torrent of arrows sped down but stopped abruptly as three figures entered the area from the opposite side.

"It's them!" Teah called. "The priests won't be far behind."

Lyaren rapidly discharged arrows towards the nearest of the lizards, while Grun and Rudley carved their way through any he missed.

Ela pushed forwards to help but Calin grabbed her from behind and pulled her back. "Sorry lass, I promised Ly."

She glared at him. "I can handle myself."

Calin gave her a grimace back. "I know, but so can he!"

They were almost to the gate now, with just ten or so lizard warriors standing in their way. More arrows rained down, passing over their heads, and Daniel and Danny had pushed forward to help clear the way, their swords dancing with an uncanny synchronicity of movement. Grun made the gate first, breathing hard, with Rudley fast on his heels. Lyaren was steps away when a low thrust to his right took him in the leg and he stumbled, falling to the ground, his bow spinning wildly out of his hand.

Ela stifled a scream but Rudley was on it; pivoting in one motion he threw himself back out, launching himself in Lyaren's direction. The movement distracted the closest of the lizards long enough for Ly to regain his footing and draw his blade, but now the two men stood back to back surrounded by enemies, only metres from safety. Over to the right the first of the black-cloaked priests came into view.

"Blow this!" Rudley yelled. "On three lad," and together they both turned their backs in a last-ditch effort to get inside the gate. Danny and Daniel took out two more of the lizards each, so only two now stood in their way. "Run!" Rudley shouted, and Lyaren did, cutting down the man before him and stumbling through the gate as the first of the priests' magical blasts hit the wall.

Everything seemed to slow down and stop for an instant. As Lyaren made it through, Rudley was savagely caught in the shoulder by an enemy axe; bone shattered and blood sprayed out from the wound. He swayed forward as more lizards rushed up towards him, pulling him back up to his feet. On the wall the magical ruby above the gate had begun to pulse and a strange buzzing sound reverberated through the atmosphere. In his peripheral vision Lyaren was aware of Ela falling to the floor; Calin was there ready to catch her. There was frenzied activity all around him but his eyes never left

Rudley. Blood poured from his friend's wounded shoulder, pumping wildly now. The buzzing sound intensified as his vision became distorted; it was the magic igniting the ancient spell. There was no time to think, Rudley couldn't make it inside now and to go after him would be suicide. He wouldn't want to be taken alive. Lyaren pulled his thin throwing-knife from its sheath. He looked his friend in the eye and threw, then the whole world tilted and everything everywhere went black.

Juzuk and his acolytes strode unopposed into the open square before the portcullis which marked the entrance to the keep of Stagsonton. The foolish inhabitants of the city had helpfully placed themselves inside the perfect enclosure to act as their funeral pyre. There was one last squabble going on at the gate as two of the fools attempted to get back into the keep. Some good it would do them; he and his acolytes were magnificent in their power, it pulsed through their veins and welled in their stomachs longing for an outlet. This would be glorious.

He looked again at the imbeciles by the gate; they had almost managed to get to their people. The Sandkind were even bigger fools, there were more than enough of them to deal with just two simple soldiers. No not soldiers, they were dressed differently, something about one of the men's dress drew his attention; he wore a fancy uniform which signalled him out from the other men on the wall. He was the one Juzuk had watched strutting up and down as if it was his wall! A smear twisted his mouth. *'He was their leader, the General.'* "I want the General alive!" He directed his voice to reach the warriors nearest the scuffle.

Juzuk turned his attention back to the wall. He reached out with his sensors, grasping the power of his fellow priests without regard for the consequences. Wrenching and tearing he dragged every ounce of power from them all, feeling a slipping as each of them gave their last and fell away from the chain. He began crafting the huge vat of power within him ready for the final blast. Nothing would remain of their puny wall when he let it go; it would crumble to dust. With every ounce of his concentration he released the spell. The power accelerated outwards with pinpoint precision, gaining astonishing speed as it neared the wall.

The spell was magnificent. It flew to its target, smashing against the masonry and exploding outwards on contact. There was a deafening crash – the whole city vibrated with the ricochet – and blinding white light engulfed the citadel only to be replaced, a second afterwards, by an enormous plume of dust and debris. As he waited for the dust to settle Juzuk looked down at the fallen priests around him. His body still hummed with the energy of their passing. Their sacrifice would bring him the glory he deserved.

The scene was opening up. He fought down his anticipation; there was devastation. The huge wall had crumbled to nothing, exposing the courtyard beyond. Something was very wrong. An eerie silence settled over the town and a twinge of worry passed through Juzuk's gut. He marched over, closer to the wall, his brain struggling to comprehend what his eyes were seeing.

His rage soared with his impotent frustration. Without care he threw outwards the remaining power in his body and those unfortunate souls standing closest violently exploded where they stood, their bodies splintering into quivering chunks of lightly-singed flesh, which splattered against the remaining members of their regiment.

Juzuk turned, angrily looking for the captured General. He would know what they had done, how they had achieved this. He levitated himself above the dead and dying figures all around him, over to where his men held the fool; he would tell him everything he knew and then Juzuk would fill the man with Dragath and feed on his fear until he found the inhabitants of this pitiful, filthy town.

As he reached the man he threw the lizards to either side of him out of his way and grabbed him by his clothes. The general made no attempt at resistance, his body flopped awkwardly forwards. Juzuk shook the man and pushed him backwards onto the ground. It was only as he hit the floor that he noticed the slender nick in the man's neck, which had accurately severed the main artery. His lifeblood had already sped away.

Juzuk stared at the dead man in disbelief. An icy tendril of fear began to spread throughout his body.

The darkness was absolute and the air temperature had plummeted. Deafening silence had replaced the humming sound created by the release of the enchantment. Somewhere within the main house of the keep a child was crying, and the sound seemed to echo all around them. All else was stillness.

"Light the torches!" Danny's commanding voice sounded shocking against the strangeness of their silent situation.

Torches hissed into life all around and soon there was enough light to illuminate the keep and reassure everyone that they were, in fact, still within its protective walls. Beyond the walls, however, they were surrounded by the blackness of a night with neither moon nor stars.

"Try to reassure everyone," Danny suggested to Daniel. "It's going to take me a while to get the lights on."

Daniel resisted the urge to ask how he intended to light the darkness. He could feel his own heartbeat settling into its more natural rhythm, but knew his people would be terrified. He called for the guards to bring torches closer to him and, when he felt he was clearly visible to those within sight of him, he shouted as loudly as he could so that his voice carried as far as he could make it. "My friends, I know this is all very strange but please try to stay calm. The Goddess has saved us from the evil of the Sandkind army by bringing us here to Safehelm. I suspect we have just experienced the first of the many wonders which stand before us. We are safe for the time being and so we require only those on guard-duty to remain at their posts. I urge you all, return to your families and friends. Comfort and reassure them. Your council members and I will find out as much information as we can and share it with you as quickly as we can. Go in peace, my friends and don't let the strangeness feed your fears. Today we have witnessed a miracle."

As he finished his speech a hum of voices picked up all around, swelling in volume and replacing the vastness of the silence with a more natural environment, which began to go a little way towards helping everyone relax.

Lyaren checked Ela over quickly as Calin gently cradled her in his arms. "Is it the same as before?" Calin asked.

"Yes, I think so" Lyaren reassured him. "Her breathing is natural, but the sleep is still clouded with magic. Can you carry her up to her room? I need to talk to Daniel and I'll be up straight after."

"Do what you need to do." Teah told him. "We'll watch over her until you've finished."

The courtyard was becoming less crowded as people drifted off to find their families and attempt to find more mundane pastimes or simply contemplate the events. Daniel could tell his mother had managed to spread the word and prepare the people of Stagsonton efficiently; people mostly appeared calm, if not just a little anxious.

Lyaren appeared at his side. The elf had dropped his glamour and looked exhausted. "Daniel, I need to talk to you and your mother, I need to explain."

Daniel was confused for a moment; everything had happened so quickly and he had been so focussed on the people, but then events replayed and he realised what had transpired prior to the magic. Sadness clouded his eyes. "Be easy, Lyaren. We lost a lot of good men today and the one we will mourn most deeply will be Rudley, but you are not to blame for his death. You saved our friend from the fate he feared most of all. We will miss him terribly but we will remember him, along with those of his men who also perished in the battle as the heroes who gave their lives to save ours.

Lyaren nodded sadly. "He asked me never to allow him to be taken by the Xyakahan priests. I wanted to go back for him but the spell was in motion and I dare not for fear of disrupting the magic. If they got their hands on him he would have given away the secret of Safehelm, not willingly I know, but they have their ways and I... Well, I did the only thing I could."

"You did what had to be done, Lyaren, and I thank you for that." It was Grun. "We all feel his loss, but no one here will blame you for your actions."

Emptiness settled in the pit of Lyaren's stomach. He had lived a very long life, and had made many hard decisions. Today he had made the hardest and he would carry the wound with him always.

"Torches! Torches in the distance!" The cry came from the battlements of the keep.

"Hold your fire!" Danny shouted up. "They are my people, come to help."

Daniel, Grun and Lyaren followed Danny to the open gate which was the only way in and out of the keep. Over in the distance a line of torches could just be seen, making slow progress towards them. "Safehelm is a vast cavern," Danny explained. "We had no way of knowing where the keep would materialise and so my people waited back in the labyrinth which leads to this place. When they get here we can invoke the magic which will bring illumination to Safehelm and then we can get to work establishing a sustainable society. The prophecy says we will be here for some time."

"Should we go out to meet them?" Lyaren asked.

"I dare not. In the dark I too have no way of knowing where we are. There are dangers within this cavern; I don't want to inadvertently walk off the edge of a cliff. Some of the drops are said to be bottomless."

"Then we wait." Daniel said.

They watched as the procession of light approached, making its steady way over to their position, the time it took for them to arrive giving some indication of just how vast Safehelm truly was. As they neared the lights became identifiable as individual torches, nineteen in total. Finally they entered the glow of torchlight thrown out from the keep's torches and, as they did so, the nineteen men and women spread themselves out into a straight line in front of the gateway. A woman from the centre of the group stepped forward. Even in the gloom it was obvious that she was very young and extraordinarily beautiful. Like all the others she wore a full-length white robe, cinched at the waist with a silver belt which picked up and reflected the light of the torches. Her light coloured hair was pulled back in a long ponytail and she wore a simple silver tiara on her head.

"Its fine," Danny reassured them. "These are my people; these are the Circle of the Goddess Mysta." He walked forward, out through the blackness which stood between them and into the light of the woman's torch.

"Welcome home, Lord Safehelm." The woman's voice was loud and clear and full of joy. "You certainly know how to make an entrance." Although her face maintained its formal expression, her eyes danced with laughter.

"I must admit it was rather exhilarating. However, I suspect that my companions may not see it that way. It is good to see you Salistanya."

"It's good to see you too, Daniel. You have played your part well, we are all very proud of you."

"I'm known as Danny to our new friends." he told her. "They found the idea of two Daniel Nunningtons a little too confusing. Did you bring the crystal?" Danny asked.

Two men who were also dressed in the same white robes, but without the silver embellishments, stepped forwards carrying a metal chest similar to the one which Danny had carried the rubies and ancient documents in.

Danny turned back and called over to those who watched from the gate. "These are my people; together we are the Circle of Mysta, she is our Mother Goddess and it is in her name and at her bidding that you are saved this day from the evil which stands far above our heads. Here, deep below the surface of this world, we are safe but Mysta would not have us living in darkness. This crystal is embedded with power akin to that of the enchantment which brought you here. When I place it into the wall we will have light. I cannot give you a cycle of night and day, but this light will be soft and adequate. Please spread the word to everyone. After the darkness it will take a moment for all our eyes to adjust." Danny opened the chest and took a huge emerald from inside. The stone glowed softly in his hands. Reverently Danny carried it over to the keep but this time stopped outside the wall. Just as he had before he used magic to levitate the stone up into the air where it gently floated above the portcullis to an arched niche carved into the stones. The emerald gently settled into a perfectly shaped position. As it did, the glow of its light intensified and, high above their heads in the roof of the mighty cavern, tiny lights flickered into life as a myriad of crystals took up the same soft glow. From those above the wall there was a communal intake of breath as the alien beauty of their subterranean refuge revealed itself fully for the first time to its new inhabitants. The cavern was truly enormous; over to the left side a river cut through, passing into the wall, while to the right a huge ravine broke the cavern floor, spanned by a precarious-looking bridge of stone. Numerous tunnels could just be made out in various positions around the main body of the cavern. The cavern itself hosted a variety of stalagmites, stalactites and columns, and was dotted with colours from the softly-glowing crystals and a variety of leafy lichens and mosses which blanketed the rocks. The whole effect was beautiful and exotic.

Daniel pulled his eyes away from the dazzling beauty of the cavern, to look at Danny who stood only a matter of metres in front of him. "Safehelm is beautiful, Danny. How can we ever thank you and your people for what you have done, your family have sacrificed everything to bring us to this moment."

"Don't pity me, Lord Nunnington, my life has not been as hard as you might think, the Goddess has blessed me and my ancestors in many ways. It is a great honour to serve the Goddess and custodianship of

Safehelm is only part of my responsibility. If it is alright with you I would like to speak with my people and get a good appreciation of the how the arrival of the keep in Safehelm has impacted on this place. I suggest you do investigations of your own, ensure the whole of the citadel was transported; I have no idea what effect the spell would have on the dungeon and cellars of the keep. I would suggest we meet together tomorrow and my people can work with yours to help establish and craft your new society."

"That would be more than acceptable." Daniel said. "Can we offer rooms to you and your people, we have some space and I know mother will find comfortable accommodation for you all."

Danny smiled. "That is kind, Daniel, but don't forget this is my home. I already have a very comfortable room of my own here in Safehelm, as we all do. Tomorrow we will show you around your new home and some of your men can begin to learn the ways of the labyrinth, which lead to surface caves hidden deep within the woods. From here we can begin to launch our attacks on those creatures above our heads."

"I am overwhelmed by all of this, Danny, as I know my people are. I can't wait to explore this place."

"Then tomorrow I will collect you and the council; the Circle will work with some of your key citizens to begin sharing our knowledge."

"Thank you, cousin." Daniel held out his hand.

"You are welcome, cousin." Danny took the offered hand and the two men stood for a moment, both of the same mind. The future was very exciting and full of promise.

Calin and Teah sat with Lyaren as he waited for Ela to wake. It was strange how ordinary the sounds from her bedroom window were. Outside life was

405

quickly returning to some semblance of normality. True enough the people had lost their homes, but they had shelter and food and an odd comfort, which they had brought with them. Before long the sounds of music and laughter began to emerge from a populace who simply needed to celebrate the wonder of their escape.

"So you think that by getting married here in Maldora it will force your father to accept Calin?" Lyaren asked Teah.

"Nothing and no one will force my father into anything, but it will make it more difficult and he will be forced to take Calin's claim seriously. As my husband, he has a right to defend his position; as a suitor without my father's blessing, he has no rights at all."

"And what do you think Tarrin would say if he was here?"

"I think he would be angry for a while," Teah admitted. "Tradition is important to all clansfolk, but I know he likes Calin and he understands the bond which ties us. He would give us his blessing in the end."

"Very well then," Lyaren said. "Then I will also stand by you both if this is what you want. There are priests of the Goddess and the Gods here in the keep; we can organise the ceremony quite quickly if you are happy to keep it intimate and simple."

"Who's getting married?" Ela asked drowsily as she began to come around.

Lyaren smiled warmly at her. "Glad to see you awake, dear one." He stroked her head feeling for a temperature but found none. Calin and Teah. They plan to marry tomorrow and then leave by the secret tunnel which leads into the woods and make their way to the clans."

"Oh damn!" Ela cursed; a habit she had picked up from the clanswomen. "Are we here? Did we make it to Safehelm? Did I pass out again?"

"Indeed you did," Calin told her. "The moment those rubies began to glow you were out like a light."

Her memory of the events prior to her fainting began to re-emerge. "I remember the stone shining and a loud buzzing." She stopped and grabbed hold of Lyaren's hand. "I remember you falling; I thought you wouldn't make it."

"So did I for a moment," Lyaren confessed. "But thanks to Rudley I just got through in time. He wasn't so lucky. He didn't make it." Lyaren chose not to go into detail, he was fairly sure that Calin and Teah wouldn't have seen what he did and he was far too ashamed to tell Ela.

"Oh how sad, poor Simeon," Ela said, emotion thickening her words. "He was a good man."

"Yes he was, and he wouldn't want us to dwell on things." Calin said, cryptically placing a supportive hand on Lyaren's back. "So what will you two do now? I get the feeling Lord Daniel won't need your services so much now he has a wizard cousin to help him."

Lyaren stopped thunderstruck. He was so caught up in the drama of the past few days that he had failed to notice that he and Ela were now free to carry on their journey. "Well I suppose..." he said thoughtfully, "Tomorrow we will learn all we can about Safehelm and how to leave here, then we will celebrate our friends' union and, on the following day, we shall make preparations to leave."

After a good night's rest Daniel had called an early council meeting in order to organise the day's work. It was agreed that Grun, Rothenburg, Grimsore, Samuel, Hayal and Sally would organise meetings with the appropriate people for the members of Danny's Circle, to ensure information was disseminated effectively. Sahain would organise preparations for the clanswomen's departure and the remaining members would accompany Danny on his tour of their new home. Daniel was saddened to hear that Teah and Calin planned to leave but their wedding plans softened the blow. When Lyaren declared that his and Ela's plans were also to leave there was silence; they had become so enmeshed within the running of the city that everyone had forgotten that they had their own agenda, and a heavy mood descended over the room. Before the sadness had time to settle a loud knock at the door interrupted their brooding and Danny entered, along with the entire Circle of Mysta – twenty men and women all, with the exception of Danny, wearing the white ceremonial robes of their order.

"Good morning." Danny beamed at everyone, obviously excited at the prospect of the day.

"Good morning and welcome." Daniel said to his guests. He looked towards Danny but his eyes were constantly drawn to the beautiful young woman who stood at his side. She was dazzling in her perfection. Her eyes were the purest blue he had ever encountered, and her bone structure was soft and full, giving her features a warm yet striking quality. Her white gown clung tightly to her slender body, hugging her figure and accentuating her graceful curves. She was truly the most perfect person he had ever seen and he was determined to get to know her better.

The Circle were efficient in their organisation, each one carrying responsibility for one of the essential requirements for the functioning of the keep. As they each stated their responsibility they were placed with a council member whose role it was to ensure they were paired with the right person or group of people from within the keep. Soon, only Danny and Salistanya and two older men remained, the first of whom stepped

408

forward. My name is Jacob Livingwood and this is my brother, Thomas; we are the keepers of the histories. As Lord Safehelm will show you, this place is far more than just a safe-haven for your people. We are keepers of the knowledge of our order and one of the items we tend are the histories of man, rescued from the catacombs in Sidmore before the fires were able to engulf them.

Daniel, Ronald and Lyndon had all studied at the University in Sidmore, as had the sons of most of the nobles in Maldora. The three of them looked at Jacob in disbelief.

Jacob smiled at their expressions. "I know, gentlemen, you have been led to believe that these ancient documents were lost to us forever, but our Goddess Mysta would not allow such a loss. There are many things here in our custody which mankind fears lost; it is our responsibility to protect them for the time when they will be of most importance. The prophecy says that two members of the council will have the skills needed to join my brother and I in our work while they are in this place.

The three friends' jaws dropped even lower.

It was Lyndon who found his wits first and offered. "My friend Ronald and I are still in the service of the University of Sidmore; it would be our honour to help you with your work. Indeed, I doubt you would be able to stop us."

"Just so." Ronald had regained his wits also. "This is a remarkable revelation. Just how much of the documentation was rescued from the fires?"

"Oh all of it," Jacob smiled. "They make up about a tenth of the works we have here in our libraries."

Both men were up and out of their chairs without thought for the rest of the council.

"So we will see you later?" Daniel said, his words laced with friendly sarcasm.

409

"Yes." the sarcasm was completely lost on the two men. "Well, maybe," Ronald said absently. "We'll go see what this is all about."

As the men left the room Daniel gave way to the merriment building inside and laughed whole heartedly. "Danny my friend, I think you have just provided those men with the one thing which will help them deal with their grief. I am in awe of the wonders we have witnessed already here in Safehelm."

"With respect, My Lord, there is still much to share with you; with your permission, Salistanya and I would like to do just that." Danny told them.

The beautiful woman by Danny's side introduced herself. "I am Salistanya of Triwold Isles, my father,"

Daniel cut in. "You are Lord Triwold's oldest daughter, the whole kingdom was informed of your disappearance, your father was distraught at your loss, we thought you taken by pirates!"

Salistanya laughed a beautiful, tuneful laugh full of wonder and joy. "Indeed I was taken by pirates, though the situation was quite amicable and my father knew full well it was my intention to go with the Midnight Lord and his men. My family, as you know, is influential in the shipping industry. We have held an accord with the Midnight Lord for centuries, perhaps as long as he has held the title to Safehelm."

Now all the remaining council members stared with open astonishment at Danny, who just beamed at them.

"I told you when we first met that I was not a good man; I told you I have many names and many responsibilities. I am Daniel Nunnington, Lord of Safehelm, Keeper of Time, Midnight Lord of the Pirates, Death Lord to the Assassin's Guild and Overlord of the Thieves. As I told you yesterday I have not lived a bad life, in fact it has been one of privilege, albeit unorthodox. Our family, Daniel, has its roots in the darkness of the underworld. When the King first bestowed the title of Stagsonton upon our ancestor, he had assumed he would be able to walk away from his less-savoury responsibilities. This in truth was never an option, and so it was that my branch of the family came into being, distancing this side of the family business from the legitimate side."

"Good God, you are the Devil incarnate!" Daniel stated in horror.

"Please don't misunderstand me, Lord Daniel. There will always be thieves, murderers and brigands with their own code of order and honour. Without such there would be anarchy; innocents would never be safe. I govern that which cannot be governed by those outside. You could say you have me to thank for the equilibrium of your city being maintained so well for so long."

"This is true, My Lord Nunnington." Salistanya spoke on Danny's behalf. "Your family histories are kept here in our vaults along with many other treasures collected over the years. The first Daniel Nunnington, along with his mother the first Myllasanndia Nightburry, set up an honourable and efficient organisation to oversee and govern the criminal element of this city and, today, that power stretches far beyond the city walls. I hope your prejudice will allow you to see the sacrifice which Danny's family made and have continued to make, generation after generation in the name of the Nunnington family and at the bidding of the Goddess Mysta, so that the balance of light and dark could always be maintained. We are good people carrying out those jobs which must never be trusted to one with a black heart, for that would be the ruin of us all."

"She makes sense," Lyaren advised. "We of the elves see the laws that your people operate under as

411

stifling as they often do not allow for the balance of light and dark which Salistanya describes. Having this mechanism of control in place addresses the discrepancy in the laws and stops all the power from being placed in the hands of the rich minority. I would not advise you to view Danny too harshly; he has saved our lives and is just about to share with you a birthright you did not know you had. See this as an opportunity, nothing more, and be grateful that you have not had to govern a city without this mechanism for control in place."

"Very well," Daniel said cautiously. "What other revelations do you have for us today?"

"The prophecy speaks of the chosen ones – a group of individuals who will play a key role in the events which are currently unfolding in this world. Although nothing is said of the role each person plays, we do have gifts for each of these people. The prophecy names the Sleeper and the Eagle, Animage and the Beast, Keeper of Time and Keeper of Dimension, Keeper of Wisdom and the Keeper of Emotion. I believe we are those individuals, which the prophecy calls the Inner Circle. Some are obvious: Lady Elayna is the Sleeper; Master Lyaren, I believe, the Eagle?"

"Yes," Lyaren was listening intently now. "That would make sense."

"Princess Teah is the Animage and that makes Calin the Beast?"

"What are you trying to say?" Calin was less than amused.

"Don't be insulted," Teah told him. "You have the size and strength of a bear and I am not objecting to that."

"Yes, and the wisdom of the owl and the stealth of the fox, the loyalty of the hound and the heart of a lion. The beast is spoken of with love and respect; it is

412

not intended with disrespect, but as an honour." Danny told him.

"Very well." Calin said. "Then that makes Myllasanndia the Keeper of Emotion and I guess you the Master of Time, because of the history thing?"

"Yes, I think so. Salistanya is the Keeper of Wisdom, which makes Daniel the master of Dimension, although I must confess I'm not sure yet what that means." Danny completed the list. "I am instructed to show you the deepest secrets of Safehelm."

"And I am instructed to hold a marriage ceremony; it is foretold that the Beast and the Animage must be bonded by the Keeper of Mysta's wisdom." Salistanya looked at Teah and Calin; now it was their turn to show amazement.

"It says this in the prophecy?" Teah asked.

"Yes, why?"

"Because we only just announced our intentions to our friends this morning." Calin was beginning to feel a little suspicious.

"Good, then we'll not have to change any plans if you haven't got around to making them." Salistanya's voice carried the unmistakable tone of authority. "Shall we get on with the tour, there is rather a lot to show you."

Danny and Salistanya led the group out of the keep and into the cavern beyond. They made a point of identifying the more dangerous areas and then headed down to the river. Here there were a number of small boats and nets. Danny explained that the river only spent a part of its journey underground and that higher up stream it ran in the open air; as a result it carried fish. They then led them to the first of the tunnels which opened out of the main cavern. In fact for the most part these were not tunnels at all but smaller chambers which had been stocked up with a whole host of items. One was laid out as a hospital with extensive medical supplies, one as a store room with grains, herbs and basic provisions. Another was a huge wine cellar, while one was hung with fresh-caught game and cured meats. As they made their exploration the party encountered many of the townsfolk also being shown around specific areas by the white-robed priests. Everywhere there were exclamations of wonder and surprise. They came to the entrance to the labyrinth which, once mastered, led under the forest and out into a secluded grove through a remote cave. Here they encountered Grun with a large group of Elite guards, who were beginning to learn the complex network of tunnels which would lead them out. Danny explained that one of the tunnels which led off the labyrinth came out into a valley which was totally surrounded by an inaccessible rock-face. He explained that as the area could only be seen from the air they would be able to farm some fresh vegetables to supplement their food supplies. He then showed them a large cavern full of strange moss and mushrooms, all of which Danny told them were edible and ranged from tasteless to delicious; the people of Stagsonton would not starve while they dwelt in the depth of Safehelm. Finally Danny led them to a natural tunnel which they walked down for about half a mile. This tunnel then opened up into a large vault which was set up like a library. Enormous shelves housed thousands of books and large tables were laid out with lanterns, parchment and inks. Both Lyndon and Ronald were already engrossed in huge tomes and only when Daniel addressed them directly did either of the men realise they were not alone.

"Oh Daniel this place is magnificent!" Ronald exclaimed to his friends. "This is the actual history of the first kings of our land, before Maldora was set up! Can you believe it? And Lyndon's reading about the birth of Maldora and Graydon the First's rise to power and the formation of the Quarrels. We thought these books were long destroyed; it truly is a miracle."

"Indeed it is, my friend," Daniel agreed. "A true miracle.

"This way," Salistanya urged them. "We have much more to show you and it is getting late." They crossed the huge library chamber and over to the far side of the room where a large wooden door had been set into the wall. Danny placed his hand on the door and it vanished from view. As it did so, Elayna began to feel the telltale tug of magic and a crashing pain rang through her skull. She grabbed Lyaren's arm for support and felt him catch her just as everything went black.

"This part of the cave system is where the magical items are kept," Danny told Lyaren. "I did wonder if Ela might have a problem entering. Our home is close to here; perhaps we should take her there, she will be comfortable there while we go on."

Lyaren looked at Ela's beautiful sleeping form – she was so light in his arms. "Very well," he agreed. "Lead the way."

Danny led them back through the library and out into the tunnel, this time turning left. A short way further they took a turn into yet another large cavern; this one had many small caves leading off from the main, most of which had curtains pulled across to provide privacy. Danny led them to one of the closer curtains which he drew back and, as he did so, the laughing sound of children's voices could be heard within. A little surprised they followed him inside to find a homely little room with a small fire blazing in a hearth placed under a natural chimney. There was the smell of fresh baking and an elderly lady sat in a large, comfortable chair with two young children at her feet playing happily with an assortment of small toys. "My Grandmother." Danny introduced.

The woman smiled at the visitors and said "Welcome, all of you, I have waited a long time for this day and am proud to be here to see it come." She noticed Ela in Lyaren's arms and, rising from the chair, bid him follow her to another small room where there was a comfortable bed covered with woollen blankets and soft furs. Once Lyaren was satisfied that Ela was comfortable he followed the woman out into the main room.

"Thank you Mama." Salistanya said to the older woman warmly, then, turning back to her guests, "These are our children, Jamie and Sofia, they are twins."

"Oh, you are married," Myllasanndia exclaimed. "We didn't realise."

"We didn't seem to know how to explain." Salistanya confessed. "After all, I disobeyed my father to be with Danny; I was worried you would think me shameful."

"In the great scheme of things, this is not something we need to dwell on my dear" Myllasanndia placed an arm around the delicate young woman. As Danny's wife that makes you family too. I am a very happy woman to finally be surrounded by such a large family, don't you think Daniel?"

Daniel looked a little like he had been slapped in the face. He quickly schooled his expression as everyone turned towards him. "Indeed it is," he said politely. "Welcome to the family, Salistanya." Deep inside he felt his heart break, but he never let a glimmer of the pain show on his face.

Danny suggested they take refreshments while they were in his home and Salistanya brought in cups of warm sweet tea and homemade biscuits. The party chatted quietly, Danny and Salistanya describing their day-to-day lives in Safehelm, each with a young child sat upon their knee. Once the refreshments were gone they bid farewell to Danny's grandmother and the children. Then Danny led them back to the library and the huge wooden door in the back of the room. Once again Salistanya placed her hand upon the door. The magic hummed and there was a blast of cold air. The door seemed to shimmer before them and then it was gone. Beyond a brightly-lit corridor was revealed, lined with a warm comfortable carpet and thick bright tapestries on the wall. They were, for all intents and purposes, entering a castle.

"Welcome to the seat of Mysta," Salistanya told them. "Sometimes known as the true temple of the Mother, or Womb of the Goddess. Any will suffice. Please enter, only the chosen will be able to pass within so I urge you enter of your own free will. For any without the Goddess's blessing, trying to get into this part of Safehelm can be quite painful."

Salistanya entered first, followed by Danny, then the two of them turned to wait for the rest of the party to follow. Daniel held out a hand to his mother and the two entered together without a problem. Calin and Teah also entered together and Lyaren came last. As he crossed the threshold the humming started up again and the door shimmered back into life. Salistanya led the party down the corridor, passing numerous large oak doors.

"What's behind the doors?" Daniel asked curiously.

"We don't know for most of them," Danny confessed. "They have always been locked for us, although a few I can open. These lead to locations within the city where I have work to carry out. They allow me to move quickly and so fulfil my many roles and obligations effectively."

"Such secret passageways would be of much use to thieves and murderers." Daniel commented, a little

417

darkly. Learning of Danny and Salistanya's relationship had returned his mistrust of his new found cousin.

"Yes I agree they would be," Danny replied conversationally. "But I am the only one who can enter them – even Salistanya cannot cross the threshold – and so I use them only as they are intended. It would not be right to offend the Goddess by using her gifts for evil."

"So one of these doors leads to the infamous Hall of Assassins?" Myllasanndia asked.

"Yes, and one goes to the Thieves' Guild hideout and others lead to a few other key locations in and around town. Then there is the one which leads to the pirates' headquarters of the Midnight Lord in Tallowbridge."

Lyaren whistled under his breath. "That is some door; Tallowbridge must be over a month's journey away by horse. How long does it take you to get there on foot?"

"Over land it would take many months, but through the door a few minutes." Danny ignored the looks of astonishment on their faces. "I had hoped the Keeper of Dimension might be able to explain it to me but I suspect Daniel is as clueless as I am. Like I say, the doors are a gift from the Goddess herself and magic is her specialty."

The group had reached an ornately-carved set of double doors which, unlike the others they had passed, seemed less foreboding and more welcoming. "We are here,"

Salistanya told them. "Please come in and take a seat."

The room within was modest and its walls were lined with shelves, each of which held a metal box of varying sizes. A number of wooden chairs stood in a semi-circle to the centre of the room around an ancient-looking stone altar. The group each took one of the

418

chairs while Salistanya reached up to remove a small chest from one of the shelves. She carried the chest carefully over to the altar and placed it reverently upon it. There was an air of anticipation amongst the group.

"This box holds the gifts I mentioned." Salistanya told them all. "There is one for each of you. My Goddess bids me to hand them to their rightful owner, though I know nothing more of their purpose. In the name of the Goddess Mysta I bestow these tokens of love to each of you. Hold them close and they will serve you well when your need is greatest." She took a small wrapped package out of the box and handed it to Myllasanndia who was sat closest to her, then repeated the process until all but Danny held a package. Once they all held their gifts she bid them open them. They each had been given an identical ring, made of a silver-like metal and engraved with strange markings.

"This is beautiful," Calin told her as he held up his huge hand. "But I don't think mine will fit."

Salistanya remained calm and patient. "Try it on, Master of Beasts." she told him.

Calin shrugged his shoulders and pushed the ring onto his middle finger; it slipped easily on, sitting comfortably in place. The others all followed suit and Salistanya smiled contentedly. "Good." she said simply. "Now let's go wake Ela. There is no ring for her, I think the magic in them would react with her and trigger the trance." She looked towards Calin who was still staring at his finger in wonder. "I hope you have a liking for rings." she told him. "Let's go get you and Teah another one. I think we could all do with a party."

419

Chapter 15
Goodbyes

Calin pulled the front of his formal shirt smoothly into place. The softness of the fabric felt strange after the weeks he had spent in travelling clothes. Something about the fabric made him think of his mother, who had always insisted they dress smartly for festival days. She would approve of the beautiful clothes Myllasanndia had given him for today, but thinking of his mother brought pain so he pushed his melancholy to the back of his mind; *Mam would not want sadness to spoil this day.* The only thing he had known since the moment he set eyes on Teah was that their lives were somehow linked at the deepest of levels. He had been confused by it all at first, expecting her to reject him (she was a princess after all and he was just a simple smith) but the moment he realised she felt the same way an explosion had turned his perspective upside down and the world had ignited with possibilities and potential, despite their dire situation.

On one level he should fear the choice he was making today. By taking her as his wife he would antagonise a whole nation and he could not expect them to approve, not on any level. He knew all too well that he did not have the magic which would enable him to meet their challenges as an equal, but somehow none of this worried him. In his heart was an acceptance that today he and Teah would solidify their feelings for each other into something real and that the power of their union would not yield – not under any amount of pressure.

A knock at the door distracted him from his musings. Lyaren, who looked equally stunning in a fitted black suit with a jade waistcoat and gleaming black boots, smiled broadly at his friend.

"Don't you scrub up well boy?" Lyaren teased. "I think I can see what Teah sees in you." Lyaren felt a genuine wave of pride. Just weeks ago he had met a boy and now he stood by a man.

"I guess I don't look too bad." Calin laughed sincerely, he had got used to Lyaren's sense of humour. "You look quite lordly yourself, for an elf."

Lyaren nodded approvingly of the banter. "Salistanya sent me to fetch you, it's almost time, that is, if you have not changed your mind? I mean, no one would blame you."

"I've never been surer about anything." Calin said simply, letting all his emotions sound in his words.

"Yes we know," Lyaren assured, equally sincere. "That's why we are all so happy to be a part of this."

The two men made their way down to the keep's gate and out into the cavern of Safehelm. The Circle of Mysta had created a beautiful area for the ceremony, with an arrangement of simple furnishings and decorations strung from the surrounding rock formations. Tiny lanterns and torches threw lights around the area, which played off the richly-coloured crystals abounding the cavern. The overall effect was breathtakingly beautiful.

All his friends were there: Daniel, Myllasanndia and the other council members, almost the whole town of Lower Gonfiels, the women from Waydonfield and the clanswomen, who had formed a guard of honour along the aisle down which he now walked. Spread out in a semi-circle before him was the Circle of Mysta in their formal white robes. Calin noticed Danny now stood amongst them, also dressed as a priest of their Goddess.

As he and Lyaren drew closer, Salistanya stepped forward to greet him. Her voice rose above the hum of excited voices which hovered over the gathered crowd. "Welcome in the name of the Goddess, child of the light. Do you come this day of your own free will to join in this life-journey with your one twin soul in a union of unconditional love?"

Calin had never heard the words said in such a way before, but the greeting was similar to that he remembered from weddings in the village and so he answered as he hoped he should. "I come in the name of the Goddess and of my own free will to bind my soul with its one true love."

Salistanya smiled and then she began to sing. Her beautiful, pure voice soared through the air, amplified by the natural acoustics of the cavern, and then the music soared as her fellow priests added their voices to the song. The words were ancient and difficult to follow but the meaning was clear to all. As he listened to the song, Calin became aware of gasps and murmurs behind him; she was here.

For a second he could not move, totally lost in the atmosphere of reverence created by the Circle, but curiosity won out and he turned to look upon the woman he loved.

If Teah was anything it was not orthodox; he wouldn't have been surprised to turn and see her striding towards him in her warrior leathers, but nothing would

423

ever have prepared him for how she looked. Her dress was made out of the same soft fabric as his shirt, cut in an ancient style with a slender-fitting gown caught tight at the waist and long flowing sleeves which added a simple elegance. At the back the gown trailed out, falling softly in pools of fabric which gave a sense that she glided towards him. Ela and Sahain followed, also wearing elegant dresses in soft green tones, but his eyes were focused only on Teah. As she reached his side Calin realised he had stopped breathing. He forced his lungs to take a breath just as the song came to its end.

"Welcome in the name of the Goddess, child of light. Do you come here this day of your own free will to join in this life-journey with your one twin soul in a union of unconditional love?"

Teah smiled at Calin and her face lit up with mischief. She turned and looked directly at Salistanya with uncompromising confidence. "No!" she declared clearly.

Calin felt his heart stop beating in his chest.

Teah continued. "I come this day at the bidding of the Universe, to join my soul with its one twin soul from now to eternity in the name of the Goddess."

Yet again Calin forced a breath. He had never heard these words before either and, judging from the murmur of voices behind him, neither had anyone else; even the white robed priests looked taken aback.

Salistanya, however, was not fazed by her words. "You invoke the ancient rite that will ignite the power of Mysta. Should your souls not be truly twinned your union will be forbidden by the Goddess. Yet should you be indeed twin souls, no mortal can remove the bond formed, from now unto eternity. Is this your wish Teah of the Clans?"

"It is my wish." Teah's voice was heavy with emotion, her eyes held back tears, straining to spill.

424

"And what of you, Calin of Waydonfield? Would you also call on the Goddess to tie your souls for eternity, knowing that if they are not truly twinned the Goddess will forbid their joining?"

All was silent as Calin fought to find the words, but then they were there as if placed in his mind by the Goddess herself. "I call on the Goddess as I am so bound to re-join that which has always been one and create the whole from two halves."

Pure joy flared in Salistanya's eyes. She held out her arms to either side and, with her head held high, called in a loud, clear voice. "Mysta, how do you judge these souls of man and woman, will you bless this union as true and absolute?"

There was absolute stillness, not a soul moved as the tension grew; Salistanya seemed to be waiting for an answer.

Then out of the surrounding darkness a light so bright no one could look directly at it flared into being, and from deep within a woman's voice replied. "These souls need no joining, they are already one. Accept my blessings this day beloved ones, as you did in the beginning and will to the end."

As quickly as the light appeared it was gone, leaving the air with a strange metallic tinge to it and shocked awe upon the faces of all present.

"The Goddess has spoken and no mortal can undo her words. In the name of Mysta you are now wedded." As she spoke these words, Salistanya took a strip of white cloth from the belt of her robe and tied it around Calin and Teah's hands. Tied to the ends of the cloth were two plain, silver rings which she undid and placed on both their fingers. Before she stepped away she drew closer and, for their ears only, spoke "Your path will not be easy in this life, man cannot break the bond which you share but it can be tested and it could be parted. Enjoy each other while you can, and know the Goddess blesses this match, for you will be joined for all eternity." Then she turned back to the waiting crowd beyond and announced in her crystal-clear voice, "Let the celebration begin, a new life is forged where once were two now stand one, rejoice in the name of Mysta!" As her voice carried over the congregation she turned and made her way back to her fellow priest.

Calin had not once taken his eyes off his bride. "Well, wife?" he asked. And then she was in his arms and the claps and whistles of their friends were lost in the smells and taste of his twin soul.

The celebration of Calin and Teah's marriage was the tiny spark needed to ignite a population-wide party as the whole of Safehelm rejoiced in the revelry. Music, dancing, laughter and delight filled the cavern for the night. The musicians of Lower Gonfiels performed their most joyous of tunes and Calin found himself spinning and turning from partner to partner as everyone young and old wished him well. By the time Samuel came to his rescue with a brimming cup of ale he was red-faced and dizzy.

"May you be always blessed with happiness and many strong children to come." Samuel said; his face a picture of pure delight. "I am proud of you, Calin; you have proven yourself many times over these past weeks. You deserve to be happy."

"I'll make sure he is," Teah said, sneaking up behind the two men and hugging her husband affectionately. "I am very proud of him also."

Calin smiled, deliriously happy. "I don't think things can get much better. I have a beautiful wife and had a real Goddess at my wedding, what more can there be?"

Teah kissed him softly on the cheek then

playfully caught his ear with her teeth. "I will show you more!" she whispered loudly.

Even with the volume of the music Samuel had a good idea what she had said – he could tell by the beetroot flush in his friend's cheeks. He laughed loudly and clapped Calin on the shoulder. "Don't look so worried boy; I'm sure she won't do any serious damage!" They all shared the joke, but then Samuel sobered a little and he asked, "Do you still plan to leave?"

"We hope to set out tomorrow," Calin told him. "We just need to get Danny to agree to show us the way."

"Show you the way to where?" Danny asked; he had been on his way over with Salistanya to pay his respects.

It was Teah who answered. "Through the maze so we can begin our journey back to the Grassland."

"We expected that you would want to leave soon," Salistanya said softly. "Although there will be much sadness when you do. We can do better than take you through the maze though. There is a passageway which leads north-west; it will take you a little out of your way and comes out in the Bleak, which will mean considerable risk, but this path should see you well on your way before you need fear running into lizard warriors."

"How far into the Bleak?" Teah asked soberly. "It will be summer you know, the packs will be banding."

"This is so," Salistanya agreed. "And I am not sure just how deeply into the Bleak the tunnel runs, but I do know that to travel over land in the direction of the Grasslands is certain death. There are too many lizards to count already and our sources inform us that more are

427

coming down through the woods all the time, but they do not enter the Bleak."

"I can't say I blame them." Teah exclaimed. "Our people only enter the Bleak when they know it is close to their time."

Teah and Calin looked at each other, they both understood the risks. "We'll talk to the clanswomen tomorrow," Calin said. "If they are in agreement then we will leave the day after, it will give us time to say our goodbyes."

"I will make arrangements for provisions to be packed for you both, a journey through the tunnels, has slightly different requirements to one over ground." Salistanya smiled.

"That's very kind." Teah thanked her.

"It's the least we can do." Salistanya admitted earnestly. "Because of you we got to hear the voice of our Goddess today, and that is something which hasn't happened in hundreds of years. Today my people were just as blessed by that experience as your union was. Consider this our wedding present to you both."

Danny laughed. "Perhaps a honeymoon in the Bleak is not the cheeriest of gifts my wife could offer, but with the rings which the Goddess gave you both you need not fear the Bleak; you will lead your people safely through I'm sure."

"Thank you," Calin said simply. "Now I suggest we go and let Lyaren and Ela know what we are thinking before it gets any later; I want to make sure we have a proper chance to say goodbye before we have to go."

"Good idea." Teah yawned theatrically, her voice the tone of pure virtue. "I think we should plan to meet up tomorrow, but first we should get an early night. After all, if we don't have many more nights left to sleep in a real bed, we should be sure to get plenty of..."

To her delight Calin didn't give her chance to finish her sentence, catching hold of her playfully and easily lifting her into his arms. "Let's go tell them quickly." he said and set off towards the table where Ela and Ly sat, leaving his new friends and old friends laughing heartily.

Lyaren was stunned to hear of the tunnel leading north. "I wonder if we should take that path too," he suggested. "It would mean a heavy hike through the forests and the mountains, but I suspect with all the lizard warriors roaming around it could mean we make faster progress."

"Still, that's a long way from the Silent Forest; it will take months for you to cut across the mountains and in the summer the path will be very dangerous, even without the lizard warriors roaming about." Teah advised.

"True, but it could still be worth the risk." Lyaren pondered for a moment and the group fell silent.

"It would be nice to travel together," Ela said simply. "I will miss you all very much when we all leave. In fact, I sort of wish we could all just stay here; I have never felt quite so much like I belong anywhere as I do here."

"Yes I know what you mean," Calin agreed. "It's like we all came together and made an instant little mismatched family that helped everyone to deal with unbelievable events and come out the other side stronger."

Teah smiled. "Calin, you never cease to amaze me... I will miss you all too, even the elf who sent my brother away."

Lyaren sobered. "I know Tarrin is alive, Teah. I'm not sure how but I can sort of still feel his magic in the world."

"It's alright, I'm teasing, I know he is fine, I would know if he died, like I did with Sardan when he was killed back at the peace camp. Tarrin knew what he was getting himself into and, besides, he would never have let me marry Calin so it's all worked out just fine!"

"Oh Goddess now she tells me!" Calin exclaimed.

"You better start calling on Mysta for help," Ela told him. "She seems to have adopted you two and I think she will do everything in her power to keep you together."

"I have to agree." Myllasanndia said, coming over to join them. "That was a very impressive blessing, everyone is talking about it; I don't think I have ever attended a wedding like this one."

Before long Daniel and Grun, Danny and Salistanya, Alyha and Sahain, and Samuel and Dina had all made their way over and the group sat chatting. The crystals above seemed to dim a little and, as they did so, more than one member of the group yawned. Eventually Calin and Teah made their goodnights and retired for the evening. The rest of the group poured more wine and continued to share their thoughts and plans for the future. Ela remained pensive; since her mother died she had known only loneliness. Now, just as she was surrounded by friends, she was about to find herself alone once more. Ly would do his best but she doubted he would be able to fill the gap created by the loss of these wonderful new companions.

It was cool in the bedroom which Teah had been using since she arrived at the keep. Outside, the music and voices were loud and clear and she knew they would go on long into the night. As much as it was their celebration, all the inhabitants of Safehelm had much to celebrate and be thankful for and so everyone was part of the party.

It felt a little strange to have Calin's gear in her room – her status as a princess of the clans had meant that she had never had to share her space with anyone. Calin came out from the small water closet off the main bedroom; he had taken off his shoes and his shirt was loose, the fastening open casually. He crossed to where she sat on the slim chair by the dressing table and put his large gentle hands on her shoulders, then leaned over and tenderly kissed her neck. As he did so, Teah felt the bond swell and tighten alarmingly. She jumped a little and, misinterpreting her reaction, Calin pulled away. "No, don't." she whispered, standing and turning to face him. Fear, excitement and longing all welled within her. "Don't stop. It's just when you touch me like that I can feel you so strongly, it's the…"

"The magic, I know, I think I can feel it too." He took a step towards her, their bodies touching; he had been close to her before but never this close, never so that he could feel so much of her body pressed against his. He looked deeply into her eyes. "It feels like little twists of me are wrapping around you and, at the same time, little twists of you are wrapped around me, like every nerve in my body stretches out of me when you are there and… well, I can't really describe it, it's like I just need you, I need you like I need air to breathe or food to eat." He stopped talking; Teah was trembling in his arms. "I'm sorry," he said. "We don't need to, I mean we can wait, everything happened so –"

She stopped him with her mouth, kissing him so deeply and intensely the world seemed to cartwheel around them. The kiss was long; intense. When she pulled away he saw that tears rolled down her cheeks. "You are the part of me I didn't know about until you came into my life. You are as necessary to me as the air I breathe and the food I eat; nothing between us has happened too fast and nothing is going to stop what happens now. Calin, I love you and nothing will ever change that." She placed her fingers on his chest and pulled the fastening so that his shirt fell open.

Calin smiled an open and honest smile which lit up his whole face. "I love you too, and I hope you still feel the same way tomorrow because I really don't have a clue how to do this."

Teah loosened the clasp on her gown and, as she shrugged her shoulders, it slid down her body to the floor. She stepped over the fabric, her naked skin responding to the chill air. "Let's see if we can work it out together." she suggested, stepping back into his arms, and then they were both truly lost as the longing took over and their world was consumed by passion.

Danny drank deeply from the coffee cup, it was the third cup of the thick rich drink which he had acquired a taste for back when he was actively sailing. Back then he had used it to cut through the headache brought on by the thick brown liquor his men insisted on feeding him each night. Now it was to help deal with the after effects of far too much wine. "Was it worth it?" Salistanya asked a little acidly.

"Probably not, but it was good to celebrate with our new friends." he smiled.

She smiled back. "Yes it was, but today you have much to do before they all leave to play out their parts in this unravelling drama."

"I know, I'm going to make the arrangements now and then I will go and tell Lyaren." He laughed impishly, "I can't wait to see the expression on his face, he was so curious about the doors; when I tell him that they can use one of them too – well, I think it will make his day."

432

"It will be good to know they have made it to the coast at least, even if it is a little further south than they want to be. They stand a much better chance if they can travel by sea; I can't imagine those Xyakahan priests even considering the existence of the oceans, let alone taking to a ship."

"I know, everything is working out just right isn't it?" He kissed his wife fully on the lips and held her in a tight hug. "No sneaking off to see my cousin while I'm away; I've seen the way he looks at you and I know you fancy him cos he looks just like me."

Salistanya laughed merrily. "He is very handsome, I must admit, but one Daniel Nunnington is quite enough for me to deal with thank you very much."

"Alright, I will trust you." He winked and grinned at her then left for the mysterious doorways.

Salistanya stared after him for a long while, lost to her thoughts. It was difficult carrying the knowledge she had been born with; she knew she couldn't warn him, it wouldn't be fair, it wasn't what was agreed, but even so, everything was going to change. Then one of the twins cried out from their bedchamber behind her and, a little melancholy, she turned to attend to her children.

Danny quickly covered the ground needed to get him to the Seat of Mysta and followed the corridor down to the door he used in his capacity as Pirate Lord. As he opened the door he looked into the molten whirlpool of energy shimmering before him. Danny was no fan of the trip, it had taken months after his first try for his father to get him to do it again, but it was the only way to get where he needed to be and so, closing his eyes, he stepped into the vortex and then he was no longer in Safehelm.

Ela had woken late after the party but dressed quickly and headed straight down to the barrack buildings to spar with the clanswomen. Alyha had been happy to see her and, within minutes, they were going through the warm-up dance and preparing to spar. Teah and Calin were nowhere to be found, and most of the Waydonfield women were still abed, but the clanswomen were up and preparing their gear for the journey home. Alyha called a halt after about half an hour and they both took a drink of water. It was warm here in Safehelm, despite being so far underground. Danny had explained that there were huge furnaces of molten rock far beneath their feet and that the heat from these came up through the floor of the cavern to keep the temperature comfortable. Safehelm truly was a wonderful place.

"Sahain says you and Lyaren also plan to leave soon," Alyha stated. "Is this true?"

"Yes, we were on our way to the Silent Forest, to Lyaren's people, when all of this started. We need to continue with that journey and then I hope the elves will be able to work out what's wrong with me and maybe cure it so that I can use my magic without passing out."

"Then I am glad I have had the chance to train and work with you, I have seen you grow immeasurably; you are a very fast student, Elayna. You should be able to hold your own in a fight."

"Thank you, I mean for the comment and for the teaching, I owe you a great deal. What about you, Alyha? I mean when will you be leaving, do you know?"

"I think that Teah will want to set out tomorrow, but I will be staying. I have no family back in the clans; the best I can hope for there is to become a warrior's wife but, after what the lizards put me through, I want no part of having a husband. A few of us have chosen to stay here. We are going to work with the Waydonfield women; Sahain and Grun have been cooking up a part for the women to play in the war and they will need leaders with some experience. I doubt they will want to work for men, so a few of us have offered to stay and lead them."

Ela was genuinely happy for Alyha. "I am glad for you and for the women. They deserve their revenge and you all have a lot to offer the people of Stagsonton." She paused, "I mean Safehelm."

Alyha nodded her agreement. "Yes they do. Their company is to be named the Widows' Blade; they have been working out uniforms and everything. I can't wait to see them in uniform, I mean us. We will be a stealth unit: sneak in, kill and get out – deadly and fast. It will feel good to be fighting again."

"Yes, they need a purpose and I don't see how they can ever go back to a life like the one they were robbed of after all that's happened. How does Teah feel about you staying?"

"She's fine, a little grumpy but she understands really. She's the daughter of our overlord, she has responsibilities to the clans; I'm the daughter of a shepherd, our positions are very different. I suspect if her background was like mine she would stay here with Calin and make babies, but her honour won't allow that, so she will do what she must, but she understands those who do not want to go."

"Your magic will be very valuable to Grun also, and the women if you are to work silently."

"Yes, I think Grun is pleased we have chosen to stay. As is Sally, she says that she is relieved that she will still have a friendly face on the council with her. I think I will like living here, I feel needed."

"Yes I know what you mean." Ela's sentiment echoed Alyha's. "This is a good place to call home."

435

Lyaren sat at Daniel's desk in his father's old office. Daniel had offered to let him use it to try and contact his master, Kiam. He had placed a large bowl of water on the desk before him and gone through the meditation ritual in his mind but when he tried to call out to Kiam, as he had done a thousand times before, he felt nothing. This was the sixth time he had tried today and each time was the same. It was as if his magic couldn't penetrate the confines of Safehelm. He would just have to wait until they left the cavern system to update Kiam on their situation.

A knock on the heavy wooden door interrupted his musings and Lyaren called out for the visitor to enter. The door swung open and in walked Daniel. *'No'* Lyaren corrected himself, *'It was Danny, by the Mother the two men looked alike.'*

"I heard you were here," Danny said. "I hope I'm not interrupting anything."

"No, I can't seem to make my magic stretch beyond the confines of Safehelm so, as it turns out, you are interrupting nothing at all." Lyaren told him.

"I have never tried to use magic in that way but the cavern is protected by the Goddess Mysta so it stands to reason your magic wouldn't penetrate the protective boundary. Why? Was there something important you wanted to do?"

"Like you, I play my part in an ancient prophecy, passed down by my people from the same Goddess that you worship. I have not checked in with my people in many days; they will be concerned. I simply wanted to let them know that all is well." He paused as a thought hit him. "I wonder if I could use my magic once I left the main cavern, perhaps in the tunnels of the maze or the tunnel which leads to the Bleak. We were considering that as a route to get us into the mountains and from there back to my people."

436

"Well actually that's why I'm here. I know that you need to get to the Silent Forest, it is sort of mentioned in the prophecy."

Lyaren rolled his eyes. "Of course it is."

Danny carried on, ignoring his sarcasm. "Well I have an alternative means to get you where you need to go, if you don't mind me helping you?"

"Go on." Lyaren urged him.

"Well, I've been through the doorway which holds a portal to Sidmore, I have connections there with a number of...Well, let's call them sailors. I've secured you and Elayna passage north by ship; the journey should take about three weeks, but that is considerably less than it would take if you took the tunnel with Calin and Teah and crossed the mountains. My sources tell me there are no lizards upon the seas yet."

"That's good of you, Danny, but how do you propose we get to Sidmore? That's a good two weeks' ride and my guess would be that, by now, our enemy are teaming all over that part of the country."

Danny's grin almost split his face. "That's the best bit," he exclaimed excitedly. "The door to Sidmore is different to the others; most of them will only let me through, but this door is the one my ancestors used to get the books out of the University. Mysta made it so a group of people could use it and so, because of that, you and Ela will be able to go through. I suspect Ela will have to travel in her sleep with the doors – they can be a bit disconcerting – but in all the journey takes about three seconds, that is, if you want to take it?"

Lyaren's jaw hit the ground. "You're serious?"

"Absolutely."

"You do know, Lord Safehelm, that you are amazing!"

"Yes I am aren't I? So when do you want to get out of here?"

"Tomorrow, I'll go and tell Ela!" Lyaren jumped up and grabbed Danny in a tight hug. "Thank you, Danny, this is yet another miracle."

"Oh don't thank me, I'm just doing my bit. Thank Mysta, she's the one who took care of all the details."

Ly grinned like a child, his excitement unmistakable. "I must tell Ela!" he stated, virtually running from the room to find her and leaving a grinning Danny looking out after him.

Lyaren almost ran straight into Calin and Teah, who approached from the other side of the keep and were also heading to the barrack buildings, where Ly knew he would find Ela. The couple matched each other's strides, purposefully. He had never noticed before just how much taller Calin was than Teah, it was almost as if the smith had grown overnight, but Ly realized that in fact Calin simply stood more confidently today. He felt such genuine warmth for the couple, finding each other had strengthened them both and they were already formidable, easily fit to lead others and Lyaren had no doubt that in the war to come they would do just that.

"Are you heading to see the clanswomen?" Lyaren asked them.

"Yes," Calin answered. "We need to make our preparations and consult the women on the idea of crossing the Bleak. What about you?"

Lyaren joined them and they all continued walking. "I'm looking for Ela, she'll be with Alyha or Sahain, I thought you would be there by now; are you still planning to set out tomorrow?"

Calin's cheeks reddened a little and Lyaren was surprised to see Teah also looking a little flushed. "We thought we could allow ourselves a little time before we set out." Teah said softly.

"Good." Lyaren smiled. "You needed to. Who knows when you will be alone again?"

A thought hit Calin as Lyaren spoke and the words were out of his mouth before he thought them through. "Are you married, Lyaren?" he asked. "You never speak of your family."

Lyaren considered shrugging off the question but he knew that, on Calin's part, it came from a genuine desire to know his friend better. "I was married once, yes. We elves live long lives, longer than humans, and I have lived a long time. I once had a family and I have a son, but that part of this life is over now; I have no family ties."

"I'm sorry," Calin said. "I had no right to pry."

Lyaren shrugged his shoulders. "It's not a secret, I just haven't been asked about my old life before. Humans tend to forget that we age differently to them; I guess most think I'm too young to have been married, had a son and then stated a new life. In fact my son is almost one hundred years old; my age, if you don't mind, I will keep to myself."

"That's fine." Calin laughed.

Myllasanndia and Daniel listened silently as first Teah and then Lyaren shared their plans to leave. Ela placed her arm affectionately around the older woman's shoulder. Her emotions were playing over her face like a mirror into her soul. "I'll be fine," Myllasanndia told her firmly. "I had just got used to having you all around, that's all, but I've got Daniel and now we have Danny and Salistanya and there is so much to be done here in Safehelm I'm sure I won't have time to miss you all. Still, I will worry. Promise me you won't do anything too reckless."

"We'll be as careful as our circumstances allow." Lyaren reassured her.

439

"Right!" Daniel exclaimed, digesting the information. "So that means tonight we will eat together for one last time and tomorrow we will part company."

They spent the rest of the day saying their goodbyes to good friends and then finished packing. Their last meal with Daniel and Myllasanndia was a warm and friendly family meal, but overshadowed by sadness. The next morning Tilly had been unable to speak as she had packed the last of Ela's things and when Ela thanked her for her kindness and hugged her fondly the poor woman had burst into tears and fled from the room. Her guards escorted her for the last time down to the ornate front doors of the castle where Lyaren waited with Daniel and Myllasanndia. They said their farewells there, no one wanted to prolong this goodbye, then joined Calin and Teah at the front gates of the keep. The clanswomen all stood with their horses ready to leave. Elayna couldn't help thinking of Fire and Hurricane. Daniel had promised to take good care of their horses and Myllasanndia herself had said she would brush and ride them both weekly so they felt loved and cared for. It helped to know that later today they were to be moved to the caverns closer to the enclosed valley where they would be able to have some time in the outdoors each day.

Danny and Salistanya were waiting with Teah and Calin, ready to escort them all to their respective exits. First they made the journey to the northern tunnel which the clansfolk were to take. It took about half an hour to make the trip, with the muffled, rhythmic drumming of horse's hooves filling the cavern. The women and Calin had all wrapped the horse's hooves in cloths to protect them from the hard stone floor. The creatures seemed to know their enforced confinement was coming to an end and Ela was aware of all the women whispering softly in the creatures' ears to calm

440

them. Finally they arrived at the entrance of a large, dark tunnel, wide enough for four riders to travel side by side. Danny passed torches around, some of which were lit but most of which were stored for later.

"The tunnel does narrow," Danny told them. "And there are parts where you won't be able to ride; you will need to use your magic to keep the horses calm in these smaller areas. I suspect, with the horses, you should reach the end of the tunnel in around five days. Don't leave the tunnel if it is night time. That's when the worst of the predators hunt. Use the stars to find your bearings and travel quickly at first light. If you are attacked call on the Goddess Mysta, she will hear you and she will not desert you."

"Thank you." Teah said, kissing the Lord of Safehelm affectionately on the cheek then turning to do the same for Salistanya. The other clanswomen also said their last goodbyes, Sahain wiping tears from her cheeks. Each hugged Elayna fondly and Ela found that she also shed silent tears. Then Calin was there, hugging her like he was squeezing the life out of her and finally she faced Teah. Although her eyes were full of sorrow the woman didn't cry. She looked Ela firmly in the eye and said formally "May the blessing of the Gods of war go with you always, sister of the sword." Then she leaned in and the two women embraced.

Lyaren couldn't hear what Teah said as she hugged Ela but whatever it was it had a profound effect on the girl. Even in the alien lighting of the cavern he could see the colour drain from her face followed by an expression of sheer shock. Ela quickly pulled herself together and wished Teah luck for the journey, but she was clearly unsettled by whatever Teah had said. Once the clansfolk had all followed Calin and Teah into the darkness of the tunnel she still seemed stunned, even confused and a little out of sorts. Lyaren shook off his concern; he was being silly, Ela was bound to be upset, she cared very much for the friends they were leaving behind today. In so many ways this parting was much harder than their flight from Ladaston.

Perhaps Ela was simply apprehensive about what was to happen next. After all, she knew that the magic of the portal would knock her out and that when she woke she would have to face a journey by sea – something, she had confessed, that equally excited and terrified her.

They followed Danny and Salistanya as they retraced their steps across the cavern and down the passageway which led to the Seat of the Goddess. When Danny placed his hand on the doorway in the great library, Ela fainted and Lyaren was ready to catch her. He cradled her closely in his arms, breathing in the fresh scent of the flowers which she had taken to using in her daily baths. Danny picked up Ela's pack and led them down the corridor past a number of the extraordinary doors until he came to one which was carved with images of waves and ships. He opened the door to reveal a portal of effervescent molten silver which shimmered and bubbled as if it was a living thing.

"Safe journey," Salistanya said. "Take care of each other."

"We will, and thank you, there are not enough words to express what we all owe you both."

"You ready?" Danny asked.

"I'm not sure." Lyaren answered truthfully.

"I don't blame you!" Danny pulled a face. "I find it easier to close my eyes, but if you have a problem I've told Salistanya to give you a push from behind!" Danny didn't wait for Lyaren's answer. He turned back to the door, closed his eyes, stepped into the silver pool and disappeared.

Lyaren took one last deep breath. "There will be no need to push." he told Salistanya, smiling fondly at the woman. Then he too closed his eyes, took a leap of faith and stepped confidently into the unknown.

Salistanya opened her eyes. She knew the hour was late, but she felt the unmistakable tug of magic and knew it was time. She looked over to where her husband lay sleeping soundly beside her. Danny had spent the afternoon with Ela and Lyaren in Sidmore; settling them into the inn and ensuring that all his contacts were ready to play their parts in helping the couple on their journey. As Pirate Lord his influence was considerable. When he had finally returned he had been exhausted and fallen quickly into a deep sleep. Salistanya, on the other hand, had been troubled and as the night wore on she began to recognise the sensations she felt as the magic of an ancient spell springing back into life.

"Are you ready?" a man's voice asked softly.

"Yes," she said sadly. "Though it will be hard to leave behind all that we have created here."

"It won't be lost." the man told her. "It will all still be there, just there will be more."

"Will it hurt him?"

The man laughed softly. "He's had worse."

"Very well, do what you have to do." She felt the unmistakable ripple of magic and, as she looked at her beloved husband's sleeping form, she watched him vanish, the sheets falling onto the bed in the position where he had laid. "You will bring him back?"

"I know you and I have had our differences, Salistanya, but I am true to Mysta. This is her will; I will bring him back to you, just as soon as you do what you have to do."

Salistanya nodded and pulled on her shawl. Despite the thermals, the tunnels turned cold at night.

After the sadness of the morning Daniel and Myllasanndia had thrown themselves into the mountain of mundane tasks which had mounted up over the past few days. Together they saw the numerous petitioners, who asked for everything from compensation for loss of properties (these Daniel gave short shrift) to those with suggestions for improving the living conditions of their new surroundings, some of which were inspired. They then set to work on the piles of paperwork left by Grun, the household staff, and the council. Eventually they both gave into exhaustion and allowed sleep to take them.

Daniel felt the presence of someone sit at the side of him and was instantly awake. He kept his eyes closed, all his other senses straining to gather as much information as possible. The figure was slight, a woman, but not his mother, the scent was wrong. He knew that smell though, a heady mixture of oils and incense. A hand gently touched his arm and a soft voice whispered, "Daniel, don't panic, it's only me."

Daniel's eyes shot open and he found himself looking into the absolute perfection of Salistanya's beautiful face. She smiled as he opened his eyes and kissed him lightly on the lips.

He allowed himself for a moment to feel her mouth on his, to taste her. He so wanted to respond, but she was his cousin's wife and he pulled away.

"Have I shocked you?" she asked. "I have done nothing wrong, you will understand soon. Come, we need to get your mother; I have a lot to explain and not much time to do it."

"Is something wrong?" Daniel asked. "Is it Danny?" He could make no sense out of the situation.

"Nothing is wrong, everything is working out perfectly. Come, let's get your mother."

444

Daniel walked barefoot with Salistanya down the corridor to his mother's suite. The guards who stood at her door both looked firmly ahead, neither of them noticing the presence of the two intruders. Salistanya wiggled her fingers, as Danny had once done to indicate that magic was in play. Then she led him past the guards and into his mother's room. Daniel woke Myllasanndia who was equally shocked and confused and the three of them sat by the small fire in her room.

"I am known in the Circle as the Keeper of Secrets. When I was born I held an ancient knowledge deep within me. The prophecy you hear us speak of is not written in a book. I am the book." She smiled. "It's hard to explain but it is as if I wake each morning with the instructions I need to get me through the day. It's how I knew to seek out the Pirate Lord and marry him, how I knew to find you and what to do to help you. Tonight something new happened. Tonight I woke and I knew everything. I remember so many things, things from this life but things from many more lives also. It is because of this that I know what has to happen next. She held her hand out to Daniel. "I want you to take my hand and listen with your heart to what I am about to tell you. I have no way to prove to you that I am telling the truth, but I know how deeply you love me and I believe that your heart will confirm that I am telling you the truth.

Daniel wanted to deny his feelings, tell her he would never disrespect this cousin's wife, but he could still feel the touch of her lips on his, the warmth of her body; the smell of her body. He took her hand and she smiled.

Salistanya held her other hand out to Myllasanndia. "You on the other hand have the gift necessary to know that I am telling the truth." Myllasanndia scowled slightly at the woman. She most certainly did not approve of the way she had just spoken to her son. She was a married woman, what was she playing at?

As Myllasanndia took the offered hand she was overwhelmed with emotions: sadness and joy in equal measures, uncertainty and duty, love…the deepest of loves, both for her and for Daniel, then desire to succeed at all costs and the fear of failure, the fear of the horror which failure would unleash. Myllasanndia's eyes opened wide. "Oh my dear, what on earth is wrong?"

"Safehelm is not yet truly safe, there is a great task I must burden you both with for which I am truly sorry. In order to save your city and your people I must ask you to sacrifice yourselves and give up all that you hold dear, but please hear me out for the gifts which await you on the other side far outweigh all that you will be leaving behind."

Xyakah sat comfortably in his huge throne. His High Priest Talistorium stood proudly beside the enormous creature which Xyakah was now inspecting. The creature still had some of the characteristics of the other lizard warriors; its skin resembled scales and its face was elongated, with the characteristic split tongue which flicked nervously in and out of its mouth, tasting the unusual environment of Xyakah's palace. But that was where the similarities stopped. This creature was easily twice the size of the biggest lizard warrior he had ever seen and it had powerful arms. Xyakah was in no doubt the creature would be formidable in battle. It had longer legs than its predecessors and the eyes were not split, as the others' were. This creature had humanoid eyes, with eyelids and eyelashes, which would solve the problem of poor vision in bad weather and in the woodlands.

"Open your mouth!" Talistorium instructed the creature, which complied revealing a maw of razor sharp teeth. "One hundred teeth" Talistorium informed his master. "And the two front fangs contain a venom which paralyses the victim when it enters the bloodstream."

"Very impressive," Xyakah admired the creature. "You have done well, Talistorium. What about the mortality? You were having difficulty getting them to live more than a few months."

"That is still a problem, Master." the priest admitted. "In order to achieve the number we require to support the war in the south we are having to accelerate the growth process significantly. This puts a strain on the creature's hearts and they have been expiring under exercise. However, in this particular specimen we have adapted the heart and we are hopeful we may have overcome that problem. The added bonus of accelerating the growth process means we have creatures with extreme strength and power, but they have immature brains and limited intelligence. In short the perfect war machine."

"So tell me specifics, how long did this creature take to make? How long will it live? And how long will it take you to make more?"

"This specimen was conceived in the breeding pens three months ago. We accelerated the gestation period with magic and then mutated the foetus at birth. Again, we accelerated the growth and have been building muscle and strength alongside teaching battle skills and obedience. It takes about four months in all and we are hopeful it will live for three to four years. We have one hundred of the creatures battle-ready and a further two thousand in various stages of growth. The only thing slowing the process is the rate that the bitches in the breeding pens can knock out their yelps."

"Then we need more females in the pens!" Xyakah let his frustration at their ineptitude flavour his tone. "Get me that bitch of a Priestess up here; she'll just have to give up more of her whores."

"We tried that, Master, she says the other females are too immature – they have not yet bled."

"Don't be such a gullible fool, Talistorium; we all know that bitch hides their brats in her temple. Threaten to have the building torn down, she'll soon find you new flesh for your ..." He stopped mid-sentence, holding his hand in the air to halt any interruption as he reached out to the tug of magical power he felt draining from his connections to his priests. "Do you feel that?" he asked his high priest.

"Yes, Master, Juzuk has initiated the final destruction of their northern city."

"The man is sloppy; he has drained all of his initiates. What does he propose to do if he needs more power? I need to get a more powerful priest out there with the army. Do what you have to do Talistorium; I want twenty thousand of these creatures battle-ready and marching on that infestation of rancid humans in the south within four months from now, and I don't care how many of the lizard brats your stallions need to screw to do so! Do you understand?"

Talistorium prostrated himself at his master's feet. "At your command, oh Mighty Xyakah." The priest made the formal supplication; he could feel his master's disquiet, something was not right with the war effort, they should both be feeling the power-boost created by the passing of more souls by now.

Xyakah growled softly under his breath and Talistorium quickly rose and fled to do his master's bidding.

Kala stirred from her position on the floor at his side; she knew all too well when Xyakah was unhappy and it was her purpose to console him at such times. Standing, she laid her naked form over his lap, offering her unprotected body up to him. Xyakah did not look at her; he was lost to his thoughts, reaching out with all his awareness for some form of information as to what had transpired in the south. Today was to be his first major victory; he would achieve the eradication of that filthy city's inhabitants. He absently ran his hand over the exposed skin of Kala's abdomen, his claws carving deep scratches into her flesh. Kala did not react to the pain; her master did not like that to happen too quickly. Instead she purred softly and reached her own hand into his lap, heightening his arousal. Still he did not react. Somewhere deep inside herself Kala felt the terror rising. He had been still for an awfully long time. When his anger came it would be terrible and she knew it was her burden to bear the worst of it.

Epilogue

Alextrallion Nunnington paced the short length of his private study impatiently. Worry etched his face and he clenched his hands into fists. Things were getting out of hand. His father had managed all this so much better than he did! Not for the first time Alextrallion cursed Bordin Nunnington and his decision to accept the seat at Stagsonton from the King. The man was a fool! No one could expect to rule over a city as a true and noble lord, a benefactor and protector of the people, while simultaneously running a major criminal organisation. A hundred and fifty years ago the King knew what was going on, Bordin and his sons were protected by the throne, but no one remembered that which wasn't written down and when this house of cards came tumbling down it would be his son, Warren, who would suffer the consequences. Warren was a good boy. He would make a fine lord of Stagsonton, but he would make a lousy lord of thieves, pirates and assassins.

Blast the woman! Where was she?

It was hard enough that he was about to give up his family's claim to the less-legitimate side of the business. Bad enough that he would be forced to break the oath his forefathers took when Stagsonton was nothing more than a village – an oath which stretched back over the generations. Bad enough that – Mysta knows who – would be stepping into his shoes, one of the less ethical of men, and bad enough to think of the fighting and squabbling which would unfold by his absence; all hell would be unleashed on his city!

Where was she! Why did she insist on making him wait?

A tapping came from the concealed door at the back of the study.

At last!

Alextallion opened the door and the High Priestess stepped out into his room. She smiled brightly at him and he scowled deeply in return.

"About bloody time! Well, did you speak to her? Will she help?" he snapped.

"Why does everything have to be such a drama with you, Alex? You need to lighten up!" she said brightly. "Mysta is very aware of the burden she placed on your family, she knew you would need help and it is on its way."

"I don't need staff I need a replacement." he snapped.

"Oh in the name of the Creator and the Destroyer don't be so damned melodramatic. You are not getting staff or a replacement, you are getting help. Come on, they'll be here soon, we have to go and meet them. Oh, and try to find a smile. You might even find you get a pleasant surprise."

The High Priestess stepped back through the doorway and into the hidden passageway. She glared at the Lord of Stagsonton, a challenge to defy her, and he followed, intrigued despite his better judgement.

The secret corridor twisted and turned until it came to a solid stone wall, made to appear as if you had

452

reached the exterior of the house. The priestess touched the stone with the palm of her hand and there was a slight buzzing sound followed by a high-pitched ting; the stone disappeared and was replaced by the whirling silver expansion of the portal. Alex followed the woman through the vortex without hesitation and instantly they were both stood in the corridor which was affectionately known as the Seat of Mysta.

"Is it longer?" Alex asked, looking up and down the length of the long straight corridor which stretched out before him.

"You should know." she answered cryptically and marched up to the large doors which led to the inner chamber. Once inside, they both waited.

Alex felt calmer here, he always did. The presence of Mysta had that effect on him. He remembered when he had met her as a boy. His father had brought him here and told him all about his responsibilities and he had been scared and overwhelmed. Then she had appeared before him and told him he was to be brave. She explained that he had an important role to play, but that he would be blessed with great happiness and a long life. He wondered if his father had been made the same promise. The poor man had died of an attack of the heart at thirty - two.

The hum of magic rippled through the air and he looked expectantly at his companion but, as he did so, saw her gasp and fall to her knees. Alex moved towards her to help but was caught by a blast of energy, which washed through his whole body so suddenly he, too, felt his legs give way beneath him. He held his breath as the power surged into his body and flooded his mind. When it passed they both remembered. They looked at each other with truly open eyes and the animosity between them slipped away.

"They're coming, really coming aren't they."

"Yes, Alex, they are and we are going to have so much fun. It will be good to lead one lifetime with the knowledge of who we are and what we strive to achieve."

The buzzing sound returned, but this time neither of them flinched as a portal opened in the centre of the room, not silver this time but a lustrous galaxy of glittering translucent colours. There was a shimmering on the surface of the portal and two figures emerged hand in hand, stepping out into the room. As they did so the same energy-blast hit them both and the waiting pair rushed forward to support them, while their memories also were fully returned. The new arrivals stood slowly, digesting the immensity of what had just been deposited into their minds.

Myllasanndia caught her wits fastest and stepped up to the current Lord Nunnington. Curtsying elegantly she said in a loud clear voice, "My Lord, we have travelled across time to be at your side as you build an empire below the ground which, in years to come, will save the world above."

Lord Alextrallion Nunnington ignored the formality of her performance and grabbed her firmly around the waist; laughing merrily he pulled her roughly into his arms. "I've missed you." he breathed desperately into her ear.

Myllasanndia laughed. "But darling, until a moment ago you had no memory of who I was and what we are."

"I might not have remembered, but I knew you weren't there." The creases and worries of the past few months slipped away from his face in an instant and were replaced by a radiance of pure joy. "Mysta promised me a life of happiness, but I hadn't expected to be so blessed." He looked past his beloved Myllasanndia and to their beautiful son, reborn as they all were in their

454

current forms. "You look well, Daniel, it's good to see you boy."

"Thank you, Father; it's good to see you too." He smiled broadly then turned to the beautiful young woman who still held his hand. "A little while ago," he told her. "You kissed me and I thought it was outrageous behaviour for a married woman, especially as you were married to my cousin! But now I see what you meant when you said you had done nothing wrong. There were two of me! In the future there will be two of me, both living simultaneously, and without knowledge of the fact that we are the same person. How in the world will we manage to manifest something like that?"

"An interesting dilemma to ponder over for a few years." Alextrallion said. "Perhaps we will need to find a way to combine our magic, create a partial time / partial dimensional paradox." He looked at Myllasanndia. "What do you think Milly?"

"I think you two will work it out together but, in the meantime, can we go and get some food? We didn't have breakfast this morning and I'm starving!"

"Oh lord how the hells do I explain you two to the people upstairs?"

"All sorted," Myllasanndia said. "I am your mistress of spies, you will introduce me to your son as such and, over the next few months, I will prove my loyalty and dedication to you and the family name. He will see our relationship grow and, when the time is right, happily accept me into the family. Daniel, however, will live apart from us but he has other distractions to keep him occupied." She raised her eyebrow and smiled at him affectionately.

Daniel looked from his mother into Salistanya's eyes. She had turned towards him too and kissed him lightly on the lips. "Welcome home, Lord Safehelm, I have been waiting for you." she said, her voice choked with emotion. He caught her in a fierce embrace and kissed her back, remembering fully the myriad of times he had done so before, both with and without his memories of each and every life. "It's good to have some of my family back," he grinned. "Now, Lord Nunnington, I believe this is where you get to name me Lord Safehelm for the first time, and I start having some fun! I've got just over five hundred years and a couple of reincarnations to get a cavern ready to hold a whole city and I suspect the assassins are, by now, in need of a firm hand and a little organisation, but nothing we can't manage and I really can't wait to go and prove myself as the Pirate Lord. But first," he grinned excitedly. "I think I need to go and steal the entire contents of the library of Sidmore, well all the histories and magical bits at least. And build our own magical archive down here in the caverns. It's so exciting! Father, do you think you could make me a doorway? It's such a long way to Sidmore."

Salistanya made her way back to the cavern which she and Daniel had called home for many happy years and untold lifetimes. It had been so hard carrying on their life together with so many of her memories, while Daniel had been denied his for so long, but soon the prophecy would reach its apex and the fate of the world be decided once and for all.

As she entered her room she saw Alex was sat waiting on the bench holding the sleeping form of her daughter in his arms.

"She woke up hungry, Salistanya, I hope you don't mind, I am sort of her grandfather."

"No not at all, thank you for tending her, she gets grumpy if she doesn't get enough sleep."

"Is it done?" he asked.

She smiled her eyes full of sadness. "Yes, they have just crossed through."

"Why so sad? You know where they have gone, you must remember that time, it was so perfect."

Salistanya shook off her melancholy and grinned at her father-in-law. "Yes it was wonderful, but I'm not there. Here it is just Daniel and I; for a short time our family were almost all back together, we all felt the power of our union but we didn't know who we were. Just as my memories are returned to me, they have all left, all fulfilling their own parts of the prophecy. Alex I'm so worried, they are out there with hardly any magic in a world on its knees and I feel so small and powerless to help them."

"You are far from small, daughter of my heart." He tutted at her. "Let's wake the boy, he always knows how to make you smile."

She smiled but her eyes were so sad. "I want him back, Alex, I mean *really* back. He knows me, he loves me, but there is so much he can't remember and it breaks my heart each time I think of all he has lost."

"Nothing is lost. Daniel has been working in the confines of a complex spell which has required him to expend a huge amount of energy. He needed to be in two places at once and acquire two lifetimes of experience simultaneously – don't imagine for a moment that it was easy for him or me. But once the spell is ended he can be the one and only Daniel Nunnington once again, and he can digest both his lifetimes and assimilate them into who he will be when he wakes up. He can only do that and stay sane if he knows who and what he is."

Hope flared in Salistanya's eyes. "You mean?"

Alex waved his hand and Daniel slipped fully back into this dimension, reoccupying the exact position in their bed from which he had disappeared.

"Go wake him and see, but don't forget to activate the spell you and Milly made. You'll need it to slip back into your twin roles as Lord and Lady

Nunnington and Lord and Lady Safehelm. Now stop worrying about what ifs and get on with living, something tells me you will be just fine." He kissed her fondly on the forehead. "We will be together in the Greenlands."

She hugged him. "See you soon, grumpy old man."

His chuckle echoed around the cavern as he disappeared from sight.

'Right,' she told herself. *'Let's see what he remembers.'*

Appendix 1
Characters' names

Alex Nunnington VII *nineteenth Lord of Stagsonton, father of Daniel, husband of Myllasanndia*

Alexia *princess and heir to the throne of the Kingdom of Maldora*

Alextrallion Nunnington I (Alex) *fourth lord of Stagsonton husband to Myllasanndia*

Alyha *clan's woman*

Anna *housekeeper at Gallowheart Keep*

Bayzar *acolyte to Juzuk*

Bordin Nunnington *the first Nunnington to be lord of Stagsonton*

Calin of Waydonfield *son of Sara of Waydonfield, Blacksmith*

Dalhain *Clan's woman, Sahain's younger sister*

Damian *head butler at Gallowheart Keep*

Daniel Nunnington XII *the twentieth Lord of Stagsonton, son of Alex and Myllasanndia*

Danny Nunnington *lord of Safehelm*

Desca *Xyakahan priest*

Dina Youngwood *wife of Samuel, mother to 6 children 2 girls Sally and Polly, 4 boys, Aaron, Brin, Byron and William*

Edric III *King of Maldora father of Alexia*

Elayna Of Ladaston *daughter of Gadon and Rebecca Ladaston, sister of Gaylon*

Fire *Lyaren's chestnut stallion*

Gadon *Elayna's father, husband to Rebecca*

Gaylon *Elayna's brother*

Greg *Calin's carthorse*

Griss *general of the legion stationed at Stagsonton*
Grum Highlord *lieutenant in the Stagsonton Elite guard, son of Baron Glynn Highlord, warden of the King, from Summer Garden, brother to six younger sisters Lydia, Lucinda, Layla, Lauren, Lorral, Laura*
Jemima *Waydonfield woman*
Hayal Longfellow *village elder from Lower Gonfiels, father to Kayel*
Horkins *jailor at Stagsonton keep*
Hurricane *Elayna's dappled grey stallion*
Juzuk *Xyakahan priest*
Kala *plaything of Xyakah*
Kayel Longfellow *archer from Lower Gonfiels, son of Hayal*
Kiam *first of the Elvin Warlocks*
Kizin *Xyakahan priest*
Loquin *supreme God of order*
Lyaren *elf from the Silent Forest*
Maginus *dragon warlock who challenged the Gods*
Myllasanndia Nunnington *mother to Daniel, wife to Lord Alex Nunnington, daughter of the Nightburry family*
Mysta *Mother Goddess of the Elves, Goddess of a secret order of humans.*
Sahain *clan's woman*
Salistanya *high priestess of Mysta, wife to Danny Nunnington*
Sally Dorkins Waydonfield villager
Samuel Youngwood *smith from Lower Gonfiels*
Sara *Waydonfield villager, mother to Calin, herbs woman*
Sardan *brother to Tarrin and Teah*

Savarna *elf servant of Mysta in dragon form*
Simeon Rudley *colonel to the army stationed at Stagsonton*
Tain *head steward for Lord Nunnington*
Tarrin Strong Arm *prince of the Wolf Moon Clan, son of Tarrin True Heart, brother to Sardan and Teah*
Tarrin True Heart *king of the Grass Lands and leader of the Horse Clan Warriors, father of Sardan, Tarrin and Teah*
Taya *childhood friend of Elayna*
Teah *princess of the Grassland clan's, sister to Tarrin*
Tilly *maid at Stagsonton keep*
Trancmean *lord of a small estate to south east of Stagsonton, wife and two daughters*
The Spinner *mystical creature who controls the wheel of life and death*
Xyakah *evil demi-god Leader of Xyakahan cult*
Zuqule *supreme God of destruction*

Appendix 2
Place names

Galloheart Keep *family home to the Ladaston family*

Ladaston *village in the North of Maldora*

Lower Gonfiels *village North West of Stagsonton*

The Kingdom of Maldora *land of the human's - known as Maldorans - divided into regions called Quarrels*

Each Quarrel is ruled over by a lord and the largest Quarrel is ruled over by the King.

Mount Tystar *mountain in the Eastern Desert- hidden deep in the mountain is Xyakah's palace and seat of power*

The Eastern Desert *also known as the Lizard's Desert east of the Grasslands beyond the Northern drop*

Peace Camp *trading camp in the Wayfinder Forest*

Riversway *hamlet on the northern boarders of Maldora*

Sidmore *university sea town*

Stronghold *capital city Maldora located in the southeast*

Stagsonton *northern city*

The Silent Forest *home to the Elves of Mysta*

Tallowbridge *coastal town*

Tormenton *Maldora city and port on the west coast*

Torr-Arron Keep *northern Maldoran keep in the Boarder Mountains*

Wezle *remote fishing town on the north west coast*

Waydonfield northern Maldoran village

Tribes and people

Sandkind *peaceful people, with lizard like features, living isolated from other societies, in the harshest most remote areas of the far North Desert*
Horse Lords *nomadic tribes living in the Grasslands*
Horse Clan Warriors *a gathering of the Horse Lord clans in order to raise an army*
Wolf Moon Clan *Horse clan*
Silent Sabre Clan *Horse clan*
Elves *ancient magical people who live in the Silent forest*

Made in the USA
Columbia, SC
05 June 2017